James Seaton Reid

The History of the Presbyterian Church in Ireland

Vol. I

SALZWASSER VERLAG

James Seaton Reid

The History of the Presbyterian Church in Ireland

Vol. I

1st Edition | ISBN: 978-3-75253-343-9

Place of Publication: Frankfurt am Main, Germany

Year of Publication: 2021

Salzwasser Verlag GmbH, Germany.

Reprint of the original, first published in 1834.

THE HISTORY OF THE PRESBYTERIAN CHURCH IN IRELAND,

COMPRISING

THE CIVIL HISTORY OF THE PROVINCE OF ULSTER,

FROM THE ACCESSION OF JAMES THE FIRST:

WITH

A PRELIMINARY SKETCH OF THE PROGRESS OF THE REFORMED RELIGION IN IRELAND DURING THE SIXTEENTH CENTURY,

AND

AN APPENDIX CONSISTING OF ORIGINAL PAPERS.

BY

JAMES SEATON REID, D.D.

MINISTER OF THE PRESBYTERIAN CHURCH, CARRICKFERGUS.

Though thy beginning was small, yet thy latter end should greatly increase. For inquire, I pray thee, of the former age, and prepare thyself to the search of their fathers:—shall not they teach thee, and tell thee, and utter words out of their heart?

BOOK OF JOB.

VOL. I.

WAUGH AND INNES, EDINBURGH;

W. CURRY, JUN. AND CO. DUBLIN; W. M'COMB, BELFAST;

AND WHITTAKER AND CO. LONDON.

MDCCCXXXIV.

PREFACE.

I SUBMIT the following work to the public, as the first attempt towards filling up a chasm, which has long existed in the Ecclesiastical History of the empire. While the origin and progress of the churches of England and of Scotland, of the Puritans, Baptists, Quakers, and almost every other denomination, have been fully and frequently traced, it is singular that no history has yet appeared of any branch of the Protestant church in Ireland. Of this church, the Presbyterians have long formed an extensive and influential section, and have, at the same time, possessed many strong claims upon the notice of the historian. Their history is so intimately connected with all the more important changes in the civil affairs of Great Britain during the last two centuries, and the cause of constitutional freedom is so much indebted to their noble efforts at the Revolution—they have been planted in the north of Ireland for so long a period, and have passed through so many interesting vicissitudes, both as a church and people—their settlement in Ulster, where they constitute the large majority of the population, has rendered that province so remarkable a contrast, in point of wealth, intelligence, and tranquillity, to the other parts of the empire—they occupy so singular and anomalous a position, a non-conforming yet an endowed church—and they have been so generally characterised by probity, peaceableness, and industry, as well as firm and enlightened attachment to the principles of civil and religious liberty; that while it is surprising these peculiarities in their condition have not long ago led to an inquiry into their history, it is, at the same time, far from being creditable to ourselves that our forefathers' services and sufferings should have remained so long unrecorded.

The present work originated in a desire to rescue the history of our church from this obscurity, in which it has so long and so unaccountably lain. To accomplish this object, has been a work of more difficulty than I at first anticipated, owing as much to the loss of the earlier records of the church, as to the want of an accurate history of the kingdom, and especially of the province of Ulster. These defects I have endeavoured to supply by diligent and extended inquiries; in the prosecution of which, neither labour nor expense has been spared, while every accessible source of information has been carefully explored in search of materials—with what success, it becomes not me to say. If the reader, however, wishes to form an estimate of it, let him consider how much he knows of the history of Ulster, and the early state of the Presbyterian Church, before he enters on the following pages; and having perused them, let him examine how much has been added to his knowledge of these subjects—the difference, if any, may be assumed as a fair criterion of the success with which the investigation has been conducted.

To render the work more generally interesting, I have prefixed an Introduction, comprising a view of the state of the Romish Church in Ireland prior to the Reformation—a brief narrative of the progress of the reformed religion during the sixteenth century—and an examination of the causes which rendered it less successful here, during that period, than in either of the sister kingdoms. As this Preliminary Sketch embraces subjects not previously investigated, I trust it will be found no unimportant addition to the value and interest of the work; while it will prepare the reader for a more profitable perusal of the subsequent narrative.

In compiling the history of our church, I found it impossible to present a satisfactory view of its circumstances and progress, without more extended references to civil affairs, especially to those of Ulster, than I either intended or wished. Some, I am aware, may be ready to condemn the work as embracing too much of civil history, and containing accounts of political and military transactions, incompatible with its character as an ecclesiastical history. But the affairs of church and state were so intimately connected, particularly during the period embraced in this volume, that I found it impracticable to separate them in the narrative. And when it is considered, that the civil affairs of Ulster have been as imperfectly explored, and are, at the present day, as imperfectly known as its religious changes, I hope the attempt I have made to furnish, for the first time, an ample and accurate account of both, will be the more favourably received.

From the nature of the following work, I could not avoid noticing the character and procedure of other churches in Ireland. But while I have expressed myself without reserve on these subjects, and have neither disguised the principles nor repressed the feelings of a conscientious presbyterian, I am not aware of having unnecessarily obtruded my sentiments, or employed language which ought to be offensive to those who cannot adopt my views. My 'plainness of speech' may provoke and irritate the bigot; but it will not annoy or displease the candid reader, how widely soever he may differ from me in political or religious matters. I have exposed corruption and error, and reprobated intolerance and persecution, with unreserved freedom, wherever they were displayed; but assuredly, with no hostile feelings towards the adherents of the churches whose conduct may have been censured; and certainly under no political prejudice against any one class of my countrymen, nor with the remotest intention of implicating the present generation, either of Romanists or Protestants, in the guilt of former transactions. While I have 'nothing extenuated,' I can sincerely say, I have not 'set down aught in malice;' and though 'not afraid to blame,' the awarding of praise to all parties, had the truth of history permitted, would have been to me a much more congenial occupation.

The reader will observe, in perusing the following pages, that my materials have been collected from various quarters, and from widely different sources. In addition to the ordinary histories of Ireland and Great Britain, and such other historical and biographical works as I could obtain, I have made use of several rare pamphlets relating to Irish affairs, which I consulted in that noble institution, the British Museum, and which have enabled me to throw additional light upon the transactions recorded in this volume. To these various publications I have carefully referred in the notes, as occasion required. My references might indeed have been easily increased, and my array of authorities rendered more imposing; but where the facts stated were generally known and uncontroverted, I did not conceive any reference necessary; while out of the numerous works which might have been produced to corroborate the same fact, I preferred referring to that only which appeared to be the original authority.

I also consulted—though I regret my limited time permitted me to do so only partially—the manuscript collections, in the British Museum, London; in the Advocates' Library, Edinburgh; and in Trinity College, Dublin, to which last I obtained ready access through the kindness of the Rev. S. J. M'Clean, one of the Fellows of that learned body. From all these sources I derived important information, illustrative of the early state of Ulster. A few interesting papers, which have not been published before, are inserted in the Appendix.

As my professional duties retard the progress of an undertaking like this, I am able to offer to the public only the FIRST volume of the work, which brings down the narrative to the period of the Solemn League and Covenant. A still more interesting portion of the history of our church yet remains; which, should this volume be favourably received, I shall endeavour to complete as speedily as possible.

CARRICKFERGUS,
December 19, 1833.

CONTENTS OF VOLUME FIRST.

INTRODUCTION.

SKETCH OF THE PROGRESS OF THE REFORMED RELIGION IN IRELAND DURING THE SIXTEENTH CENTURY.

HISTORY OF THE PRESBYTERIAN CHURCH IN IRELAND.

CHAPTER I.

CHAPTER II.

CHAPTER III.

CHAPTER IV.

CHAPTER V.

CHAPTER VI.

CHAPTER VII.

CHAPTER VIII.

CHAPTER IX.

CONTENTS

OF

APPENDIX TO VOLUME FIRST.

ERRATA.

N. B.—The author's distance from the press will satisfactorily account for the following errata:—

Page 20, line 13 of note 48. The notice of archbishop Brown, which concludes this note, ought to have been attached to the subsequent note, 49.

—— 77, — 7, *for* it, *read* they.

—— 109, — 17, *for* prophets, *read* prophet.

—— 153, — 23, *for* this, *read* his.

—— 173, — 13, *for* his, *read* this.

—— 173, — 6 of note 25, *for* their, *read* these.

—— 174, — 2 of note 27, *for* this, *read* his.

—— 177, — 17, *dele* he.

—— 185, — 20, *for* present, *read* pervert.

—— 186, — 13 of note 9, *for* chap. iii. *read* chap. ii.

—— 248, — 2, *for* letter, *read* letters.

—— 280, — 5 of note 25, *for* Life of Vesey, *read* Life by Vesey.

—— 295, — 20, *for* as the view, *read* with the view.

—— 314, — 2 of note 26, *for* soubriquet, *read* sobriquet.

—— 342, — last line of note 4, *for* Claneboy, *read* Chichester.

HISTORY

OF THE

PRESBYTERIAN CHURCH IN IRELAND.

INTRODUCTION.

Early purity of the Irish church—Subjugated to the see of Rome—State of the Romish Church in Ireland before the sixteenth century—Arrogance and turbulence of the clergy—Their rapacity—ignorance—and immorality—Consequent prevalence of superstition—error—and irreligion—among the nobles—and the people—The kingdom unprepared for religious reformation—Brown made archbishop of Dublin by Henry VIII.—The Pope's supremacy renounced by Parliament—Opposition of the Romish clergy—Accession of Edward VI.—Endeavours to introduce the English liturgy—Alleged violence of the Irish reformers—Shown to be unfounded—Unwillingness of English ministers to remove to Ireland—Bishop Bale—His character and conduct vindicated—Reign of Mary—Accession of Elizabeth—Proceedings of her first Parliament—Impropriety of the measures adopted by Government—A second Parliament called—Its acts on the subject of religion—Irish types introduced—Great want of reformed ministers—General indifference to the advancement of the truth—Establishment of Dublin college—Principles on which it was founded—Spenser's description of the religious state of the country—Slow progress of the Reformation—Causes thereof—Unfavourable state of the kingdom—Opposition of the Romish clergy—Inadequacy of the means employed for promoting the Reformation—Harsh and summary proceedings of Parliament—Exclusive employment of English agents and of the English language—Timidity and indecision of the Irish reformers—Want of adequate ministers—Progress of the truth consequently slow and partial.

THE early state of religion in Ireland is involved in deep obscurity, rendered still more impenetrable by the violent and protracted controversies which it has occasioned. It is uncertain when Christianity was first introduced into the kingdom, or to what period its ultimate triumph over the druidical superstition is to be assigned. The very existence of St. Patrick, the celebrated apostle of Ireland, has been plausibly impugned; and the period of his mission, the character he sustained, the form of Christianity he introduced, and the success he experienced, are to the present day vigorously contested. On one point, however, and that happily the most important, there is considerable unanimity. It is now generally admitted, that the primitive church of Ireland, though not free from error, differed most materially and for a length of time, from that of Rome. The free and commanded use of the Scriptures—the inculcation of the doctrines of grace and of the efficacy of the sacrifice and intercession of Christ, without any allusion to the mass, to transubstantiation, purgatory, human merit or prayers for the dead—the diversity in the forms of celebrating divine worship—the rejection of the papal supremacy—the marriage of the clergy—the scriptural character of the early bishops, each having the charge of only one parish, and being labourers 'in word and doctrine'—the presbyterial order of the Culdees and their singular piety and zeal—all these important points of doctrine and discipline which were maintained and practised in the ancient Irish church, clearly indicate its opposition to the papal system. [1]

The corrupting influence of the church of Rome, however, was gradually extended to this sequestered island, long before the papal authority was formally recognised. Several unsuccessful attempts were indeed made by the Roman pontiffs to subject to their domination the Irish church, the last of the national churches of the West which preserved its independence. It succeeded in resisting these attempts until the middle of the twelfth century, when it was at length unhappily sub-

[1] Ussher's Discourse of the Religion anciently professed by the Irish, Lond. 1631, *passim*. Jamieson's Hist. Acc. of the Culdees, Edin. 1811.

jected to the see of Rome. Considerable opposition was at first made to the new establishment, principally by the inferior clergy and the native chieftains. But pope Adrian IV., having arrogantly claimed the sovereignty of the kingdom, by a bull issued in the year 1155, formally conferred it on Henry II. of England, on condition of his reducing his newly acquired dominions to unqualified subjection to the pope's supremacy and conformity with the Romish church. By the aid of this powerful auxiliary, all opposition to the papal innovations was silenced, the Irish church was completely assimilated in doctrine and discipline to that of Rome, every remaining trace of its primitive purity and independence was speedily obliterated; and after the lapse of a century, Ireland presented the same religious aspect as the other countries of Western Europe.

As the value and importance of the Reformation can only be justly appreciated from a knowledge of the previous state of religion, it will therefore be the first object of this preliminary sketch to describe the religious condition of Ireland, during the period that elapsed from the full establishment of the papal system, till the commencement of the sixteenth century. In this country, religion had an ample share of those corruptions by which it was so lamentably defaced, and its benign influence so generally counteracted, through the rest of Europe. Here the authority of the Roman pontiff and his degenerate church, reigned supreme, as well over a bigoted and obsequious priesthood, as an ignorant and enslaved people; while the political circumstances of the country aggravated the evils which had universally resulted from such an uncontrolled and unscriptural jurisdiction.

The turbulent state of the island, and its remoteness from the seat of government, prevented the British monarch from exercising with effect that control which he claimed over the appointment of prelates to the Irish sees. These dignities were almost invariably bestowed by the pope, without the reference to the king required in the sister kingdoms, either for his previous license or his subsequent approbation. When a vacant see lay contiguous to the English Pale, [2] or promised to be a lucrative preferment, the interposition of the sovereign was occasionally entreated by a rival candidate, and the paramount claims of the pope, though after much contention, were as often overthrown. But this salutary check was seldom exercised; and the Roman pontiff was permitted to fill all the influential offices in the church, and not unfrequently in the state, with the most obsequious of his adherents. The ready communication which, by way of France and Spain, existed between Ireland and the court of Rome, by facilitating the carrying of appeals thither, and the procuring thence of indulgences and other expensive articles of papal manufacture, contributed still further to extend and increase the power of that court, and proportionably to oppress and impoverish the people.

The prelates, therefore, were entirely devoted to the interests of the mother-church on which they were so dependent, and with which they possessed such facilities of intercourse. In other countries, allegiance to the sovereign generally counteracted, if it did not supersede, this unqualified subservience to the authority of the pope; but the royal power was too weak in Ireland to oppose with success the continued extension of ecclesiastical domination. Accordingly, the bishops carried the authority of the church, and the privileges of their order, to an extravagant and intolerable height. They spared neither king nor people. The encroachments on the rights of the crown occasionally roused the indignation of the sovereign; [3] but

2 The Pale included the few counties immediately contiguous to Dublin, where the English first settled. This district was more or less extensive, according as they were more or less successful in their incursions on the neighbouring septs. It included the counties of Dublin, Kildare, Meath, with part of Louth, and occasionally extended as far northward as Newry.

3 Ware's Works, i. 199. The curious case here related between the bishop of Down and Edward I., clearly evinces the usurpation of the clergy in the beginning of the fifteenth century. The king called him to account, 1, for excluding, in conjunction with the primate, all clerks born in Eng-

owing to the troubled state of the kingdom and the weakness of the royal authority, these were generally unnoticed. They filled the chief offices in the civil government of the kingdom, in which they were often guilty of shameless fraud and oppression.[4] They arrogantly claimed that their persons should be exempted from arrest for debt;[5] and their properties from being taxed without their own consent. On one occasion, the prelates of an entire province threatened to depose their clergy, and to excommunicate the people, because they had, without special consent of their superiors, contributed to a subsidy laid on by Parliament for the exigencies of the state.[6] They exercised the right of pardoning felons within their dioceses, or of commuting their punishment for

land from the monasteries within his diocese; 2, for exercising in his manors all the pleas of the crown except four; 3, for claiming the eiric, or ransom, for killing a mere Irishman, or committing felony within his jurisdiction. After he had been deprived of these exorbitant encroachments, he was again brought under censure for breaking into the convent at Down, stealing thence the king's letter of license to the prior, &c., to elect a new abbot, and then forcibly advancing one of his own creatures to that dignity.

4 Ware, i. 331. Bicknor, archbishop of Dublin in the fourteenth century, was lord treasurer of Ireland for many years. He was excommunicated by the Pope, at the instigation of Edward II., for refusing to give any account of his administration of the public revenues. The sentence, however, was pronounced merely *pro forma*, to satisfy the king; and the delinquent was permitted to join in the performance of divine service at Rome, whilst under its operation; dishonesty being, in the opinion of his Holiness, no very flagrant crime. The archbishop was afterwards pardoned for sundry false writs and acquittances which he had fraudulently inserted in his account as treasurer; so that when he did render an account of his administration, it had not been a very correct one. The office of lord chancellor was at this time almost exclusively filled by bishops.

5 Ware i. 482. Cox. i. 222. It was not till the year 1529, that this exemption began to be limited. Power was then given, by a provincial synod held at Limerick, to the mayor of that city, to imprison clerical debtors without danger of incurring the sentence of excommunication—the usual penalty for so heinous a sacrilege. "The clergy made," as might be expected, "a grievous outcry against this canon, as an infringement and violation of their ecclesiastical privileges."

6 See this case in Ware, i. 478.

money.[7] To increase their influence, they studied to transfer almost every litigated case from the civil to the ecclesiastical tribunals. Their own disputed claims, however, were sometimes adjusted, not by the verdict of the law, but by the chances of single combat, in which bishops did not hesitate to engage by delegated champions.[8] The various orders of the clergy, too, were repeatedly encroaching on the privileges of each other, and were frequently embroiled in the most unseemly contentions. Bishops opposed the jurisdiction of their metropolitans;[9] and the latter, in their turn, oppressed, and sometimes even openly assaulted, their suffragans.[10] The inferior orders were not less refractory and disputatious than their superiors.[11] The regular or monastic clergy laboured to undermine the popularity and diminish the dues of the secu-

7 See note 3.

8 Cox, i. 76. Ware, i. 406. A bishop of Ossory, in the year 1284, prosecuted his right to a manor by combat, and gained it, his champion overcoming that of his adversary.

9 Ware, i. 508. The following charges, exhibited against a bishop of Limerick in the latter end of the fourteenth century, will corroborate the above assertion.—" That when Torrington, the archbishop of Cashel, came to redress the grievances of the Franciscans, and cited this bishop to answer them, he laid violent hands on the archbishop, and tore the citation from him with such force that he drew his blood—that the bishop having been a long time excommunicated for debts due to the apostolic see, paid no regard thereto, but acted as usual—that the archbishop having cited him for heresy, was, together with his attendant clergy, in danger of being assaulted, if he had not run away; and that, after he had retired, the bishop, clothed in his pontificals, entered the city of Limerick, and by bell, book, and candle, publicly excommunicated every person who had supplied the archbishop with food or entertainment." See also Ware, i. 528-9, for the turbulent conduct of a bishop of Waterford towards the bishop of Lismore and the archbishop of Cashel.

10 Ware, i. 533. An archbishop of Cashel, in the middle of the fourteenth century, assaulted a bishop of Waterford, by night, in his lodgings, grievously wounded him, and many others who were in his company, and robbed him of his goods. See also Cox, i. 91.

11 So late as 1525, a bishop of Leighlin was murdered by his archdeacon, on the high-way, " because he had reproved him for his insolent obstinacy and other crimes, and threatened him with further correction." Ware, i. 461.

lar or parochial clergy; while the latter inveighed in the bitterest terms against the idleness and profligacy of the mendicant orders.[12] The clergy of native extraction opposed their English brethren, and did not hesitate to charge them with corrupting the entire clerical order, by the vices which they introduced into the country.[13] To so great a height were these animosities carried, that the king was frequently obliged to interfere, in order to secure admission for his countrymen into vacant benefices in the Irish church.[14] They who thus invaded the rights of the sovereign and of each other, could not be expected to be very scrupulous in their encroachments on those of the laity. The people, indeed, were the victims of unmitigated oppression; and both their persons and their properties were treated by the priesthood, as if placed at their absolute disposal.

The wealth of the Irish clergy, the chief cause and evidence of their corruption,[15] was not so exorbitant as in Britain, in consequence of the general poverty of the kingdom. The

12 See these contentions related at large, in Ware, i. 92 and 332; ii. 86. Cox, i. 148, and in Mason's history of St. Patrick's cathedral, 133-4. Fitzralph, archbishop of Armagh from 1347 to 1359, was the most vigorous opponent of the mendicants, for which he was charged with heresy, and suffered no little hardship. It is remarkable that the year in which he died, Wycliffe, who was acquainted with his writings, took up the same controversy in England, which was the first occasion that brought this celebrated reformer into prominent notice, and led him to adopt that cardinal principle of Protestantism—the sufficiency of Scripture for all purposes of faith and duty. Bellarmine charges Fitzralph with heresy, and states that Wycliffe derived from the archbishop's writings several of his alleged errors. Bishop Davenant gives the following as an opinion of Fitzralph:—"Armachani opinio est, quod si omnes Episcopi essent defuncti sacerdotes minores possent ordinare." Several very interesting particulars in his life may be seen in Anderson's "Sketches of the Native Irish," pp. 14—18.

13 Ware's Annals, ad an. 1185, and Works, i. 439.

14 See the interference of the king, in the case of the bishop of Down, in note 3. It thence appears that both the primate and he excluded all Englishmen from benefices in their dioceses.

15 It was an old saying and a true one, "Ecclesia peperit divitias, et filia devoravit matrem."

devastations occasioned by the perpetual contests of the native chieftains impoverished the country, and left but little for the priesthood to amass. A northern bishoprick in the fifteenth century was so poor, that no occupant could be found for it during more than twenty years.[16] Several prelates were obliged to have recourse to inferior occupations for support; though, in the mean time, their fees to the pope were exacted with such unsparing rigour, that even the churches were stripped of their ornaments to satisfy his exorbitant demands.[17] In proportion, however, to the general poverty that prevailed, the clergy became the more rapacious and oppressive. The most unjustifiable measures were employed to increase their revenues. In the thirteenth century, an archbishop of Dublin destroyed in the fire all the leases which his tenants, at his own order, had laid before him, and by which alone they held their respective properties, that he might by this iniquitous procedure the more readily augment his income.[18] One of his successors in the same century laid the metropolis under an interdict, because the mayor and citizens had attempted to limit the exactions of his clergy, and to subject their offerings to the priests to certain reasonable regulations.[19] In addition to their stated support derived from tithes, which were rigorously exacted, numerous other expedients for amassing wealth were adopted. Ecclesiastical censures were commuted for money. Penances were liberally enjoined, that they might be superseded by extravagant fines. Fixed dues were demanded for almost every religious office performed; indulgences were regularly set up to sale, and every op-

16 The bishoprick of Dromore. See Ware, i. 188, 263, 408, for similar instances of poverty.

17 Cox, i. 61. A. D. 1229. "Now came over Stephen, the pope's chaplain, to demand the tenth of all moveables, to support the Holy See against the Emperor Frederick. It was so hard a tax in Ireland that they were fain to part with not only their *cadows* and aquavitæ, but also with their chalices and their altar-cloathes." See also ibid. p. 75. *Cadows* were the Irish mantles, the chief article of dress.

18 Ware, i. 319–20.

19 Ware, i. 322–3.

portunity of extorting money was eagerly embraced.[20] In favourable situations, therefore, the prelates and inferior clergy shared among them much of the wealth of the country, a very small proportion of which was consecrated to the advancement of useful learning or the encouragement of education among the people.

Learning, which had formerly flourished in Ireland to a considerable extent, was now reduced to a very low ebb. The want of colleges contributed materially to this national degeneracy. The higher orders of the clergy were generally educated at Oxford, and a large proportion at Paris, and other places on the Continent, and a few of these were undoubtedly men of considerable attainments and extensive erudition. But the priesthood were content with the scanty instructions which they received at cathedral or collegiate churches, and which scarcely fitted them for the celebration of divine service.[21] Attempts had been frequently made to establish colleges at Dublin, Drogheda, and Armagh; but after a brief existence they were soon abandoned through the want of that fostering patronage which wealthy prelates might have afforded. The numerous monasteries that were scattered through the island scarcely relieved the general gloom. The knowledge existing among their indolent inmates was confined to the dreams of martyrology, the subtleties of the canon law, or the conceits of scholastic theology. Hence the works which were produced in Ireland during the two or three centuries preceding the Reformation, so far as they are known, were both few in number and trifling in matter. Their authors

20 I may mention, as an instance of prelatical rapacity, the rigour with which archbishops levied from the heirs of their suffragan bishops, some of their most valuable possessions which they claimed as heriots due them. In the fifteenth century an archbishop of Armagh prosecuted this claim on the heirs of two of his suffragans, for their best horse, ring and cup. Ware, i. 185, 253.

21 See in a subsequent part of this introduction, the descriptions given by archbishop Brown and Sir Henry Sydney, of the wretched ignorance of the inferior orders of the clergy even in their times.

were almost exclusively ecclesiastical, yet scarcely any of their writings had reference to the sacred volume, or tended to advance the knowledge or promote the practice of religion. The lives of imaginary saints and the compilation of fabulous annals—commentaries on the works of the scholastic doctors, and poems in honour of deceased prelates, composed the principal part of their writings.[22]

The standard of their morals was not higher than that of their learning. Canonical obedience, everywhere a leading feature in the character of the Romish clergy, was grossly violated in Ireland by the occasional insubordination of the prelates, and the frequent contumacy of the inferior orders. It was no unusual spectacle to see rival bishops and priors contending for their preferments by force of arms; and in opposition to both pope and king, persisting for years in these degrading contests.[23] Their conduct was characterised by

22 See Ware's writers during the centuries above mentioned. I may here observe, that I have searched in vain for any satisfactory notices of the contents of the monastic or cathedral libraries in Ireland, immediately prior to the Reformation. The following are the only gleanings I have met with. 1305. An archbishop of Armagh bequeathed several books to the church there. Ware, i. 71.—1369. A southern chieftain is obliged to restore to the church of Limerick, among other things, the books which he had taken from it. Cox, i. 129.—1438. Mr. Martin White, rector of Liscarton, left to the monastery of Navan a book of the decretals and a small Bible. Monast. Hiber. 559.—1483. An archbishop of Dublin left to the abbey of Osney a portiforium, (probably a liturgical book) the mass-book, a book called "Pupilla Oculi," and two books of physic. Ware, i. 343.—1500. Dean Alleyne bequeathed to Christ church, Dublin, the works of Panormitan, (a celebrated canonist) with the great repertory thereon; also the great repertory of Philip, bishop of Brescia. Mason's St. Patrick, 142.

23 Thus, in the year 1250, there were for a time two bishops of Meath contending for that see. Ware, i. 143.—In 1489 there were two bishops of Culmore, and the clergy not being able to terminate their disputes, both were permitted to enjoy the dignity for many years. Cox, i. 183.—In the end of the fifteenth century, the priory of Kilmainham, a dignity equal to that of a bishop, was stoutly contested by two candidates, even by force of arms, for a considerable time. See this curious case in Ware's Annals, ad an. 1485.

the keenest animosities among themselves, and the most tyrannical oppression towards their people when charged with crime; though at the same time guilty themselves of many scandalous violations of the moral law.[24] Whilst chastity was lauded and professed by the priesthood as the chief of virtues, they were notorious for the most shameless profligacy. Bishops openly kept their harlots, and alienated the property of their sees by prodigal grants to their illegitimate progeny.[25] Their metropolitans occasionally interfered to repress such scandalous excesses; but while the offenders were under the prescribed discipline, the crime was perhaps repeated, and a new penance had again to be endured.[26] Even the provincials of the regular clergy were not exempt from this general incontinence, and their offspring sometimes attained the highest

24 A sample of these prelatic oppressions may be seen in Ware, i. 408-10, in the case of a bishop of Ossory who caused two persons to be burned for witchcraft, and imprisoned a supposed accomplice. This man being set at liberty by the interposition of one Poer, the indignant bishop excommunicated the latter for heresy, and had him imprisoned in Dublin. He being humanely treated by the lord justice, the bishop again took fire, and accused the lord justice himself of heresy—the never-failing expedient, in those days, of all discomfited priests. The lord justice, however, freed himself from this charge, and convicted the arrogant prelate of gross partiality and injustice, who was now, in his turn, accused of heresy by his metropolitan, and obliged to fly. Having effected his return, however, he excommunicated the lord treasurer of the kingdom, and gave abusive language to the chief justice while sitting in court. He was tried for being an accomplice in the murder of one Le Poer, and in the burning of his castle; but escaped by pleading the king's pardon.

25 In 1434, a bishop of Down openly cohabited with a married woman whom he kept in his palace; nor was it till seven years after his metropolitan had noticed his immorality, that he was punished for persisting in this flagrant conduct. Ware, i. 202. In 1370, a bishop of Kilmore is described by another prelate, as "much blackened on account of his lusts." Ibid. 227. In 1469, a bishop of Raphoe was proceeded against for incontinence and other offences, "quæ propter religionis et dignitatis scandalum subticemus." On submitting to due penance, he was absolved. Ibid. 274. Two successive bishops of Ferns laid waste the revenues of that see by grants to their bastards. Ibid. 448.

26 See this statement exemplified in the case of a bishop of Derry. Ware, i. 290.

dignities in the church.[27] The inferior orders of the clergy did not fail to improve on the example so openly set them by their bishops, and to take ample advantage of the license afforded by the lax morality of their superiors.[28] Sometimes, indeed, a prelate arose, who, detesting such profligacy, subjected the conduct of his clergy to stricter scrutiny than usual, and thereby revealed, in the number of the offenders, the great extent to which these crimes had prevailed.[29]

Under a clergy, so ignorant and dissolute, it is no wonder that the spirit of true religion had been altogether banished from the kingdom. The doctrinal and practical errors which defaced the communion of the Romish church need not be

27 An illegitimate son of a provincial of the Carmelites became archbishop of Cashel. Ware, ii. 85. See also the preamble to the bill passed by the Irish Parliament in 1569, which will be afterwards given. It may be added, that when Bale, in the beginning of the year 1553, came to Knocktopher in the county of Kilkenny, the parish priest boasted to him that the last prior of the suppressed monastery in that town was his father. "I asked him," said Bale, "if that were in marriage? He made me answer, No; for that was, he said, against his profession. Then counselled I him that he never should boast of it more. Why, saith he, it is an honour in this land to have a spiritual man, as a bishop, an abbott, a monk, a friar, or a priest, to father. With that I greatly marvelled, not so much of his unshamefaced talk, as I did that adultery, forbidden of God and of all honest men detested, should there have both praise and preferment; thinking in process, for my part to reform it." Vocacyon of Johan Bale, apud Harl. Mis. i. 340. Lond. 1809. 8vo.

28 So lately as the beginning of the sixteenth century, the state of the morals of the inferior clergy in Galway was such as to call for the following enactments on the part of the corporation of that town. A. D. 1520. "That no priest, monk, canon, or friar shall have a w——e or leman in any man's house within this town; and that man which keepeth said, &c. shall forfeit 20s." 1530. "Enacted, that any priest or vicar of the college found with any fault or crime, to lose one hundred shillings and their benefice; and also if he or they keep any w——e being with child, or bearing him children, to pay the above penalty." Hardiman's Galway, 202, 238.

29 "An archbishop of Dublin," says Ware, "in the end of the twelfth century, was such an enemy to incontinence in his clergy, that at one time he sent a hundred and forty clerks to Rome, who had been convicted of the same, in order to obtain absolution from the Pope, although he had power of granting it to them himself." Ware, i. 314.

enumerated. It is enough to state that they flourished in Ireland in their most fatal luxuriance, accompanied by their inseparable attendant, the grossest superstition. In proportion as this baneful spirit extended itself over the kingdom, a multitude of monasteries sprang up, which, though originally designed for pious and benevolent purposes, speedily degenerated, and in their turn increased the evil that had given them birth. Nearly six hundred religious houses, belonging to eighteen different monastic orders, were scattered over the entire island, the inmates and members of which were calculated to be as numerous as all the other inhabitants of the kingdom. [30] These individuals derived their chief support from the superstitious feelings of the laity, which were, therefore, the more studiously fostered. A continual rivalry existed between the monks and friars on the one hand, and the parochial clergy on the other; each party struggling for the pre-eminence in deluding and impoverishing the people. Hence the importance that was attached to the sight and touch of consecrated relics, to the possession of papal indulgences, and to devout visits to the shrines of favourite saints. Crowds of Irish pilgrims resorted to Italy, Spain, and the sister kingdoms, many of whom not unfrequently perished in these dangerous journies. [31] The Irish clergy, however, possessed a station at home, the unrivalled merits of which they failed not to publish through the most distant countries. St. Patrick's purgatory, situated in an island in Lough Derg

30 Monast. Hiber. Pref. p. xi.

31 In 1451, above fifty persons went out of the diocess of Dublin to Rome, to celebrate a jubilee, seven of whom were pressed to death there in a crowd, and many more died on their return. Ware, i. 341. We find the mayor and bailiffs of Waterford going in pilgrimage to St. James', of Compostella, in Spain. Ware's Annals, ad an. 1483. In 1508, Lady Margaret Athy went on a similar pilgrimage. Hardiman's Galway, 272. Like "the wife of Bath," she

"Thries hadde ben at Jerusaleme,
She hadde passed many a strange streme;
At Rome she hadde ben, and at Boloine,
In Galice, at Seint James, and at Coloine."

in the county of Donegal, was long a favourite resort with the superstitious Romanists. It was set forth as containing a passage, through which the devout worshipper might enter into the other world, and behold, in all their reality, the felicities of the heavenly state, as well as the torments of purgatory and the pains of hell.[32] Penances performed at this privileged station were represented as of special efficacy to purge away the deadliest sins, and restore the soul to spotless purity. No wonder then that it was annually visited by crowds of devotees, not only from the remoter districts of Britain, but even from the most distant parts of Europe. So shameless, however, were the impositions practised here by the priests on the credulous multitudes, that the indignation of the Holy See was excited, and it was ordered by the Pope to be demolished at the end of the fifteenth century.[33] But it was too gainful a superstition to be relinquished, even at the command of the sovereign pontiff himself; and though the government, more than once since the Reformation, attempted to suppress it,[34] it continues to the present day to attract and delude the people. Many other stations, though of

32 This celebrated station came first into notice about the middle of the twelfth century. I find in Rymer's Fœdera, folio edit. vol. iii. part i. p. 174-5, a safe-conduct granted by Edward III. on the 24th October 1358, to Maletesta Ungarus, a knight of Rimini in Italy, to visit Lough Derg, who it appears was sent thither by the pope to do penance; (Richardson's Folly of Pilg. p. 42.) and another of the same date to Nicholas de Beccario, a nobleman of Ferrara in Lombardy. In Rym. vol. iii. part iv. p. 135, there is another safe-conduct granted by Richard II. on the 6th of September 1397, to Raymond, viscount de Perilleux and knight of Rhodes, with a train of twenty men and thirty horses. There is also a testimonial extant from Octavianus, archbishop of Armagh, so late as the year 1485, certifying that John Garhi, Francis Proly, and John Burgess, three French pilgrims, had visited this station, and performed the usual penances. Jones's St. Pat. Purg. p. 58-9. I may add that James Young, a notary-public of Dublin, wrote " A History of the pilgrimage of Laurence Rathold, a knight and baron of Hungary, to St. Patrick's Purgatory, an. 1411." Ware, ii. 88.

33 By Pope Alexander VI. in the year 1497.

34 By the Lords justices of Ireland in the year 1632, and by act of Parliament in the reign of Queen Anne.

inferior celebrity, existed in various parts of the kingdom, where the prescribed penances of the church were performed, and where crowds of infatuated votaries sought to obtain absolution, by rigorous acts of mortification to which they subjected themselves at these hallowed spots. In these and similar degrading observances nearly the whole of practical religion was made to consist; while, at the same time, the doctrinal truths of the Bible were altogether obscured, and 'made of none effect' by human traditions. The majesty of Jehovah was insulted by the worship of images, pictures and crosses; and his holy law made void by the profligate doctrine of venial, as distinguished from mortal sin. The atonement of the Redeemer was superseded by the idolatrous sacrifice of the mass; and the sufficiency of his intercession denied by the intervention of the Virgin Mary and a crowd of saints, as additional and indispensable mediators. The efficacy of the Spirit, in purifying the soul from sin, was undervalued by the lucrative figment of a purgatorial process after death, which it was in the power of the clergy to shorten, when bribed by an adequate remuneration. Repentance was understood as synonymous with bodily penance, and faith with dependence on the clergy, who blasphemously claimed the prerogative of forgiving sin. Piety was confined to the repetition of unmeaning ceremonies or of prayers in an unknown tongue; and inward purity of heart was exchanged for external conformity with the rites of the church. Nothing remained of the 'Glorious Gospel of the Blessed God' but the name; and even this could scarcely be recognised under the mass of superstitious follies and abuses with which it was encumbered.

In reverting to the situation of the laity, it will be found to have been most deplorable. Without education, without even ordinary civilization, enslaved by error and debased by superstition, the dupes of designing monks, and the slaves of haughty and bigoted priests, what could be expected but the grossest ignorance and irreligion? No rank or station could be exempted from this general character. Even the chiefs and nobles were proverbially turbulent and licentious, devoid of either religion or education,[35] and characterised, even in those unsettled times, by a more than ordinary degree of violence and insubordination. The history of Ireland during this period is only a record either of disgraceful combinations among these petty despots for the purposes of rapine or revenge; or of dishonourable conspiracies, sometimes against known allies, marked by the basest treachery and the most revolting cruelty. Even religion, which usually commands the superstitious veneration of the most lawless chieftains, was frequently outraged. Neither its temples nor its ministers were secure against their violence. So late as the fifteenth century, the chief of a northern clan destroyed above forty churches in Ulster, and was himself soon after massacred in one of them, to which he had fled for refuge, but which his own previous spoliations had rendered insecure.[36] Noblemen of the highest rank in the kingdom did not hesitate to avenge themselves on neighbouring bishops, by the ruin both of their cathedrals and their palaces;[37] while they who were less profane or violent, only rushed into the opposite extreme of superstition. It is lamentable to read of noblemen sending embassies to Rome for permission to translate the bones of favourite

35 Cox relates, that even so late as the end of Henry VIII.'s reign, "most of the letters of the great Irish Lords, (even some of English extraction) were subscribed with a mark, very few of them being able to write their names." i. 281.

36 MacGilmore was the name of this "*corbi*," as he was called, or unbaptized Irishman. He had rifled the church of the Minorites in Carrickfergus, and taken away the iron bars by which the windows were secured; and having afterwards fled to it for refuge from the hostile clan of the Savages, he was easily captured and massacred. Ware's Annals, ad an. 1408. Cox, i. 147.

37 In 1369, a southern chief rifled the church of Limerick of its books, ornaments, and chalices, which he was afterwards obliged to restore. Cox, i. 129. The earl of Kildare being offended with the archbishop of Cashel, burnt his cathedral to the ground. Ware's Annals, ad an. 1503. His excuse for this wanton outrage was, "that he would not have done it, but that he thought the archbishop was in it." Cox, i. 9.

saints to more attractive shrines; (38) and to hear their occasional reverses of fortune ascribed to their having altered the patron saint of some sacred edifice. (39) But it is still more lamentable to find them, after lives marked by the deepest guilt, confidently resorting to the erection of a chapel or the endowment of a monastery, as an infallible passport to the divine acceptance. The chief magistrates of the first cities in the kingdom were content to perform public penances, and to go on distant pilgrimages, as atonements enjoined by the clergy for ecclesiastical misdemeanours. (40) Inferior delinquents were lustily cudgelled for their sins, and bore with patience this degrading discipline, being taught to consider it as indispensable to the welfare of the soul. (41)

The mass of the people were, if possible, sunk still deeper in ignorance and superstition. To keep the people in profound darkness has indeed been, when practicable, the policy of the Romish church in all countries. But the attainment of this object was unhappily facilitated in Ireland by the jealousy of the British court, who prohibited the use of the Irish language, through the vain idea of banishing it altogether from the kingdom, to make way for the adoption of the English tongue. (42) Though this absurd project failed,

38 In 1185, John De Courcy sent an embassy to Rome to Pope Urban III., for permission to translate the bodies of St. Patrick, Columba, and Bridget, just then discovered, as it was thought, at Downpatrick. Ware's Annals, ad an. 1185.

39 By the above De Courcy the Cathedral of Down, previously dedicated to the Trinity, was dedicated to St. Patrick, which, says a contemporary annalist, as quoted by Ware, "many believed was the cause of all those misfortunes that afterwards fell upon him." Ware's Annals ad an. 1183.

40 The mayor of Dublin, in the year 1512, was compelled to go barefoot through the city, on account of the citizens having, in a riot, defaced some of the images in St. Patrick's Cathedral. Cox, i. 202. See also in note (31) the mayor of Waterford sent on a pilgrimage to Spain.

41 In the year 1268 it was ruled in Dublin by the clergy, that an offending citizen should, for the first sin, be fined—for the second, be cudgelled about the church—and for the third, be cudgelled in front of the public religious processions annually made through the city. Ware, i. 323.

42 So early as 1367, the use of the Irish language was punished with the

yet its natural consequence, in the mean time, was to retard the instruction of the people, who were, as far as possible, prevented from obtaining either teachers of their own nation, or books in their own language. The benefits of the art of printing were not extended to the Irish language till after the Reformation, when books were first printed in that character.[43] The clergy had therefore little difficulty in retaining the people in that profound ignorance, which renders them at all times fit subjects of priestly domination. The instruction professedly given by their clergy was both extremely scanty in itself, and calculated only to deepen the gloom in which they were involved. Preaching constituted no part of the clerical office; and what occasionally assumed the name, was a tissue of silly fables, or of legendary tales of saints and martyrs. The inculcation both of religion and of morality was neglected, and their high sanctions were superseded by the mere terrors of bodily penances. The priests were often non-resident,[44] and the churches deserted or ruined. The Sabbath was systematically profaned,[45] and holidays of human institution alone kept sacred. And when to all these circumstances are added the example both of the civil and spiritual rulers, and the facilities afforded to the most abandoned, of obtaining absolution at their dying hour, need we wonder at the violence, insubordination, and profli-

loss of lands. Cox, i. 127. It had, however, spread so extensively, even over the English Pale, that in 1494 this penalty was withdrawn. Ibid. 188.

43 Irish types were introduced into the kingdom in 1571; and the first book printed with them was a catechism written and printed by John Kerney, treasurer of St. Patrick's, Dublin, entitled, "Alphabeticum et ratio legendi Hibernicam et Catechismus in eadem lingua." 8vo. It was not till the year 1602, that the New Testament was printed in this character. See subsequent note.

44 So early as 1357, enactments were made by the Irish church to remedy the evil of non-residence; (Cox, i. 24) an evil which has never existed in Presbyterian, nor been cured in Prelatical, churches.

45 In the fourteenth century, markets were held principally on the Lord's day. Cox, i. 103.

gacy by which the wretched population of Ireland were so generally characterized? [46]

Such was the state of the Romish church in Ireland prior to the Reformation. The slightest consideration of its melancholy details will be sufficient to show the paramount necessity that existed for overthrowing its arrogant authority, and reclaiming it, if possible, to the purity and simplicity of the church of Christ. The measures adopted for this purpose during the reigns of Henry, Edward, and Elizabeth, will now be briefly detailed.

The spirit of religious inquiry did not display itself in Ireland so early as in either of the sister kingdoms. The turbulent and distracted state of the island, its limited commercial intercourse with the more civilized countries of Europe, its want of colleges and schools, and of books printed in the native language of the country, were all extremely unfavourable to the introduction of new ideas in science or religion. The ancient faith, consecrated by time and defended by power, maintained an unquestioned sway over the minds of the ignorant and uninquiring natives;—while the English settlers of the same faith, being chiefly intent on extending their conquests, were equally indisposed to indulge in controversial disquisitions. A profound silence, therefore, on the subject of religion, universally prevailed. While the most important controversies were everywhere agitating the Romish church to its centre, Ireland alone, among the states of Europe, was involved in the stillness of death. Here there were no external circumstances to provoke or cherish a spirit of inquiry. There was no political opposition to the temporal encroachments of the Pope to pave the way, as in Britain, France, and Germany, for overturning his spiritual domination. There were no extraordinary exactions to rouse the indignation of the people long habituated to the most grievous oppression. There were no educated nobles to en-

[46] See a shocking instance of their sacrilegious conduct recorded by Cox, i. 109.

courage inquiry, or patronize opposition to the ambitious claims of the priesthood. Nor were there any poets to expose the vices of the clergy, and by the powerful aid of ridicule and satire, to open the eyes of men to their venality and corruption.(47) We accordingly find here none of those precursors of the Reformation, discernible in the suppression of books and the punishment of heretics, in the increased vigilance of the priests and in enactments against free inquiry,(48) which in other countries both indicated and hastened the progress of the truth.

The kingdom was thus totally unprepared for the meditated change in religion, when Henry VIII., anxious not for the doctrines of the Reformation, which he had never received or professed, but merely to overthrow the authority of the Roman pontiff, sent his commissioners hither to proclaim the royal supremacy, and demand the subjection of the Irish prelates to his own ecclesiastical power. The chief agent employed in

47 The great influence which poetry had in paving the way for the Reformation in other counties, is illustrated with his characteristic accuracy and learning, by Dr. M'Crie, in note K appended to the first volume of his "Life of Knox." The Irish bards, prior to the Reformation, do not appear to have strung their harps in censure of their clergy.

48 No legislative notice was taken of the reformed doctrines till the reign of Queen Mary, in the year 1556; when an act was passed for reviving three statutes enacted for the punishment of heretics in England, but not previously in force in Ireland; for the preamble runs thus:—"For that the ordinaries have wanted authority to proceed against those that were infected therewith; therefore be it enacted," &c. The statutes revived were 5 Rich. II. chap. 5—2 Hen. IV. chap. 15, and 2 Hen. V. chap. 7. This last statute is "concerning the suppression of heresy and Lallardy." The latter was a name of contempt for Protestantism before the Reformation. Leland indeed states, that "in the famous Parliament held in the tenth year of Henry VII. (A. D. 1495) laws had been revived to prevent the growth of Lollardism and heresy." Hist. ii. 158. But I cannot find any such laws among the printed statutes of that Parliament. Henry's writ constituting George Brown,—who is described as professor of theology, and provincial of the Augustinians of the city of London,—archbishop of Dublin, is dated March 12, 1536. Rym. Fœd. vol. vi. part 2, p. 222. There is an error in the year here given; it ought to be 1535, or more accurately 1534-5.

this important negociation was George Brown, who was consecrated archbishop of Dublin on the 19th of March 1535.[49] His opposition to some of the doctrinal errors of the church of Rome, while provincial of the Augustinian order in England, had attracted the notice of Henry, and pointed him out as a fit instrument for accomplishing his designs in Ireland. Charged with the royal commission, he hastened to Dublin, and in a conference with the principal clergy and nobility of the kingdom, laid before them his instructions, and required them to acknowledge the king's supremacy. To a similar demand in England, a ready acquiescence had been given, because the spirit of religious inquiry had already detected many of the errors of Popery, while the clergy had long been habituated to bow to the authority of the sovereign to whom they owed their preferments. But as a totally opposite state of things existed in Ireland, so a different result followed.

The proposal of Archbishop Brown met with the prompt and decided opposition of Cromer, archbishop of Armagh, and of his suffragan clergy. Cromer defended with vigour the papal supremacy. He rested his chief argument on the assumption, that the British monarch owed his authority over Ireland entirely to the liberality of the Pope; and concluded with boldly pronouncing a curse on all who should dare to own the supremacy of the heretical and ungrateful king. He indignantly withdrew himself and his bishops from the metropolis, sent messengers to Rome to apprize the Pope of these proceedings, and laboured to excite both the nobility and the clergy to resist the attempted usurpation. These vigorous measures, which were well adapted to the circumstances of the country, were met, on the other

49 The subsequent notices of Brown in the text, are taken from a rare tract, entitled, "Historical Collections of the Church in Ireland, &c. set forth in the Life and Death of George Brown, some time Archbishop of Dublin." Lond. 1681, 4to. pp. 18. This tract is to be found in Ware's works, Dub. 1705, fol. and in the fifth volume of the "Harleian Miscellany."

side, with the most reserved and cautious opposition. For nearly a whole year, no means were taken to disseminate the truth, or excite a spirit of religious inquiry in the kingdom. Every thing was permitted to remain in its former state, till, at the suggestion of Archbishop Brown, a parliament was called in May 1536, to take the necessary measures for having the king's supremacy,—the chief object of anxiety,—formally and efficiently acknowledged. This assembly ultimately acceded to the wishes of the Government, then administered by Lord Leonard Grey. Brown was the first to vote for the acknowledgment of the royal supremacy. He defended this measure, not on those great principles of religious liberty which were urged by the English Protestants, but upon some ancient precedents that had been set by the Romish see; and he endeavoured to persuade the other peers to adopt it, by this characteristic argument,—"he who will not pass this act as I do, is no true subject to his majesty." Though the proposal was at first resented both by the nobility and the commons, yet the government party succeeded in silencing their opposition, and in procuring the enactment of all the laws deemed necessary for the required alteration of the national faith. Of these the following are the most remarkable :—The king was declared the supreme head of the church on earth; the authority of the Pope was solemnly renounced; the supporters of the papal supremacy were declared guilty of high treason; all appeals to Rome were strictly forbidden, together with the payment of dues and the purchasing of dispensations; several religious houses were dissolved, and their revenues vested in the crown; and the projected alteration was completed by the enactment of severe penalties against those who should slander the king, or, on account of those innovations, style him usurper or tyrant, heretic or schismatic.

So far, therefore, as legislative enactments could avail, and so far as one monstrous dogma of popery was concerned, the Reformation had successfully commenced. But this first step was productive of little real benefit. Though public opposition was silenced in all places where the British power prevailed, which included a very limited portion of the island, yet secret discontent only increased the more; and throughout the remainder of the kingdom, the partizans of the Romish church became more zealous and more devoted to her cause. The supremacy of the Pope was indeed formally renounced; but it was only to transfer the same unscriptural power to the king; while the rest of the grosser errors and corruptions of that church were permitted to remain unquestioned and unreformed.

During the two years subsequent to this meeting of Parliament, no account has been preserved of the progress which the Reformation was making, even in the metropolis. The inferior clergy had not imbibed the spirit or acceded to the measures of Archbishop Brown; nor does he himself appear to have as yet aimed at any other object than the acknowledgment of the king's supremacy. But in the beginning of the year 1538, at the express command of Lord Cromwell, the king's favourite minister in England, he ordered the images and relics to be removed from the cathedral and the other churches of his province. So little alteration, however, had as yet taken place in the minds of the clergy, and so limited was the authority of the archbishop, that his order was successfully evaded.[50] Perplexed by this opposition in his own diocese, he wrote, in the month of April, to his patron and chief adviser, Lord Cromwell, informing him of the difficulties which had occurred in the execution of his commission,

50 It would appear, however, by the following extract from Ware, that in some other parts of the country this order had been partially complied with: "Also, about the same time, (i. e. May, 1538) among other famous images whereunto pilgrimages were designed, the statue of the Blessed Virgin Mary was burnt, then kept at Trim, in the abbey of the canons regular. The image of Christ crucified in the abbey of Ballibogan, and St. Patrick's staff in the cathedral church of the Holy Trinity at Dublin, underwent the like fate. The same was done in many other places, according to the example of England." Ware's Annals, ad an. 1538.

and requesting a renewal of the order, with additional power to enforce its observance. The following extracts from this letter will more clearly evince the state of religious matters at this period than any formal description. In a previous letter he had said: "This island hath been for a long time held in ignorance by the Roman orders; and as for their secular orders, they be in a manner as ignorant as the people, being not able to say mass or pronounce the words, they not knowing what they themselves say in the Roman tongue." He now repeats the same statement. "The people of this nation be zealous, yet blind and unknowing; most of the clergy, as your lordship hath had from me before, being ignorant and not able to speak right words in the mass or liturgy, as being not skilled in the Latin grammar, so that a bird may be taught to speak with as much sense as several of them do in this country.—The Romish reliques and images of both my cathedrals in Dublin took off the common people from the true worship; but the prior and the dean find them so sweet for their gain, that they heed not my words. Therefore send, in your lordship's next, to me an order more full, and a chide to them and their canons, that they might be removed. Let the order be, that the chief governors may assist me in it." He also informs Lord Cromwell that several of his clergy had resigned their benefices, but that he would not supply their places till he received further orders. At the same time, he apprizes his lordship, probably with the view of rousing him to more vigorous measures against the Romanists, of their contemptuous treatment of himself,—"the country-folk here much hate your lordship, and despitefully call you, in their Irish tongue, the blacksmith's son."(51)

But scarcely had this letter been despatched, when information reached Dublin, that the primate, Cromer, had received from Rome the strictest injunctions, as well as the most extensive commission, to maintain the authority of the

51 This was literally the fact. His father was a blacksmith at Putney, near London.

Pope, to resist the usurpations of the king, and to declare those accursed who acknowledged any power superior to that of the mother-church. By the same emissaries who conveyed these orders to the archbishop, the northern chieftains were excited to take arms against the heretical English, and to invade the territories of the pale. This opposition was promptly quelled by the vigorous measures of the lord-deputy, who routed the insurgents in May, 1539, and effectually intimidated all the military partizans of the Pope's supremacy.[52]

But the opposition of the Romish clergy could not be so promptly or effectually silenced. So far, indeed, as power could avail, it was freely employed. The monasteries and other religious houses were now formally suppressed, and the abbots and priors who had voluntarily surrendered, were pensioned by the king.[53] But in the remoter parts of the kingdom, the order for their dissolution was disregarded, and these powerful allies of the proscribed faith existed for half a century longer.[54] The oath of supremacy was now freely taken by clergy and nobles, but as freely broken when the power which enforced it was removed. As the more important bishopricks became vacant, the new prelates were willing enough to receive the formality of their preferment from the king, and promise conformity to his views. But most of them, notwithstanding, continued attached to the interests of the Romish church; and in the remoter districts,

52 Leland, ii. 115.

53 Ware's Annals, ad an. 1539. By the parliament in 1541, the full and free disposal of all the abbeys, &c. was vested in the king. By the same parliament it was enacted, "that laymen and boys should not be admitted to ecclesiastical preferments," thus plainly intimating that such perversions of church-offices had frequently taken place.

54 Sir John Davis relates, that "the abbies and religious houses in Tyrone, Donegall, and Fermanagh, though they were dissolved in the 33d year of Henry VIII. were never surveyed nor reduced into charge, but were continually possessed by the religious persons;" and this state of things existed till the reign of James I. Leland, ii. 185.

even this formality of royal investiture was neglected or disregarded, and the sees were, as formerly, disposed of by the Pope, without interruption or control.(55) The inferior clergy remained unenlightened in their views, and undisturbed in their preferments; and where the more devoted adherents to Rome had resigned, few reformed pastors could be found to occupy their places and excite a spirit of religious inquiry among the people. The reverses, too, which at this period occurred in the progress of the Reformation in England, by the passing of the "Six acts" in the year 1538,(56) and the unjust execution of Lord Cromwell two years afterwards,(57) extended their influence to Ireland, where both the reformed clergy and laity, as yet few in number, were but too well disposed to yield to their disheartening effects. At the death of Henry VIII., therefore, in the year 1547, the Reformation can scarcely be said to have been effectually introduced into Ireland. In England, notwithstanding the discouragements experienced in the latter years of Henry's reign, the Pope's supremacy had been completely overthrown, an influential proportion of the clergy had received the knowledge of the truth, and many of their people far exceeded their rulers in attachment to the reformed doctrines. But in Ireland, the contrary was the case. The civil authorities alone supported the cause; the rest of the influential classes were either obstinately attached to the Romish see, or sunk in ignorance and unconcern.

55 The sees of Clogher, Derry, and Raphoe, were thus disposed of till the year 1605. Ware's bishops.

56 These acts decreed, (1) the doctrine of transubstantiation; (2) communion in one kind; (3) the celibacy of the clergy; (4) vows of chastity; (5) private masses for souls in purgatory; and (6) auricular confession. The penalties annexed to a breach of these articles were, for the first, to be burned as an heretic; for the others, to be hanged as a felon, and to forfeit lands and goods as a traitor! Collier, Ecc. His. ii. 168-9.

57 Lord Cromwell, the patron and friend of Archbishop Brown, was a great pillar of the Reformation in England. "He was beheaded July 30th, on a bill of attainder, without being brought to trial, or allowed to speak for himself." Neal, i. 28.

The reign of Edward VI. proved more favourable to the advancement of the truth. Its beneficial influence, however, was far from being immediately felt in Ireland. During the first four years after his accession to the throne, no steps were taken to carry forward the work that had been so imperfectly commenced by his capricious and tyrannical father; while in England, during the same period, the Reformation was anxiously fostered, and advanced with rapid strides. Thus a book of instructive homilies was composed for the use of the inferior clergy, as yet unaccustomed to the work of public preaching. English Bibles were placed in every parish church; the mass was changed into the communion in both elements, and tables in the centre of the church were substituted for altars; divine worship in all its parts was appointed to be conducted in English, and a book of common prayer compiled; while learned foreigners were placed in the universities, and zealous preachers were employed in itinerating labours among the awakened and inquiring people.[56]

But in Ireland only one of these rational and effective plans of reform was introduced, and that, too, by no means the most urgent. On the 6th of February, 1551, King Edward issued a proclamation to the lord deputy, requiring the English common prayer-book to be used throughout the kingdom in the celebration of divine worship. A remarkable variation, indicative of the pusillanimous spirit in which the Reformation was pressed in Ireland, is observable between this proclamation and that by which the same measure was carried in England. In the latter country, the British Parliament did not hesitate to describe the new liturgy as altogether different from that used by the Romish Church,—as 'an order of divine worship agreeable to Scripture and the primitive church, and concluded on by the bishops with the aid of the Holy Ghost.' But in the proclamation for

[56] Burnet's History of the Reformation, fol. ii. 71.—Coll. Ecc. His. ii. 263.—See also period iii. of M'Crie's Life of Knox. Knox was a preacher in England from 1549 to 1554.

Ireland, the timid council did not venture to set forth the book in its real character. They merely state, in the name of the king, that they had caused the liturgy and prayers of the church to be translated into the mother-tongue of the realm of England by the assembly of divines lately met there; and as such,—a mere translation of the Romish service,—they require it to be adopted in all the churches in Ireland. Distrusting this artifice, however, as insufficient to impose on the wary clergy, and desirous of facilitating the adoption of the new service by more effectual means, Sir Anthony Saintleger, the lord deputy, called an assembly of the prelates and clergy in the month of March, to whom he submitted the service-book previous to its general circulation, and at the same time required their co-operation in effecting the wishes of the king. Of the proceedings of this conference a contemporary annalist has preserved the following narrative. It is necessary to premise that at the death of Cromer, in the year 1543, George Dowdal had succeeded to the primacy at the recommendation of Saintleger, and on the nomination of Henry VIII.; but that nevertheless, he continued to be the zealous partizan of the Romish church. "Sir Anthony Saintleger having spoken," in support of the prayer-book, "George Dowdal stood and laboured with all his power and force to oppose the liturgy, that it might not be read or sung in the church, saying, 'then shall every illiterate fellow read service or mass,' as he, in those days, termed the word service. To this saying of the archbishop's Sir Anthony replied, 'No, your grace is mistaken; for we have too many illiterate priests amongst us already, who can neither pronounce the Latin nor know what it means, no more than the common people that hear them: but when the people hear the litany in English, they and the priest will then understand what they pray for.' Upon this reply, George Dowdal bade Sir Anthony beware of the clergy's curse. Sir Anthony made answer, 'I fear no strange curse so long as I have the blessing of that church which I believe to be the true one.'

The archbishop again said, 'can there be a truer church than the church of St. Peter, the mother-church of Rome?' Sir Anthony returned this answer, 'I thought we had all been of the church of Christ, for he calls all true believers in him, his church, and himself the head thereof.' Then George Dowdal rose up and several of the suffragan bishops under his jurisdiction, and left the conference. Sir Anthony then took up the order and held it forth to George Brown, archbishop of Dublin, who, standing up, received it, saying: 'this order, brethren, is from our gracious king, and from the rest of our brethren, the fathers, and clergy of England who have consulted herein, and compared the Holy Scriptures with what they have done; unto whom I submit, as Jesus did to Cæsar, in all things just and lawful, making no question why or wherefore, as we own him our true and lawful king.'" (59) After this characteristic conference, the liturgy was adopted only by four other prelates. On easter-day it was solemnly used, for the first time, in Christ church, Dublin, in presence of all the civil and ecclesiastical authorities; and was soon after printed, with annexed rules for ecclesiastical habits and ceremonies. (60)

59 Hist. Coll. of the church in Ireland, p. 9.

60 This is said to be the first book printed in Ireland, its printer, Humphrey Powell, having come from England the same year in which it appeared.—"In 1548 and 1549, he dwelt above Holborn Conduit in London; from thence he went to Ireland in 1551, and is said to have been the first who introduced the art into that kingdom." Ames' Typ. Ant. ii. 709.—The title of the book runs thus:—"The boke of common prayer and administration of the sacramentes and other rites and ceremonies of the churche, after the use of the church of England. Dubliniæ, in officina Humfredi Poweli, cum privilegio ad imprimendum solum. Anno Domini M.D.LI." Among the annexed rules, it was ordered, "as touching kneeling, crossing, holding up of hands, knocking upon the breast, and other gestures, they may be used or left out, as every man's devotion serveth, without blame." Again,—"If there be a sermon, or for other great cause, the curate by his discretion may leave out the litany." The early history of printing in Ireland like many other branches of our national antiquities, has not, as yet, been satisfactorily explored; the sketch given in Ames' Typ. Ant. being very imperfect. Very little printing was executed in

Little advantage accrued to the truth from this change in public worship, especially when unsupported by the other reforms with which the same measure was accompanied in England. Its actual adoption, too, was extremely limited. Of the four bishops by whom it was formally received in Dublin, one being blind, resigned his see in the following month.[61] Another was extremely unpopular, being described by his contemporaries as cruel, avaricious, and oppressive even to his clergy.[62] The dioceses of the other

Dublin before the year 1600; and after that date it appears to have been carried on for a length of time, by persons employed by the London Company of Stationers. Bolton's "Statutes of Ireland" was so printed in 1620; and this is the earliest English book that I can find, printed here after the commencement of the century; though there can be little doubt there were many of an earlier date. Sir John Davis' "Primier Reports des Cases, &c." purports to be printed at Dublin in 1615; but, not having seen a copy, I presume from the title it is written in Norman-French. Bolton's Statutes was followed by Sibthorp's "Friendly Advertisement to the Pretended Catholics of Ireland," 1623. Leslie's Treatise tending to Unity, 1623. Jerome's Ireland's Jubilee, 1624. Andrews' Quaternion of Sermons, 1625. Sibthorp's reply, 1625; and his Surreplication, 1627. These are a few of the English books that I have met with printed in Dublin before 1630, after which period they become too numerous to be specified within the limits of a note. Several of Ussher's works printed at London in 1630 and 1631 are stated to be "printed in London for the partners of the Irish stock." Parr, in his life of Ussher (p. 36) says, that Ussher's Life of Gotteschalcus, published in 1631, was the first Latin book printed in Ireland. This statement has been copied without inquiry by all succeeding writers of the primate's life; but it is manifestly incorrect, as I find two Latin works, by Sir James Ware, were previously printed here, viz. "Archiepiscoporum Cassiliensium et Tuamensium vitæ," Dub. 1626; and "De Præsulibus Lageniæ, liber unus." Dub. 1628. What better subject for a prize-essay could be proposed by the learned societies of Dublin, than an inquiry into the history of printing in Ireland, with a catalogue raisonné of the more curious books, and sketches of Irish printers?

61 John Coyn, or Quin, bishop of Limerick, originally a Dominican friar, being blind and disabled by infirmities, resigned his see, April 9th, 1551. Ware's bishops.

62 Robert Travers had been, the year before, made bishop of Leighlin. "His chancellor," says Ware, "gave him the character of a cruel, avaricious man, and an oppressor of his clergy."

two lay contiguous to the metropolis; and in the most extensive of them, scarcely any of the churches were occupied by reformed ministers.[63] This single measure, therefore, though it had even been more excellent in itself, could have scarcely any effect in accelerating the reformation of the kingdom. The enemies of the truth, too, were at this period encouraged in their opposition to it, as well by the vigour and boldness of the primate Dowdal on the one hand, as by the remissness of the deputy in supporting it on the other. At the suggestion, however, of archbishop Brown, who, it is alleged, accused him of treason, Saintleger was recalled from the Government. Though no specific acts have been mentioned on which this accusation was founded; yet, from his having been the person afterwards selected by Mary for restoring the Romish faith in Ireland, it may be fairly inferred that, notwithstanding his able reasoning in defence of the Reformation against Dowdal, he had been an insincere professor of its doctrines.

Saintleger was succeeded by Sir James Croft, who, in the month of April, 1552, assumed the reins of Government. His first anxiety was to ensure the general reception of the English liturgy, and thereby accomplish the object in which his predecessor had failed. But though he employed for this purpose the most conciliatory methods, he did not prove more successful. In the month of June, he despatched a respectful letter to Dowdal, who had retired in disgust to

63 Edward Staples, bishop of Meath, warmly adopted the liturgy; but from the state of his diocese, as represented by Sir Henry Sydney twenty-five years afterwards, it could scarcely have been used for want of ministers. Thomas Lancaster, of Kildare, was the fourth prelate that supported Brown. He had been consecrated about half a-year before; and, it is probable, that the new service was not used beyond the precincts of his own cathedral. When Bale came to the diocese of Ossory, two years afterwards, he complains that his clergy obstinately refused to use it: "I had earnestly," he says, "ever since my first coming, required them to observe and follow that only book of common-prayer; but that would they at no hand obey."—Bale's Vocacyon, *ut supra*, p. 343.

Mary's Abbey, then in the suburbs of the city, reminding him of the obedience which he owed to the king; and in the hope of inducing him to join with the other prelates in adopting the liturgy, he requested Dowdal to appoint a place, "where," as Sir James artfully expressed it, "he might conveniently have an opportunity of appeasing wrath between the fathers of the church and his grace." With this request the primate complied, though he declined appearing at the deputy's palace, and at the same time expressed his apprehensions of the inutility of the proposed conference. "I fear," he said, "that it is in vain for me to converse with an obstinate number of churchmen, and in vain for your lordship to suppose the difference between us can be so soon appeased, as our judgments, opinions and consciences are so different."(64) But Sir James, anxious to secure the co-operation of one who held the highest station in the Irish church, appointed the conference to be held at the temporary residence of Dowdal. Staples, bishop of Meath, advocated the reformed mode of worship; while the primate, at the head of his suffragan clergy, undertook to defend the service of the mass. Like all similar discussions, the conference terminated without effecting any change in the sentiments of either party, both of whom retired more firmly attached to their previous opinions. In October following, the primacy of Ireland was transferred from Armagh to Dublin, with the view of mortifying Dowdal and his partizans, and, at the same time, of encouraging Brown and the reformed clergy. This expedient, inadequate as it was to meet the exigencies of the case, had the desired effect. Dowdal soon after fled to the continent, and the popish party were thus, at a very critical period, deprived of their most influential leader.(65)

Notwithstanding this partial triumph, the cause of the Reformation advanced but slowly. None of the other important measures, already adopted with success in England,

64 Harris's MSS. Roy. Dub. Soc. vol. iv. p. 472.
65 Leland, ii. 197—9.

were even attempted to be introduced into Ireland; nor did the lord deputy, though he commenced his government with apparent zeal, continue to exert himself in behalf of the truth. Though it was an express article in his instructions from the British court, to have the service of the church translated into Irish for general use throughout the kingdom, yet no steps were taken to carry into effect this most wise and salutary proposal. Neither was the want of preachers, even in the metropolis, yet supplied. The lord chancellor Cusack, in a letter to the duke of Northumberland, in the year 1552, states that they had no preaching throughout the year, and justly ascribes to this lamented deficiency the ignorance and insubordination which prevailed in all parts of the kingdom.[66]

To account for the slow progress of the truth at this period, it has been asserted, that the indiscreet violence of the persons who were commissioned to remove the idolatrous images out of the churches, but who, at the same time, stripped them of their most necessary furniture, tended to inflame the prejudices of the people against the reformed faith. No evidence of such precipitate zeal can be discovered. One of Sir James Croft's instructions doubtless was, to "prevent

66 Quoted by Leland (ii. 193,) from the original in Trinity College, Dublin. I examined this MS. in the College Library. It is in F. 3. 16, No. 6, and is dated May 8, 1552. It is a long and very important document, giving a geographical and statistical account of the entire kingdom; but I could not meet with the passages quoted by Leland. As a sample of its contents I subjoin a paragraph, descriptive of the county Antrim at that period, p. 72.—"The country of Claneboy is in woods and bogs for the greatest part; wherein lies Carrickfergus and so to the Glynns, where the Scotts do inhabit such of this country as is near the sea, a champaign country of twenty miles in length, and not over four miles in breadth or little more. The same Hugh (Oge O'Neill) hath two castles; one called Belfast, an old castle standing upon a ford that leadeth from Ards to Claneboy, which being well repaired (being now broken down) would be a good defence betwixt the woods and Knockfergus. The other called Castlereagh is four miles from Belfast, upon the plain in the midst of the woods."

the sale of bells, church-goods, and chauntry lands."[67] These, however, had been, as in England, fraudulently laid hold of by the laity, sometimes even by the clergy, who, in the midst of the confusions produced by the change of the national faith, were desirous of enriching themselves at the expense of some neglected and forsaken church or monastery. It is not even hinted that these spoils had been seized by the outrageous zeal of popular fury against popery. On the contrary, the mention of "chauntry lands" plainly intimates that they had been surreptitiously obtained; and it was against this private peculation, that the deputy was instructed to guard. Only one instance of that indiscreet ardour, which some historians deplore, is produced to justify their censure. But the spoliation alluded to did not proceed from religious but military zeal. In the contests between Sir Nicholas Bagnall and an Irish chief, in the year 1552, the garrison of Athlone obtained a temporary triumph at Clonmacnoise; when in revenge for some losses which they had previously sustained, they plundered the country, and, in this work of retaliation, pillaged the church and destroyed what they could not carry away. The Irish annals, which contain the only authentic narrative of this transaction, describe it, agreeably to the translation of an eminent Roman Catholic ecclesiastic, as the work of foreigners, not of protestants.[68] Such a spoliation, therefore, cannot surely be ascribed to religious fury, or afford any just ground for the lamentations in which even protestant historians have joined, over the ruthless and sacrilegious zeal

67 Cox, i. 290.

68 The late Charles O'Connor, D. D. librarian to the duke of Buckingham, the very highest authority on points of this nature, has given (Hist. Address, part ii. p. 307) the following translation of the original passage from the Irish Annals.—"Cluanmacnoise plundered and ravaged by the Gals—*i. e. the Foreigners not the Protestants*—of Athlone, and the great bells carried off from the steeple. They did not leave a small or a great bell, an image or an altar, or a book, or hardly a pane of glass in any of the windows from one end to the other of the church which they did not carry off." The explanatory clause initalics is inserted by Dr. O'Connor.

of the early reformers.[60] In truth, the prejudices of the Romanist party, instead of being at this period unnecessarily shocked, were but too studiously consulted; and so far from there being an excess, there was a most deplorable want, of sincere and earnest zeal in all the measures adopted for the advancement of true religion. None of the reformers, not even archbishop Brown himself, seems to have been impressed with a deep or honest conviction of the pernicious nature of the errors of popery; nor did any of them advance a single step in the work of reformation, to which they had not been previously urged by the English government.

The primacy and several of the Irish sees being now vacant, efforts were made at the English court to procure adequate persons to fill these influential situations. Application was

[60] It affords a curious illustration of the origin and progress of historical error, when we discover a leading author on any side taking a particular view of a transaction, to observe how those who follow after him, instead of examining the accuracy of his statement, unhesitatingly adopt it. This is strikingly exemplified in the present case. Leland assumed that the destruction of the church at Clonmacnoise was owing to "the barbarous and heathen fury" of those who were commissioned to remove the idolatrous images from the churches. Upon this view of a solitary transaction, he does not hesitate to brand the reformers, generally, as sacrilegious spoilers of "all the most valuable furniture of the churches." Stuart, in his valuable "History of Armagh," (p. 239,) adopts the same view, and states that they executed their commission "in the most violent, outrageous, and indecent manner." But he gives us no additional facts or authorities. Taylor, another Protestant writer, in his "Civil Wars of Ireland," (i. 168,) forming No. 73 of Constable's Miscellany, refers to this never-failing case of Clonmacnoise, as teaching the Romanists that "the new system sanctioned sacrilege and robbery;" and, he adds, that "similar excesses were committed in other parts of the country." But still we are not furnished with any specific cases. Until such therefore be pointed out from authentic sources, I cannot join with these and various other protestant writers in condemning the Irish reformers on the solitary case of Clonmacnoise, which, I trust, I have satisfactorily shown ought not to be attributed to religious "fury." I may remark that, at least in Waterford, there could have been no great spoliation, as we find the dean and chapter, in 1577, selling two hundred pounds worth of plate, the property of the cathedral—no inconsiderable sum in those days.—Ryland's Waterford, p. 135.

made to archbishop Cranmer to nominate a few individuals whom he might conceive to be not only qualified to be bishops, but willing to undertake the office in this remote and turbulent country. Having stated in his reply, that he "knew very few that would gladly be persuaded to remove to Ireland," he, at the same time, named four, whom he "thought for conscience sake would not refuse to bestow the talent committed unto them wheresoever it shall please the king's majesty to appoint them." One of these, W. Turner of Canterbury, owing to the character given him by Cranmer,[70] was selected by Edward in the month of August to be archbishop of Armagh. When he was apprised of the dignity intended for him, he was most unwilling to accept it. The following account of Cranmer's endeavours to persuade him to go to Ireland, has been happily preserved, and is strikingly illustrative, not only of the aversion which faithful men felt to enter, even as bishops, on the ministry in this country, but also of the sound views which were entertained of what was requisite for constituting a successful preacher in Ireland. "Now at last," writes Cranmer to Sir William Cecil, "against his will, Turner is come up unto the court. He preached twice in the camp that was by Canterbury, for which the rebels would have hanged him; and he seemed then more glad to go to hanging than he doth now to go to Armachane, he alleged so many excuses. But the chief is, that he shall preach to the walls and stalls, for the people (he says) understand no English. I bear him in hand, yes; and yet I doubt whether they speak English in the diocese of Armachane. But if they do not, then I say, that if he will take the pains to learn the Irish tongue, which with dili-

70 The following is Cranmer's character of Turner;—"Who besides that he is merry and witty withal, nihil appetit, nihil ardet, nihil somniat, nisi Jesum Christum; and in the lively preaching of him and his word, he declareth such diligence, fruitfulness and wisdom, as for the same deserveth much commendation."—Strype's Memorials of Cranmer, Oxf. 1812, vol. i. 905.

gence he may do in a year or two, then both his person and doctrine shall be more acceptable not only unto his diocese, but thorowe all Ireland."(71) The archbishop's efforts, however, proved unavailing, and Turner altogether refused to remove to Ireland. At length, in the end of the year, two of the vacant sees were accepted by men eminently qualified for the office, both of whom were at that period chaplains to the bishop of Winchester, and well known to each other. On the 27th of October, John Bale was nominated to the see of Ossory, and on the 4th of November, Hugh Goodacre to that of Armagh; and letters of the same dates were despatched from court to the lord deputy and council of Ireland in commendation of these bishops elect.(72)

Of Goodacre, little could be known, as he died within three months after his appointment to the primacy; "having been poisoned at Dublin," according to Bale, "by procurement of certain priests of his diocese, for preaching God's verity and rebuking their common vices."(73) Of Bale, we have many authentic memorials which show him to have possessed not only the fidelity, learning and piety of a reformer, but also the zeal, energy and courage essential to the character of a champion of the truth. Deeply convinced of the ruinous errors of popery, he attacked and exposed them without reserve. For this honest boldness he had been twice imprisoned in England by the ruling clergy. Owing to the favour of lord Cromwell, already mentioned, he obtained his liberty; and, after the melancholy death of his patron, he retired to the continent, where he spent eight years in habits of intimacy and friendship with Luther, Calvin, and other celebrated con-

(71) Strype's Cranmer, i. p. 907.

(72) Ibid. p. 393.

(73) Bale's Vocacyon, ut supra, p. 343, who styles him "that godly preacher, and virtuous learned man." In his Scrip. Illus. Mag. Britt. Basil. 1567. Pars sec. p. 231, Bale thus describes him;—"Virum doctrinæ sinceritate ac vitæ integritate conspicuum D. Hugonem Goodacrum, beatæ memoriæ, concionatorem in Hybernia vigilantissimum, ac theologica eloquentia non immerito commendatum."

tinental reformers. At the accession of Edward VI. he returned to England, and in August, 1552, was offered the see of Ossory. He could not, however, for some time, be prevailed on to accept it, alleging his age, being then nearly sixty, his poverty, and his ill health, as sufficient to excuse him from undertaking so arduous a charge. At the personal solicitation of the sovereign himself, Bale at length consented; and in conjunction with his friend and colleague Goodacre, was solemnly set apart to his office on the 2d of February, 1553. His determination to refuse all conformity to the ceremonies of the ancient superstition was manifested at his consecration, in an incident, which at the same time still farther displays the timid and temporising policy that continued to actuate the other dignitaries of the church. Lockwood, the dean of the cathedral, insisted on using the popish form of consecration, and refused to adopt the form set forth in the book of common prayer, though this book had, two years before, been regularly received by the reformed clergy. He alleged that the use of the new form would excite a tumult, and that not having been yet ratified by parliament, it could not be deemed binding. In this opinion, strange to tell, he was joined by archbishop Brown, Lancaster of Kildare, and the other assembled prelates. Goodacre, the primate elect, differed from these brethren, though for the sake of peace he was willing, on this occasion, to acquiesce in the use of the Romish ritual. But Bale opposed it in the most decided manner. He would not, in any degree, consent to adopt the ritual of so corrupted a church. His firmness prevailed. The reformed ritual was adopted. No tumult ensued. The timid supporters of the Reformation were abashed and confounded. They were taught the weakness of those apprehensions by which they had been kept in awe of the multitude, and restrained from exposing, with sufficient energy, the monstrous errors of popery. And an example was set them of uncompromising fidelity to the truth, which, had it been generally followed, would have soon changed the religious aspect of Ireland, and laid the foundation for the ultimate triumph of the reformed faith. The people would have seen and appreciated the whole extent of the difference that existed between the Romish and Protestant churches, which was studiously concealed from their eyes by the temporising conduct of their teachers; and though their prejudices might have been shocked, and the passions of a few roused, yet, from the manifest importance of the change proposed to them, a more serious inquiry into the grounds of their faith would have been the result—which is all that TRUTH requires to ensure her ultimate triumph. It was on this principle that Luther, Calvin, Knox, and the more successful of the early reformers acted—a principle from which Bale never deviated through the whole course of his ministry.

Immediately after his consecration, he repaired to his diocese, where he was a constant and faithful preacher. He has left on record the following interesting notices of his ministerial labours at this period. "My first proceedings were these;—I earnestly exhorted the people to repentance for sin, and required them to give credit to the gospel of salvation: To acknowledge and believe that there was but one God; and him alone, without any other, sincerely to worship: To confess one Christ for an only Saviour and Redeemer, and to trust in none other man's prayers, merits, nor yet deservings, but in his alone, for salvation. I treated at large both of the heavenly and political state of the Christian church; and helpers I found none among my prebendaries and clergy, but adversaries a great number. I preached the gospel of the knowledge and right invocation of God. But when I once sought to destroy the idolatries and dissolve the hypocrites' yokes, then followed angers, slanders, conspiracies, and in the end, the slaughter of men."[74] While he thus faithfully proclaimed the truth, he also laboured, with the utmost diligence, to correct the vices of his clergy, whom he found

(74) Vocacyon, ut supra, p. 342.

plunged in the grossest licentiousness. He at once abolished the idolatrous service of the mass, and sought to lead the people to the knowledge and love of true religion. For this purpose he considered no lawful means improper to be employed. The present age may smile to hear of a bishop writing metrical interludes on religious subjects, and causing them to be acted in public places for the edification of the public. But though manifestly unsuitable to the taste and circumstances of the present generation, it proved at that period a most successful means of exposing error and conveying truth in a lively and affecting manner.[75] In this useful course, however, he was permitted to continue but a very few months. By the premature death of Edward VI., in the month of June, and the subsequent accession of queen Mary, the Romish party in Ireland assumed new courage, and ventured on acts of violence which they would not otherwise have attempted. Accordingly, Bale, who had been hitherto secure and unmolested, and who, had Edward lived, would doubtless have continued so, now became the object of virulent persecution. In the month of September, five of his servants were barbarously murdered beside his residence, which he was consequently forced to abandon. Protected by a strong escort, he was conveyed in safety to Kilkenny, " the young men," as he relates, " singing psalms and other godly songs in rejoice of my deliverance, the people in great number stood on both sides of the way, both within the gates and

(75) Bale tells us that on the day on which queen Mary was proclaimed at Kilkenny, " the young men in the forenoon played a tragedy of God's promises in the old law, at the market-cross ; in the afternoon again they played a comedy of Saint John the Baptist's preachings, of Christ's baptizing, and of his temptation in the wilderness, to the small contentation of the priests and other papists there." Vocacyon, ut supra, p. 345. The latter of these is printed in the Harleian Miscellany, (i. 202, et seq.) and is thus entitled, " A brefe Comedy or Enterlude of Johan Baptystes preachynge in the wyldernesse ; openynge the craftye assaultes of hypocrytes, compyled anno M.D.XXXVIII." He wrote at least twelve other comedies on Scriptural subjects. Biog. Brit. art. *Bale.*

without, with candles lighted in their hands, shouting out praises to God for delivering me from the hands of these murderers :" a pleasing and satisfactory evidence that though persecuted by the more bigoted, he had secured the affectionate regard of a large portion of his people. Here he maintained his ground with firmness for some time longer; till at length finding it impossible to remain, his life being daily endangered, he reluctantly withdrew; and after encountering many difficulties, succeeded in reaching the continent in safety.(76)

This violence which Bale encountered after the death of the king, is assumed by several Protestant historians as decisive evidence of the impropriety of his conduct; and many severe reflections are made on his uncompromising opposition to the errors and superstitions by which he was encompassed, and by which, like the apostle, "his spirit was stirred in him when he saw the city wholly given to idolatry."(77)

(76) Some very narrow escapes occurred in his flight, which may be seen in the Biog. Brit. art. *Bale;* and in Brooke's Lives of the Puritans, i. 105-6. On the accession of Elizabeth, he returned to England, but declined acting as a bishop, and refused to accept his former preferment, his principles inclining him rather to join with the Non-conformists. He died at Canterbury, of which cathedral he was a prebendary, in November, 1563. His voluminous and valuable writings are prohibited by the church of Rome, and placed in the first class of heretical books. The following epigram, by a contemporary, shows the opinion then entertained of the value of his labours in the cause of truth :—

Plurima Lutherus patefecit, Platina multa,
Quaedam Vergerius, cuncta Balæus habet.

A friend has favoured me with the following metrical verson of these lines;

Most of the errors of the Church of Rome
Luther exposed—Platina *many* told;
To *some*, Vergerius held the lamp of truth,
But Bale, with matchless lore, does *all* unfold.

77 Leland sarcastically styles him, "the violent and acrimonious impugner of Popery," and describes him as "insulting the prejudices of his flock without reserve or caution." Yet he confesses he could not discover what imprudencies Bale committed, or what "was the intemperate conduct which his adversaries retorted with such shocking barbarity." Why then,

But these reflections are certainly unmerited. For it ought to be remembered, that being the only active and zealous prelate in the kingdom, his solitary and successful exertions were the more obnoxious to the Popish clergy, and drew down upon him their special indignation. At the same time, he was secretly disliked by many of his reformed brethren, whose indolence was exposed, and whose timidity was alarmed, by his undaunted fidelity and perseverance. Let it be remarked, too, that no violence was offered during six months, when it might be expected the irritation of his bigoted opponents would have been greatest; nor was it till the death of Edward, and the accession of a Romanist to the throne, that he experienced any annoyance. It is truly deplorable to observe the severity and injustice with which Protestant writers have reflected on the character of the only sincere reformer that the church in Ireland enjoyed, at this critical period of her history.

The accession of Queen Mary proved fatal, for a time, to the progress of the Reformation in Ireland. Under her inauspicious sway, the Roman Catholic religion was formally restored by Parliament. The supremacy of the Pope was re-established. Dowal was recalled with honour to his see, and restored to the envied primacy of all Ireland. The prelates who favoured the Reformation and had married, were, on the latter pretence, ejected from their sees. These were Brown of Dublin,[78] Staples of Meath, Casey of Limerick, Travers of Leighlin, and Lancaster of Kildare. Eight other prelates, who had equally acknowledged the royal supremacy and professed the reformed doctrines, quietly acceded to the changes now introduced, and became the adherents of the church of Rome, which they again abandoned to embrace,

we may ask, should the historian have reflected so severely on his conduct? Was it possible, at that period, for any sincere Protestant prelate to do his duty, and escape the factious opposition of the Popish clergy?

78 "Queen Mary's writ constituting Hugh Curwen, Archbishop of Dublin, in room of George Brown deprived, is dated April 25, 1555. Rym. Fœd. vol vi. part iv. p. 37."

under Elizabeth, the Protestant faith.[79]—The people relapsed into their former state of blind subjection to the Papal see, from which they had been as yet scarcely severed; and as there was none to disturb the government in their measures, or provoke the indignation of the clergy, so there was less apparent persecution in Ireland during this reign than in England. The ruling powers were satisfied that they had replaced the Romish faith in all its former security. A day of jubilee was observed throughout the kingdom for its happy restoration.[80] Whatever number of Protestants may have remained, were deemed too few and insignificant to excite any alarm for its uninterrupted establishment in this favoured "island of saints." Ireland, therefore, strange as it may appear, became an asylum for the persecuted Protestants of England, who resorted thither to escape the fury of their Romish countrymen. Some of these little colonies brought with them their ministers, who privately officiated among them, even in the metropolis; and thus, while Ireland appeared to be doomed to the most hopeless sterility, the seeds of reformation, by the fostering care of Providence, whose "ways are not as our ways," were springing up in it more extensively than when under the protection of a nominally reformed government.[81] Preparation was indeed made for introducing into Ireland the persecuting measures which cha-

79 These were Magennis of Down and Connor, Devereux of Ferns, Walsh of Waterford, Magennis of Dromore, Bodekin of Tuam, De Burgo of Elphin, Nugent of Kilmore, and Tirrey of Cork. The two latter died in the end of Queen Mary's reign, but the others, under Elizabeth, once more reverted to the reformed faith!—a remarkable evidence of the little care that had been taken to fill the vacant sees with faithful or conscientious ministers.

80 Ware's Annals, ad an. 1554.

81 "1554. This year several of the Protestants of England fled over into Ireland, by reason Queen Mary began to prosecute them for their religion, viz.—John Harvey, Abel Ellis, John Edmonds, and Henry Haugh, all Cheshire men; who bringing over their goods and chattels lived in Dublin, and became citizens thereof; it not being known wherefore they came

racterised this reign in England. In the month of October 1558, Dr. Cole, Romish Dean of St. Paul's, was despatched by Mary with a commission to Lord Deputy Fitzwalter, authorising him to proceed with vigour in the detection and punishment of Protestants within his jurisdiction. The dean having arrived at Chester, was waited on by the mayor, to whom he showed with exultation his commission, and boasted of the severities which it would be the means of inflicting on the heretics in Ireland. This intelligence alarmed his hostess, who had several Protestant friends concealed in Dublin. Watching her opportunity, she removed the commission out of the box in which it was deposited, and substituted in its place a parcel of similar size. Cole, ignorant of this exchange, proceeded to Dublin, and having presented himself before the deputy and council, he explained at length the pious intention of the queen in support of the church, and concluded with handing his box to the secretary that the commission might be formally read. But to the dismay of the dean, and the surprise of the council, instead of the commission, the box contained only a pack of cards, with the knave of clubs faced upwards. The deputy, probably not displeased that he was so unexpectedly freed from the invidious office of a persecutor, humorously replied,—"Let us have a new commission, and we will shuffle the cards in the mean time." Cole returned and succeeded in obtaining a new commission, but the death of the queen, in the month of November, happily and providentially defeated the design.[88]

hither, until Queen Mary's death. These families having one Thomas Jones, a Welshman, a Protestant priest, privately amongst them, who read service and the Scripture to them upon Sundays and other days secretly; all this not being discovered until Queen Mary's death."—Ware's Annals.

[88] Hist. Coll. of the church in Ireland, pp. 17, 18. The woman's name was Elizabeth Edmonds, sister to John Edmonds, mentioned in the preceding note—Leland seems to discredit the authenticity of this singular occurrence, but, in my opinion, without sufficient grounds.

The peaceful and unobstructed accession of Elizabeth to the throne was a most auspicious event to the persecuted Protestants in England. It was equally so to the interests of the truth in Ireland, though, from the unhappy state of the kingdom, it was some time before its beneficial effects were visible. The flattering prospects presented in the reign of Edward had been blighted by the bigotry of Mary. Scarcely any traces were discernible, on the face of the church, of the previous reformation, which had been too superficial to withstand the storm of Popish violence. The work had therefore to be commenced anew; but the individuals to whom it was intrusted profited little by the experience of former years. The same fatal error into which former rulers had fallen, of forcing external conformity, unsupported by adequate instruction, was still persisted in; though its futility had been exposed, and its pernicious effects fully developed, to the English court by some of its most influential advisers. Owing to this radical error, less progress was made in reviving and extending the Reformation than might have been reasonably expected.

Though Queen Elizabeth was known to be attached to the reformed faith, the news of her accession to the crown was received in Dublin without any symptoms of dissatisfaction. The event was celebrated in the usual manner, and for more than six months every thing continued as in the preceding reign. The first indication of the religious sentiments of the court was manifested in an order sent in May 1559, to the dean of Christ-church, to remove from his cathedral all relics, images, and pictures, and to substitute in their place, appropriate passages of Scripture.[83] This order was soon after followed by an important gift conferred on the metropolis by an English prelate. Dr. Heath, archbishop of York, sent a large English Bible to each of the two cathedrals of St. Patrick and

83 Thomas Lockwood was the name of this dignitary, and like his superiors was a genuine *Vicar of Bray*. At the consecration of Bishop Bale,

Christ-church, to be fixed in the centre of the choirs, and not only to be read in divine service, but to be left open for public perusal. The avidity with which the people availed themselves of this privilege, plainly indicated that it was the first of the kind with which they had been favoured. They came in crowds to hear the word of God read, and both before and after divine service, they shewed great impatience to peruse it for themselves. Once acquainted with its contents, their desire for further knowledge rapidly increased. The archbishop's seasonable gift prepared the way for a subsequent demand for Bibles, which must have had an important influence in promoting the cause of the Reformation. For in the year 1566, John Dale, a Dublin bookseller, encouraged by the growing desire of the people to become better acquainted with the sacred volume, imported from London a supply of small Bibles, then first printed; and so urgent was the demand, that in less than two years he disposed of no fewer than seven thousand copies.[m]

So soon as circumstances permitted, which was not until the beginning of the year 1560, a parliament was held in Dublin, for the purpose of again transferring the sanctions of the law from the Romish to the Protestant faith. With the exception of the opposition given by the nobles, which, however, was so alarming as to induce the deputy to prorogue the

the reader has seen his anxiety to see the Romish ritual. At the accession of Mary he relapsed into Popery, if indeed he had ever abandoned it; and now, at that of Elizabeth, he retains his dignities and emoluments, and has so little of even decent consistency, that he is willing to be employed in pulling down the former objects of his adoration. Men were set to work for this purpose, May 23rd, 1559. Ware's Annals. Yet even this order was only partially complied with. From a note at p. 181. of Mason's St. Patrick, it would appear, that so late as the year 1630, images still remained in some parts of that cathedral. In October 1578 the Bishop of Cork publicly burned St. Dominic's image at the high cross of that city, "to the great grief of the superstitious people there." Ware's Bishops, p. 566. Cox, i. [illegible].

m Ware's Annals, ad an. 1566.

parliament in a few weeks, this important change was speedily effected. Of nineteen prelates who had conformed to Popery under Mary, only two now adhered with steadfastness to their profession, thus exhibiting another degrading instance of clerical tergiversation. The commons, consisting of representatives from ten counties out of thirty-two, and from about twenty towns, principally under the influence of the crown, acquiesced more readily, though not without evident reluctance, in the proposed measures; so that the whole ecclesiastical fabric was again overthrown as promptly as it had been constructed at the accession of Mary. By this parliament, "the ecclesiastical jurisdiction was restored to the crown, and a new oath of supremacy appointed; the use of the common prayer was enforced, and all subjects obliged to attend the public service of the church."[85] A most absurd enactment was passed, respecting the use of the common prayer-book by those who might be ignorant of the English language. It was one of the essential principles of the Reformation, that divine service should be conducted in the language of the worshippers. As English was not a spoken language, except in the metropolis and some of the principal towns, one of the most obvious measures of the court ought to have been to have the liturgy translated into Irish, and ministers speaking this tongue provided for that vast majority of the population who knew no other language. Accordingly, one of the instructions given to Sir James Croft, in a preceding reign, had been to procure such a translation; but no efforts had been made for that purpose.[86] Instead, however, of reviving this wise and salutary measure, and giving it the sanction of legislative authority, it was inconsistently enacted, that where the minister, and, by implication, the people, did not understand English, the public service should be per-

[85] Leland ii. 224-5.

[86] According to Cox, (i. 290) the first instruction given him was,—"to propagate the worship of God in the English tongue, and the service to be translated into Irish to those places which need it."

formed, not in the Irish tongue known to both parties, but in the Latin language unknown to either! The reasons assigned for this singular order was as insufficient, as the measure itself was absurd and ridiculous. They were founded on the pleas, that the Irish language was difficult to be printed; and that, if printed, few even of the native reformed clergy could be found competent to read it. [87] And thus for the sake of these temporary obstacles, which prudent and zealous rulers would soon have found means of removing, the dissemination of the truth through the country was effectually impeded, and the most ignorant as well as the most numerous class of the community were cut off from the benefits of divine worship, and attached more strongly to their ancient errors.

The deputy, the Earl of Sussex, perceived the visible reluctance with which these ecclesiastical changes were received. After hastily dissolving the parliament, in the beginning of February he retired to England to consult Elizabeth and her council on the subsequent measures which he should adopt for rendering effectual the recent acts of the legislature. He returned in the following month, and, by the Queen's directions, summoned a general meeting of the clergy of the kingdom, to tender to them the new oath of supremacy, and excite them to introduce the reformation into their respective dioceses. As already stated, only two bishops had refused to conform. Walsh of Meath, not only declined taking the oath, but attacked with violence the book of common-prayer, and persisting to warn his clergy and people against it, he was deposed from his dignity, and cruelly imprisoned for many years. Leverous of Kildare, also declined the oath, and defended his refusal principally on the ground of the sovereign's sex. Being asked, by the lord deputy, the cause of his declining an oath already taken by many learned and illustrious men, he replied, " that all ecclesiastical jurisdiction was

87 2 Elizabeth, chap. 2, sect. 15.

derived from Christ—that since he thought not fit to confer such authority on the blessed Virgin his mother, it could not be believed that he would delegate supremacy to any other person of that sex—that St. Paul had forbidden any woman to speak in the church, much less to preside and rule there—and, that the same doctrine was maintained by Chrysostom and Tertullian," whose sentiments he quoted. (88) To these reasons no answer was returned but one—an argument, with the force of which, in Queen Mary's days, he had himself been familiar—that, if he refused to comply, he must be deprived of his office. This sacrifice he willingly made. He was deposed from the prelacy, and for many years supported himself by filling the humble office of a schoolmaster. (89)

The example set by these two prelates was followed by many of the inferior clergy; who resigned their dignities, and either abandoned the kingdom or retired to the more remote districts, where they remained without molestation. The government was extremely remiss in filling the vacancies thus created. The see of Meath, a most extensive diocese in the immediate vicinity of Dublin, continued vacant for two years. Clogher enjoyed a bishop for only one year during a period of above half a century—from the year 1557 to 1610! Even the primacy was vacant for four years, while the remoter dioceses still remained at the uncontrolled disposal of the Pope. When the more lucrative and influential stations in the church were thus permitted to remain unoccupied, it will not appear surprising that the inferior benefices should share a similar fate. So protracted indeed was the interruption of divine service in many places, that even the churches fell into decay, and when incumbents at length took possession of them, they were generally so ruinous as to be unfit for use. (90)

88 Extracted from a rare work, printed at Cologne in 1649, entitled—"De processu martyriali," &c.

89 Mason's Cathedral of St. Patrick, pp. 163-4.

90 Leland ii, 226. This desolation of the churches was completed by the continual wars in which the country was involved, throughout the

This shameful neglect was scarcely less injurious to the progress of the Reformation, than were the harsh measures employed to press external conformity on the prejudiced and uninstructed people. The penalties for neglecting to frequent the church were, for a time at least, strictly inflicted.[91] But many attended merely to escape the fine, and consequently in a state of mind that unfitted them for receiving instruction. Others endeavoured to 'serve two masters,' by attending the mass in the morning, and the authorized service afterwards; while the greater number refused altogether to attend. To remedy these defects, the churchwardens were directed to call over the list of householders in every parish, and exact the fines from the absent. And where these measures were found ineffectual, soldiers were not unfrequently quartered on a refractory parish, till by their violence and rapacity, the people were harassed into a reluctant and ineffectual conformity.[92] Proclamations were issued against Popish priests and friars, forbidding them to meet in Dublin or reside within the walls. If they were apprehended they were unceremoniously cast into prison, and treated with the combined rigour due to both recusants and rebels.[93] These severities, especially at the commencement of a reign, served only to alienate the people more and more from the reformed faith; and their animosity being studiously inflamed by the priests, while no means were taken, either by the Protestant clergy or the state, to inform their minds or win their confidence, a powerful barrier, rendered every year more formidable, was raised against the progress of the Reformation.

whole of this reign. In the commencement of the following century, the state of the parish churches was most deplorable. In 1538, the cathedral of Down was burned by the lord deputy Grey; and in 1566, O'Neill burned that of Armagh. See note (96.)

91 We find Sir William Drury, when lord deputy, in October 1578, binding several citizens of Kilkenny, "by recognisance of forty pounds, to come to church to hear divine service every Sunday." Cox, i. 354.

92 Chronicle of Chichester's government, in Desid. Cur. Hib. i. 252.

93 Ware's Annals, ad an. 1563.

In truth, strange as it may appear under a government proverbially vigorous in civil affairs, neither Elizabeth nor her ministers, after the first formal change of the national faith, ever seriously entered on the consideration of the religious state of Ireland. In thirteen letters of instruction to various lords deputies during her reign, the subject is passed over in almost total silence, and when noticed, it is in a very vague manner.[94] The most important of the enactments passed in parliament respecting religion were, for the most part, suffered to slumber on the statute-book, as if they had been intended for no other purpose than to give unnecessary irritation to the Romanist party. The same silence respecting religion is observable in nearly all the contemporary pamphlets published relative to Ireland;[95] while, during the same period, no other topic engrossed so much of the literature of both the sister kingdoms. This silence may, in part, be accounted for by the turbulent state of the country, and by the frequent and formidable rebellions, which, at the instigation of the Pope, were organized against the authority of Elizabeth. It was in Ireland, during this reign, that the head of the Romish church, deprived of his influence both in England and Scotland, made his most pertinacious and successful opposition to the power of the queen and the progress of the truth. His excommunication of Elizabeth, which was despised in Britain, had in Ireland a formidable effect in exciting to rebellion a bigoted nobility and a superstitious people. By his influence, too, the king of Spain, on several occasions, sent forces to cooperate with those Irish chiefs who were ambitious of distinguishing themselves in support of the Holy See. Thus the discord which had ever subsisted between the English and the natives, and which had been fomented by the selfish policy of the British court, and by the insolent rapacity and in-

94 These letters may be seen in the first volume of Desid. Cur. Hib.

95 These were indeed comparatively few; but it is extremely mortifying to the inquirer to find them all so destitute of facts or references relative to the state and progress of religion here during this reign.

justice of its adherents, was still further aggravated by religious rancour; so that the government was almost exclusively occupied in taking measures for its own defence, and had scarcely leisure to attend either to the civil improvement or the religious reformation of the kingdom. These circumstances prepare us to expect, during the remainder of this reign, no very zealous or successful exertions in support of the truth. Where it did spring up, it was not without countenance and protection. But its progress was confined solely to the cities and principal towns, many of which now made profession of the reformed faith;[96] while the rural population of the kingdom remained unnoticed and unenlightened, in a state of wretched ignorance and delusion.

In the year 1569, a second parliament was convened under the auspices of Sir Henry Sydney, an able and enlightened statesman. By this assembly two acts were passed, which, had they been brought into operation, might have been of considerable benefit. But they were soon forgotten amidst the tumults of civil war. By one of these, all presentations to cathedral dignities in the provinces of Munster and Connaught, with the exception of four dioceses, were, for ten years, put into the hands of the chief governor of the kingdom, who was strictly enjoined to present none but duly qualified persons, "who can speak English and will reside." The reason alleged for transferring this extraordinary power to the lord deputy is assigned in the preamble of the bill, the following summary of which will serve to illustrate the state of religion in those extensive provinces: "Whereas persons have been admitted to ecclesiastical dignities which had

96 There is great difficulty in ascertaining the time when the reformed religion was introduced into the cities and towns of Ireland. Galway is said to have received it in the beginning of Edward VI.'s reign, though the celebration of mass in public was only first prohibited in 1568. Hardiman, 85, 240-1. It appears from the charter of Queen Elizabeth, granted to the town of Carrickfergus in the year 1569, that the inhabitants had, several years before, embraced the reformed faith. M'Skimin's Carrickfergus, p. 180;—one of the very few valuable works illustrative of the local antiquities of Ireland.

neither legitimacy, learning, English habit or English language, but were the issue of unchaste abbots, priors, deans, chantors, and such like, getting into the same dignities by force, simony, or other undue means: therefore the chief governor of Ireland shall, for ten years to come, have the sole nomination of all deans, archdeacons, chantors, chancellors, and treasurers of cathedral churches in Munster and Connaught, those of Waterford, Cork, Limerick, and Cashel excepted."[97] By a second act, schools were ordered to be erected in the principal town of every diocese, under the direction of English schoolmasters, of whose salary one-third was to be paid by the bishop and the remainder by his clergy. Another act "for the reparation of parochial churches," had been transmitted by the council in England for the approbation of the parliament here. But it never passed into a law, having been either opposed by the popish party, or considered as too expensive, and therefore impracticable.[98]

A much more promising measure was shortly after attempted by private zeal and enterprise. A printing press, together with a set of Irish types, the first that had been cast, were brought into Ireland by two dignitaries of St. Patrick's cathedral, Dublin, who also procured an order for printing the

97 Cox, i. 331. See note (97.)

98 Leland, ii. 245. The following preamble to a proclamation, issued by Sir John Perrot, lord deputy, above fifteen years after the passing of these acts, furnishes another proof of the wretched state of the parish churches, and at the same time shows that the above act, on the subject of schools, had not been carried into effect. "4 March, 1584. Whereas it appeareth unto us, that churches and chauncels, for the most part, within this realm, are not only decayed, ruinated and broken down, to the great hindrance of God's divine service, whereby the people are for the most part, and in most places, left without instruction to know their duty to God and the prince; but also we find that free-schools, which are to be maintained and kept for the education and bringing up of youth in good literature, are now, for the most part, not kept or maintained, &c., &c.," therefore commissioners were apppointed to "make inquiry into the same." Here the matter ended, according to the established custom of Irish reforms, and nothing further was done. Hardiman's Bard. Rem. ii. 409-10.

liturgy in that character, and for setting apart in every principal town, a church in which divine service might be conducted, and a sermon preached in the Irish tongue.[99] It is doubtful whether any part of this most judicious plan was, at this period, carried into execution. There was, indeed, some preaching in the Irish tongue,[100] but the book of common-prayer was not published in that language till the reign of James I. Various books, however, were successively printed in Irish and partially circulated. A translation of the New Testament was in considerable progress, when it was unhappily interrupted by the murder of the translator, the bishop of Ossory, in the year 1585.[101] It was not completed until twenty years afterwards. This important though unsuccessful attempt, it is in the highest degree pleasing to contemplate, as it not only afforded a promise of better things to come, but was a gratifying proof that although the civil authorities were inattentive and negligent, there were individuals who deeply felt for the ignorance and error by which they were surrounded, and were anxious for the removal of these evils by the legitimate means of reasoning and instruction.

Such zealous and benevolent individuals, however, whether among the clergy or laity, were extremely few. The greatest

99 Ware's Annals, ad an. 1571: These dignitaries were Nic. Walsh, chancellor, who was afterwards bishop of Ossory, and John Kerney, treasurer. See note (43.)

100 This is evident from the statement of Ware, who says that these sermons in Irish "were instrumental in converting many of the ignorant sort in those days." Annals.

101 Nic. Walsh, mentioned in note (99), was surprised and murdered in his own house, on the 14th of Dec. 1585, by a man whom he had cited before his court for adultery. His translation of the New Testament was completed by Wm. Daniel, archbishop of Tuam, out of the original Greek. Ware's Bishops, p. 616. It was printed in 1602; at least this is the date upon the title-page. But as the work is dedicated to James I. after his accession to the English throne, it was probably only put to press in that year. A copy is in Trinity College library, Dublin. Archbishop Daniel also translated the book of common-prayer into Irish, which was printed in 1608, and dedicated to Sir Arthur Chichester, then lord deputy.

disadvantage under which the cause of truth now laboured, was the want of learned and pious ministers. This sad deficiency has been already alluded to, as characterizing the earlier periods of the Reformation. It was, no doubt, impossible that it should at once be supplied, even by the most diligent exertions to procure individuals fitted for the work of evangelizing the country. But these exertions were not made. The evil continued to exist, and even to increase. In the year 1576, Sir Henry Sydney feeling the want of a well-instructed ministry, was induced to write to Elizabeth herself on the subject, pointing out the magnitude of the evil, and entreating her to adopt the means which, at the same time, he suggested for its removal. In this letter he details the wretched situation of one diocese in the most populous and civilized part of the kingdom, and leaves his royal mistress to conjecture how destitute the remoter districts must be of an adequate ministry.

The following extracts, from this important document, are necessary for enabling the reader to form a correct idea of the ecclesiastical state of Ireland at this period. "I would not have believed, had I not for a great part viewed the same throughout the whole realm, and was advertised of the particular estate of each church in the bishoprick of Meath, (being the best inhabited country of all this realm) by the honest, zealous, and learned bishop of the same, Mr. Hugh Brady, a godly minister of the Gospel, who went from church to church himself, and found that there are within his diocese 224 parish churches, of which number 105 are impropriated to sundry possessions now of your Highness, and all leased out for years, or in fee farm, to several farmers, and great gain reaped out of them above the rent which your Majesty receiveth, no parson or vicar resident upon any of them, and a very simple or sorry curate for the most part appointed to serve them: among which number of curates, only eighteen were found able to speak English, the rest are Irish priests, or rather Irish rogues, having very little Latin and less learning and civility: all these live on the bare alterages (as they term them) which,

God knoweth, are very small, and were wont to live upon the gain of masses, dirges, shriving and such like trumpery, goodly abolished by your Majesty, no one house standing for any of them to dwell in. In many places the very walls of the churches down, very few chancels covered, windows or doors ruined or spoiled. There are fifty-two parish churches more, residue of the first number of 224, which pertain to divers particular lords; and these, though in better estate than the rest commonly are, yet far from well. If this be the estate of the church in the best peopled diocese and best governed country of this your realm, (as in truth it is) easy it is for your Majesty to conjecture in what case the rest is, where little or no reformation, either of religion or manners, hath yet been planted and continued among them. ——— Your Majesty may believe it, that upon the face of the earth, where Christ is professed, there is not a church in so miserable a case: the misery of which consisteth in these three particulars, the ruin of the very temples themselves, the want of good ministers to serve in them when they shall be re-edified, and competent livings for the ministers when well chosen." Sir Henry then proceeds to suggest the most practicable methods for supplying these deplorable deficiencies. He recommends that the churches be forthwith repaired; that search be made in the English Universities for reformed ministers, especially for such as can speak Irish; that if these cannot be found there, application be made to the Regent of Scotland, in whose dominions he states there were many persons thus qualified; and that some of the grave and well-beneficed English clergy be sent hither, "to undertake this apostleship, and that upon their own charges. They be rich enough," he adds, "and if either they be thankful to your Majesty for your immense bounty done to them, or zealous to increase the Christian flock, they will not refuse the honourable and religious travel."(102) These recommendations, how-

102 Sydney Papers, i. 112, et seq.

ever, though coming from so influential a quarter, and urged with so much earnestness, do not appear to have met with the least attention. There is no notice taken of them in the instructions given to subsequent deputies; and in the Parliament held a few years afterwards, at which were present four archbishops and twenty bishops, not a single enactment was passed bearing on the subject of religion! Such was the fate of all the good plans so often projected for advancing the Reformation in Ireland! They were neglected and forgotten. How could the Gospel be expected to prevail in the face of interest, prejudice, and passion, without the agency of ministers and missionaries to teach its doctrines, illustrate its excellence, and defend its truth against sophistry and misrepresentation?

But while the measures recommended by Sir Henry Sydney for obtaining a supply of faithful pastors were thus neglected, one obvious means for attaining this object, though unaccountably overlooked in his letter to the queen, was soon after adopted. This was the establishment of a University in Dublin. Such a measure had indeed been projected by Sydney in the year 1569, but like many similar plans, it had failed through the neglect or indifference of the English ministry. It was now, in the year 1590, revived. By the exertions of the archbishop of Dublin and the lord deputy Fitzwilliam, this important establishment was completed, and students were, for the first time, admitted on the ninth of January 1593.[103] One chief object of its erection was to afford facilities for the education of candidates for the national church. For this purpose the study of the Irish language was very judiciously encouraged, and endowments called "natives' places," which still exist, were set apart for the support of those who applied themselves to this pursuit. The college was founded on more liberal principles than those on which it has been subsequently conducted. The distinction

103 Leland, ii. 324—6.

between conformists and non-conformists, which had already been carried to so great an extent in England, was at this period happily unknown in Ireland. Conformity to the many rites and ceremonies which originated in human authority alone, was not as yet pressed upon the Irish Protestant clergy. The rulers of the church willingly received all the reformed ministers offering themselves, who were sound in the faith, and possessed the requisite zeal and learning. Nor was it until the inauspicious reign of Charles I. that the scheme was formed for bringing all the members of the church to an absolute and entire conformity. Nothing, indeed, save such a charitable comprehension as existed at this period, would have ever brought the Protestant church to any degree of stability in Ireland.

This liberal spirit was displayed in the early history of the University of Dublin. Its first elected fellows were two Presbyterians from Scotland, who had settled in the metropolis about five years before.(104) They were professedly engaged in teaching school; but, under this pretext, they were political agents of James I., employed by him in conducting a confidential correspondence with certain of the English nobility, and in forming a party in Ireland attached to his interest, in case of any competitor starting for the crown of England on the demise of Elizabeth.(105) Their names were Fullerton

104 They settled in Dublin in 1587. Lodge, iii. 1. It is singular, that in this same year, it was ordered by the state, "that no grammar but Lilly's should be taught in Ireland." The reason assigned for this minute act of legislation was, the variety of grammars previously used in schools, by which the progress of youth, moving from one school to another, was greatly impeded. Ware's Annals, ad an. 1587.

105 Cox, i. 397. Birch, in his "Life of Prince Henry," p. 178, states that they were first brought into notice by conveying the letters of some of the English lords "who worshipped the rising sun," to and from King James in Scotland; "that way being chosen as more safe than the direct northern road," in order to escape the vigilance of Elizabeth. Several other learned Scotchmen were also employed by James as political agents in Ireland at this period, Dr. Robert Maxwell, afterwards Dean of Armagh, was one of these. Lodge, iii. 390.

and Hamilton. The former was knighted and made a member of the royal household, on the king's removal to London. The latter had been master, and, in college, was tutor to the celebrated Ussher. He was afterwards ennobled by the title of Lord Claneboy, and for a time proved, as will be seen, a zealous patron of the Presbyterian interest in Ulster, where the king had conferred on him considerable estates.(106) The first two regular and official provosts of the college were also Non-conformists. The former of these was Walter Travers, one of the most celebrated of the English puritans. Though silenced for his non-conformity by Whitgift, archbishop of Canterbury, he was invited over to Ireland by Loftus, archbishop of Dublin, who had been his fellow-student at Trinity College, Cambridge, and who now vacated his honorary provostship, that he might provide for his persecuted friend. Travers accepted of the office in 1594, and presided over the college for several years.(107) He was much respected by Ussher, who under his guidance and the tuition of Hamilton, not only laid the foundation of his immense learning, but also imbibed those liberal sentiments towards Presbyterians by which he was distinguished. The successor of Travers

106 See M'Crie's life of Melville (ii. 405-8) for several interesting particulars relative to these Scotchmen. According to the Montgomery manuscripts, (Belfast, 1830, p. 30,) Sir James Fullerton was knighted and in favour at the English court so early as 1604-5. I find that the priory of Holm-patrick in the county of Dublin, and the monastery of friars of the blessed Virgin Mary at Ramullan, in the county of Donegall, were granted by James I. to Sir James Fullerton,—another evidence of his influence at court. The former he disposed of to the Earl of Thomond, and the latter to Sir Ralph Bingley. Ware, ii. 262, 283.

107 In 1598, the civil wars forced Travers to leave the college and the kingdom, when he returned to England, and died there in poverty and obscurity some time after the year 1624. Archbishop Ussher continued to respect him till his death. The pious prelate frequently visited him in England, when both old and poor, and offered him presents of money, but the good old man thankfully declined to accept them. Fuller's Church Hist. b. ix. p. 215-6. Brooke's Puritans, ii. 314-30. Those who wish to know the early part of Mr. Travers's history and his troubles in England, may consult the first volume of Neal's "History of the Puritans."

was Henry Alvey, B. D., an equally zealous puritan. He had been fellow of St. John's college, Cambridge; and, like his predecessor in the provostship, had been so persecuted by Whitgift for his non-conformity, that he resigned his fellowship and removed to Ireland, where so much greater freedom was enjoyed. He came to the college in February 1601, and in October following entered on the office of Provost, which he continued to fill until the year 1609, when he was elected the first vice-chancellor of the university.[108]

Some time necessarily elapsed before the beneficial effects resulting from the erection of the college were discernible in the church. The melancholy description, therefore, which Spenser gives of the Irish clergy and the religious state of the kingdom in the year 1596, need not excite surprise. In some respects it is even more gloomy than that given by Sir Henry Sydney twenty years before. A few extracts will suffice to show how much yet remained to be done in the work of instructing the people, and of purifying and reforming the clergy themselves. Of the *people* he states, " not one amongst an hundred knoweth any ground of religion, or any article of his faith; but can perhaps say his pater-noster or his ave-maria without any knowledge or understanding what one word thereof meaneth."[109] Among the *clergy*, he adds, " ye may find gross simony, greedy covetousness, fleshly incontinence, careless sloth, and generally all disordered life in the common clergymen;—they neither read scriptures,

108 Brooke's Puritans, ii. 85. Dub. Univ. Calendar, for 1833.

109 Spenser's State of Ireland. Dub. 1763. p. 129. Though written in 1596, this treatise was not printed until the year 1633.—The reader will probably be surprised to find Spenser in the above passage describe the professed Protestants as repeating the ave-maria, or the Romish prayer to the Virgin Mary, as a stated part of their daily worship. Yet such was the case even in England above half a century after this period. For Baxter, speaking of the state of religion in Worcestershire about the year 1640, says, that some of the people " on going to bed would say over the creed, or the Lord's prayer, and some of them the ' Hail Mary,' or ave-maria." Life by Silvester.

nor preach to the people, nor administer the communion. But baptism they do, for they christen yet after the Popish fashion." (110) Of the *bishops* he says, "in the remoter dioceses they do not at all bestow the benefices, which are in their own donation, upon any, but keep them in their own hands, and set their own servants and horseboys to take up their tythes and fruits." (111) In a strain of eloquence characteristic of the poet, he thus contrasts the zeal of the Romish, with the apathy of the Reformed clergy:—"It is a great wonder to see the odds which is between the zeal of Popish priests and the ministers of the Gospel; for they spare not to come out of Spain, from Rome, and from Rheims, by long toil and danger travelling hither, where they know peril of death awaiteth them, and no reward or riches is to be found, only to draw the people to the church of Rome: whereas some of our idle ministers having a way for credit and esteem thereby opened unto them, without pains and without peril, will neither for the same, nor any love of God, nor zeal of religion, nor for all the good they may do by winning souls to God, be drawn forth from their warm nests to look out into God's harvest which is even ready for the sickle, and all the fields yellow long ago." (112)

Such was the wretched state of the Irish church in the latter years of Elizabeth, and such it continued till her death, though her council were fully apprized of the method by which its condition might have been ameliorated. (113) But

110 Spenser, p. 131. 111 Ibid. p. 132. 112 Ibid. p. 245.

113 In the year 1601, the celebrated Lord Bacon wrote in the following terms to Mr. Secretary Cecil, at that time the most influential minister in the court of Elizabeth. After speaking of the civil reformation of the kingdom, he adds: "But there should go hand in hand with this, some course of advancing religion indeed, where the people is capable thereof; as the sending over some good preachers, especially of that sort which are vehement and zealous preachers, and not scholastic; to be resident in principal towns: endowing them with some stipend out of her Majesty's revenues, as her Majesty hath most religiously and graciously done in Lancashire; and the recontinuing and replenishing the college begun in Dublin—

the formidable rebellions which, during this period, agitated the kingdom and desolated its fairest provinces, occupied exclusively the attention of government. The miserable population were sadly diminished by the combined ravages of war, famine, and pestilence; and, except in the cities and principal towns, they were living ignorant of the common arts of life, and devoid of order or civilization. After great exertions and incredible expense, peace was at length restored. For the first time, during four centuries, the opponents of the English power were completely subdued, and the authority of the laws was extended throughout the entire island. Under these circumstances, highly auspicious so far as the civil administration of the kingdom was concerned, Queen Elizabeth's reign terminated by her death in the month of March, 1603. A nobler work, however, remained to be accomplished by her successor, for which her military triumphs had paved the way,—the work of promoting the civilization of the inhabitants, infusing into them a love of peace and social order, and circulating among them the blessings of education and of true religion.

During the long period of seventy years which has now been reviewed, how slow and partial was the progress of the Reformation in Ireland! When it is remembered that, during the same period, the reformed faith had taken a deep and firm root in both the sister-kingdoms, and had therein effectually supplanted the ancient superstition, an important inquiry is suggested—what are the causes that retarded its growth in Ireland? The preceding narrative may have enabled the reader to detect several of these causes. The importance of the subject, however, will justify a more detailed investigation.

the placing of good men to be bishops in the sees there, and the taking care of the versions of Bibles, and catechisms, and other books of instruction into the Irish language; and the like religious courses, both for the honour of God, and for the avoiding of scandal and unsatisfaction here, by the show of toleration of religion in some parts there." Works, fol. 1740; iv. 552.

The slow and limited progress of the Reformation in Ireland may be traced principally to two causes—the condition of the kingdom, which was peculiarly unfavourable to the spread of the truth; and the inadequacy of the measures employed for its propagation.

A country such as Ireland was at the commencement of the sixteenth century—nominally subject to England, but really governed by a number of petty despots inflamed with a deadly hatred against the British, and involved in perpetual hostilities among themselves; its native inhabitants treated with cruelty and oppression, as a proscribed and inferior race, without education, commerce, enterprise, or even ordinary civilization—presented a most unpromising field for the propagation of the reformed faith. Though introduced by the authority and supported by the power of the state, the Reformation derived no assistance from this circumstance. For the English Government, long prior to this period, had not only rendered itself justly odious to the nation, but, by repressing the authority of the feudal nobility, had deprived itself of all power of acting with effect on the minds or habits of the people. In other countries the aristocracy, acting in concert with the supreme power of the state, as in England, and sometimes even in opposition to that power, as in Scotland, effectually secured the admission of the truth to the minds of their vassals. But, in Ireland, the unfortunate policy of the British court had been to destroy, as far as possible, the influence of the aristocracy, whereby the truth was deprived of the aid of an important ally which it elsewhere enjoyed. Nor was this the only evil attendant on such a short-sighted policy. By this means also, the authority and influence peculiar to an hereditary nobility were transferred to the priesthood. The Romish clergy became the real and effective aristocracy of the country, and were thereby invested with additional facilities for opposing the progress of the truth, and preventing its access to the minds of the enthralled population. Originating in Britain, too, it shared in all the hatred with which the Irish contemplated the inhabitants of that country, whom they knew only as violent oppressors; and the people to whom it was proposed, being rude and uncultivated, were unable, as much from ignorance as from prejudice, to discern or appreciate its excellence.

In addition to these difficulties peculiar to Ireland, the Reformation had moreover to contend with those obstacles common to other countries, originating in the exorbitant power and selfish policy of the Romish priesthood. These obstacles, however, were not more formidable here than in the sister kingdoms. The clergy were, indeed, ignorant and bigoted in the extreme, their authority over the people was supreme and despotic, and their zeal in maintaining the lucrative forms and doctrines of Popery vehement and relentless.[114] But this was universally the character of the Roman Catholic hierarchy previous to the Reformation. In every country they contemplated the reformed faith with aversion, and resisted its progress with all their influence; yet this interested opposition, though for a time it may have retarded the advancement of the truth, never ultimately prevailed against it where it was disseminated with zeal, fidelity, and perseverance. Unfortunately, however, it was not

114 I find a bishop of Ferns thus describing the opposition given to the truth in his diocese in the year 1612. "As for the poorer sort, some of them have not only discovered unto me privately their dislike of popery and the mass, in regard they understand not what is said or done therein, but also groaned under the burden of the many priests in respect of the double tythes and offerings, the one paid by them unto us, and the other unto them. Being then demanded of me why they did not forsake the mass and come to our church, their answer hath been, (which I know to be true in some,) that if they should be of our religion, no popish merchant would employ them being sailors, no popish landlord would let them any lands being husbandmen, nor set them houses in tenantry being artificers; and therefore they must either starve, or do as they do. As for the gentlemen, and those of the richer sort, I have always found them very obstinate, which hath proceeded from the priests resorting unto their houses and company, and continual hammering of them upon their superstitious anvil." Extracted from a curious paper in Reports of Com. of Pub. Rec. in Ireland, vol. i. p. 264.

in this manner that the attempt was made to propagate the reformed faith in Ireland. It was offered to the people and pressed on them in a way which would have defeated any cause: and to this mismanagement, still more than to the unfavourable circumstances of the kingdom, may be attributed its slow and partial advancement. Had the clergy been even more formidable, the people more enslaved, and both more exasperated against the English than they really were; yet Christian prudence could have disarmed their hostility, while faithful diligence and intrepidity would have planted the true standard of the cross among the most remote or turbulent septs.

But there was neither ordinary discretion nor reasonable activity employed in conducting this important and critical work. The Romish faith was summarily condemned by acts of parliament, and profession of the Reformed religion enforced under the heaviest penalties, before any attempts were made to convince the people of their former errors, and thus prepare them for accompanying the court in the projected reformation. That authority, therefore, which might have been usefully exercised at a subsequent stage, in protecting and encouraging those who had been won over by the force of reasoning and of truth, became highly injurious when it was violently resorted to at the very commencement, and employed as the chief instrument of conversion.

Another error consisted in employing exclusively, as the agents in this work, the natives of a kingdom against which the Irish were deeply and justly incensed. By this means the reformed religion became unhappily identified with England, and the most violent prejudices were unnecessarily excited against it in the minds of the people. Had native converts from Popery been advanced to the dignities and offices which were conferred exclusively on Englishmen—had they been sent forth among their countrymen and their friends, to whom they would have had the happiest facilities of access, and with whom they would have enjoyed the auspicious opportunity of reasoning in a spirit of affection and impartiality, a greater measure of success might justly have been expected to result.

But perhaps a still more fatal error was that of attempting to propagate religion through the medium of a foreign language. Nothing could be more preposterous or absurd than this attempt, which was persisted in by the government through the vain desire of banishing the Irish, to make way for the adoption of the English tongue. This change, however, as might have been anticipated, the natives unanimously and successfully opposed. They utterly refused to relinquish their national language—endeared to them by so many powerful associations; much less to adopt in its room that of their oppressors—the most degrading badge of servitude a people could wear. Had there been even any rational prospect of effecting this favourite object of British policy, its accomplishment ought not to have been preferred before that of enlightening and converting the nation. But unfortunately this preference was given. The native population were not to be addressed in their own tongue; nor were Irish books permitted to be printed for their use. Divine service was to be performed solely in the English language; and where the bishops could find no readers, but those who spoke the vernacular language of their parishioners, instead of permitting them to conduct the reformed worship in the Irish tongue, it was most absurdly provided that they should officiate in Latin. How could the Reformation be expected to prosper by such measures as these! Ecclesiastical history furnishes no instance in which they have been successful; but, on the contrary, its records clearly evince—what indeed is sufficiently obvious in itself—the necessity of employing the native language of every country both orally and in writing, to instruct or convert the inhabitants. [115]

115 The case of Wales furnishes a striking corroboration of the truth of these observations. Although the inhabitants of the Principality were, perhaps, as violently prejudiced against the English government as the

But besides overlooking these obvious means of promoting the Reformation, neither sufficient vigour nor intrepidity was displayed in the measures which were actually adopted. The agents employed, both civil and ecclesiastical, were too timid and pusillanimous to effect any thing like a general or permanent reformation of the national faith. The errors and absurdities of Popery were very cautiously exposed, and condemned only in the most measured terms. The prejudices of the people were most studiously humoured, and the slightest possible alterations in their former ritual were permitted to be made. The transfer of supremacy from the Pope to the king, and the appropriation of the monastic revenues to the crown, appeared to be the sole objects of the commissioners intrusted with the nominal charge of reforming Ireland: and in effecting these objects, their reasoning was founded not on scriptural considerations, but on Popish precedents; and their most convincing arguments were drawn from the exercise of the civil power. The prelate, to whom was assigned the office of presiding over the national reformation, was unequal to its discharge. When we compare archbishop Brown with those illustrious reformers, who, in Britain and on the Continent, had been the instruments, under Providence, of emancipating their respective countries from Popish thraldom, we find him palpably deficient in those qualifications which had enabled them to triumph so signally over power and prejudice, and to establish their countrymen, so generally as they did, in the profession of the reformed faith. He was far from possessing that promptitude

Irish were, and spoke also a different language; yet by the judicious measures adopted in reference both to their civil and their religious reformation, especially by the circulation of the Scriptures in Welch, the employment of native preachers, and the use of their vernacular tongue in public worship, they speedily became incorporated with England, and firmly attached to the Protestant church. Much important information on this, as well as on almost every other topic connected with the spiritual amelioration of Ireland, may be found in "Sketches of the native Irish," by the Rev. C. Anderson, Edinburgh.

and intrepidity which the important station he held so manifestly required. He had courage to attempt the removal of only the grosser abominations of Popery. The personal danger to which he was occasionally exposed, repeatedly cramped his exertions and repressed his zeal; while the fear of offending his patron at the English court led him to act with fatal caution and indecision. His timidity betrayed him into the delusive expectation of subverting the ancient superstition by conciliatory measures;—a procedure which, however promising and desirable it may be in theory, has seldom succeeded in practice.[116] Affected philanthropists have reprobated the bold and energetic manner in which Knox assailed the errors and triumphed over the power of Popery in Scotland, and have descanted on the superior success which would have been attained by a more gentle and pacific reformer. But the result would assuredly have been the same as in Ireland. The moral disease may, perhaps, be mitigated by soothing treatment; but it is too virulent and inveterate to be subdued by any but the most active and powerful applications.[117]

116 From an attentive consideration of the letters and proceedings of Brown, I had been reluctantly led, in opposition to all preceding writers, to adopt the views of his character stated in the text. I have since met with Bale's account of him in his 'Vocacyon,' and find that these views are too amply corroborated. In fact, Bale, from personal knowledge, speaks of him as worldly, selfish, and "gluttonous;" and further states, that at the trying period of the accession of Mary, he was willing enough to relapse into popery, "becoming then, of a dissembling proselyte, a most pernicious papist." His marriage, however, was a bar to his continuing in office in the Romish church; and he was removed from his see, not for any alleged heresy, but solely on account of his having been married. He died unmolested, not long before the accession of Elizabeth.

117 Let it not be imagined by any of my readers that I am either here, or in any part of this introductory sketch, an advocate for the use of civil penalties or external force in repressing error or propagating the truth: "for the weapons of our warfare are not carnal, but mighty through God, to the pulling down of strong holds." 2 Cor. x. 4. The 'applications' alluded to in the text, as alone effectual for overturning Popery in Ireland were,—and I may say, *are*, for the work has yet to be performed,—the 'active' dissemination of the Bible in the vernacular language of the coun-

The cautious policy of the archbishop was adopted by his colleagues in office. The several lords deputies who presided over the government of the kingdom, were indifferent, if not secretly hostile, to the cause of the Reformation; or they hoped to establish it by the summary agency of royal proclamations and legislative enactments. By one of these governors, the reformed liturgy was recommended to the people as a mere translation of their former service, the mass; as if he were afraid or ashamed to own its real character: and by another, the Romish primate was invited to a conference, through the extravagant hope of bringing him to such an amicable compromise as might terminate all the differences between the rival churches. Nor were the bishops, who had accompanied Brown from England and been preferred to Irish sees, possessed of a different spirit from their superiors. They were distinguished for neither learning nor zeal; nor do they appear to have ever united in any active or combined efforts for promoting the Reformation, beyond removing the pictures and images from their respective cathedrals. One honourable exception, indeed, occurred in the bishop of Ossory, who alone was endowed with the talents and actuated by the spirit of a reformer. But being unsupported in his vigorous measures by the other prelates, while his rigid adherence to Protestantism was condemned by his more timid and complying brethren, his insulated efforts were not attended with that success which would otherwise have undoubtedly followed. When Queen Mary ascended the throne, these cautious and wary advocates of the Reformation, as might be anticipated, either fled in dismay, or, under a profession of Popery, concealed their attachment to the truth. During her inauspicious reign, not a single opponent of the Romish faith appeared in Ireland; not a Protestant noble or prelate was intrepid enough to protest against its re-establishment, and

try; the 'powerful' preaching of the word; the 'bold' and honest exposure of error; and the 'energetic' labours of a learned and faithful, and adequate ministry, throughout the length and breadth of the land.

extremely few were conscientious enough to refuse conforming to its superstitious ritual. Even under Elizabeth, the civil and ecclesiastical authorities were neither so prompt nor so vigorous in advancing the Reformation as were their contemporaries in England. No wonder then that so few inroads were made on the Romish superstition. Could it be expected that the people would forsake their ancient religion, supported as it was by the combined influence of habit, education, language, prejudice, and antiquity, and adopt the Protestant faith, which they saw so reluctantly preached and so feebly urged? Even had they understood the language of the reformed teachers, how could they be convinced of errors which were so timidly exposed, or forsake a course the danger of which was so cautiously intimated?

To complete this picture of mismanagement in conducting the Reformation, much culpable negligence was manifested in providing persons sufficiently qualified to carry forward the work. It was no doubt impossible to procure at once an adequate number of zealous preachers. But no earnest exertions appear to have been made by the rulers, in either the church or the state, to supply this deficiency. The superior clergy who favoured the Reformation were, at first, not more than five, and little care was taken to increase their number, the remaining sees being occupied by Romish prelates exercising unrestricted jurisdiction. Most of the northern dioceses enjoyed no Protestant bishops before the commencement of the seventeenth century. Even then, three of the most extensive were held by one individual; (118) and, until the year 1610, there were only the primate and two suffragans to preside over the seven sees included in the province of Ulster. (119)

118 The sees of Derry, Raphoe, and Clogher, were held by Geo. Montgomery, a native of Scotland, for several years. In 1610, he resigned the former two, and obtained that of Meath, which he held in conjunction with Clogher till his death.—Ware's Bishops.

119 These were Henry Ussher, archbishop of Armagh; John Todd, bishop of Dromore, Down, and Connor; and the above George Montgomery, bishop of Derry, Raphoe, and Clogher.—Ware's Bishops.

Equally, if not more, deplorable was the state of the reformed church in the southern and western provinces, where the succession of Protestant bishops was so carelessly maintained and so frequently interrupted, that even their names soon sunk into oblivion.

Still more lamentable was the want of inferior clergy. When the priests in the metropolis, who opposed the Reformation, resigned their charges, and a most favourable opportunity was thus afforded for zealous preachers to disseminate the truth in this important station, archbishop Brown would not venture to fill up their benefices, lest he might excite a still more formidable opposition to his measures. The persons afterwards employed were not only unfitted by their nation and their language for the office of enlightening the people; but were also indolent and worldly, and many of them openly immoral. Even had they been better qualified, their number was quite disproportioned to the work necessary to be done in so extended and uncultivated a field. No inducements were held out to honest and faithful ministers to remove to Ireland, nor sufficient protection and maintenance secured to those who were labouring in the cause of truth. No pains were employed to discover native teachers, or to bring over from Scotland, where there were many such, some of those who could use the Irish tongue. Neither were there, for a long time, any facilities afforded to those who were desirous of qualifying themselves for the exercise of the ministry in this country. Hence the grossest darkness continued to cover the land. Nothing can be more distressing than to read the descriptions that contemporary writers have given of the ignorance which prevailed among the bulk of the people, and which they invariably trace to the scarcity of ministers and their inadequacy to their office. "Hard it is," saith a chancellor of Ireland, writing to an English nobleman in the reign of Edward VI., "that men should know their duties to God and to the king, when they shall not hear teaching or preaching throughout the year." And in the same letter he farther complains; "preaching we have none, which is our lack, without which the ignorant can have no knowledge."

Such were the measures pursued in the earlier stages of the Reformation in Ireland; and to their manifest inadequacy must, in a great degree, be ascribed its limited progress. They were insufficient for promoting the cause of religion, even under the most favourable circumstances, when opposed by neither power, prejudice, nor interest. Need we wonder, then, at the failure which ensued, when, under the palpable mismanagement already described, the truth had to combat with all the obstacles presented by a powerful and crafty priesthood, a turbulent and bigoted nobility, and an ignorant and superstitious people! Under these peculiar disadvantages, nothing but uncompromising fidelity and consummate prudence, accompanied with unshrinking zeal and perseverance—qualities which the Irish reformers seldom displayed,—could have ensured the success of the reformed faith, or prepared the country for reaping the full benefit of the judicious measures adopted in the succeeding reign.

HISTORY

OF THE

PRESBYTERIAN CHURCH IN IRELAND.

CHAPTER I.

Accession of James I.—His measures for civilizing Ireland—State of the Province of Ulster—Its moral and religious condition—Early attempts to plant colonies on the Eastern coast—James's project for colonizing the six forfeited counties—Progress of the Northern plantation—Settlement of the Hamilton and Montgomery families—Proceedings of the Parliament in 1615 *—And of the Convocation—Articles of religion—General character of the first Colonists—Arrival of Scottish ministers—Brice—Hubbard—Glendinning—Ridge—Cunningham—Blair—Hamilton.*

The accession of James I. to the British throne was proclaimed in Dublin, with the usual solemnities, on the fifth of April, 1603. All parties in Ireland recognised his claims to the crown, and readily received him as their rightful sovereign. The victories of Elizabeth had invested him with the undisturbed possession of the entire island, while his love of peace and attachment to religion both disposed and enabled him to improve this important advantage, which none of his predecessors had ever enjoyed.

He accordingly resolved to lay the foundation of a permanent peace by wise and conciliatory measures. He received, with readiness, the submission of the northern rebels, conferred on them new titles, and established them securely in the possession of their estates. He proclaimed a general pardon to all who were concerned in the late rebellions, and restored those who had not been attainted to their former possessions. The ancient customs which had prevailed through the kingdom in place of law were judiciously abolished, and the natives were admitted, for the first time, to the privileges of subjects, and placed in all respects on an equality with the English residents. The estates of their lords, previously held on very precarious titles, were secured to them with all the formalities of law. Itinerating courts of assize were renewed in the southern provinces, after an interruption of two centuries, and in the north, they were for the first time established; so that the arm of the law was now extended over the entire kingdom, and the administration of justice secured to all classes of the people.[1]

James was no less anxious to promote the religious than the civil reformation of the kingdom. He was at first considered by the Roman Catholic party as favourable to their cause. They were consequently encouraged, in the southern parts of the kingdom, to eject the Protestant ministers with violence, and openly to celebrate their religious rites in the places dedicated to the reformed worship. But the promptitude and vigour of the lord deputy speedily quelled this insurrection; and as the priests were studiously inflaming the mortification and disappointment of the people into hatred and hostility against his government, a proclamation was issued commanding the Popish clergy to depart from the kingdom or conform to the law. In his measures against Popery, however, James appears to have been actuated more by his dread of their tenets relative to the temporal power of the Pope, than by a conscientious abhorrence of their doctrinal errors. The private exercise of their worship was therefore connived at, and would have been soon openly tolerated, had

[1] Cox's History of Ireland, ii. 9, 10.

not the discovery of the gunpowder plot in England, and the detection of some Romish emissaries in Ireland about the same period, roused the king's apprehensions of foreign interference, and determined him to refuse all public countenance to a religion so hostile to the rights of princes. Irritated at this resolution of James, and urged on by the disaffected clergy, several of the northern nobles, who had been previously favoured by him, and had sworn fealty to the crown, entered into a conspiracy against his government, and applied to the courts of France and Spain to aid them in subverting the English power in Ireland. This plot, however, was happily discovered before the time appointed for its execution had arrived. Its chief promoters, the earls of Tyrone and Tyrconnell, fled in dismay, leaving their estates at the mercy of the king; and, shortly afterwards, a second insurrection being raised in Ulster, in which its leader, O'Dogherty, was slain, another extensive portion of that province reverted to the crown. In consequence of these and other forfeitures, about half a million of acres, and nearly six entire counties in Ulster, were placed at the disposal of the king. The principal part of these territories James wisely resolved to plant with English and Scottish colonies, with the combined view of rendering the lands more profitable, establishing the peace and prosperity of this part of the kingdom hitherto the most turbulent, and securing the more general and speedy dissemination of the reformed faith.

That the wisdom and value of this memorable scheme of colonization may be clearly understood and appreciated, it will be necessary to describe the civil and religious state of Ulster at the accession of James.

This province having been the chief seat of the rebellions which disturbed the latter years of the reign of Elizabeth, was reduced to the lowest extremity of poverty and wretchedness. Though no longer distracted by intestine war, the peace which it enjoyed was solely owing to the desolations which it had suffered. The descriptions which contemporary writers have given of its wretched state would appear incredible, were they not unfortunately too well authenticated to admit of any rational doubt. The country was almost depopulated, and wasted in all its resources. The wretched remnant of its inhabitants who had survived the ravages of an exterminating contest, suffered the combined horrors of its ghastly attendants—pestilence and famine.[2] With the exception of the few fortified cities which it contained, its towns and villages were levelled to the ground, and scarcely any building remained, save the insulated castles occupied by the English, or the pitiful cabins of the natives, too poor to be plundered.[3] The face of the country was intersected by immense woods, and covered with numerous marshes. Cultivation was occasionally visible only in some favoured spots, but so wretchedly conducted as scarcely to yield the necessaries of life.[4] Its products of grain and cattle, in which alone consisted the wealth of the country, had been swept away by the wars; and the few proprietors who survived were reduced to such poverty, as to be altogether unable to resume with profit the labours of the field: while many betook themselves to the woods, where they lived almost in a state of nature, supported by

[2] Morrison, ii. 172, 200, 283.

[3] The following list of garrisons held by the British in Ulster, in May, 1608, compiled from Morrison, (Hist. i. 73, 155, 253; and ii. 131, 184, 208, 336,) will convey some idea of the military state of the province:—*Down.*—Newry, 100 men; Lecale, or Downpatrick, including Dundrum and Ardglass, 200; Narrow-water; Greencastle. *Antrim.*—Carrickfergus, 650; Toome; Olderfleet. *Armagh.*—Armagh, 150; Mountnorris, 150; Ennislaughlin. *Monaghan.*—Monaghan and Ruske, including some other castles, 300. *Cavan.*—Cavan, 100; Cloughoughter; Ballinicargy. *Fermanagh.*—Enniskillen and some castles garrisoned from Ballyshannon. *Tyrone.*—Omagh, 100; Charlemont, 150; Mountjoy, 350; Newtonstewart, 100; Dunman, 150; Augher. *Derry.*—Derry, 350; Culmore, 20; Anagh, 100; Coleraine, 100. *Donegall.*—Donegall, Asheraw, Ballyshannon, including castles in Fermanagh, 900; Lifford, 350; Dunalong, 150; Kilmacrenan, 100; Ramullan, 100; Doe, 100; Cargan, 100; and Burt, 150.

[4] Morrison, ii. 270.

plunder, and secure amidst the general poverty and desolation by which they were surrounded.[5]

The moral and religious state of Ulster, it may well be supposed, was scarcely less deplorable. Though, during the reign of Elizabeth, the reformed doctrines had reached a few of its principal cities, and been openly professed in them; yet so far as the general population was concerned, it can scarcely be said to have passed, at the accession of James, the frontiers of the province. A Roman Catholic historian[6] describes Ulster, at this period, as "the most constant in maintaining its liberty, and in preserving the Catholic religion;" while, at the same time, he acknowledges that his religion had disappeared from many other parts of the kingdom. The sees of Derry, Raphoe, and Clogher, which comprised the greater part of the province, were occupied, even so late as the year 1605, by Roman Catholic prelates, around whom were necessarily collected numerous priests and friars; and the abbeys, though formally dissolved half a century be-

5 Cox, ii. 3. The following brief notices, taken from Sir Henry Sydney's account of the state of Ulster in 1575, exhibit a deplorable picture of even the best parts of the province:—"*Lecale*, much of the country waste, but on the mending hand.—*Dufferin*, or White's country, all waste and desolate—the *Ardes*, much impoverished, but in good hope of recovery; for that there are many freeholders of English race, of ancient habiting there—[All these districts are in the county Down]—County of *Clandeboy* utterly disinhabited—town of *Knockfergus* much decayed and impoverished, no ploughs going at all, where before were many; and great store of kyne and cattle belonging to the town, now few or none left, church and houses, saving castles, burned, the inhabitants fled, not above five householders of any countenance left remaining—the *Glynnes* and the *Route*, possessed by the Scots, now governed by Sorly Boy." These districts include the whole of the county Antrim. The Scots here mentioned were piratical marauders and Roman Catholics from the western islands, and must not be confounded with those who came over at the plantation of Ulster. Sir Henry describes Armagh town as "miserable, the fort imperfect, and the church all down." He says, that "at the passage of the water at Belfast, by reason of the tide's extraordinary return, our horses swam, and the footmen waded very deep." Sydney papers, i. 76—9.

6 Du Pin, in his Ecc. Hist. folio, iii. 663.

fore, were not actually resumed by the crown, nor their useless inmates ejected till about the same period. The continual wars, of which this province had been the seat, prevented the access of reformed ministers to its scanty and reduced population; while many of those who were thinly scattered over the country were more detrimental than useful to the advancement of the truth.

A protestant minister, who afterwards became a prelate in Ulster, and who cannot be suspected of any inclination to undervalue the character of his brethren, has given a sad description both of the paucity and inadequacy of the northern clergy about this period. "In many places, there is no minister at all; in many places, a minister as good as none, even a dumb dog that cannot bark, an idol [idle] shepherd who is not apt to teach, nor able to confute; in other places, a lewd and scandalous minister whose not Gospel-like behaviour is a stumbling-block to them that are without. Even as the prince of Cuba in India said, he would not go to heaven if the Spaniards went thither, because he thought that could be no good place where such cruel tyrants were: so, many of this country will not be of our religion, because they think that can be no true religion which hath so unconscionable professors and ministers."(7) In consequence of the indolence and insufficiency of such a clergy as are here described, as well as owing to the ruinous state of the churches which had shared in all the ravages of war, "divine service had not for years together been used in any parish church

7 Extracted from a sermon on 1 Tim. ii. 5, by Henry Leslie, at this time curate of Drogheda, afterwards the noted bishop of Down and Connor. It is entitled "A Treatise tending to Unitie, in a sermon preached at Droghedah on Whitsunday, being on the ninth of June 1622, before the King's Majestie's Commissioners for Ireland." 4to, Dublin, 1623, pp. 52. This sermon, now very rare, appears to have been the earliest of his productions; for, in his dedication to Primate Hampton, he modestly calls it, "the first fruits of my weak engine." The reader will afterwards be presented with more matured, though less agreeable 'fruits,' from the same stock.

throughout Ulster, except in some city or principal towns."[8] This province thus appeared to be the most secure refuge of the ancient superstition, at the very time when, by the projected introduction of British colonists, it was upon the eve of becoming the most permanent seat of the reformed faith.

This project, though perhaps the most extensive and successful, was not the first that had been formed for the colonization of Ulster. So early as the year 1559, it was one of the instructions given to the Earl of Sussex, when he came over as lord deputy, to "people Ulster with English;"[9] and not many years afterwards, Queen Elizabeth took measures for carrying this object into effect, in the counties of Down and Antrim. In the former, by the rebellion of Shane O'Neill, a large tract of country in the Ards was forfeited to the crown; and, in 1572, was granted to Sir Thomas Smith, on condition of planting it with English settlers. But his son, whom he sent over to conduct the settlement, being killed by a neighbouring chief, the design was very partially executed; and James finding, at his accession, the conditions of the former patent not duly fulfilled, recalled it, and granted the lands to other proprietors. In Antrim, Elizabeth had also attempted to place an English colony. The greater part of this county, especially that bordering on the coast, was possessed by marauding clans from the islands of Scotland, chiefly of the Macdonnells, who had forcibly wrested it from the natives.[10] In time, however, these Scots intermarried

8 Carte's Ormond, i. 17. 9 Cox, i. 313. Des. Cur. Heb. i. 2.

10 The following extract from a scarce work entitled, "The Government of Ireland under Sir John Perrott, Knt.," &c. Lond. 1626, 4to. pp. 136, shows how these Highland clans obtained a footing in Antrim. About the year 1584, "the deputy received intelligence of the approach of a thousand Scottish islanders, called Redshanks, being of the septs or families of the Cambiles, Macconnells, [Macdonnells] and Magalanes, drawne to invade Ulster by Surleboy, one of that nation, who had usurped, and by power and strong hand, possessed himself of the Macquilies, [M'Quillans] and other men's lands in Ulster, called the Glinnes and the Route; meaning to hold that by force, which he had gotten without right, by violence,

with the Irish, and frequently joined in rendering their opposition to the English power much more formidable than it would otherwise have been. Elizabeth, therefore, determined to curb, and, if possible, eject these turbulent intruders, by establishing an English settlement in that part of the country. Accordingly, in 1573, she apprised the lord deputy that, "in the month of August, the Earl of Essex, with 2000 men would come to inhabit the forfeited lands in the Glynns, Route, and Clandeboy, which she had granted to them;" but, at the same time, she desired the deputy to give notice that "Essex came to expel the Scots, and not to hurt the Irish." He soon after arrived at Carrickfergus, with numerous persons of quality in his train, as intended settlers; but owing to the lateness of the season, and several unexpected difficulties in the execution of the plan, many of his followers returned in disgust to England.(11) Having succeeded in driving the Scots only out of Claneboy, he, not long after, altogether abandoned the design.(12) The lands therefore reverted to their former occupiers; and in 1603, James I. confirmed Sir Randal Macdonnell in the possession of the territory of the Route.(13) In various other parts both of Down and Antrim, James had granted estates to his favourite officers, on condition of planting them with British occupants, several years before that great plantation took place, the circumstances of which will now be detailed.

The chief agent employed in conducting this memorable scheme was Sir Arthur Chichester, on whom the king had conferred a considerable estate in Antrim. He was appointed lord deputy of the kingdom in February 1605. He was peculiarly

fraud and injury." Page 12. Surly Boy, that is, Charles the yellow, was the Gaelic or Irish name of the chief of the Macdonnells.

11 Several, however, of Essex's officers remained in the country, so that the enterprise was not entirely fruitless as a colonizing experiment. Of these I may notice the founders of the noble families of Downshire, Templetown, and I believe Massareene; and also of the Dalways, Dobbs, &c.

12 Cox, i. 339, 341.

13 Cox, ii. 8.

liarly well qualified for executing with success the task assigned him; possessing, as he did, sound judgment and discretion, combined with a just sense of religion, and great experience in conducting affairs of state. His first care was to have the six forfeited counties minutely surveyed; and having satisfied himself of their extent, capabilities and situation, he drew up the plan by which their subsequent plantation was principally regulated. They were allotted to three classes of persons—British undertakers, who voluntarily engaged in the enterprise—servitors of the crown, consisting of civil and military officers—and natives, whom it was expected this confidence and liberality would render loyal subjects. The lands were divided into three proportions of two thousand, fifteen hundred and one thousand acres. The occupiers of the largest proportion were bound, within four years, to build a castle and bawn,(14) and to plant on their estates forty-eight able men, eighteen years old or upwards, of English or Scottish descent. Those of the second class were obliged to build, within two years, a strong stone or brick house and bawn; and those of the third a bawn; while both were bound to plant a proportionable number of British families on their possessions, and to have their houses furnished with a sufficiency of arms. Various other judicious restrictions and limitations were prescribed, under which the escheated lands were disposed of to one hundred and four English and Scottish undertakers, fifty-six servitors, and two hundred and eighty-six natives, who gave bonds to the state for the fulfilment of their covenants, and who were required to render an annual account of their progress in carrying on the plantation. In this enumeration

14 A *bawn* was simply a walled enclosure, usually with towers at the angles. Within it was placed the house or castle, and it was sufficient to secure the inmates and their stock of cattle from the incursions of the marauding Irish. A specimen of the better kind of these bawns may be seen in tolerable preservation, at Bellahill near Carrickfergus, the seat of Marriott Dalway, Esq.

of undertakers, the corporation of the city of London deserve particular notice from the extensive possessions which were committed to their care. Nearly the whole of the county of Coleraine—now called, in allusion to this circumstance, the county of Londonderry—was allotted them, on condition of their building and fortifying the cities of Londonderry and Coleraine, and otherwise expending twenty thousand pounds on the plantation.(15)

In this liberal distribution of the forfeited lands, the king took especial care to provide for the support of the church, to the poverty of which was ascribed much of the ignorance and superstition which then pervaded the province. He restored to the sees all their ecclesiastical possessions, the greater part of which had been alienated by the violence and cupidity of the nobles; and for the maintenance of the inferior clergy, he induced the bishops to resign their impropriations, and to relinquish the tithes formerly paid them, by the parishes, in favour of the respective incumbents. Parochial churches were ordered to be repaired, and glebes allotted to the ministers; and for the revival and encouragement of learning, a free school was endowed in the principal town of every diocese.

In the year 1610, the lands began to be generally occupied, agreeably to the plan now briefly detailed. Owing to the vicinity of Scotland to Ulster, as well as to the hardiness and enterprise of its natives, the principal part of the settlers came from that kingdom. The north-eastern parts of the province were first occupied by them, whence they spread

(15) So great was James's regard for his favourite servant Sir A. Chichester, that he assigned to him, by writ of Privy Seal dated June 21st, 1610, the entire territory of Inishowen, with all the manors and rights formerly possessed by the O'Dogherty's—a larger portion than fell to the lot of any other undertaker. But in this liberal grant, several of those salutary conditions required of the other undertakers, were dispensed with; in consequence of which the lands were never sufficiently planted, and that district of country remains, even at the present day, inferior to the rest of the county in the arts of civilization, and the possession of the re- [illegible]

themselves over the remoter districts. The southern and western parts were chiefly planted with the English, between whom and the Scots there existed the most friendly co-operation. The decayed and almost deserted cities[16] were now replenished with inhabitants; the lands were gradually cleared of the woods; towns were built and incorporated; houses erected through the cultivated country; and in every direction there was ample testimony afforded of the peaceableness and industry of the new occupants. Their situation, however, was not without its difficulties. The woods and fastnesses were still frequented by bands of the irreclaimable natives, who plundered their possessions as often as a favourable opportunity occurred. A contemporary writer states, among similar

16 Blennerhassett, in his "Direction for the Plantation in Ulster," Lond. 1610, thus describes Armagh: "How exceedingly well standeth Ardmath, better seat for rich soil there cannot be, but so poor, as I do verily think, all the household stuff in that city is not worth L.20. Yet it is the primate of all Ireland, and, as they say, for antiquity, one of the most ancient in all Europe. It is also of so small power as forty resolute men may rob, rifle, and burn it. Were it a defenced corporation, it would soon be rich and religious, and the security would make one acre more worth than now twenty be." The town of Clogher is thus described in the "Memorial of the life and death of Bishop Spottiswoode," printed by the late unfortunate Sir Alexander Boswell, from a manuscript in the Auchinleck Library. "The Bishop of Clogher had now begun to settle himself at Clogher, in the county of Tyrone, which was of old an ancient city, decored with two churches and a great number of inhabitants: but in the late wars was utterly ruined, the churches undermined and fired, the bishop's, and the abbott's, and canons' houses were demolished; and, at the bishop's coming to dwell there in the year 1628, there were no more than ten or twelve poor people dwelling in cottages patched up with skreas and wattles," Mem. p. 66. I may add, that I procured this "Memorial" in the hope that much interesting matter, illustrative of the religious state of Ulster, would certainly be found in the life of a northern bishop, extending from 1621 to 1641. But though frequently disappointed before in similar purchases, I never was so mortified as on this occasion. There is not a single fact, in the eighty quarto pages of which it consists, relating to the state of religion, or the affairs of the church, though, with the exception of the few concluding pages, the bishop himself was evidently the writer.

instances, that "Sir Toby Caufield's people are driven every night to lay up all his cattle, as it were, in ward; and do he and his what they can, the woolfe and the wood-kerne within culiver shot of his fort, have oftentimes a share;" even "in the English pale," he adds, "Sir John King and Sir Henry Harrington, within half a mile of Dublin, do the like, for those forenamed enemies do every night survey the fields to the very walls of Dublin."[17] The difference of climate, too, occasioned by the insular situation of the country, and by the many woods and marshes which covered its surface, was severely felt by the settlers, and tended for a time to retard the plantation.

Notwithstanding these and other hinderances peculiar to such an enterprise, it flourished amazingly. The following notices from an unpublished manuscript by a Presbyterian minister, whose father accompanied the first settlers, [18] will serve to illustrate its progress in the north-eastern parts of the province. Of the English, he states, not many came over, "for it is to be observed that being a great deal more tenderly bred at home in England, and entertained in better quarters than they could find here in Ireland, they were very unwilling to flock hither, except to good land, such as they had before at home, or to good cities where they might trade; both of which in these days were scarce enough here. Be-

17 Blennerhassett's Direction, &c.

18 This manuscript history was written by the Rev. Andrew Stewart, minister of Donaghadee from 1645 to 1671, son to the Rev. A. Stewart, whom the reader in Chap. II. will find settled at Donegore It is entitled, "A short account of the Church of Christ as it was (1) among the Irish at first; (2) among and after the English entered; (3) after the entry of the Scots." The third part is chiefly valuable, but it unfortunately extends no farther than the formation of the monthly meeting at Antrim, in 1626. It is deposited among the Wodrow MSS., in the Advocates' library, Edinburgh. (Rob. iii. 4. 17. No. 3.) Prefixed to it, is a letter from the Rev. Andrew Crawford, minister of Carnmoney, dated Sept. 7th, 1724, in which he states that he had faithfully transcribed the copy, therewith sent to Wodrow, from the original in the handwriting of Mr. Stewart, his maternal uncle.

sides that the marshiness and fogginess of this Island was still found unwholesome to English bodies, more tenderly bred and in a better air; so that we have seen, in our time, multitudes of them die of a flux, called here the country disease, at their first entry. These things were such discouragements that the new English came but very slowly, and the old English were become no better than the Irish." He then adds, that "the king had a natural love to have Ireland planted with Scots, as being, beside their loyalty, of a middle temper between the English tender and the Irish rude breeding, and a great deal more like to adventure to plant Ulster than the English, it lying far both from the English native land and more from their humour, while it lies nigh to Scotland, and the inhabitants not so far from the ancient Scots manners: so that it might be hoped that the Irish untoward living would be met both with equal firmness, if need be, and be especially allayed by the example of more civility and Protestant profession than in former times had been among them."

The progress of the plantation is thus described: "The Londoners have in Lagan a great interest, and built a city called Londonderry, chiefly planted with English. Coleraine, also, is built by them, both of them sea-ports, though Derry be both the more commodious and famous. Sir Hugh Clotworthy obtains the lands of Antrim, both fruitful and good, and invites thither several of the English, very good men, the Ellisses, Leslies, Langfords and others. Chichester, a worthy man, has an estate given him in the county of Antrim, where he improves his interest, builds the prospering mart Belfast, and confirms his interest in Carrickfergus, and builds a stately palace there. Conway has an estate given him in the county of Antrim, and builds a town, afterwards called Lisnegarvy, and this was planted with a colony of English also. Moses Hill had woodlands given him, which being thereafter demolished, left a fair and beautiful country, where a late heir of the Hills built a town called Hillsborough. All these lands and more were given to the English gentlemen, worthy persons, who afterwards increased and made noble and loyal families in places where formerly had been nothing but robbing, treason, and rebellion. Of the Scots nation, there was a family of the Balfours, of the Forbesses, of the Grahames, two of the Stewarts, and not a few of the Hamiltons. The Macdonnells founded the earldom of Antrim by King James's gift, the Hamiltons the earldoms of Strabane and Clanbrassil, and there were besides several knights of that name, Sir Frederick, Sir George, Sir Francis, Sir Charles his son, and Sir Hans, all Hamiltons; for they prospered above all others in this country after the first admittance of the Scots into it."

The writer then gives the following account of the settlement, in the county of Down, of the Hamilton and Montgomery families, who proved the most successful promoters of the Scottish plantation, and were intimately connected with the subsequent vicissitudes of the Presbyterian church in Ulster:—

"There had been one of the O'Neills, called Con O'Neill, a man of great lands in that country, both in Down and Antrim. This man being rebellious, and his land falling to the king, was apprehended by the then deputy Chichester, and was laid up in the king's castle at Carrickfergus; a drunken, sluggish man, but he had a sharp nimble woman to his wife. The deputy thought to have him to suffer according to law, and to be chief sharer in his lands. But divine providence had otherwise appointed. For the woman, his wife, in the greatness of her spirit, taking in high indignation that her husband was not only captive, but appointed to an ignominious death, soon resolved that the saving his life with a part of his estate was better than to lose all. Therefore this she strongly intends and diligently endeavours. But in a throng of thoughts how to accomplish her desire, she lights on this expedient, viz., to pass secretly to the next Scottish shore, and there light, if she could, on some good instrument for making good her design. And God leading her to Mr.

Hugh Montgomery, of Broadstone, in Scotland, a man sober, kind, humane, and trusty, to whom she revealed her husband's case and her own desire, saying, if Mr. Montgomery would be at pains and charge to purchase from the king her husband's life and liberty, with a third part of the estate for him and her to live on, the said Montgomery should, with their great good-will, have the other two parts, to be purchased by the king's grant. Montgomery considering the matter wisely and maturely, entertains the gentlewoman with all kindness, till he was ripe to give her answer, which, in short, was this, that if she should find the way to deliver her husband Con out of the deputy's hands, and let him have the secure keeping of his person, with such assurance as he could give that the articles should be performed which she had proposed in her husband's name; then would he make adventure and labour for the said Con's life and liberty.

"On these beginnings they proceed. The wife endeavours her husband's delivery, and Montgomery to have a vessel ready to send for him upon notice given. The woman therefore returning with what speed she could to Ireland; had access, when she would, into the castle of Carrickfergus, where her husband was; sometime to bring in clothes, sometime drink, sometime meat, and never almost without some appearance of a good errand. At last she had appointed a boat to come from Bangor, which being light, might even come under the castle and receive Con out at a window, at a certain hour, and thus to effect it. For one day she came into the chamber with two big cheeses, the meat being neatly taken out, and filled with cords well packed in, and the holes handsomely made up again. Those she brought to him without any suspicion of deceit, and left him to hank himself down from the window at such a time when, by moonshine, he might see the boat ready, and so begone as was already contrived. All this is done accordingly, and Con brought over to the church of Bangor, where in an old steeple he is hid, and kept till such time as Hugh Montgomery might be advertised to send a relief for him. And indeed, it was not long till, wind and weather serving, there is a boat sent with Patrick Montgomery, afterwards of Creboy in Ireland, to carry Con away. And away he went, and was well and kindly entertained in Scotland by the family of Broadstone, till Hugh made ready and went to London, to do what he could to bring his desire to pass."

Stewart then proceeds to state that Montgomery applied to Mr. James Hamilton, who had relinquished his fellowship in Dublin College, and who, with Sir James Fullerton, was in high favour at the English court, to forward the application on behalf of O'Neill, promising—"a half of his two parts, if by his friends and means he might have access to work out Con's pardon, and have the king's gift of the lands to be divided among the three; for it was thought sufficient for them all. Mr. James Hamilton, glad of this, makes way first with the Hamiltons, then with others of the English and Scottish nobility; that now Montgomery is well heard and especially respected by his majesty, and in a word the grant is given out—Con has his life and a third part, Montgomery has a third part, and Mr. James Hamilton has a third part of Con O'Neill's estate in Down.[19] Hugh Montgomery and James Hamilton are both made knights; but the king's pleasure was that Montgomery should have the precedency, being not only a gentleman as the other was, but an inheritor under him, and his vassal in Scotland. Besides, that he perceived that Hamilton, through the efficiency of wit and friendship, had obtained the better share of the dividend. For besides that in the patent he engrossed many more church lands than the other, he was so wise as to take, at easy terms, endless leases of much more of Con's third part, and from other despairiug Irishes, than Sir Hugh had done. And so it was, indeed, the one had the precedency in possession, the other priority in honour, and thus the king

[19] The date of this transaction is the 16th of April, 1605. Montg. Manus. p. 32.

tried to satisfy them both; but all that did it not, for they quarrelled afterwards to their this day's loss, and to their great cost. These two knights having received their lands, were shortly after made Lords Montgomery of Ards, and Hamilton of Claneboy. But land without inhabitants, is a burden without relief. The Irish were gone, the ground was desolate, rent must be paid to the king, tenants were none to pay to them.[20] Therefore the lords having a good bargain themselves, make some of their friends sharers, as freeholders under them. Thus came several farmers under Mr. Montgomery, gentlemen from Scotland, and of the names of the Shaws, Calderwoods, Boyds, of the Keiths from the North. And some foundations are laid for towns, and incorporations, as Newton, Donaghadee, Comber, Old and New Grey-Abbey.[21] Many Hamiltons also followed Sir James, especially his own brethren, all of them worthy men; and other farmers, as the Maxwells, Rosses, Barclays, Moors, Bayleys, and others, whose posterity hold good to this day. He also founded towns and incorporations, viz., Bangor, Holywood, and Killileagh, where he built a strong castle, and Ballywalter. These foundations being laid, the Scots came hither apace, and became tenants willingly and

20 "Let us pause awhile, and we shall wonder how this plantation advanced itself, especially in and about the towns of Donaghadee and Newton; considering that in the spring-time, 1606, those parishes were more wasted than America when the Spaniards landed there; for in all these three parishes aforesaid, thirty cabins could not be found, nor any stone-walls; but ruined roofless churches, and a few vaults at Grey-Abbey, and a stump of an old castle in Newton." Montg. Manus. p. 49.

21 In addition to what is stated above, the following paragraph, showing the way in which Sir Hugh provided for the church, is supplied from the Montg. Manus. p. 47—"He considered that the contentions which too frequently happen concerning tythes, might breed dislike and aversion between the people and minister. Therefore he gave unto the incumbents salaries, with glebes and perquisites for marriages, christenings, burials, and easter-offerings; the clerk and sexton also had their share of dues; and the people in those days resorted to church, and submitted to its censures, and paid willingly their small ecclesiastical dues; and so were in no hazard of suits in the ecclesiastical courts." Sir James Hamilton adopted a similar plan.

sub-tenants to their countrymen, (whose manner and way they knew,) so that in a short time the country began again to be inhabited."[22]

The progress of the plantation in the other parts of Ulster was not so rapid as it thus appears to have been in Down and Antrim. It advanced so slowly in the forfeited counties, that frequent inquiries, by order of the crown, were made into its progress. The last and most important of these surveys was made by Pynnar in the year 1618, from which it appears that "though 8000 men of British birth and descent, able to bear arms, were settled in the country; yet the fourth part of the land was not fully inhabited." He also states, that there had been erected one hundred and seven castles with bawns, nineteen castles without bawns, forty-two bawns without castles or houses, and one thousand eight hundred and ninety-seven dwelling-houses of stone and timber—a very insufficient number, when the extent of country, and the time which had elapsed from the commencement of the plantation, are considered.[23] The success of the undertaking would have been still greater, had the original condi-

22 This account by Stewart differs, in some important points, both from that given by Lodge in his "Peerage of Ireland," and from the "Montgomery Manuscripts," first printed at Belfast in the year 1830. The latter two being interested accounts, I prefer that by Stewart, who was unconnected with either the Montgomery or the Hamilton family, and therefore most likely to be an impartial narrator.

23 The extent of the forfeited lands is stated by Carte at "above half a million of acres;" but Pynnar, who is much more accurate, gives it at about 400,000 acres, situated in the counties of Derry, Donegall, Tyrone, Armagh, Fermanagh, and Cavan,—the whole extent of these six counties being above two millions of acres. The remaining million and a-half of acres comprised not only the unprofitable lands, but also large tracts of country held by the native proprietors, who, either being not implicated in the revolt of 1607, or having made timely submission, were unmolested in their estates. From a careful examination of Pynnar's valuable Survey, alluded to in the text, and first printed by Harris in his "Hibernica," fol. Dub. 1747, I find that of the 400,000 forfeited acres, 100,000 were granted for church, school, and corporation lands; above 60,000 were regranted to the native Irish; and the remaining 240,000 were disposed of to the British undertakers or colonists, the majority of whose tenants were

tions been strictly adhered to. But, as might be anticipated, in so extensive a scheme, interfering with so many former claims, conferring so many new rights, and intrusted to so many agents, it appears from Pynnar that numerous deviations from the original project took place, notwithstanding all the vigilance of the lord deputy; and that these contributed in many places to mar the prosperity of the undertaking, and to disappoint the expectations which had been formed of its beneficial influence on the province. At the same time these exceptions only rendered more apparent the general wisdom and propriety of the plantation. For, at the present day, we can easily discern in their inferior improvement and civilization, those districts where the prescribed conditions were neglected, and a departure made from the original plan.

Soon after the commencement of the plantation, a parliament was summoned to give the sanction of law to its various arrangements. Numbers of the Scots had come over to Ulster, while many of the native Irish had been permitted to occupy lands in the midst of the new settlers. It therefore became necessary to repeal those injudicious acts which, in former times, had been passed to prevent the English inhabitants of the kingdom from maintaining any communion either with the Irish or the Scots. This was accordingly done, to the great joy of all parties. With regard to the native Irish, all the odious edicts which had marked them out as the natural enemies of Government, and forbade them, under the penalties of high treason, to intermarry with the English; and which made it felony in the latter to hold intercourse with them, or employ them in the fostering of their children, were specifically repealed, though they had long

also Irish, the original inhabitants of Ulster. These facts it is necessary to bear in mind, as Roman Catholic, and sometimes Protestant, writers represent the forfeited lands as comprising the whole of the six counties, and speak of the colonization of Ulster as having dispossessed and displaced the entire native population of the province. Both of these statements are decided exaggerations.

before become obsolete. And with regard to the Scots, the statute of Queen Mary was repealed, by which the Anglo-Irish were forbidden to introduce them into the kingdom, to intermarry with them, or to retain them in their service. For though this act was originally applied only to those Scottish marauders from the Highlands who infested Ulster, and kept it for many centuries involved in turbulent contests, yet as the act describes these intruders by the general name of Scots, it was now necessary for the satisfaction and security of the late settlers from that kingdom, that it should be formally rescinded, lest in the hands of future legislators, its penalties might be brought to bear upon those peaceable, loyal, and industrious emigrants. The Earls of Tyrone and Tyrconnell, with O'Dogherty and the other rebels, whose lands were possessed by the British, were now also attainted, and the confiscation of their properties was sanctioned by law; that no shadow of a doubt might remain, with regard to the legality and security of the late plantation.

In conjunction with the parliament, a convocation of the clergy was summoned to meet in 1615. The church had now attained such stability and influence in the kingdom, that, for the first time, it became both necessary and practicable to hold such an assembly. The sees were all filled with Protestant prelates, whom the peaceful condition of the kingdom enabled to assemble in the metropolis; while the state of the church, as a national establishment independent of that in England, rendered it necessary that its faith should be formally declared, and its future government regulated. The statutes already in force in the kingdom respected solely the celebration of public worship, which had been made conformable to that of the English Church. Bishops were consecrated, and the sacraments dispensed according to the same ritual, and the ecclesiastical courts were similarly constituted. But as yet the Irish Church had adopted no distinct confession of faith; and it was principally to supply this defect that the clergy were now convoked. By some of the prelates it was proposed to adopt the thirty-nine articles of the sister-church of England. But the majority conceived it more consistent with the character and independence of their national church, to frame a new confession of their own. Such at least was the ostensible reason assigned for taking this step, though the real cause most probably was a secret dislike to many of the English articles. The individual to whom was intrusted the drawing up of the confession, was Dr. James Ussher, who had already been distinguished for his theological learning, and who at this period was professor of divinity in the college in Dublin.(94) This important task he executed to the entire satisfaction of the parliament and both the houses of convocation. The confession thus unanimously adopted was transmitted to England, where it was approved by the king in council. The same year it was solemnly ratified, in his Majesty's name in Dublin, by the lord deputy Chichester, and formally published as the accredited standard of the national faith.

This important document merits particular attention, as clearly evincing the doctrinal principles on which the Irish Church was founded, and the scriptural maxims by which it was then regulated. In England contrary views and principles were at that period unhappily predominant. There, even under James, the most rigid conformity continued to be urged with extreme violence. The heads of the hierarchy indignantly refused to consult the scruples of the puritans; and instead of seeking, by some comprehensive and charitable scheme, to continue them in communion with the church, and thus give it the benefit of their zeal and learning, they laboured to detect them by new tests, that they might more effectually exclude and punish these conscientious though nonconforming brethren. They would neither render their doctrinal articles more explicit, nor reduce the number or

94 Ussher was at this time professor of divinity, not provost, as stated by Neal, in his account of these articles.

authority of their canons. Their claims of ecclesiastical power were quite as extravagant as those of the Romish Church, and were pressed with almost as high a hand. The non-conformists had been consequently obliged to leave the kingdom. Many of them fled to Ireland, and were advanced to influential situations, both in the university and the church; for provided they were removed out of England and Scotland, where they so frequently opposed his arbitrary measures, James cared little for their existence and influence in this remote and turbulent country.

These exiles, in conjunction with the Scottish clergy, who had accompanied their countrymen in the late plantation of Ulster, and had been promoted to bishopricks and other ecclesiastical dignities, gave that tone to the religious sentiments of the kingdom, by which it was distinguished from the sister country.[25] Their influence appeared in the proceedings of this first convocation, especially in the Confession, which was evidently framed with the view of compromising the differences existing between the high-church clergy and the non-conformists. It was digested into no less than nineteen sections, and one hundred and four

25 Peter Heylin, the celebrated champion of the English church, thus laments over the progress of puritanism at this period in Ireland; while, at the same time, he unconsciously bears testimony to the exemplary care of the Presbyterians to maintain the public preaching of the Gospel wherever they settled. "Hereupon followed the plantation of Ulster, first undertaken by the city of London, who fortified Coleraine and built Londonderry, and purchased many thousand acres of lands in the parts adjoining. But it was carried on more vigorously, as more unfortunately withal, by some adventurers of the Scottish nation, who poured themselves into this country as the richer soil: and, though they were sufficiently industrious in improving their own fortunes there, and set up preaching in all churches, wheresoever they fixed, yet whether it happened for the better or for the worse, the event hath showed. For they brought with them hither such a stock of puritanism, such a contempt of bishops, such a neglect of the public liturgy, and other divine offices of this church, that there was nothing less to be found among them than the government and forms of worship established in the church of England." Hist. Presb. p. 393. Collier's account (Ecc. Hist. ii. 708.) is abridged from Heylin, and furnishes no additional particulars.

articles or propositions. It is as decidedly Calvinistic in doctrine as that which was subsequently compiled by the Westminster divines; and includes, in almost the same words, the nine articles of Lambeth, which the English puritans had in vain requested to be adopted at the Hampton-court conference in 1604. The morality of the Sabbath is strongly asserted, though a tenet well known to be at variance with the sentiments of the king[26]—the validity of ordination by Presbyters is clearly implied—the doctrine of absolution is condemned, and the forgiveness of sins by the clergy taught to be only declaratory—lent is disclaimed as a religious fast, and the Pope is unhesitatingly pronounced to be Antichrist,[27]—all which tenets were then characteristic of the puritan party in the church, and eagerly defended by them in opposition to the high-church clergy. At the same time no authority is claimed for framing or enforcing ecclesiastical canons, or decreeing rites and ceremonies, and no allusion is made to the mode of consecrating the higher orders of the clergy; as if on purpose to avoid maintaining that distinction between bishops and presbyters, which was so much opposed by the non-conformists. And the confession is summed up by a decree of the Synod, forbidding the public teaching of any doctrine contrary to the articles now solemnly agreed upon.[28] On

26 Leland, in noticing this peculiarity in the Irish articles, seems to regret that the opinions of the king, in reference to the Sabbath, had not been treated with more respect by Usher. His word are, " And without any condescension to the sentiments of king James, he declared in one article that the Lord's day was to be WHOLLY dedicated to the service of God." Hist. ii. 459. This looks very like making the king something more than the mere *civil* head of the church. In the view of the reverend historian, the professor of divinity ought, out of pure condescension, to have adapted his religious sentiments more closely to those of his royal master!

27 Heylin in his Hist. Presb. p. 394, thus speaks of this article, " the Pope was made to be antichrist, according to the like determination of the French Hugonots at Gappe, in Dauphiny." This Synod was held in October, 1603. Quick, i. 227.

28 The reader may see these articles in the Appendix to Neal's History of the Puritans, (No. 6.) where they are fully, and I may add, correctly

this comprehensive foundation the Irish church was formally settled. Its terms of communion were limited only in respect of doctrine, a subject on which there then existed almost universal conformity throughout the three kingdoms. It embraced all the faithful ministers of the gospel who coincided in their views of divine truth; neither compelling them to submit to objectionable ceremonies, nor unchurching them at once if they could not conscientiously approve of all the minute arrangements of government and worship then established in England. This spirit of mutual forbearance was no less agreeable to scripture than it was happily adapted to the existing state of the kingdom; for the country was involved in such ignorance and viewed with such aversion, that it was necessary to induce faithful ministers to settle in it, by affording them every facility for the exercise of their office, whatever might be their views respecting the controverted points of ecclesiastical discipline.

Encouraged by the result of this convocation, many ministers removed to Ireland, and especially to Ulster, where they were likely to enjoy the greatest security, and where there existed a more urgent necessity for their services. This province was now occupied by settlers, who were willing enough to receive and respect them when sent; but who were far from being generally characterized by a desire for enjoying religious ordinances. On the contrary, a great number of those who accompanied the original proprietors and who occupied their lands, were openly profane and immoral in their conduct, and were generally inattentive to the sacred institutions of the Gospel. The following description of their conduct and character, though probably a little overcharged, is given by Stewart:—"From Scotland," he says, "came many, and from England not a few; yet all of them generally the scum of both nations, who, from debt, or breaking

given, having compared them with an early copy in my possession, published by authority. Lond. 1629. 4to.

and fleeing from justice, or seeking shelter, came hither, hoping to be without fear of man's justice in a land where there was nothing, or but little as yet, of the fear of God. And in a few years there flocked such a multitude of people from Scotland, that these northern counties of Down, Antrim, Londonderry, &c., were in a good measure planted, which had been waste before. Yet most of the people were all void of godliness, who seemed rather to flee from God in this enterprise than to follow their own mercy. Yet God followed them when they fled from him. Albeit at first it must be remembered, that as they cared little for any church, so God seemed to care as little for them. For these strangers were no better entertained than with the relics of popery, served up in a ceremonial service of God under a sort of antichristian hierarchy, and committed to the care of a number of careless men, who were only zealous to call for their gain from their quarter; men who said, 'come ye, I will bring wine, let us drink, for to-morrow shall be as this day, and much more abundant.' Thus on all hands atheism increased, and disregard of God, iniquity abounded with contention, fighting, murder, adultery, &c. as among people who, as they had nothing within them to overawe them, so their ministers' example was worse than nothing; for, 'from the prophets' of Israel profaneness went forth to the whole land.' And verily at this time the whole body of this people seemed ripe for the manifestation, in a great degree, either of God's judgments or mercy. For their carriage made them to be abhorred at home in their native land, insomuch, that 'going for Ireland' was looked on as a miserable mark of a deplorable person. Yea, it was turned into a proverb; and one of the worst expressions of disdain that could be invented was, to tell a man that 'Ireland would be his hinder end.' While thus it was, and when any man would have expected nothing but God's judgment to have followed this crew of sinners; behold the Lord visited them in admirable *mercy*, the like whereof had not been any where for many generations."

This account is also confirmed by Blair, who says: "Although amongst those whom divine providence did send to Ireland there were several persons eminent for birth, education, and parts; yet the most part were such as either poverty, scandalous lives, or at the best, adventurous seeking of better accommodation had forced thither: so that the security and thriving of religion was little seen to by those adventurers, and the preachers were generally of the same complexion with the people." (29)

The *mercy*, alluded to by Stewart, consisted in the band of faithful ministers who were now encouraged to take their lot in Ulster, and whose labours were remarkably blessed to the converting of many out of so profane and godless a multitude. Of these servants of God, a few are so eminently distinguished by their zeal and fortitude, and are so frequently referred to as the founders of the Presbyterian Church in the province, that their history merits and demands especial notice. (30)

Of these the first, in point of time, is Edward Brice, M. A. He had, for many years, been minister of Drymen in Stirlingshire. But having, in the year 1607, resolutely opposed the motion for making Spotiswood, archbishop of Glasgow, permanent moderator of the Synod of Clydesdale—the expedient then adopted for securing the introduction of prelacy into Scotland—he was marked out for persecution, and was shortly afterwards obliged to leave the kingdom. (31) His views were naturally directed to Ireland, whither many of his countrymen had already resorted; and among others William Edmonstone of Duntreath, in Stirling-

29 Blair's Life, p. 51. Edin. 1754.

30 On this topic, some of my readers may conceive that I have gone into a minuteness of detail, more appropriate to the biographer than the historian. But the novelty and interest of the subject encourage me to lay before the public all that I could glean respecting the settlement, character, and fate of these fathers of the Presbyterian Church in Ireland.

31 Balfour's Annals, ii. 22.

shire, who in 1609 had settled in Broadisland, in the county of Antrim. Having been minister in his vicinity in Scotland, and doubtless known to him there, Brice directed his steps to his former acquaintance; and having been received and acknowledged by Echlin, bishop of Down and Connor—himself a Scotchman—he began, in the year 1613, to exercise his ministry in Broadisland, a district of country lying between Larne and Carrickfergus. In September 1619, he was promoted by the bishop to be prebendary of Kilroot, but continued to officiate in his first settlement, which was part of the prebend. His new dignity, which was little more than nominal, did not tempt him to abate his zeal in the ministry, or renounce his former principles. Ten years afterwards, Livingston thus describes him:—"He was an aged man ere I knew him, and came not much abroad. In all his preaching he insisted most on the life of Christ in the heart, and the light of his word and Spirit on the mind; that being his own continual exercise." [32]

In the adjoining parish of Carrickfergus, Mr. Hubbard, a puritan minister from England, was settled. He was episcopally ordained; but he had forsaken the communion of the English Church, and taken charge of a non-conforming congregation at Southwark, London. In this situation, being much oppressed by the intolerant measures of that period, both he and his people resolved to remove to Ireland. Having been, under the celebrated Cartwright, a fellow-pupil of Sir Arthur Chichester at Cambridge, and having apprized him of his determination, he was invited by Sir Arthur to Carrickfergus, where he and the members of his congregation who accompanied him, were peaceably settled about the year 1621. Blair speaks of him "as an able, gracious man;" but he was not long spared to the church. He died in the

[32] Livingston's Life, p. 78, 18mo. Edin. 1754. This valuable little work was originally printed in quarto in the year 1727. I have a copy of this edition, but my references are to the former, as being more generally accessible.

beginning of the year 1623, scarcely two years after his removal; and his people, having lost their pastor, returned to their native country, and settled again in the vicinity of London.[33]

Shortly after the death of Hubbard, JAMES GLENDINNING, A. M. is noticed as residing and lecturing in Carrickfergus. He was a native of Scotland, and was educated at St. Leonard's college, in St. Andrews; but at an early period he had removed to Ireland. In the visitation book of the diocese of Down and Connor in 1622, he is returned as incumbent of the adjoining parish of Coole or Carnmoney, and as serving the cure there; though, at the same time, the parish church is described as being in ruins.[34] It is probable, therefore, that he resided altogether at Carrickfergus, in the capacity of lecturer—an office now almost wholly laid aside in the established church in Ireland: at all events he continued to preach here with great applause for several years.

At Antrim was settled JOHN RIDGE, A. M. a native of England. On the sixth of March 1611, he had been admitted to the order of deacon by the bishop of Oxford; but having no freedom for the exercise of his ministry in England, without submitting to impositions which were contrary to his conscience, he removed to this country, and was admitted on the seventh of July 1619, to the vicarage of Antrim, on the presentation of Sir Arthur, now Lord Chichester, being another of those eminent ministers patronized by that pious and public-spirited nobleman. Blair styles him, "the judicious and gracious minister of Antrim;" and Livingston says of him, "he used not to have many points in his sermon; but he so enlarged those he had, that it was scarcely possible for any hearer to forget his preaching. He was a great urger of charitable works, and a very humble man."

Contemporary with these ministers, there were others in

33 Brooke's Lives of the Puritans, iii. 517. Wilson's Dissenting Churches in London, iv. 124.

34 Ulster Visitation Book, MSS. E. 3. 6. Trin. Coll. Dub.

the county of Down equally distinguished for their piety and zeal. The first settled there was ROBERT CUNNINGHAM, A. M. He had been chaplain to the Earl of Buccleugh's regiment in Holland; but removing to Ireland on the return of the troops to Scotland, he was, on the ninth of November 1615, admitted to the ministry by bishop Echlin. He is returned on the diocesan roll in 1622, as curate of Holywood and Craigavad, and as maintained in this office by a stipend from Sir James Hamilton, now Lord Claneboy. "To my discerning," says Livingston, "he was the one man who most resembled the meekness of Jesus Christ in all his carriage that ever I saw, and was so far reverenced of all, even by the wicked, that he was oft troubled with that scripture, 'Wo to you when all men speak well of you!'"

In the neighbouring parish of Bangor was soon after settled the celebrated ROBERT BLAIR. He had been a regent or professor in the college of Glasgow; but being much opposed by Dr. Cameron,—who had been appointed principal with the view of bringing the college to approve of prelacy,—he resigned his situation; and being invited over by Lord Claneboy, he came to Ireland in May 1623. He thus narrates the circumstances of his settlement at Bangor. "When I landed in Ireland, some men parting from their cups and all things smelling of a root called rampions, [35] my prejudice was confirmed against that land. But next day travelling towards Bangor, I met unexpectedly with so sweet a peace and so great a joy, as I behoved to look thereon as my welcome thither; and retiring to a private place about a mile above Craigfergus, I prostrated myself upon the grass to rejoice in the Lord, who proved the same to me in Ireland which he had been in Scotland. Nevertheless, my aversion to a settlement there continued strong; and when my noble patron renewed his invitation and offer, I was very careful to

35 This is the *Allium Ursinum*, a species of wild Garlic. I have found it growing in the vicinity of Carrickfergus.

inform him both of what accusations had been laid against me of disaffection to the civil powers, and that I could not submit to the use of the English liturgy nor episcopal government, to see if either of these would prevail with him to pass from his invitation. But he having been informed by a minister present of my altercations with Dr. Cameron, he said, 'I know all that business;' and for the other point, he added, that he was confident of procuring a free entry for me, which he quickly effectuated. So all my devices to obstruct a settlement there did evanish and took no effect, the counsel of the Lord standing fast in all generations; yea, his wisdom overruled all this, both to procure me a free and safe entry to the holy ministry; and that when after some years I met with trials for my non-conformity, neither patron nor prelate could say that I had broken any condition to them.

"Having been invited to preach by the patron, and by Mr. Gibson, the sick incumbent, [the first protestant dean of Down, but resident at Bangor,] I yielded to their invitation, and preached there three Sabbath-days. After that, several of the aged and most respectful persons in the congregation came to me by order of the whole, and informed me, that they were edified by the doctrine delivered by me; intreated me not to leave them; and promised, if the patron's offer of maintenance was not large enough, they would willingly add to the same. This promise I slighted, being too careless of competent and comfortable provision, for I had no thoughts of any greater family than a boy or two to serve me. But on the former part of that speech importing the congregation's call, I laid great weight; and it did contribute more to the removing of my unwillingness to settle there than any thing else. Likewise the dying man, [Gibson,] did several ways encourage me. He professed great sorrow for his having been a dean. He condemned episcopacy more strongly than ever I durst do; he charged me in the name of Christ, and as I expected his blessing on my ministry, not to leave that good way wherein I had begun to walk; and then drawing my head towards his bosom with both his arms, he laid his hands on my head and blessed me.[36] Within a few days after he died; and my admission was accomplished as quickly as might be, in the following way. The Viscount Claneboy, my noble patron, did, on my request, inform the bishop,[37] how opposite I was to episcopacy and their liturgy, and had the influence to procure my admission on easy and honourable terms. Yet, lest his lordship had not been plain enough, I declared my opinion fully to the bishop at our first meeting, and found him yielding beyond my expectation. The bishop said to me, 'I hear good of you, and will impose no conditions on you; I am old and can teach you ceremonies, and you can teach me substance, only I must ordain you, else neither I nor you can answer the law nor brook the land.' I answered him, that his sole ordination did utterly contradict my principles; but he replied both wittily and submis-

36 The following account of this interview is given by Robert Fleming in his "Fulfilling of the Scripture," vol. i. p. 435. Mr. Blair "found the dean was lying sick, and though a most naughty man, he made him not only welcome upon his visit, but encouraged him to hold on his way, and told him he was to succeed him in that charge. Yea, he spoke so unlike himself, and in a strain so different from what was usual unto him, that a gentlewoman standing by said to some others—'An angel is speaking out of the dean's bed to Mr. Blair,' thinking it could not be such a man."—I subjoin a copy of his epitaph, constructed, perhaps, on the well-known principle, '*De mortuis nil nisi bonum*,'—"Heir lyes beloue ane learned and reverend Father in Gode's church, mester John Gibson, sence reformacione from Popary, the firest deane of Down, send by his maiestie into this kingdom, and receved by my Lord Claneboy to be preacher at Bangor. At his entry had XL communicants; and at his departour this lyf 23 of Junii 1623, left 1200; being of age 63 years. So Chyrst was his advantage bothe in lyf and death."

37 Stevenson, the editor of Blair's Life, has here erroneously inserted in the printed copy (p. 52,) the name of Knox, bishop of Raphoe, as the person to whom Blair applied for ordination. No name is given in the original MS. in Blair's hand-writing, which I examined in the Library of the Writers to the Signet, Edinburgh. It was manifestly Echlin of Down, as appears not only from the context, but also from the entry on the diocesan roll of 1633, in which Blair is set forth as having been ordained by this prelate.

sively, 'whatever you account of episcopacy, yet I know you account a presbytery to have divine warrant; will you not receive ordination from Mr. Cunningham and the adjacent brethren, and let me come in among them in no other relation than a presbyter?' This I could not refuse, and so the matter was performed"—on the tenth of July 1623.

Blair was one of the most eminent ministers at this time in Ireland, and contributed, more than any other, to the revival and establishment of true religion in the province. "He was a man," says Livingston who knew him intimately, "of notable constitution both of body and mind; of a majestic, awful, yet affable and amiable countenance and carriage, thoroughly learned, of strong parts, deep invention, solid judgment, and of a most public spirit for God. His gift of preaching was such, that seldom could any observe withdrawing of assistance in public, which in others is frequent. He seldom ever wanted assurance of his salvation. He spent many days and nights in prayer alone and with others, and was vouchsafed great intimacy with God."

Shortly after his settlement at Bangor, he was the means of inducing another minister to devote himself to the service of the church. This was JAMES HAMILTON, nephew to Lord Claneboy, who, though educated for the ministry in Scotland, had as yet held only the situation of steward or agent to his uncle. Mr. Blair, perceiving his learning and growing piety, proposed to him to enter the ministry, and, in conjunction with Mr. Cunningham, made private trial of his endowments. "Being satisfied with his gifts," continues Blair, "I invited him to preach in my pulpit, in his uncle's hearing, who, till then, knew nothing of this matter. For Mr. Hamilton having been his uncle's chamberlain, and chief manager of his affairs, we were afraid the viscount would not part with so faithful a servant. But he, having once heard his nephew, did put more respect upon him than ever before. Shortly thereafter, [about the year 1625,] Mr. Hamilton was ordained [by bishop Echlin] to the holy ministry at Ballywalter, where he was both diligent and successful. And notwithstanding he had many temptations to espouse episcopacy, and might easily have obtained promotion in that way, yet the Lord did graciously preserve him from being ensnared with those baits, and made him very instrumental in promoting his work." Livingston describes him "as a learned and diligent man;" and adds, that "his gift of preaching was rather doctrinal than exhortatory."

These seven brethren constituted the first band of ministers who laboured with apostolic earnestness to remove the ignorance, formality, and profaneness which characterised the greater part of the early colonists. Possessed of the true missionary spirit, and inspired with a holy zeal to propagate the Gospel, they commenced with vigour the work of evangelizing the land; and though few in number and beset with many difficulties, they were favoured with an extraordinary, if not unprecedented, measure of success.

CHAPTER II.

Revival of religion—Circumstances which occasioned it—Establishment of a monthly meeting at Antrim—Arrival of additional ministers from Scotland—Welsh—Stewart—Dunbar—Colvert—Livingston—Notices of MacClelland and Semple—Their labours and success—Their maintenance of the Presbyterian worship and discipline—Monthly meetings at Antrim—Influence in promoting the revival of religion—Testimonies respecting its extent and reality—Difficulties it encountered—General non conformity of the northern clergy—Jealousy of bishop Echlin—His insidious opposition to Blair.—Is defeated—Afterwards suspends two ministers.—They apply to Archbishop Ussher and are restored.—Echlin again silences four ministers.—Blair goes to London—Applies for relief to Charles I.—Their case referred to the lord deputy of Ireland—who refuses to relieve them.

It was not long before the zealous labours of the ministers, whose names are recorded in the preceding chapter, began to be visibly blessed. A remarkable improvement in the habits and demeanour of the people was speedily effected. The thoughtless were roused to serious inquiry on the subject of religion, and the careless were alarmed, and at the same time urged to anxious self-examination. The profane were, in a great measure, silenced, and the immoral reclaimed; while the obstinate opposers of the Gospel were converted into its willing and decided supporters. The revival of religion which occurred at this period subsequently attracted considerable attention both in Scotland and in England. The fame of it extended even to America, and it has been repeatedly referred to by religious writers of the last century, as one of those sudden and extensive manifestations of the power of divine grace upon a careless people, with which the church has been occasionally favoured.

This spirit of religious inquiry and reformation, which in a short time pervaded a considerable portion of the counties of Down and Antrim, was no doubt the natural, as it is the promised, result of that devotedness and fidelity by which the Presbyterian ministers in this part of Ulster were so eminently distinguished. Yet it appears to have first manifested itself under the ministry of the weakest of these brethren, whose limited attainments and ill-regulated zeal were providentially over-ruled 'for the furtherance of the Gospel.'

The singular circumstances connected with the origin of this religious revival, the first important incident occurring in the history of the Presbyterian church in Ulster, deserve to be noticed, and are thus fully narrated by Stewart. "Mr. Blair coming over from Bangor to Carrickfergus on some business, and occasionally hearing Mr. Glendinning to preach, perceived some sparkles of good inclination in him, yet found him not solid but weak, and not fitted for a public place and among the English. On which Mr. Blair did call him, and using freedom with him, advised him to go to some place in the country among his countrymen: whereupon he went to Oldstone [near the town of Antrim] and was there placed. He was a man who would never have been chosen by a wise assembly of ministers, nor sent to begin a reformation in this land. For he was little better than distracted; yea, afterwards, did actually become so. Yet this was the Lord's choice to begin with him the admirable work of God; which I mention on purpose that all men may see how the glory is only the Lord's in making a holy nation in this profane land, and that it was 'not by might, nor by power, nor by man's wisdom, but by my Spirit, saith the Lord.' At Oldstone God made use of him to awaken the consciences of a lewd and secure people thereabouts. For seeing the great lewdness and ungodly sinfulness of the people, he preached to them nothing but law-wrath, and the terrors of God for sin. And in very deed for this only was he fitted, for hardly could he preach any other thing. But behold the success! For the hearers finding themselves condemned by the mouth of God speaking in his word, fell into such anxiety and terror of conscience that they looked on themselves as altogether lost and damned; and this work appeared not in one single person or two, but multitudes were brought to understand their way, and to cry out, men and brethren, what shall we do to be saved? I have seen them myself stricken into a swoon with the word; yea, a dozen in one day carried out of doors as dead; so marvellous was the power of God smiting their hearts for sin, condemning and killing. And of these were none of the weaker sex or spirit, but indeed some of the boldest spirits who formerly feared not with their swords to put a whole market-town in a fray; yet in defence of their stubbornness cared not to lie in prison and in the stocks; and being incorrigible, were as ready to do the like the next day. I have heard one of them, then a mighty strong man, now a mighty Christian, say that his end in coming to church was to consult with his companions how to work some mischief. And yet at one of those sermons was he so catched, that he was fully subdued. But why do I speak of him? We knew, and yet know, multitudes of such men who sinned and still gloried in it, because they feared no man, yet are now patterns of sobriety, fearing to sin because they fear God. And this spread through the country to admiration, especially about that river, commonly called the Six-mile-water,[1] for there this work began at first. At this time of people's gathering to Christ, it pleased the Lord to visit mercifully the honourable family in Antrim,[2]

1 This river runs past the towns of Ballynure, Ballyclare, and Templepatrick, and empties itself into Lough Neagh at Antrim.

2 Blair also notices this eminent family. "At Antrim, Sir Hugh Clotworthy was very hospitable to the ministers who took part in that work; and his worthy son, the first Lord Massareene, with his mother and spouse, both of them very virtuous and religious ladies, did greatly countenance the

so as Sir John Clotworthy, and my lady his mother, and his own precious lady, did shine in an eminent manner in receiving the Gospel, and offering themselves to the Lord; whose example instantly other gentlemen followed, such as Captain Norton[(3)] and others, of whom the Gospel made a clear and cleanly conquest."

These religious agitations continued for a considerable time. The ministers were indefatigable in improving the favourable opportunities thus afforded for extending the knowledge and influence of the Gospel. The people, awakened and inquiring, many of them desponding and alarmed, both desired and needed guidance and instruction. The judicious exhibition of evangelical doctrines and promises by these faithful men was, in due time, productive of those happy and tranquillizing effects which were early predicted as the characteristics of Gospel-times. Adopting the beautiful imagery of the prophets,—the broken-hearted were bound up and comforted; the spirit of bondage and of fear gave

same." Sir Hugh, here mentioned, was the first of this family who settled in Ireland. He was here in 1603, and died at Antrim in February 1630. His wife was Mary, daughter of Roger Langford, Esq. of Muckamore. He left an only daughter, Mary, married in 1628 to Captain Henry Upton, of Templepatrick; and a younger son, James, who was settled at Moneymore in the county of Derry. His eldest son was John, whose 'spouse' was Margaret, daughter to Lord Ranelagh, and who became the first Viscount Massareene. The reader will find him, as Sir John Clotworthy, frequently mentioned in these pages, and uniformly distinguished, through the most trying times, for his ardent attachment to Presbyterianism and the cause of civil liberty. The student of English history will also be familiar with his name and character, as a prominent member of the Long Parliament. Lord Viscount Ferrard is the present representative of this ancient family, and the title of Lord Massareene, having been for some time dormant, is once more revived in his eldest son.

[3] Captain Humphrey Norton was settled at Templepatrick. His daughter, probably his only child, having displeased him by an imprudent marriage, he sold his estate to Captain Henry Upton, son-in-law to Sir Hugh Clotworthy, who became the founder of a family, now ennobled by the title of Viscount Templetown, who long continued to be the generous and ardent patrons of the Presbyterian interest in Ulster.

way to a spirit of freedom and of love; the oil of joy was poured forth instead of mourning; and the spirit of heaviness exchanged for the garment of praise and thankfulness. As the people emerged from the anxiety and alarm produced by the stern preaching of the law, and gradually experienced the hope and joy of the Gospel, they would be naturally led to maintain among themselves a closer religious fellowship than they had done in their previous state of unconcern. This proved to be the case. In addition to the stated exercises of the Sabbath, a day which they strictly observed, they assembled for devotional purposes at other special seasons. Hence originated those monthly meetings at Antrim, which afterwards attracted so much attention, and which, in the mean time, tended materially to strengthen and consolidate the good work that had commenced. Stewart, in the last portion of his narrative which has been preserved, thus details the origin of these meetings.

"When, therefore, the multitude of wounded consciences were healed, they began to draw into holy communion and meeting together privately for edification, a thing which in a lifeless generation is both neglected and reproved. But the new life forced it among the people, who desired to know what God was doing with the souls of their neighbours, who, they perceived, were wrought on in spirit, as they had been. There was a man in the parish of Oldstone, called Hugh Campbell, who had fled from Scotland; him God caught in Ireland, and made him an eminent and exemplary Christian until this day. He was a gentleman of the house of Duket-hall.[4] After this man was healed of the wound given to his soul by the Almighty, he became very refreshful to others who had less learning and judgment than himself. He therefore invited some of his honest neighbours who fought the same fight of faith, to meet him at his house on the last Friday of the month; where and when, beginning with a few,

[4] The reader will find him again mentioned in chapter v.

they spent their time in prayer, mutual edification and conference on what they found within them: Nothing like the superficial superfluous meetings of some cold-hearted professors, who afterwards made this work a snare to many. But these new beginners were more filled with heart-exercise than head-notions, and with fervent prayer rather than conceity gifts to fill the head. As these truly increased, so did this meeting for private edification increase too; and still at Hugh Campbell's house, on the last Friday of the month. At last they grew so numerous, that the ministers who had begotten them again to Christ, thought fit that some of them should be still with them to prevent what hurt might follow."— "Accordingly," says Blair, who fortunately carries on the narrative from this period, at which that of Stewart abruptly terminates, "Mr. John Ridge, the judicious and gracious minister of Antrim, perceiving many people on both sides of the Six-mile-water awakened out of their security, made an overture that a monthly meeting might be set up at Antrim, which was within a mile of Oldstone, and lay centrical for the awakened persons to resort to, and he invited Mr. Cunningham, Mr. Hamilton and myself to take part in that work, who were all glad of the motion, and heartily embraced it. Mr. Glendinning was also at the first glad of the confluence of the people. But we not having invited him to bear a part in the monthly meeting, he became so emulous, that to preserve popular applause, he watched and fasted wonderfully. Afterward he was smitten with a number of erroneous and enthusiastic opinions—and embracing one error after another, he set out at last on a visit to the seven churches of Asia."

The removal of this minister was no loss to the cause of religion, although he had happily been made the instrument of awakening many to a sense of its supreme importance. Had there not been judicious ministers at hand able to control and improve the agitations and alarms which he excited, and to warn the weak of his errors, the good work might have been disgraced and overthrown, and formality and indifference might have resumed their fatal influence over the people. His place was soon after supplied by equally zealous, though more prudent and faithful brethren from Scotland; who, hearing of this great revival of religion and of the freedom with which they would be permitted to exercise their ministry, willingly removed hither, and became valuable fellow-workers with their brethren in extending the influence of the gospel and in promoting the interests of the church of Christ in Ulster.

The first of these was JOSIAS WELSH, son of the celebrated John Welsh, minister of Ayr, and consequently grandson to JOHN KNOX, the Scottish Reformer, by Elizabeth, his third daughter. He was educated at Geneva, and on his return to his native country was appointed professor of humanity in the university of Glasgow. This situation he filled until the same cause which had driven Mr. Blair from the college, —the introduction of prelacy under Dr. Cameron,—soon after compelled him also to resign his chair. "A great measure of that spirit," says Blair, "which wrought in and by the father rested on the son. The last time I had been in Scotland I met with him, and finding of how zealous a spirit he was, I exhorted him to hasten over to Ireland, where he would find work enough, and I hoped success too." He accordingly came over about the year 1626, and took up his residence with Mr. Shaw, a gentleman from Ayrshire, who had been probably known to his father, and who was now settled near Templepatrick on the opposite side of the Six-mile-water. Welsh preached for a time at Oldstone, vacant by the departure of Glendinning; and having been ordained by his kinsman Knox, bishop of Raphoe,[5] he was soon after

5 Bishop Knox was of the same family with the Reformer Knox; consequently Welsh was his relative. The bishop was educated at Glasgow; (M'Ure's Glas. last ed. p. 197,) and was minister, first at Lochwinnoch and then at Paisley. On the second of April 1606, he was made bishop of the Isles by King James, where he was distinguished for his attention to the

settled at Templepatrick as chaplain to Captain Norton. "Here," writes Livingston, "he had many seals to his ministry. He was much exercised in his own spirit, and therefore much of his preaching was an exercise of conscience." "He did with great eagerness," adds Blair, "convince the secure and sweetly comfort those that were dejected."

After him came over ANDREW STEWART in the year 1627. He succeeded John Stirling, A. M. as minister of Donegore, a parish adjoining both Templepatrick and Antrim. According to Livingston, "he was a man very streight in the cause of God;" and Blair styles him, "a learned gentleman and fervent in spirit, and a very successful minister of the word of God."

The next who followed from Scotland was GEORGE DUNBAR, A. M. He had been, for a length of time, minister of Ayr, and had been twice ejected in Scotland by the High commission court for his resolute attachment to the presbyterian cause which James I. was then labouring to subvert. "When the messenger [of the court] came to his house [at Ayr] the second time, a young daughter of his turning said, 'and is Pharaoh's heart hardened still?' while all that Mr. George said was to his wife to provide the creels again. For the former time, the children being young, they behoved to carry them away in creels upon horseback."—

propagation of religion. Keith's Scott. Bish. p. 308. When in this see he appears to have enjoyed a pension from the king of L.100 per annum, as I find this pension withdrawn in May 1620, when he was probably on the eve of being removed to Ireland. Rym. Fæd. vol. vii. part 3, p. 147. He was translated to the see of Raphoe in 1622, where he died on the 7th of November 1632. Ware's Bishops. I may add that both the bishop and the reformer were of the house of Ranfurly in Renfrewshire, a title which now appears in the British peerage, as borne by the family of Knox of Dungannon in the county of Tyrone, who are descended from Marcus Knox, of the family of Selbiland and of Ranfurly, a zealous merchant in Glasgow at the period of the Reformation, and the donor of the great bell in the high-church, which still bears his name. The representative of this family was first ennobled by the title of Viscount Northland, which has been recently exchanged for the higher dignity of Earl of Ranfurly.

"He was," says Stewart, "for a long time prisoner at Blackness; but being released from this confinement, he was banished by order of the privy-council, and soon after came to Ireland. He first preached at Carrickfergus [after the removal of Glendinning;] but having no entertainment there, he staid a while at Ballymena and then came to Inver or Larne; by whose means all that country heard the word and were first gathered to the Lord." He ultimately settled at Larne, where he proved a most diligent minister.

His congregation participated in that awakening spirit of religion which had already manifested its striking effects in the vicinity of Antrim. The good old man having witnessed some of its fruits in that quarter, had one day in his sermon at home been "regretting with great grief that he thought none of his people had gotten good by his ministry; when one Robert Brown rose and said before them all that he had gotten good. So, after that, there appeared a blessed change wrought on him and several others." Among these, the singular case of Andrew Brown, as related by Livingston, deserves to be specified. "He was born deaf and dumb, and had been a very vicious, loose man. But when it pleased the Lord to work a change on several of that parish of Larne, a very sensible change was observed in him, not only in forsaking his former loose courses and company, but in joining himself to religious people, and all the exercises of God's worship in public and private. He ordinarily, morning and evening, used to go alone to prayer, and would weep at sermons; and by such signs those who were acquainted with him understood that he would express many things of the work of God upon his heart. So that upon his earnest desire and by the consent of all the ministers who used to meet at Antrim, he was at last admitted to the ordinance of the Lord's supper." As if to try the truth and reality of these changes of character, there were several persons, in this and the adjoining parish of Broadisland, who were affected with violent breathings and convulsions, especially during public worship; and who considered these questionable symptoms as evidences of the work of the Spirit. But the prudence and discernment of Brice and Dunbar soon detected the imposition, and thus rescued the cause of religion from contempt and dishonour. "When they conferred with these persons, they did neither discover any sense of their sinful state nor any panting after a Saviour. Yet not content with this trial, the minister of the place wrote to his brethren inviting them to come and examine the matter; and when we came and had conferred with them, we perceived it to be a mere delusion and cheat of the destroyer to slander and disgrace the work of the Lord."[6]

Shortly after Mr. Dunbar, HENRY COLWORT or Calvert entered on the ministry in Ireland. He was a native of England, and had been ordained by Knox bishop of Raphoe on the fourth of May 1629. He was for some time assistant to Mr. Brice at Broadisland; but in a short time he removed to Oldstone or Muckamore, having been, on the presentation of Roger Langford, Esq., admitted to this parish on the seventeenth of June 1630. "This able minister," says Blair, "being of a fervent spirit and vehement delivery in preaching, and withal very diligent, was a blessing to that people:" and Livingston speaks of him as one "who very pertinently cited much scripture in his sermons, and frequently urged private fasting and prayer."

Lastly, JOHN LIVINGSTON, A.M. was encouraged to resume the ministry in Ireland. He had been assistant to the minister of Torphichen in Scotland; but in consequence of his opposition to prelacy, he was silenced by Spotiswood, archbishop of St. Andrews, in the year 1627. He continued to preach, however, occasionally and by stealth, and calls from several parishes were presented to him; but his settlement was invariably obstructed by the bishops. At length an opportunity offered for removing to Ireland, the circumstances

[6] Blair, p. 73.

of which he thus narrates: "In summer 1630, being in Irvine, Mr. Robert Cunningham, minister at Holywood in Ireland, and some while before that, Mr. George Dunbar, minister of Larne in Ireland, propounded to me, seeing there was no appearance I could enter into the ministry in Scotland, whether or not I would be content to go to Ireland? I answered them both, if I got a clear call and a free entry I would not refuse. About August 1630, I got letters from the Viscount Clanniboy to come to Ireland, in reference to a call to Killinchy; whither I went and got an unanimous call from the parish. And because it was needful that I should be ordained to the ministry, and the bishop of Down, in whose diocese Killinchy was, being a corrupt humorous [7] man, and would require some engagement; therefore my Lord Clanniboy sent some with me and wrote to Mr. Andrew Knox, bishop of Rapho; who when I came and had delivered the letters from my Lord Clanniboy, and from the Earl of Wigton and some others, that I had for that purpose brought out of Scotland, told me he knew my errand; that I came to him because I had scruples against episcopacy and ceremonies, according as Mr. Josias Welsh and some others had done before; and that he thought his old age was prolonged for little other purpose but to do such offices: That if I scrupled to call him 'my Lord,' he cared not much for it; all he would desire of me, because they got there but few sermons, that I would preach at Ramallen [8] the first Sabbath, and that he would send for Mr. William Cunningham [9] and

7 This is "timorous" in the edition of 1727, which is evidently a more correct and appropriate epithet than "humorous."

8 This was Ramullen, on the northern side of Lough Swilly, where the bishop resided in preference to Raphoe, probably on account of the protection afforded by the castle and garrison there. I find his Report for the diocese of Raphoe, dated from the same place so early as the 31st of May 1622. Ulster Visitation Book, MSS. Trin. Coll. Dublin. The family of Knox of Prehen, near Derry, still hold considerable property at Ramullan, and are probably descendants of this bishop.

9 This Mr. William Cunningham I find was minister of the parishes of Tullaghfernan, (now Tully,) and of Gartan in the diocese of Raphoe. The

two or three other neighbouring ministers to be present, who after sermon should give me imposition of hands; but altho' they performed the work, he behoved to be present; and altho' he durst not answer it to the state, he gave me the book

former parish has been united to that of Aughnish, and is known by the name of Tully-aughnish, the parish church of which is now situated at Ramelton, within four miles of Ramullan, where the bishop resided. But at the period mentioned in the text, the church of Tully was "ruined and decayed;" while that of Aughnish, then called "Athinish," and held by another minister, Mr. William Patton, is described by the bishop in his Report of 1622, as "being in former times built in an island in an arm of the sea called Lough-Swilly, and therefore inaccessible but by water. It is fitting," he adds, "to be transported to Ramelton, where Sir William Stewart, Knt., hath built a fair castle and made a plantation of an hundred and more British houses, being in the midst of said parish." This was accordingly done, and it became the parish church for both Augnish and Tully. The bishop in his Report, already mentioned, gives the following account of Mr. Cunningham and of the glebe allotted to Tully. "Mr. Wm. Connyngham, M. A.,—a good scholar and preacher of God's word, and of godly and unspotted life and conversation. The glebe granted by his Majesty to this church is half a quarter of Ballyare, where there is a good sufficient house builded for the incumbent; together with two half-quarters, Larmado and Clandidall." Mr. Wm. Patton, M. A., the minister of Augnish, was at the same time incumbent of Ray, near Letterkenney, where he resided. He occasionally visited Ramelton, but had no other curate there than "Brian O'Downey, a converted priest."—Sir William Stewart, mentioned by the bishop, first obtained lands here in November 1610. They formed part of the forfeited estate of O'Donnell, of which Sir Richard Hansard was the first patentee. In 1618, according to Pynnar, Sir William had erected at Ramelton, "a large and strong tower 80 feet square, 16 feet high, with four flankers; and a fair strong castle, being three stories and a half high; and had made a large town consisting of 45 houses, in which there are 57 families, all British, (*i. e.* English or Scotch.) He hath also begun a church of lime and stone, which is built to the setting on of the roof. There is also a water-mill for corn. It is a market town, and standeth very well for the good of the country and the king's service." Ramelton and its church were burned and pillaged by the Roman Catholics in the beginning of the rebellion of 1641; but the Lagan forces under Sir William recovered possession of the castle a few months after. The elder branch of Sir William Stewart's descendants were ennobled by the titles of Viscounts Mountjoy and Earls of Blessington, but became extinct in 1769, when the baronetage reverted to a younger branch, and is now enjoyed by the present baronet, Sir James Stewart of Fort-Stewart, Ramelof ordination, and desired that any thing I scrupled at, I should draw a line over it on the margin, and that Mr. Cunningham should not read it. But I found that it had been so marked by some others before, that I needed not mark any thing: so the Lord was pleased to carry that business far beyond any thing that I had thought, or almost ever desired." Livingston was among the most learned and laborious of the brethren in Ireland, and suffered more than any other for his unshaken adherence to the Presbyterian cause.

Before concluding these brief notices, there are two other ministers who, though never settled in congregations, are entitled, from their diligence and sufferings as preachers, to be specially mentioned. One was JOHN M'CLELLAND. "He was," says Livingston, "first schoolmaster at Newton-ards in Ireland, where he bred several hopeful youths for the college. Being first tried and approven by the honest ministers in the county of Down, he often preached in their churches. He was a most streight and zealous man; he knew not what it was to be afraid in the cause of God, and was early acquainted with God and his ways." The other was JOHN SEMPLE. He officiated for a time as clerk or precentor to some of the brethren who were settled in the county of Down. His entering on the ministerial office arose out of the following incident. According to the mode of commencing public worship customary at that period, he was, on one Sabbath morning, "singing a psalm before the minister came in that was to preach; he thought he tarried long, and he had an impulse to speak something to the psalm he was singing; and as he told me himself," adds the narrator of this incident, who was his relative, "he was carried out in great liberty. These wor-

ton. I trust I shall be pardoned for the disproportionate minuteness of my references to this neighbourhood in the present note. My only excuse is, that here my boyhood was passed, and youthful associations lent an interest to the investigation of its parochial antiquities, and I have here recorded the result, chiefly for the gratification of many early and valued friends at Ramelton. The general reader will, I hope, excuse the appropriation of *one* note to such an object.

thies, [the ministers in Down,] considered there was speciality in this, took some private trial of him, and being satisfied of his edifying gift, gave him license to exercise the same in private houses and families. Having obtained this liberty, he went through the country, and was so much followed, that they filled the whole house, and sometimes barns, and was a happy instrument in converting many souls to God."(10)

These additional ministers proved most valuable auxiliaries to the brethren already settled in the country. The aim of all was the same—the revival and extension of true religion in this waste and desolate land. Through their honoured instrumentality, the gospel shot forth its branches in Ulster with wonderful rapidity, till, like the grain of mustard, from being the least of all seeds, it became a great and noble tree, which, after the lapse of two centuries and the beating of many bitter storms, stands, at the present day, more firm and vigorous than ever. Rarely has the church of Christ in any land experienced so sensible an increase, in so limited a period, as under the ministry of these brethren; and the reason is obvious—rarely has she enjoyed such faithful servants. Their labours for the instruction of the people were truly indefatigable, and were rendered more conspicuous when contrasted with the supineness and indifference of the surrounding clergy. At this period, there were about thirty other protestant ministers resident in the diocese of Down and Connor, which extended over almost the entire counties of Down and Antrim; while within the same limits, there were only fourteen churches in a state of repair,—the remainder being either decayed or ruinous.(11) Of these ministers, several had

10 Life of Gabriel Semple, MS. *penes* Rev. Dr. Lee, Edinburgh.

11 Report for the diocese of Down and Connor, in Ulst. Vis. Book. MSS. Trin. Coll. Dub. I have inserted, in the Appendix, appropriated to unpublished papers, a summary of the names and residences of all the ministers in the dioceses of Armagh, Raphoe, Derry, Down, and Connor, in the year 1622, taken from this valuable and authentic record. See Appendix, No. I.

the nominal charge of from three to seven parishes each. Some were consequently non-resident; many were indolent and remiss, if not "lewd and scandalous;" while even the most regular appeared to have contented themselves with the performance of the mere routine duties of their profession.

Far different was the conduct of those ministers whose names have been specially recorded in these pages. They were truly 'instant in season and out of season,' labouring to instruct their people and promote vital religion with a singleness of purpose, an intensity of desire, and an untiring diligence, which, if ever equalled, have at least been seldom surpassed. Blair thus describes his ministerial labours at Bangor. "My charge was very great, consisting of about six miles in length, and containing above twelve hundred persons come to age, besides children who stood greatly in need of instruction. This being the case, I preached twice every week besides the Lord's day, on all which occasions I found little difficulty either as to matter or method. But finding still that this fell short of reaching the design of a Gospel-ministry, and that the most part continued vastly ignorant, I saw the necessity of trying a more plain and familiar way of instructing them; and, therefore, besides my public preaching, I spent as much time every week, as my bodily strength could hold out with, in exhorting and catechising them. Not long after I fell upon this method the Lord visited me with a fever; on which, some who hated my painfulness in the ministry, said scoffingly, that they knew I could not hold out as I began. But in a little space it pleased the Lord to raise me up again, and he enabled me to continue that method the whole time I was there. The knowledge of God increasing among that people, and the ordinance of prayer being precious in their eyes, the work of the Lord did prosper in the place; and in this we were much encouraged both by the assistance of holy Mr. Cunningham, and by the good example of his little parish of Holywood. For knowing that diversity of gifts is entertaining to the hearers, he and I did frequently preach for one another; and we also agreed to celebrate the sacrament of the Lord's Supper four times in each of our congregations annually, so that those in both parishes who were thriving in religion, did communicate together on all these occasions."

In celebrating the communion, both Blair and the other ministers who have been specified, adhered to the ritual of the church of Scotland. They used tables placed in the centre of the church, and they communicated in a sitting posture. Blair's patron, Lord Claneboy, accustomed at court to the forms of the English church, was with difficulty persuaded to adopt this scriptural method. "The first time," says Blair, "I dispensed the Sacrament of the Lord's Supper, the solemnity was like to have been disorderly on this account. My noble patron and his lady would communicate kneeling; and even after reasoning, his lordship continued obstinate; so that I parted from him with sorrow, and resolved to delay that work until another time. But his lordship remembering that his pew joined to the upper end of the table, and was so enclosed that only one's head could be discovered in it, he promised not to kneel on condition he received the elements within his own pew. For peace sake, I rashly yielded to this offer, but was so much discomposed by it next day, that when I came to the public, I was for half an hour so much deserted of God, that I was about to give over the work of that day. But the Lord in great mercy pitied and helped me. For preaching upon the words of the institution, 1 Cor. xi. chap. and handling these words 'This cup is the New Testament in my blood,' as soon as I began to discourse of that New Testament or Covenant, I found light and life flowing in upon my soul, enlarging it, and opening my mouth to speak with comfort and courage; and with this assistance I went to the table and administered the Sacrament. The action being ended, my patron and especially his lady, professed their great satisfaction with that day's service, and proved my most tender and real friends ever after."

Blair and his brethren were equally firm in maintaining the other peculiarities of the Presbyterian discipline, which are not merely empty forms, capriciously adopted in opposition to other churches, but important institutions, founded on Scripture, by which the efforts of the ministry to repress sin and encourage holiness are materially assisted. "In my congregation," writes Blair, "we had both deacons for the poor, and elders for discipline; and so long as we were permitted to exercise it, the Lord blessed that ordinance. Of this, I shall only give an instance. A cunning adulterer, who had continued long in that sin before I went to Bangor, and by bribing the bishop's official, had concealed his wickedness, having been present at a sermon which I had on the parable of the sower, it pleased the Lord so to reach his conscience, that he made confession of his great sin with many tears, and sought to be admitted to the public profession of his repentance. This the session did readily agree to, and he appeared publicly, for several days, under very deep conviction, to the great affecting of the congregation, and lived ever after a reformed man, so far as could be perceived. Others also did willingly submit themselves to discipline, till a proud youth, the heir of a considerable estate, falling into a scandal, proved refractory, and appealed to the bishop: After which the order of our discipline was broken, and it became fashionable for the rich to compound with the bishop's official; and though the poor were sent to do public penance, as they call it, yet I never saw a blessing accompany that ordinance thereafter, nor edification to the people."

Livingston, as might be anticipated, adopted a similar course in Killinchy, where much ignorance and formality prevailed. Speaking of the time immediately subsequent to his ordination, he writes,—"That winter following I was often in great heaviness; for although the people were very tractable, yet they were generally very ignorant, and I saw no appearance of doing any good among them; yet it pleased the Lord that in a short time some of them began to understand somewhat of their condition. Not only had we public worship free of any inventions of men, but we had also a tolerable discipline. For after I had been somewhile among them, by the advice of the heads of families, some ablest for that charge were chosen elders, to oversee the manners of the rest, and some deacons to gather and distribute the collections. We, [*i. e.* the session,] met every week, and such as fell into notorious public scandals we desired to come before us. Such as came were dealt with, both in public and private, to confess their scandal in presence of the congregation, at the Saturday's sermon before the communion, which was celebrated twice in the year. Such as after dealing would not come before us, or coming, would not be convinced to acknowledge their fault before the congregation, upon the Saturday preceding the communion, their names, scandals, and impenitency were read out before the congregation, and they debarred from the communion: which proved such a terror, that we found very few of that sort. We needed not to have the communion oftener; for there were nine or ten parishes within the bounds of twenty miles or little more, wherein there were godly and able ministers that kept a society together, and every one of these had the communion twice a-year, at different times, and had two or three of the neighbouring ministers to help thereat, and most part of the religious people used to resort to the communions of the rest of the parishes."

The support of some of these ministers was derived from the tithes of the parishes in which they laboured; while others received a fixed endowment, paid as in Scotland, by the patron, in lieu of the tithe which was received directly by himself; and to this endowment was occasionally added a stipend from the people. Blair relates, that at his settlement "the people of Bangor promised, if the patron's offer of maintenance were not large enough, they would willingly add to the same." His predecessor, Gibson, had been maintained solely by a fixed endowment paid by Sir James Hamilton, the landlord and patron of the parish; and Cunningham of Holywood was supported in a similar manner. On the other hand, Livingston's support was derived entirely from the people; though he states, he "never had of stipend in Killinchy above four pounds sterling by year." (12)

The religious sentiments of all these ministers were those to which the epithet Calvinistic is generally applied, and which, at this period, were universally maintained throughout the three national churches of the empire. They entertained none of that hostility to creeds, covenants, or confessions, which has been sometimes assumed as characteristic of the early Presbyterian ministers in Ireland. Those who had graduated in the universities, or been admitted to the ministry, in Scotland, had signed the Scots Confession of Faith; and on entering upon the ministerial office in Ireland, while they objected to matters of government, and were particularly careful not to be ensnared into an approbation of prelacy, they cheerfully acquiesced in the confession of the Irish church, which was strictly Calvinistic, and unobjectionable either to Scottish presbyterians or English puritans.

United as these ministers were in spirit and in principle; distinguished as they were from the surrounding clergy, no less by their ardour and diligence in their profession, than by the singular success which attended their labours; and exposed, as they would thereby be, to the scoffs of the profane

12 In some manuscript copies of Livingston's Life, which I have seen, this sum is stated at *forty* pounds, probably an error of some later copyists, startled at the fact of a minister receiving only L.4 per annum, and conceiving it to be intended for L.40. But there was no mistake. In 1583, the annual stipend of John Hooke, minister at Wroxall, in Warwickshire, was L.5, 6s. 8d. Brooke's Pur. iii. 508. Rutherford's stipend in Anworth, Gallowayshire, in the year 1627, was L.11, derived partly from the teinds or tithes, and partly from the voluntary contributions of the people. Life by Murray, p. 41.

and the jealousy of their more indolent and worldly brethren; it is natural to expect that, under such circumstances, a very close and cordial intimacy would subsist among them. This was the fact. As they were 'fellow-helpers to the truth,' so were they 'members one of another;' sympathizing with those who suffered, or rejoicing with those who were honoured. Their visible bond of union was the monthly meetings which had commenced at Antrim, as already stated, about the year 1626; whither, as to a solemn and invigorating feast, they diligently resorted, accompanied by the more religious portion of their people. Livingston gives the following account of the manner in which these influential meetings were conducted, and at the same time intimates the delightful harmony which subsisted among the ministers, and the avidity for instruction by which the people were characterized.

"We used ordinarily to meet the first Friday of every month at Antrim, where was a great and good congregation; and that day was spent in fasting and prayer, and publick preaching. Commonly two preached every forenoon, and two in the afternoon. We used to come together the Thursday's night before, and stayed the Friday's night after; and consulted about such things as concerned the carrying on of the work of God; and these meetings among ourselves were sometimes as profitable as either presbyteries or synods. Such as laid religion to heart, used to convene to those meetings, especially out of the Six-mile-water [valley] which was nearest hand, and where was the greatest number of religious people; and frequently the Sabbath after the Friday's meeting, the communion was celebrated in one or other of our parishes. Among all the ministers, there was never any jar or jealousy; yea, nor amongst the professors, the greatest part of them being Scots, and some good number of very gracious English; all whose contention was to prefer others to themselves. And although the gifts of the ministers were much different, yet it was not observed that the people followed any to the undervaluing of others. Many of these religious professors had been both ignorant and profane; and for debt and want, and worse causes, had left Scotland. Yet the Lord was pleased by His word to work such a change, that I do not think there were more lively and experienced Christians any where, than were these at this time in Ireland. They were in good numbers, and several of them persons in good outward condition in the world. Being but lately brought in, the lively edge was not yet gone off them, and the perpetual fear, that the bishops would put away their ministers, made them with great hunger wait on the ordinances. I have known them come several miles from their own houses to communions, to the Saturday's sermon, and spending the whole Saturday's night in several companies, sometimes a minister being with them, and sometimes themselves alone, in conference and prayer. They have then waited on the public ordinances the whole Sabbath, and spent the Sabbath night in the same way, and yet at the Monday's sermon were not troubled with sleepiness; and so they have not slept till they went home. In those days it was no great difficulty for a minister to preach or pray in public or private, such was the hunger of the hearers; and it was hard to judge whether there was more of the Lord's presence in the public or private meetings." This statement is fully corroborated by Blair. "The blessed work of conversion, which was of several years continuance, spread beyond the bounds of Antrim and Down, to the skirts of neighbouring counties; and the resort of people to the monthly meetings and communion occasions, and the appetite of the people were become so great, that we were sometimes constrained, in sympathy to them, to venture beyond any preparation we had made for the season. And indeed preaching and praying were so pleasant in those days, and hearers so eager and greedy, that no day was long enough, nor any room great enough to answer their strong desires and large expectations."

The singular success which attended the preaching of the word at this period, is also attested by another writer in so ample and striking a manner, that this additional and independent testimony to the truth of facts which many may feel reluctant to admit, must not be withheld.[13] "I shall here instance that great and solemn work of God which was in the church of Ireland some years before the fall of prelacy, about the year 1628, and some years thereafter, which, as many grave and solid Christians yet alive can witness, who were there present, was a bright and hot sun-blink of the gospel; yea, may with sobriety be said to have been one of the largest manifestations of the Spirit, and of the most solemn times of the down-pouring thereof, that almost since the days of the apostles hath been seen. I remember, amongst other passages, what a worthy Christian told me, how sometimes in hearing the word, such a power and evidence of the Lord's presence was with it, that he hath been forced to rise and look through the church and see what the people were doing, thinking from what he felt on his own spirit, it was a wonder how any could go away without some change upon them. And then it was sweet and easy for Christians to come thirty or forty miles to the solemn communions which they had, and there continue from the time they came until they returned, without wearying or making use of sleep; yea, but little either meat or drink, and, as some of them professed, did not feel the need thereof, but went away most fresh and vigorous, their souls so filled with the sense of God."

Such was the extraordinary and well-attested success with which the preaching of these devoted servants of God was favoured. They were not, however, without their trials, nor did the important work, in which they were engaged, advance without encountering various difficulties. Obstructions from several quarters frequently threatened to impede its progress. The Romanists, who began to assume much confidence after the project of marriage between Charles and the Infanta of Spain, a Roman catholic princess, had become known in

13 By Fleming in his 'Fulf. of the Scrip.' i. 400-1.

Ireland, were the first to oppose the truth. Two friars, educated at Salamanca in Spain, challenged the ministers to a public disputation on the peculiar tenets of protestantism; and the demand was put forward with such an air of defiance, that it was accepted by Blair and Welsh. But after the topics of the intended discussion had been agreed upon, and the two brethren had appeared at the appointed time and place, the friars shrunk from their challenge, and no further opposition was offered from this quarter.

They were soon after assailed, on the other side, by a party of separatists from London, who hearing of the religious freedom enjoyed in Ulster and the success of the gospel, expected to make many converts among so zealous and religious a people. They accordingly removed hither, and settled for a time in the town of Antrim. Here they soon became known by their refusing to frequent the public assemblies for worship on the Sabbath, as well as the devotional meetings held on the other days of the week. When conferred with in relation to their religious views, they did not appear to be well informed, or at least, they concealed their peculiar tenets.[14] They failed, however, in effecting any breach in the peace and unity, by which the brethren and their people were then happily distinguished.

Thus freed from Roman catholic sophistry on the one hand, and sectarian wiles on the other, another fertile source of distraction was in danger of being opened among them. They were nearly involved in the Arminian controversy by one Mr. Freeman, "an English conformist," who had gained many followers, and was very assiduous in propagating his favourite tenets. Having accompanied his patron, Mr. Rowley, to one of the monthly meetings at Antrim, he boldly undertook to confute and silence all the assembled ministers, who unanimously maintained the opinions

14 These separatists were probably of the Baptist persuasion. The reader will find them, in chap. ix., re-appearing at Antrim after the Rebellion.

of Calvin. Mr. Blair, by appointment of the brethren, held a public discussion with him. Freeman proposed, as the subject of dispute, the decree of reprobation, the primary object of attack, to every captious Arminian and confident rationalist, to the present day; but he was wholly unable to answer the arguments of his learned antagonist. On the second day he retired in confusion from the contest, and Mr. Rowley, convinced of the ignorance and errors of his teacher, in presence of the meeting, publicly renounced his fellowship. "After which," it is added, "he was deserted of the people, and at last turned very dissolute and fell into mischievous practices." No attempt was afterwards made to introduce this distracting controversy.

These varied trials, while they did not impede the progress of the truth, served to exhibit more conspicuously the piety, learning and prudence of those eminent men, on whom alone appears to have devolved the labour of its propagation and defence. These honoured ministers, it need scarcely be added, after the full detail which has been given of their character, principles and conduct, were strictly presbyterian. Though like the English puritans, in the early part of the reign of Elizabeth, they were comprehended within the pale of the established episcopal church, enjoying its endowments and sharing its dignities, yet notwithstanding this singular position which they occupied, they introduced and maintained the several peculiarities, both of discipline and worship, by which the Scottish church was distinguished. To them, therefore, the grateful regards of their descendants in this country have, from an early period, been directed, as the founders of the presbyterian church in Ireland. Its successful progress in Ulster, in subsequent times, is no doubt to be principally ascribed to their firmness and zeal. But it would be a great mistake to suppose, because peculiar circumstances afterwards rendered these ministers conspicuous for their nonconformity, and thus gave a prominence to their names above the rest of their brethren, that they were the only persons in the ministry who were attached to presbyterianism. In truth, most of the northern clergy were at this period non-conformists, both in principle and in practice. They conformed just so far as would ensure their security and maintenance under the protection of the legal establishment. In some of the dioceses, this was all that the bishops required ; and consequently the names of those ministers who, though maintaining their peculiar sentiments, were permitted to live and die unmolested within the pale of the national church, have been necessarily lost to posterity. When succeeding prelates became more strict in exacting conformity, the clergy generally yielded, though with reluctance, the canonical obedience required of them before their superiors ; but, in the seclusion of their parishes, they continued to observe the presbyterian forms, so congenial to the habits and prejudices of their people. By this temporizing policy, however, their names also have sunk into oblivion. But the brethren noticed in these pages, having their lot cast in a diocese, over which was subsequently placed one of the most intolerant of the northern prelates, and being themselves too firm in principle to disguise their sentiments, or violate their consciences, by promising a conformity which they could not conscientiously yield, were speedily marked out for persecution ; and thus attained that unhappy but honourable notoriety, which has rescued their names from oblivion, and transmitted them to posterity, as the fathers and founders of the presbyterian church in Ulster.

To this distinction they were soon called. Scarcely had Livingston been added to their number, when their prospering labours were interrupted by bishop Echlin, once their friend and patron. He had, for some time, viewed with jealousy and dislike the increasing influence, which their zeal and fidelity had given them over the people ; and had latterly refused to ordain any more ministers, without their promising strict conformity to the order of the English church. In consequence of this refusal, Welsh, Colvert, Livingston and others were obliged to have recourse for ordination to the bishop of Raphoe. According to Blair, so early as the year 1626, Echlin began to throw obstructions in their way. "Dr. Echlin, bishop of Down, was the first whom we discovered to lay snares for us; but because the people did generally approve our labours, he did this under cover. And first he wrote to me to be ready to preach at the primate's triennial visitation; for though Dr. Ussher was then in England, two bishops and a doctor, his delegates, were to go that course for him. Before the appointed day came, bishop Echlin sent me notice by word of mouth, that another was to supply the part assigned me. But this verbal message contradicting his written order, I concluded that the last was, of purpose, calculated to leave me in an uncertainty that he might pick a quarrel with me; and therefore I prepared a discourse for that occasion. If any ask how I durst countenance these prelatic meetings? It should be considered that we were not then under an explicit covenant against them, as we are now; and being still left to our liberty as to the full and free exercise of our pastoral office, I judged it my duty to 'be instant in season and out of season.' Accordingly, having meditated upon 2 Cor. iv. 1. 'Therefore, seeing we have this ministry,' &c. I endeavoured especially to show, that Christ our Lord had instituted no bishops, but presbyters, or ministers; and proved this, first, from the holy Scriptures; next, from the testimonies of the more pure among the ancient fathers and divines, that have been seeking reformation these thirteen hundred years; and, lastly, from the testimonies of the more moderate divines, both over sea and in England; not forgetting to rank the learned Dr. Usher, their primate, among the chief: And then I concluded with an exhortation to them to use moderately that power which custom and human laws had put in their hand. And, indeed, they took with the advice, without challenging my freedom. Only the bishop of Dromore, who was brother-in-law to Dr. Usher, exhorted me privately to behave as moderately towards them, as they had done to me, and then bade me farewell.

"This snare being broken, the crafty bishop set about weaving a more dangerous web. For knowing that one of the two lords justices, who came annually to the northern circuit, was a violent urger of conformity to the English ceremonies, he wrote to me to make ready a sermon, to be delivered before them against the next assizes. And this was the more dangerous, that it being Easter, the judges were to communicate that day.(15)

"Against the time appointed, I came to the place where they sat, committing the matter to the Lord, who hath all hearts and mouths in his own hand. Some Scots gentlemen who attended the justices, knowing one of them to be well disposed, they took the freedom to hint to him the inconvenience of spending the Saturday, immediately preceding their communicating, wholly upon civil affairs; and suggested the necessity of being more religiously employed before so solemn an approach. This advice was well received by the judge, who promised to procure a hearing to any minister who had a sermon in readiness. Whereupon the gentlemen, without consulting me, undertook for my readiness. And, accordingly, one being sent to me for that purpose, I preached the same evening, and next day likewise, without ever taking the least notice of their communicating.

"After sermon, on the Lord's day, one of the judges wanting to confer with me, sent for me to his lodging; where, after professing his satisfaction with what I had delivered, especially in my last sermon, 'for therein,' said he, 'you opened a point which I never heard before, viz. the covenant

15 It is stated in the MS. life of Robert Blair, that this judge was the lord chief baron of exchequer, Sir Richard Beaton, of whom mention is made at page 134. This MS., both here and elsewhere, contains many interesting particulars which are omitted in the printed life. The day specified was Sabbath, March 25, 1627.

of redemption made with Christ the Mediator, as head of the elect;' he entreated me to go over the heads of that sermon with him. And, opening his Bible, he read over and considered the proofs cited; and was so well satisfied, that he protested, if his calling did not tie him to Dublin, he would gladly come to the north, and settle under such a ministry. In the end, he told me, that I would be sent for to supper; and warned me to be cautious in my answers to his colleague, who was zealous for the English ceremonies: And before he left the place, he sent for the bishop, and charged him to be careful that no harm nor interruption should come to my ministry. And thus the only wise Lord, to whom I had committed myself and my ministry, did break this snare also, and brought me off with comfort and credit."

Disappointed in these insidious attempts to ensnare the more eminent of the presbyterian ministers, Echlin was shortly after emboldened to oppose them more openly. To this he was urged "by the means of one Mr. Henry Leslie, dean, and afterward bishop of Down, a violent and vain-glorious man; and of Mr. John Maxwell, one of the ministers of Edinburgh, who was gaping for a bishoprick,"[16] and who strenuously supported all the arbitrary measures by which Charles was then endeavouring to impose the English prelacy and church service on the Scottish nation. These men, ever on the alert to find matter of accusation against the adherents of presbytery, were led by the following incident to solicit the interference of Echlin. In the month of June 1630, Mr. Livingston, in conjunction with Mr. Blair, then on a visit to his friends in Scotland, had assisted at the celebration of the Lord's Supper at the kirk of Shotts—a season long remembered in that country, and signally instrumental in reviving and extending vital religion. The unusual concourse of persons of all ranks who attended at that communion, and the favourable effects produced by the services, es-

16 Blair's Life, p. 73.

pecially by the sermon preached on Monday by Livingston, attracted the attention and excited the envy of the prelatical clergy, already too jealous of the popularity and influence enjoyed by their presbyterian brethren. Against the Scottish ministers, however, protected as they still were by many of the first rank in the kingdom, they dared not proceed with open violence. But the two ministers from Ireland, who had officiated on that occasion, enjoying no such protection, and being, moreover, connected with the prelatic church of their own country, presented fit objects for their envious persecution. Accordingly, Maxwell of Edinburgh, and, as Livingston adds, Mr. James Law, bishop of Glasgow, during the course of the year, informed dean Leslie of what they would doubtless style the uncanonical and schismatic conduct of the Irish ministers in their neighbourhood. They further charged them with exciting the people to ecstasies, and teaching the necessity of bodily pains to attest the reality of the new birth. The dean entered warmly into their complaints. He laid their grave accusations before Echlin, and supported by Sir Richard Beaton, lord chief baron, a violent adherent of prelacy, who occasionally came as judge on the northern circuit of assize, he at length, in September 1631, prevailed with the 'timorous' bishop to suspend Blair and Livingston from the exercise of their ministerial functions.

This was the first blow openly levelled at the permanence and prosperity of the Presbyterian ministry in Ulster. But though it happily took little effect, yet, from this period, may be dated the commencement of that systematic opposition to the brethren, which ultimately terminated in their forcible expulsion from the kingdom.

No sooner was the bishop's hasty and unjust sentence intimated to Blair, than he resolved to have recourse to archbishop Ussher, and to solicit his interference in behalf of himself and his suspended brother. He was encouraged to make this application, from his personal knowledge of the primate's liberal and forbearing spirit. Four years before, he had been introduced to his Grace by Lord Claneboy, and had conversed freely with him, on several of the topics which were then agitating the religious world. And as the minutest circumstance relative to that great and good man cannot but prove interesting, the particulars of this interview are subjoined in the words of Blair. "In March 1627, my noble patron having had a great esteem of primate Usher, would have me to accompany him to a meeting of the nobility and gentry of Ulster with the primate. Accordingly I went, and had a kind invitation to be at his table while I was in town. But having once met with the English liturgy there, I left my excuse with my patron, that I expected another thing than formal liturgies in the family of so learned and pious a man. The primate excused himself, by reason of the great confluence that was there, and had the good nature to entreat me to come to Tredaff,[17] where his ordinary residence was, and where he would be more at leisure to be better acquainted with me.

"I complied with the primate's invitation, and found him very affable and ready to impart his mind. He desired to know what was my judgment concerning the nature of justifying and saving faith. I told him, in general, that I held the accepting of Jesus Christ, as he is freely offered in the Gospel, to be saving faith. With this he was well satisfied, and by a large discourse confirmed and further cleared the same, by the similitude of a marriage, where it is not the sending or receiving of gifts, but the accepting the person that constitutes the marriage. From this he passed on to try my mind concerning ceremonies, wherein we were not so far from agreeing as I feared. For when I had freely opened my grievances, he admitted that all these things ought to have been removed, but the constitution and laws of the place and time would not permit that to be done. He added that he was afraid our strong disaffection to these would mar our ministry; that he had himself been importuned to stretch

17 The old name of Drogheda.

forth his hand against us; and that though he would not for the world do that, he feared instruments might be found who would do it; and he added, that it would break his heart if our successful ministry in the north were interrupted. Our conference ending, he dismissed me very kindly, though I gave him no high titles; and when trouble came upon us, he proved our very good friend." Such was Ussher,—kind, candid, and courteous; not more singular in his day for his immense erudition, than for his tolerant spirit! Amidst the splendour with which his rank and learning have invested him, it is delightful to obtain such a familiar glance, as this passage presents, of his private life and sentiments. Nor is it less pleasing to meet, especially in the person of Ussher, with another illustration of this instructive maxim—that while sectarian bigotry is the offspring of pride and ignorance, true wisdom and genuine piety are ever characterized by candour and charity.

Blair was not disappointed in his application to the primate. He immediately interested himself in behalf of the suspended ministers. Fully convinced of their piety and Christian prudence, he wrote to Echlin to "relax his erroneous censure." This injunction was promptly obeyed; and Blair and Livingston were permitted to resume the exercise of their ministry among their beloved and affectionate people.

Their Scottish adversaries, however, did not desist from their opposition. Baffled in their endeavours to stir up the ecclesiastical authorities against these laborious and unpretending ministers of Christ; they next endeavoured to accomplish their object through the medium of the civil powers. But dreading that the Irish government might prove as forbearing and tolerant as the primate, they resolved to apply directly to the king himself, from whom, guided as he then was in religious matters by Laud, they expected a ready acquiescence in their persecuting purposes. Maxwell, accordingly, hurried to court, and there preferred the heaviest charges of enthusiasm, turbulence, and disobedience to ecclesiastical authority, against the Scottish ministers in Ulster. He named in particular these four, Messrs. Blair, Livingston, Dunbar and Welsh, who having been censured for presumed non-conformity in Scotland, prior to their removal to Ireland, were peculiarly obnoxious to the prelatical party.

These accusations were readily entertained and acted on by Laud and his royal pupil. Letters were immediately despatched to the lords justices of Ireland, then at the head of the government, directing them to issue their orders to the bishop of Down and Connor, to try these alleged fanatical disturbers of the peace of his diocese; and, if found guilty of the charges preferred against them, to censure them accordingly. "But the bishop," says Blair, "knowing perfectly well that he would succumb in that accusation, did conceal his order, and went to work another way. He caused cite Mr. Livingston and myself, with Mr. Dunbar and Mr. Welsh before him, and urged us to conform and give our subscription to that effect. We answered, that there was then no law nor canon in that kingdom requiring this. Notwithstanding, he had the cruelty to depose us all four from the office of the holy ministry." The former two were silenced on the fourth of May 1632, and the latter two in the following week; and thus, for not yielding a conformity, from which they had been exempted when they entered on the ministry in Ireland, were these faithful men violently excluded from their offices, and thrown destitute on the world.

Undismayed, however, by the difficulties with which they were now encompassed, and ardently desirous of being restored to the exercise of their beloved calling, they resolved to use every exertion in their power to procure the reversal of this unjust sentence. "Application was again made," writes Blair, "in our behalf to archbishop Ussher. But he told us he could not interpose, because the two lords justices had an order from the king respecting us. And when we had recourse to their lordships, they remitted us to the king, from whom only remedy could be had. The brethren being thus shut up, they did weigh the expediency of an application to court. On the one hand, we saw that the tide for conformity did run very high; and we knew likewise, that bishop Laud did not only rule but domineer in England. Yet, on the other hand, we knew we were innocent of the matter wherewith we were accused. We hoped likewise that several of the Scots nobility having been friendly to us, and the lord Alexander, eldest son to the secretary for Scottish affairs,[18] having been my scholar, that by this door we would find access to his Majesty, as the ordinance of God to the oppressed. And so I was persuaded, after frequent addresses to God for direction, to undertake a journey with a petition to the king, that we might be tried in the matter laid to our charge; and if found innocent, that we might be acquitted and restored to our flocks, committing the event of all to Him who overruleth the spirits of princes, and is a King over kings, and a Lord over lords and courtiers."

In pursuance of this design, Mr. Livingston retired to Scotland, where he obtained recommendatory letters to their friends at court from the marchioness of Hamilton, and from the earls of Eglinton, Linlithgow, and Wigton. These letters he transmitted to Mr. Blair; who, having also procured additional ones from his Irish friends, immediately set out to London on this hazardous but interesting mission. The circumstances of his journey will be best narrated in his own words. "Having procured letters from several nobles

18 This secretary was William Alexander, first earl of Stirling, a poet as well as a statesman. He assisted James I. in preparing a metrical version of the book of Psalms, known by the name of the Royal Psalter. After the death of the fifth Earl of Stirling in the year 1739, the title remained dormant for a considerable period. It may not be inappropriate to add, that the title devolved on a minister of the Presbyterian church in Ireland; whose grandson has at length succeeded in establishing his claim, and is now recognised as the ninth earl of Stirling.

and gentry, both in Scotland and Ireland, to their friends at court on our behalf, I set out on my journey, leaving many holy persons wrestling with God for a comfortable issue. And indeed they were a praying people for whom I undertook this journey. At my house, two nights were spent every week at prayer, and though those who did bear chief burden therein were not above the rank of husbandmen, yet they abounded in the grace and spirit of prayer. Other places were not short of, but rather excelled in that duty; and even in congregations who yet enjoyed their own pastors, many prayers were put up on our account, as I learned at my return. After my first outset, I was suddenly afflicted with pain in my kidnies; and I cried earnestly to the Lord, that he would be pleased to spare me till I were better accommodated for such a trial; which petition was granted as soon as put up, and I went on my way rejoicing.

"When I reached Greenwich, where the court then lay, I had speedy recourse to the earl of Stirling, secretary; who promised, if my petition were sent him, to procure a despatch to my mind without expense. This he undertook the more readily, that the king being then on a progress for the hunting, he doubted not that his Majesty would be gone ere that petition were got ready. But I, supposing all the hazard lay in not getting it ready before the king set out, did bend up all the earnestness I could of prayer, with dexterity of endeavours; and getting the petition ready in due time, went with it to the secretary; and was so overjoyed in hopes of the issue, that I did literally exult and leap. But when the timorous man saw my forwardness, he, fearing bishop Laud more than God, did faint and break his promise.

"At this disappointment I was greatly dejected; and passing to a quiet place in Greenwich Park, poured out my complaint unto God; and after I had been thrice employed in that way, and in offering up myself and all my enjoyments to him for the sake of the gospel, my heaviness was removed, my prayer taken off my hand, and, as I conceived, my request granted,

"Accordingly I took courage, and found secretary Cook the mean of procuring a hearing from the king. This man being esteemed rigid for conformity, it was highly probable he would not be a happy instrument in any such matter. But the thoughts of the Lord are not as ours. The king having been then at the forest of Bewly, at a distance from the bishops, my petition was put into his hand, and met with a gracious answer. For the secretary having wrote the deliverance thereon, and addressed it to archbishop Usher, which the king reckoned improper; his majesty caused the secretary to direct it to Strafford, and with his own hand he did insert a clause which I durst not petition for, viz. 'That if the information made to him proved false, the informers should be punished.'——And so having obtained my errand, I gave the secretary's clerks, three Jacobuses, himself taking nothing, and made all the haste I could back to London, and thence to Ireland.——There I was received with great joy, especially when they heard that I had brought with me a just and favourable letter from the king's majesty. But they were much dejected, that he to whom it was directed, was yet in England, not like to come over in haste; and indeed he came not for almost a twelvemonth after this. Yet this was no great loss, but rather an advantage to us. For though this letter did not take off the sentence of deposition; yet, by putting the matter to a new trial, it did weaken the same. And therefore we went on teaching our people; only, for form's sake, I did not go up to the pulpit, but stood beside the precentor."

By this means, were the suspended brethren enabled to resume the duties of the ministry, though still under considerable restrictions. These were laid so rigorously on Livingston, that he was obliged to leave the country altogether, and retire to Scotland; and although the other ministers were enabled to remain, they enjoyed little comfort or freedom. They were supported, however, by the hope that the arrival of the lord deputy Wentworth would put an end to these privations, and that he would pay immediate attention to the royal mandate in the possession of Blair.

But they little knew the character of the man in whose hands the destinies of the kingdom were now placed. A more unfortunate choice of a deputy could not have been made for the presbyterians of Ireland; and, perhaps it might be added, for the nation at large, the subsequent calamities of which may in a great measure be attributed to the elevation of this most talented but unconstitutional statesman. Haughty and overbearing in his manner, irascible and vindictive in his temper, tyrannical in his political, and intolerant in his religious, sentiments, it was in vain to look to him for either protection against illegal oppression, or relief from prelatical severities. Viewing man as born either to rule or to obey, he was incapable of sympathizing with those who suffered for any principle of conscience; and entrusted with the care of assimilating the ecclesiastical state of Ireland to that of England, he was especially hostile to every species of non-conformity.

Though appointed lord deputy in January 1632, Wentworth did not enter on his government until July in the following year. "At last," writes Blair, "that magnificent lord having come over to the lieutenancy of Ireland, I went to Dublin, and presented his majesty's letter to him, adding, that I hoped for a ready compliance with it. But the haughty man did altogether slight that order, telling me that he had his majesty's mind in his own breast. He reviled the church of Scotland, and upbraided me, bidding me come to my right wits, and then I should be regarded: which was all the answer I could get from him. With this intelligence I went to archbishop Usher; which was so disagreeable to him, that it drew tears from his eyes; but he could not help us."

The prospects now presented to the silenced ministers were gloomy in the extreme. All hopes of relief for themselves were not only blasted, but in the tone and manner of the deputy, they discerned the storm which was gathering round the rest of their brethren throughout the kingdom. Influenced by these apprehensions, the presbyterians in Ulster began to despair of enjoying any longer their religious liberties at home, and to look out for some more favoured region abroad. Their attention was naturally directed to New-England, which had become known, at this period, as a seasonable asylum for the persecuted non-conformists of the sister kingdom. They accordingly resolved to send a minister and gentleman thither, to ascertain the condition of the country; and, if necessary, to select a place where a settlement might be most commodiously effected. The persons sent on this adventurous mission were Livingston and a Mr. William Wallace. After going to London, in the spring of the year 1634, and thence to Plymouth, they were deterred by various untoward circumstances from proceeding further; and they returned to Ulster in the month of May. They found their brethren resolved to endure, for some time longer, their religious privations, and to wait with patience for the further development of those changes, both in the civil and ecclesiastical state of the kingdom, which the bold and vigorous measures of the new deputy gave reason to expect.

CHAPTER III.

State of the kingdom at the accession of Charles I.—Irish army increased—Supplies needed—Encouragement of the Romanist party—Protested against by the Irish prelates—The 'Graces' promised—Delay in granting them—General discontent of all parties—Lord Wentworth made deputy—His arrival—Holds a parliament—Is influenced by Laud in ecclesiastical affairs—State of the English church at this period—And of the Irish church—Particularly in Ulster—Northern bishops—Bedell—His letter to Laud describing the religious state of his diocese—Laud turns his attention to Ireland—Influences Wentworth—Bramhall and Leslie promoted—Letter of the former to Laud—Alterations in Dublin college—Irish convocation meet—Adopt the English articles and canons—Wentworth's account thereof to Laud—High-Commission court erected—Gloomy prospects of the Presbyterians.

From the accession of Charles to the throne, in the year 1625, Ireland enjoyed, for a length of time, uninterrupted peace. The Romanist party were not without royal countenance and support; but owing to the zealous interference of the protestant prelates, who warmly opposed the legal toleration of popery, it was not always in the power of the king to favour them. Lord Falkland, whom Charles continued in the office of deputy, was a lenient and inactive governor; but, being married to a Roman catholic lady, he was at all times prompt enough in fulfilling the favourable wishes of the court towards the Romanists. They were accordingly encouraged to exercise their ecclesiastical jurisdiction, and observe their stated worship, with greater publicity than at any former period. New religious houses, for both monks and nuns, were opened in several parts of the kingdom; and even in the metropolis, a college was founded for the training of their priesthood, and the more extensive propagation of their religion. The kingdom swarmed with the Romish clergy, who were educated abroad, and who had imbibed the most extravagant ideas of papal power; and a bull from pope Urban VIII. in the year 1626, exhorting them to sacrifice their lives rather than take the oath of supremacy, added no little to the confidence of the recusants.[1]

The embarrassments of Charles, arising out of his expensive wars with Spain and Austria, had incapacitated him from maintaining an adequate military force in Ireland. It was necessary, however, that the Irish army should be augmented. Considerable discontent prevailed especially in the province of Connaught. Here James, before his death, had announced his intention of forming a western plantation, similar to that which he had successfully established in Ulster. But as there were no forfeitures to place this province at the disposal of the crown, it was resolved to recal the patents of the proprietors, which, though regularly passed under the great seal, were, through some trifling legal informality recently discovered, alleged to be invalid. Well-grounded apprehensions were entertained lest the numerous mal-contents, excited by this obnoxious scheme, should be encouraged to actual rebellion by the emissaries of Spain, then at war with England; while, at the same time, the growing confidence of the Romanist faction, always rendered more insolent by timid conciliation, awakened the fears of the zealous protestants. At the urgent solicitations, therefore, of the deputy and council, Charles was persuaded to augment his Irish army. But unable to furnish the necessary expense, he too willingly resorted to the unconstitutional expedient of quartering the soldiery upon the country; the inhabitants of which were bound to supply them, not only with food, but even with money and clothing on demand. To secure a readier acquiescence in

1 'Recusants' was another name for the Roman Catholics, taken from the fact, of their refusing either to take the oath of supremacy, as stated in the text, or to attend the protestant worship.

these oppressive measures, promises were freely given by the king that he was about to confer upon the nation certain favours and immunities more than sufficient to compensate them for that loyal submission which he expected and demanded.

These promises were cheerfully listened to by the landed proprietors. They had been seriously alarmed by the inquiry into defective titles, instituted by James in reference to the province of Connaught, and latterly extended to all parts of the kingdom. The Romanists conceived this opportunity to be favourable for obtaining a permanent abolition of the penal statutes. And all parties, availing themselves of the king's necessities, proposed to grant a voluntary contribution sufficient for the support of the Irish army, provided he would legally confirm the privileges which he had promised to grant. This offer was favourably entertained by the deputy on behalf of Charles. A meeting of the principal nobility and gentry of the kingdom, of whom the majority were recusants, was held in Dublin. Agents were despatched by them to London to carry on the negotiation directly with Charles. Rumours soon spread that the public toleration of the Romish faith was about to be purchased by a contribution to the state. Under this impression, archbishop Ussher, fully alive to the pernicious tendency of that system, but mistaking the means by which it was to be counteracted, consulted with the most influential of the Irish prelates assembled in Dublin, on the conduct which it was their duty to pursue in this emergency. Accordingly on the twenty-sixth of November, 1626, they drew up a strong protestation against the toleration of popery. This memorable paper, subscribed by two archbishops and ten bishops, retarded for a time the proposed project.[2] But

[2] The following is a copy of this celebrated document taken from Cox, ii. 434. "The judgment of divers of the archbishops and bishops of Ireland, concerning toleration of religion.

"The religion of the Papists is superstitious and idolatrous; their faith and doctrine erroneous and heretical; their church, in respect of both, apostatical. To give them therefore a toleration, or to consent that they may the necessities of the king were growing every day more urgent. By yielding to the demands of the Irish, which were in themselves just and equitable, he had the prospect, not only of quieting this turbulent portion of his dominions; but of enjoying, without the control of parliament, an ample supply for prosecuting the encroachments, which he was even then meditating, against the rights of his British subjects. The Irish agents, therefore, having made him the tempting offer of a voluntary subsidy of £120,000 to be paid in three years, the proposal was accepted; the privileges solicited by them, in accordance with the royal promise, he formally engaged to grant; and instructions were transmitted, in the month of May 1628, to Lord Falkland, directing him to take the necessary steps that the stipulated engagements on the part of the king might be duly and legally fulfilled.

The concessions, or as they have been denominated,

freely exercise their religion and profess their faith and doctrine, is a grievous sin, and that in two respects: For,

"First, It is to make ourselves accessory not only to their superstitious idolatries and heresies, and, in a word, to all the abominations of Popery; but also, which is a consequent of the former, to the perdition of the seduced people which perish in the deluge of the catholick apostacy.

"Secondly, To grant them a toleration in respect of any money to be given, or contribution to be made by them, is to set religion to sale, and with it the souls of the people whom Christ our Saviour hath redeemed with his most precious blood. And as it is a great sin, so it is also a matter of most dangerous consequence; the consideration whereof we commit to the wise and judicious, beseeching the God of truth to make them who are in authority zealous of God's glory and of the advancement of true religion; zealous, resolute, and courageous against all popery, superstition and idolatry. Amen."

This declaration, founded on a sad misconception of the nature of religious toleration, was signed by the archbishops of Armagh and Cashel, the bishops of Meath, Leighlin and Ferns, Down and Connor, Derry, Cork, Kildare, Kilmore, Dromore, Waterford and Limerick. According to Cox, it "called forth a remonstrance from the House of Commons in England to his majesty, to this effect; 'That the popish religion was publickly professed in every part of Ireland, and that monasteries and nunneries were there newly erected and replenished with votaries of both sexes, which would be of evil consequence, unless seasonably repressed.'" Cox, ii. 44.

The Graces, which Charles promised to grant to his Irish subjects, were of the utmost importance to the peace and prosperity of the kingdom. They were indeed so far favourable to the Roman catholic party, that permission was given to those who were lawyers to practise in the courts; and to those who held in fee from the crown, to sue out their grants upon taking an oath, in place of the oath of supremacy, in which they simply acknowledged, and engaged to defend, Charles as their lawful king. But these promised graces were generally calculated to relieve all classes and denominations, and to redress numerous grievances existing in both the civil and ecclesiastical courts. Amounting to fifty-one, they are too numerous to be inserted at length. A few, however, bearing on the reformation of the church, and the interests of the Scottish colonists in Ulster, may with propriety be noticed.

In relation to the church, it was provided by the thirty-fifth grace, that pluralities of benefices should not be conferred on incompetent ministers; and that "such as are invested therein are to be compelled to keep preaching, and sufficient qualified curates, whereby both God's glory may be advanced, poor scholars provided for, and encouragement given to students to enable themselves for that high function." By the forty-first, it was ordered, among other matters, that "such persons as have great rectories, whereunto there are chapels of ease belonging, somewhere six or seven miles distant from the mother-church, are to be enjoined to keep preaching ministers in those parts, having competent allowance to defray the same." And by the forty-ninth it was agreed, that "all unlawful exactions taken by the clergy are to be reformed and regulated," by a commission to be appointed for this special purpose.

The interests of the Scottish settlers were provided for in the twenty-sixth and fortieth graces. By the former, their titles to their estates in Ulster, which the commissioners of defective titles had rendered very doubtful and precarious, were confirmed and secured, upon doubling their rents and paying a fine of thirty pounds for every thousand acres; and a commission was directed to be issued for finally passing the necessary patents, the withholding of which, for so many years, had subjected them to serious inconvenience. By the latter of these graces, it was stipulated that "all Scottish men, undertakers in Ulster and other places, should be made free denizens of Ireland, and that no advantage for want of denization should be taken against the heirs or assigns of those that be dead."[3]

That the sanction of law might be given to these various grants, the king was induced to consent to the calling of a parliament. The third of November was the day named in the thirty-fourth grace for its assembling in Dublin, when these important favours were to be legally confirmed; a procedure by which the reformation of the kingdom, commenced by James, would have been sensibly promoted. But the disingenuousness of Charles, for which he afterwards became so unhappily notorious, and which was thus early developed in his negotiations with his subjects, interrupted this desirable consummation. Owing to a palpable informality, of which it is to be feared he was previously cognizant, the writs, summoning the parliament for the day appointed, were pronounced invalid; no new writs were issued, nor was any time mentioned when a legal meeting might take place. The graces therefore rested on the king's promise, and on that alone; but this promise he had given, and to this he stood pledged in the most public and solemn manner. Accordingly the stipulated payments were duly made in full reliance on the royal word; and as the Romanist party contributed the greater portion of this seasonable supply, the execution of the penal laws against their faith was still further relaxed. This indulgence both offended and alarmed the stricter and more conscientious protestants; and though, to allay their apprehensions, the lord deputy on the first of April 1629 issued a formal proclamation, which was wholly inoperative, forbidding the Romish clergy to exercise

[3] These graces are given at length in Strafford's Letters, i. 312—17.

their spiritual functions with that publicity and confidence which they had recently assumed, his administration, like that of all vacillating governors, became so generally unpopular, that he was soon after recalled.

The government was now intrusted to the lord chancellor Loftus and the earl of Corke, who were sworn into office on the twenty-sixth day of October 1629. These lords justices were the firm and conscientious opponents of the Romanists. Lamenting the ill-timed lenity of Falkland, and desirous of signalizing their administration by imposing some effective restraints upon that party, they threatened to execute with rigour the penal statutes against all absentees from the protestant worship. This design was, however, abandoned at the special command of the king. But a tumult having been shortly after excited in Dublin by an unsuccessful attempt to disperse a meeting of Carmelite friars, who appeared in the habits of their order, and infused sedition into the minds of their auditors, instructions were transmitted from the English council to suppress such assemblies, and to dissolve their chapels and monasteries. Fifteen religious houses were accordingly seized and confiscated; and the popish college recently erected in the metropolis was converted into a protestant seminary, and annexed to the University. The celebrated station of St. Patrick's Purgatory in Lough Derg was also suppressed by these zealous governors. Though demolished by command of the pope, above a century and a half before, it had been subsequently re-established, and continued to attract crowds of ignorant devotees, and to fill the coffers of the attendant monks. By an order of the lords justices and privy council, dated the thirteenth of September 1632, the reverend fraternity were dispersed, their cells demolished, and the mysterious cavern in which the purgatorial penances of the pilgrims were performed, was exposed to the light of day.[4]

4 Richardson's Folly of Pilg. p. 44. It is worthy of notice that in October 1638, the queen, (of the Bourbon family and a bigoted Roman catholic,) in an autograph letter to the lord deputy Wentworth, requested him

The time now drew nigh when the last portion of the voluntary subsidy became due. The necessities of the state continued as urgent as ever. None of the stipulated graces had been as yet conferred. The complaints of the people were becoming louder and more general; and the difficulty, so perplexing to Charles, again occurred, of supplying his wants without either summoning a parliament, or irrevocably granting the promised concessions. To the adoption of either of these alternatives Charles was decidedly averse. He had experienced the vexatious firmness of three parliaments in England, all of which he had been induced to dissolve under most disagreeable circumstances. He naturally dreaded a similar issue from an assembly of his Irish subjects, who, as he himself acknowledged, "had some ground to demand more than it was fit for him to give."(5) He bitterly regretted too, having consented to the petition of rights in England, the force of which important statute he was daily endeavouring to evade; and he hesitated to impose a similar restraint on the undue exercise of his prerogative in Ireland, which the confirmation of the graces would have at once effected.

In this difficulty, he had recourse to Sir Thomas, now Lord Viscount Wentworth, who had lately become one of the most confidential advisers of the crown, and had already proved himself fitted, by his political tergiversation, to support, and by his address and vigour to execute, the most despotic of its measures. This talented statesman was appointed lord deputy in January 1632; and though for a time the king could

to restore St. Patrick's purgatory; assuring him that the people would use it modestly, and that it would give her "un grand plaisir." Wentworth very dexterously evaded this indiscreet request, stating, among other reasons, that "the place was in the midst of the great Scottish plantations," and that such a procedure on his part "might furnish them [the Scots] with something to say in prejudice and scandal to his majesty's government." Straff. Lett. ii. 221. The queen had thus been early in correspondence with the Irish Romanists, by some of whom, probably the Earl of Antrim, she had been urged to make this application to the deputy.

[5] Straff. Lett. i. 233.

not spare him from his presidentship of the north of England, yet, by his advice and influence, the administration of Irish affairs was, from this period, conducted. Until he would be able personally to assume the reins of government, the English council proposed, that the voluntary subsidy should continue to be paid for some time longer. To this measure the lords justices, in common with the majority of the nation, were strongly opposed. But convinced that the Irish army must at all events be supported, they once more recurred to their favourite project, and urged the propriety of enforcing the fines ordered, by the statute of Elizabeth, to be paid by absentees from the established worship. This alternative was rejected by Charles and his deputy, as a most invidious and inefficient mode of providing for the wants of the army. After various intrigues and altercations, it was finally agreed that an additional contribution of twenty thousand pounds should be paid into the treasury in four quarterly payments. To this renewal of their burdens the nation consented the more readily, in the hope, that the arrival of Wentworth would be a signal for the final ratification of the graces, so often promised, but so long withheld.

The lord deputy at length reached Ireland, and was sworn into office, on the twenty-fifth of July 1633. It would be foreign to the present narrative, to enter into any detail of the various measures of this enterprising but tyrannical governor, in administering the civil affairs of the kingdom. Suffice it to say, that he exalted the royal prerogative on the ruin of the rights and liberties of the people; and systematically despised the restraints of law, justice and precedent, whenever they interfered with the execution of his favourite plans. Notwithstanding the previous opposition, he succeeded in prolonging the voluntary contribution for another year. In July 1634, he called a parliament, which by intrigue and intimidation he rendered most obsequious to his wishes. An extraordinary supply of about L.300,000 was freely voted; and though, in the second session, the commons presented a remonstrance addressed to the king, urging the ratification of the graces, as a reasonable return for their extraordinary liberality, Wentworth at first evaded their application; but at length, in the more important particulars, he absolutely refused to grant their request, or even to transmit their remonstrance to England. For this service, Charles was peculiarly grateful. Though repeatedly pledged to confirm the grant of these long-promised concessions, he had early resolved to violate his solemn engagement. He therefore rejoiced the more that his faithful servant had accomplished this object, and at the same time, had taken upon himself the odium of such an unprincipled transaction.[*]

In the third session of this Parliament, one of the most important of these favours, so far as the interests of the Scottish settlers were concerned, was passed into a law. The fortieth grace purported to provide, that the Scottish undertakers should be made "free denizens" of Ireland. This privilege was now secured to them by the act "for the naturalization of all the Scottish nation which were born before his late majesty King James's accession to the throne of England and Ireland;"—these persons having been previously regarded by the common law as foreigners, and therefore incapable of legally acquiring or possessing property, within the realm of Ireland. The preamble of this act contains a memorable testimony from the legislature, to the value of the Scottish colonists in promoting the peace and welfare of the kingdom. The king is assured by the parliament, that the grievance about to be removed was "a sad discouragement and disheartening unto many of your said subjects of Scotland, that otherwise would have planted themselves here, for the further civilising, strengthening, and securing this your

* On this occasion Charles thus wrote to Wentworth, under date of Oct. 23, 1634.—" Your last public despatch has given me a great deal of contentment, and especially for keeping off the envy of a necessary negative from me, of those unreasonable graces that that people expected from me." Straf. Let. i. 331.

highness' said realm, against rebels at home, and all foreign invasion." (7)

The attention of Wentworth was by no means confined to civil affairs. The state of the Irish church was commended to his especial care by Laud, now elevated to the see of Canterbury. The archbishop and the deputy were of congenial tempers and dispositions. Equally servile and despotic, Laud was, moreover, actuated by the most furious bigotry, and the most puerile superstition. Proud, arbitrary, and unfeeling, he urged conformity with a higher hand than any former prelate. The puritan party were peculiarly obnoxious to him, as well for their steady attachment to civil liberty, as for their uniform opposition to the unscriptural power assumed by the English church. He therefore opposed, and studiously avoided, the slightest approach to their sentiments, whether in matters of doctrine or of worship. With this view, he patronized the Arminian in opposition to the Calvinistic system, then universally maintained by the puritans, in common with the vast majority of the members of the established church. He encouraged the introduction of showy and superstitious rites into divine worship, and every innovation brought the protestant service into nearer approximation to the Romish ritual. Under this rule, the communion table was converted into an altar, railed in, and placed at the east end of the church, adorned with candlesticks and crucifixes, and made the object of adoration. (8) Pictures, images,

7 10 Cha. i. sess. 3. chap. 4. apud Irish Stat. ii. 100.

8 Prynne's Cant. Doom. p. 100, 1. Neal, ii. 221. The reader will be amused with the following sapient reasons, propounded by the bishop of Bath and Wells in 1633, under the sanction of Laud, to show the necessity of railing in the communion-table, which previously remained in the centre of the church, and of placing it on an elevation where the altar stood in popish times.

"2. There should be some difference between the placing of the Lord's table in the church, and the placing of a man's table in his house.

"3. It is not fit the people should sit above God's table, or be above the priest when he consecrateth.

and lighted tapers, were introduced into churches. The tutelary protection of saints and angels, and their consequent invocation, were publicly inculcated. The real presence of Christ in the communion, the necessity of auricular confession, and the efficacy of absolution, were openly maintained. While the Sabbath was commanded to be profaned by the re-publication of the 'Book of Sports,' exhorting the people to amuse themselves with certain games and recreations on this day of the Lord; holidays and festivals were revered and observed as days of especial sanctity.(9) In a word, there was scarcely an article of the church, viewed as distinct from the court, of Rome, which did not receive the sanction and support of Laud, or his adherents. No wonder then a very general impression prevailed, that under the auspicies of the archbishop, to whom the offer of a cardinal's hat had been twice made by the pope, the English church was about to apostatize from the truth, and relapse into the bosom of the mother-church.(10)

To silence the opposition so generally manifested against these unwarrantable and unscriptural innovations, the arm of spiritual power was vigorously exercised. Public lecturers, a class of preachers elected and supported by the people, and chaplains entertained by opulent private families, were alike prohibited, as not being sufficiently under prelatical control. Afternoon sermons and catechetical exercises were abolished;

"4. If it stand not thus, and be not railed in, it will be subject to many profanations and abuses; church-wardens will keep their accounts on the Lord's table; parishioners will sit round about it, and talk of their parish-businesses; schoolmasters will teach their boys to write upon this table, and the boys will lay their hats, satchels, and books upon it, and in their master's absence, sit upon the same; many will sit or lean irreverently against the Lord's table in sermon-time; glaziers will knock it full of nail-holes; and dogs will defile the Lord's table."

9 Prynne, ut sup. p. 153, et seq.

10 May's Hist. of the Parl. p. 22, 3. Heylin's Laud, p. 252. Lord Falkland, in one of his speeches, made the following just observation with respect to Laud and his party;—"it seemed their work was, to try how much of a papist might be brought in without popery."

and the privilege of public preaching was permitted only to a few approved ministers. Every book not in accordance with the prevalent spirit of error and of intolerance was suppressed, or carefully expurgated; and even those works, formerly reputed most sound and pious, did not escape.[11] The clergy who hesitated to comply with the arbitrary commands of their superiors were summarily suspended or deposed. So violent was the rage for conformity, that even the French and Dutch protestant churches in London were compelled to adopt the English ritual, in preference to that of their respective national churches, which they had used without molestation, since the commencement of the Reformation. And lest the formalities or just restraints of law might retard this career of audacious innovation, the high-commission court furnished a seasonable and appropriate engine, by which the designs of the predominant party, though ever so illegal, were carried into immediate execution. The fines imposed on conscientious non-conformists by this unconstitutional tribunal were enormous; and the punishments awarded against those who offered the slightest opposition to the tyrannical proceedings of Laud and his faction, were frequently of unparalleled severity[12] Such was the system introduced and patronized by the archbishop in England, and which he laboured to extend successively to Ireland and to Scotland. The chief aim, indeed, of the life and exertions of this 'Patriarch of the West,' as he affected to call himself, was to establish, upon the most intolerant basis, a complete uniformity in government and worship over the three kingdoms. Prelacy and the liturgy, civil and ecclesiastical despotism, he longed to see universally triumphant over the consciences and liberties of the people.

The state of the Irish church early attracted the attention of Laud. It was still in a deplorable condition, and presented, even at this period, the same general features of indolence,

[11] Prynne, 1667. Brodie, ii. 296—308. [12] Neal, ii. 137, 138.

worldliness, and consequent inefficiency, which it had exhibited in the early stages of its history. Though the sees were filled with protestant prelates, yet the majority of them appeared more solicitous to advance their private interests, than to promote the cause of true religion. The parish churches, and even the cathedrals, were, chiefly through their neglect, in a wretched state of dilapidation, and a great part of their revenues was alienated from their successors, and appropriated to the aggrandizement of their families. The incomes of the inferior clergy were reduced to an inadequate amount, and in many instances wholly enjoyed by lay-impropriators: "And as scandalous livings naturally make scandalous ministers, the clergy of the established church were generally ignorant and unlearned, loose and irregular in their lives and conversations, negligent of their cures, and were careless of observing uniformity and decency in divine worship." (13)

The ecclesiastical courts were proverbially oppressive and profligate in their proceedings. "Bribes went about almost barefaced, and the exchange they made of penance for money, was the worst sort of simony; being in effect the very same abuse, that gave the world such a scandal, when it was so indecently practised in the church of Rome, and so opened the way to the Reformation." (14) The primitive discipline of the church was entirely suppressed; and any attempt to revive even the scanty power which the English church possesses, was certain to encounter the most violent opposition. The consequences of this neglect and mismanagement were too apparent. The reformed faith had indeed been spreading, but this result was rather the effect of colonization than of conversion. All the ordinary means of its propagation were, except in a few particular districts, unaccountably neglected, while, at the same time, violent prejudices were excited against it, as well by the occasional intolerance of the state, as by the sordidness and immorality of its ministers, and the oppressions

13 Carte, i. 68.

14 Burnet's Life of Bedell, p. 69.

of its church courts. But while the reformed faith was advancing so slowly, the Roman catholic church maintained an undisturbed ascendency over the minds, and in the affections, of the people. In despite of statutes and proclamations, often indeed only formal, the Romish worship, with all its attendant ceremonials, was regularly and openly observed. The hierarchy, though almost extinct in the sister kingdoms, was complete in all its parts; every see had its prelate, and every parish its priest. Archbishops and bishops exercised, almost without control, their ecclesiastical jurisdiction; and notwithstanding the poverty of the country, they appear to have enjoyed ample revenues. Chapels were built where necessary; and where the protestant minister was non-resident, as was too generally the case, their service was conducted in the deserted church. Speaking the language of the people, and sharing in their perils and discouragements, they maintained their influence unimpaired; and easily defeated the few and inefficient efforts which were made to expose the errors of popery, and extend the knowledge of the truth.

The only part of the kingdom, in which a more pleasing prospect presented itself, was Ulster. Here the protestant ministers were more zealous and faithful; the people better instructed; religious worship was more regularly maintained; and the truth was consequently advancing with surer and more rapid steps. This superiority of the northern province is chiefly to be ascribed to the character of the colonists by whom it was principally peopled, and the diligence and labours of the pastors who accompanied them to their new abode. The influence of the bishops, who at this period resided in Ulster, all of whom were doctrinal puritans, must not be overlooked. At their head was Ussher, learned, tolerant and disinterested; the most distinguished ornament of his church and nation, and as Livingston significantly adds, "a godly man, although a bishop." He was supported by Downham, bishop of Derry, the acute and zealous antagonist of error in doctrine, and laxity in discipline; together with Knox of

Raphoe, and Echlin of Down and Connor, two Scotchmen, whose extensive dioceses were supplied with many countrymen, discharging the arduous duties of the ministry with exemplary fidelity and success. To these prelates was added Bedell, who, from being provost of Dublin college, was, in the year 1629, elevated to the joint see of Kilmore and Ardagh. He was a highly estimable prelate, and a most upright and amiable man, exemplary in his private life, laborious and strict in his public duties, a faithful and constant preacher, the decided enemy of every ecclesiastical abuse, and the generous patron of every diligent and conscientious minister. The state of his diocese, situated on the verge of Ulster, was truly deplorable. The following statement, sent by him to Laud in the month of April 1630, presents a melancholy view of the religious condition of the kingdom at this period.

"To speak much ill matter in a few words," writes Bedell, "the state of my dioceses is very miserable. The cathedral church of Ardagh, one of the most ancient in Ireland, and said to be built by St. Patrick, together with the bishop's house there, down to the ground. The church here [at Kilmore in the county of Cavan] built; but without bell or steeple, font or chalice. The parish churches all in a manner ruined, and unroofed, and unrepaired. The people, saving a few British planters here and there, which are not the tenth part of the remnant, obstinate recusants. A popish clergy more numerous by far than we, and in full exercise of all jurisdiction ecclesiastical, by their vicar-general and officials; who are so confident as they excommunicate those that come to our courts, even in matrimonial causes: which affront hath been offered myself by the popish primate's vicar-general, for which I have begun a process against him. The primate himself lives in my parish, within two miles of my house; the bishop in another part of my diocese farther off. Every parish hath its priest; and some two or three a-piece; and so their mass-houses also: in some places mass is said in the churches. Friars there are in divers places, who go about, though not in their habit; and by their importunate begging impoverish the people, who indeed are generally very poor, as from that cause, so from their paying double tithes to their own clergy and ours, from the dearth of corn, and the death of their cattle these late years, with the contributions to their soldiers and their agents: and, which they forget not to reckon among other causes, the oppression of the courts ecclesiastical, which in very truth, my lord, I cannot excuse, and do seek to reform. For our own there are seven or eight ministers in each diocese [of Kilmore and Ardagh] of good sufficiency; and, which is no small cause of the continuance of the people in popery still, English; which have not the tongue of the people, nor can perform any divine offices, or converse with them; and which hold, many of them, two, three, four or more vicarages a-piece; even the clerkships themselves are in like manner conferred upon the English; and sometimes two or three or more upon one man, and ordinarily bought and sold, or let to farm. His majesty is now with the greatest part of this country, as to their hearts and consciences, king but at the pope's discretion."—"Here was a melancholy prospect," adds bishop Burnet, his biographer, "to a man of so good a mind as Bedell, enough to have disheartened him quite, if he had not had a proportioned degree of spirit and courage to support him under so much weight."[15]

This faithful prelate, accordingly, commenced with vigour the work of reformation. He first resigned the see of Ardagh, and then persuaded the majority of his clergy to relinquish their pluralities. He rectified the abuses of the ecclesiastical courts, and met with his clergy in synod, where they drew up a series of excellent canons for the regulation of the diocese. He enforced strict residence, and exercised a minute inspection over the lives and labour of the ministers. He was principally distinguished for his judicious and zealous

15 Burnet's Bedell, pp. 35-6.

efforts to instruct the native Irish. Little, if any thing, had as yet been done for this numerous portion of the population, who were viewed as unfit for education, and capable of being restrained by force or influenced by fear alone. The New Testament and the book of Common-prayer had indeed been translated into their vernacular tongue. But the publication of these books in Irish was of comparatively little profit to the people, through the want of elementary schools for their education, and the ignorance of the language among the protestant clergy.

Bedell, who has been well styled 'the Tyndal of Ireland,' early perceived and lamented this neglect of the native population. Though an Englishman, and previously unacquainted with the circumstances of this country, he had no sooner entered on his duties as provost of Trinity College, than he established an 'Irish lecture,' for preparing young men to preach in Irish among the natives. When he removed to his bishoprick he prosecuted the same object with untiring zeal, notwithstanding the serious troubles in which his benevolent and disinterested labours involved him. Though in his sixtieth year, he commenced with ardour the study of the Irish language. The services of his cathedral were on one part of the Sabbath regularly conducted in that tongue. He compiled and printed, in English and Irish, a catechetical summary of Christian doctrine, with forms of prayer and scriptural extracts, which he studiously dispersed through his diocese. He engaged his clergy to establish schools in every parish; and to his singular praise be it recorded, he resolved to procure the translation of the whole Bible into Irish, and to publish it, at his own expense, for the benefit of his adopted countrymen. Though by profession an episcopalian, he had too much of the puritanic spirit to be generally popular with the bigoted churchmen around him. He disliked the use of his episcopal vestments, and was decidedly opposed to instrumental music in Christian worship. He preached twice every Sabbath, and catechised regularly in the afternoon. He read the psalms in divine service, like the other portions of the word of God, without responses; and though punctual in his use of the common prayer-book in the church, he never employed it in conducting his domestic worship. Like Ussher he maintained the identity of bishop and presbyter. He ordained no individual to the ministry without the consent of his clergy, whom he styled brethren and fellow-presbyters; and he deemed it irregular to exercise his episcopal functions beyond his own diocese. [16]

While these peculiarities were generally noticed to his disadvantage, the vigour and impartiality, with which he prosecuted the work of reformation, created him many enemies. His chancellor commenced a suit at law against him for presuming to sit in the courts held in his own name, and there enforce the ancient discipline of the church; a step which he had been induced to take, in consequence of the gross injustice and oppression which he found in them. This step, with several others equally decided, which he took to rectify the abuses prevailing around him, alienated from him for a time the affection of Ussher, who, as bishop Burnet alleges, "had too gentle a soul to manage that rough work of reforming abuses, and therefore he left things as he found them." [17] In this spirit, unworthy of his great name, the primate soon after apprized Bedell, that "the tide went so high against him in regard to pluralities and non-residence, that he could assist him no more." To this disheartening intimation the latter nobly replied, "that he was resolved, by the help of God, to try if he could stand by himself." This he was scarcely able to effect. His plans of reform were frequently opposed and thwarted by the civil authorities, as well as by his spiritual superiors. The clergyman whom he engaged to translate the Bible into Irish, was, for some trivial ecclesiastical delinquency, deposed without a hearing by the officials of the primate, and even imprisoned.

16 Burnet's Bedell, pp. 38, 113, 135-6, 389.

17 Ibid. p. 67.

This most important work was necessarily suspended; another half-century elapsed before it was resumed and completed; the oppressions of the church-courts were proverbially grievous; and pluralities and non-residence continued to paralyze the efficiency of the established church. Bedell's insulated and unsupported efforts, therefore, though in themselves judicious and well-directed, were of no avail to ameliorate the wretched aspect which the church presented, when he first entered on his episcopal functions.

Such was the state of the Irish church, even in the most favourable parts of the kingdom, when Laud turned his attention to Ireland, as another field on which to establish that system of doctrine and worship which he was so anxiously labouring to introduce into both the sister kingdoms. Impressed as he was with the most extravagant ideas of the wealth and splendour, the canonical subordination and rigorous conformity which ought to prevail in the protestant, as they did in the popish, church, he could not fail to be disappointed and mortified when he found the Irish establishment so destitute of these characteristics of ecclesiastical superiority. Instead of ornamented structures, he learned that the churches and even the cathedrals were, for the most part, ruined and desolate. The clergy were poor, ignorant and little respected; and what was a more serious defect, he found they entertained no great reverence for their spiritual superiors, nor were they punctual in their use of those garments, postures and other ritual observances, which Laud viewed as essential to the validity of divine ordinances. And even where the clergy were more learned, respectable and influential, he had the mortification to find them Calvinistic in doctrine and puritanical in principle, especially on a cardinal point of Laud's creed,—the extent of ecclesiastical authority. These were heresies of the darkest hue in the eyes of the intolerant archbishop, though directly taught in the public and authorized confession. He accordingly resolved to lose no time and to spare no exertion in re-modelling the Irish church; and in the prosecution of this object, he acted in the same arbitrary manner which had already characterised his conduct towards the other established churches of the empire.

The first instance in which he interfered in the religious concerns of this country was indicative of the course which he intended to pursue. In the beginning of the year 1631, Downham, bishop of Derry, published, in Dublin, a treatise on the Covenant of grace, in which he condemned the Arminian doctrines in reference to the total and final apostacy of true believers.[18] No sooner had this elaborate performance reached the hands of Laud, than, not content with causing it to be seized and suppressed in England, he wrote to Ussher in the month of August, ordering him to call in the work in Ireland also; and directing him, for the future, to take especial care that nothing be published contrary to those Arminian views which he was so anxious to uphold and propagate. It is truly painful to find the venerable primate again betrayed into servile compliance, by his timid and irresolute spirit. Through fear of displeasing this haughty and powerful prelate, Ussher meanly lent himself to the violent suppression of a work which was not only in perfect accordance with his own sentiments, but also with the accredited standards of the church of which he was the highest officer. In his letter to Laud on this occasion, dated from Drogheda on the eighth of November following, there is manifested a tone of servility, and a spirit of indifference to the truth, derogatory to his character for candour and integrity.[19]

18 Both Prynne and Collier speak of this publication as a work on "Perseverance." But the bishop wrote no work with that title, or professedly on that subject. In the year stated in the text, he published "The Covenant of Grace, or an Exposition upon Luke, i. 73, 4, 5," Dublin 1631, 8vo., which I conjecture is the work that roused the indignation of Laud. The exposition of the latter part of his text would necessarily lead him to treat of the perseverance of the saints.

19 The following is Collier's account of this affair. "This year Usher, lord primate of Ireland, published his history of Gotteschalcus. In this

To accomplish his designs in Ireland more effectually, Laud induced Charles to commit the government of it to Wentworth, as one on whose vigorous and entire concurrence in his measures he could place the fullest confidence. The new deputy did not disappoint these expectations. He never failed to support Laud in all his plans, and to carry into effect every innovation proposed by the archbishop. On assuming the reins of government, he commenced a series of preparatory inquiries into the existing state of the church; and in the month of January 1634, he communicated the result to Laud.[20] Having obtained the requisite information, he immediately proceeded to apply "the best and speediest remedies for reformation that may be." To relieve the impoverished and destitute state of the church, he issued commissions for repairing its cathedrals and other places of worship; he commenced with vigour the restitution of its temporalities; he prevailed with many of the nobility to resign their impropriations, and persecuted those who refused to comply; and, in his first parliament, he procured the enactment of various laws, by which the rights and emoluments of the clerical corporation were abundantly secured. He entered warmly into Laud's measures for discountenancing the

tract he undertook Vossius in some measure upon the Pelagian controversy; and here his pen run out a little in defence of the predestinarian scheme. Not long before, Downham, bishop of Derry, published a discourse concerning Perseverance. In this performance there were some passages that clashed directly with the king's declaration. Usher's book being written in Latin, did less disservice; and beside, some regard was shown to the eminence of his station. However, to make the primate sensible of the king's displeasure, he was commanded to call in Downham's book. But his majesty's letter not coming to hand till the middle of October, most of the copies were dispersed and out of reach. However, for preventing these prohibited sallies, Bedell, bishop of Kilmore, was ordered to overlook the press and keep it inoffensive." Ecc. Hist. ii. 750. A measure worthy of popish councils! The curious reader will find Ussher's reply to Laud on this occasion, in Pryn. Cant. Doom. p. 172.

20 Straff. Lett. i. 187, 8.

Calvinistic and puritanic clergy, against the heads of whom, Ussher and Bedell, he had been violently prejudiced, even before his arrival in Ireland. To counteract their influence, which was considerable, he brought over with him, in the capacity of private chaplain, John Bramhall, a man of decided talents and extensive erudition; but a violent and intolerant churchman, whom Cromwell, from his resemblance in spirit and temper to Laud, afterwards styled 'the Canterbury of Ireland.' This active and able minister soon proved himself an efficient auxiliary in carrying into effect the views of his patron. Shortly after his settlement in Dublin, he forwarded to Laud an account of the state of the Irish church, which amply corroborates that given by Bedell. He thus writes:—

"Right reverend father, my most honoured lord, presuming partly upon your license, but especially directed by my lord deputy's command, I am to give your Fatherhood a brief account of the present state of the poor church of Ireland, such as our short intelligence here, and your lordship's weighty employments there, will permit. First, for the fabrics; it is hard to say whether the churches be more ruinous and sordid, or the people irreverent. Even in Dublin, the metropolis of this kingdom, and seat of justice, to begin the inquisition where the reformation will begin, we find our [one ?] parochial church converted to the lord deputy's stable; a second to a nobleman's dwelling-house; the choir of a third to a tennis court, and the vicar acts the keeper. In Christ's church, the principal church in Ireland, whither the lord-deputy and council repair every Sunday, the vaults from one end of the minster to the other are made into tippling rooms for beer, wine, and tobacco, demised all to popish recusants, and by them to others, much frequented in time of divine service. —— —— Next for the clergy, I find few footsteps yet of foreign differences, so I hope it will be an easier task not to admit them, than to have them ejected.

But I doubt much whether the clergy be very orthodox,[21] and could wish both the articles and canons of the church of England were established here by act of Parliament or state; that as we live all under one king, so we might, both in doctrine and discipline, observe an uniformity. The inferior sort of ministers are below all degrees of contempt, in respect of their poverty and ignorance. The boundless heaping together of benefices by commendams and dispensations in the superiors, is but too apparent; yea, even often by plain usurpations and indirect compositions made between the patrons, as well ecclesiastical as lay, and the incumbents; by which the least part, many times not above forty shillings, rarely ten pounds in the year, is reserved for him that should serve at the altar; insomuch that it is affirmed, that by all or some of these means, one bishop in the remoter parts of the kingdom doth hold three and twenty benefices with cure. Generally their residence is as little as their livings. Seldom any suitor petitions for less than three vicarages at a time."[22]

The activity and zeal of Bramhall did not long remain unrewarded. In the year 1634, Wentworth made him bishop of Derry in place of the learned and pious Downham; as in the preceding year he had advanced John Leslie, bishop of Orkney in Scotland, another violent churchman, to the see of Raphoe, vacant by the death of the mild and tolerant Knox. All the appointments in the church were henceforth of a similar character. None but men of Arminian and intolerant principles were promoted; while, at the same time, every means was employed to discountenance and harass, not merely the professed non-conformists, but even all moderate episcopalians, who did not fully coincide in the views of doctrine, and modes of worship, now obtaining the ascendancy in England.

21 To be "orthodox," in the view of Bramhall and Laud, was to maintain anti-puritanic, Arminian, and semi-papistical principles.

22 Collier's Ecc. Hist. ii. 759.

The state of the university also underwent revision. Laud had already introduced into Oxford, of which he was chancellor, various innovations, all leading towards Arminianism and popery; and Dublin was now subjected to a similar deterioration. Wentworth had complained to Laud, among other evils in the religious state of Ireland, that the college "was extremely out of order, partly by means of their statutes which must be amended, and partly under the government of a weak provost." This disorderliness, it is more than probable, consisted solely in the leaven of puritanism which had existed in this seminary from its foundation. Its first four provosts were decided puritans. Bedell succeeded the last of these, and presided over the college for two years; during which period he was strict in his government, and exemplary for his attention to the Christian education of the young. He was succeeded by Dr. Robert Ussher, to whom Wentworth alludes as the 'weak provost.' He was related to the primate, and entertained the same sentiments with his predecessors and his illustrious kinsman, on the doctrinal points on which the church was divided. The college, thus governed, had of course exercised considerable influence in forming the minds of the Irish clergy, and rendering them averse to the innovations of Laud. Until this influence should be intrusted to other hands, it was evidently impossible to effect any extensive or permanent alteration of the national faith. A change, therefore, both in the provost and the statutes, became necessarily a part of Wentworth's plans of reformation. The former was accordingly promoted to be bishop of Kildare; and Chappell, a violent Arminian from England, who had been previously advanced by Laud to be dean of Cashel, was substituted in his place.[28] The new

[28] Chappell was of Christ's College, Cambridge. He had been tutor to Milton in 1624, 5. Johnson's Lives, i. 64. He held the divinity act with the celebrated John Cotton, afterwards of Boston, New England. Mather's Hist. of New Eng. Book iii. p. 17. He was a noted Pelagian and Arminian. Pryn. Cant. Doom. p. 359.

provost urged conformity with an unsparing intolerance; but such serious divisions were thereby created, that it became necessary, in a short time, to remove this obnoxious governor to another situation. The office of chancellor was conferred upon Laud, and the statutes of the college, being probably found too favourable to religious liberty, were subjected to his revision, and, as altered by him, were soon after established by the royal authority.

But the great object of anxiety, both with the archbishop and the deputy, yet remained to be accomplished—the complete union of the two churches of England and Ireland. To accomplish this favourite project, various changes were to be effected, and many difficulties encountered, sufficient to discourage any but the most daring innovators. Above all things, it became necessary to abolish the Calvinistic confession, compiled by Ussher, and ratified by parliament twenty years before. This measure, it was well known, would be most mortifying to the primate, and highly obnoxious to the whole body of the clergy, who were decidedly Calvinistic. Their pride would naturally be offended by the proposal, not merely to receive the articles of another church, but even to adopt its canons, to the utter annihilation of their independence as a national establishment. Yet Wentworth did not hesitate to pledge himself for the accomplishment of this delicate and difficult task. A convocation of the clergy was, by his order, summoned to meet, at the same time with the second session of the parliament, in the month of November 1634. Prior to its assembling, he took the precaution to consult Ussher on the intended union. He proposed to the primate that the Irish articles should not be in any way noticed, much less annulled, in the approaching convocation; but that, simply to manifest the agreement between this church and the sister one of England, the thirty-nine articles of the latter should be received and recognised. To this plan, thus expounded, Ussher made no objection, conceiving that the two confessions were similar in doctrine, and that the proposed arrangement would merely render them of co-ordinate authority in the Irish church. Wentworth and Laud, however, had this farther view, which was afterwards maintained by Bramhall and his partisans, but to which Ussher and his friends never assented, namely, that the intended procedure virtually and totally abrogated the Irish articles, and established the English, in their forced interpretation of Arminianism, as the sole accredited standard of the church's faith.

The deputy, relying on the concurrence of Ussher, and occupied in appeasing the indignant commons, who were warmly pressing a confirmation of the graces, had not at first attended to the proceedings of the convocation. At length having leisure to obtain information on the subject, to his great surprise he found that the lower house had, by a committee, been examining the canons of the English church, marking those which they approved, and also those which stood for farther deliberation; and that, into the fifth canon, they had introduced a recognition of the Irish articles, and enjoined them to be received under pain of excommunication. The approved canons they had digested into a series, and were about to report thereon to the House, with a view to their final adoption.

Wentworth at once perceived that these proceedings of the convocation were directly opposed to his favourite plan, and that the most prompt and vigorous measures would be required on his part to over-rule their deliberations, which savoured too much of a puritanic spirit, and especially to defeat the renewed recognition of the Irish articles. To accomplish this object, he hesitated not to employ the most unjustifiable violence. The conduct of the deputy on this occasion presents a singular and striking instance of the manner in which the proceedings of ecclesiastical councils are influenced by the civil authorities. Seldom indeed have these bodies been characterised by a firm maintenance of their authority and rights in opposition to the encroachments of the state. Presbyterian synods have perhaps been the most uniformly distinguished for the bold and fearless assertion of their independence. But the convocation sitting in Dublin permitted themselves to be over-ruled in the most insulting manner. Their deliberative acts were violently reversed by the deputy, and their freedom of discussion taken away, without a murmur.

Wentworth, exulting over his victory, forwarded to Laud the following account of the manner in which he had accomplished their favourite object. So soon as he had ascertained the proceedings of the committee of the lower house, he thus proceeded: "I instantly sent for dean Andrews, that reverend clerk, who sat forsooth in the chair at this committee, requiring him to bring along the book of canons so noted in the margin, together with the draught he was to present that afternoon to the House. This he obeyed;——but when I came to open the book, and run over the deliberandums in the margin, I confess I was not so much moved since I came into Ireland. I told him, certainly not a dean of Limerick, but an Ananias, had sat in the chair of that committee;——however, sure I was, an Ananias had been there in spirit, if not in body, with all the fraternities and conventicles of Amsterdam; that I was ashamed and scandalized with it above measure. I therefore said he should leave the book and draught with me; and I did command him, upon his allegiance, that he should report nothing to the house from that committee till he heard again from me.

"Being thus nettled, I gave present directions for a meeting, and warned the primate, the bishops of Meath, Kilmore, Raphoe and Derry, together with dean Leslie the prolocutor, and all those who had been of the committee—— to be with me the next morning.

"Then I publickly told them how unlike churchmen, who ought [owed] canonical obedience to their superiors, they had proceeded in their committee; how unheard a part it was for a few petty clerks to presume to make articles of faith without the privity or consent of state or bishop; what a spirit of

Brownism and contradiction I observed in their deliberations, as if indeed they purposed at once to take away all government and order forth of the church, and to leave every man to choose his own high place where liked him best. But these heady and arrogant courses, they must know, I was not to endure; nor if they were disposed to be frantic in this dead and cold season of the year, would I suffer them either to be mad in the convocation or in their pulpits.

"First, then, I required dean Andrews, as formerly, that he should report nothing from the committee to the house.

"Secondly, I enjoined dean Leslie, their prolocutor, that in case any of the committee should propound any question herein, yet that he should not put it, but break up the sitting for that time, and acquaint me with all.

"Thirdly, That he should put no question at all touching the receiving or not of the articles of the church of Ireland.

"Fourthly, That he should put the question for allowing and receiving the articles of England, wherein he was by name and in writing to take their votes, barely, content or not content, without admitting any other discourse at all; for I would not endure that the articles of the church of England should be disputed.

"And finally, because there should be no question in the canon that was thus to be voted, I did desire my lord primate would be pleased to frame it, and after I had perused it, I would send the prolocutor a draught of the canon to be propounded, inclosed in a letter of my own.

"This meeting thus broke off; there were some hot spirits, sons of thunder, amongst them, who moved that they should petition me for a free synod; but, in fine, they could not agree among themselves who should put the bell about the cat's neck, and so this likewise vanished.

"The primate accordingly framed a canon, which I, not so well approving, drew up one myself, more after the words of the canon in England, which I held best for me to keep as close to as I could, and then sent it to my lord. His grace came instantly unto me, and told me he feared the canon would never pass in such form as I had made it, but he was hopeful, as he had drawn it, it might; he besought me therefore to think a little better of it.

"But I confess, having taken a little jealousy, that his proceedings were not open and free to those ends I had my eye upon, it was too late now either to persuade or affright me. I told his Lordship I was resolved to put it to them in those very words, and was most confident there was not six in the houses that would refuse them, telling him by the sequel, we should see whether his lordship or myself better understood their minds in that point, and by that I would be content to be judged, only for order's sake, I desired his lordship would vote this canon (24) first, in the upper house of convocation, and so voted, then to pass the question beneath also.

"Without any delay then, I writ a letter to dean Leslie, with the canon enclosed, which accordingly that afternoon was unanimously voted, first with the bishops, and then by the rest of the clergy, excepting one man,—who singly did deliberate upon the receiving of the articles of England." (25)

24 The following is a copy of this canon, as it now stands: "For the manifestation of our agreement with the church of England in the confession of the same Christian faith, and the doctrine of the sacraments; We do receive and approve the book of articles of religion agreed upon by the archbishops and bishops, and the whole clergy, in the convocation holden at London in the year of our Lord God 1562, for the avoiding of diversities of opinion, and for the establishing of consent touching true religion. And therefore if any hereafter shall affirm, that any of those articles are, in any part, superstitious or erroneous, or such as he may not, with a good conscience subscribe unto, let him be excommunicated, and not absolved before he make a public revocation of his error." Irish Can. No. I.

25 Straff. Lett. i. 343-4.—This solitary champion of the independence of his church was probably Hamilton, minister of Ballywalter, who, it is certain, was a member of this convocation.—Bramhall in the upper, and Leslie in the lower house, were the principal supporters of Wentworth's views. Archbishop Vesey, in his life of Bramhall, prefixed to the folio edition of his works, states, that if the receiving of the English articles had been understood or suspected at the time, to be a virtual repealing of the

In this violent and summary manner was the constitution of the Irish Episcopal church, as it now stands in doctrine and in discipline, finally settled. The thirty-nine articles of the English church became the accredited standard of the former; and the latter was regulated by a body of canons, selected from those adopted in England, and framed into a new series, for the gratification of those prelates who stood out for the independence of their national establishment. These canons, the first which were in force in Ireland, amounted to one hundred in number.[26] They were ordered to be subscribed by every minister, and to be read by him publicly in his church once a-year. The indefatigable Bedell, in his convocation, brought forward the subject which had so deeply engrossed his attention,—of instructing the native Irish through the medium of their vernacular tongue. He was supported by Ussher and the great majority of his brethren. But he was opposed by Bramhall, who, like his patron and prototype Laud, was averse to the general education of the people, and who reasoned against the proposal of

Irish,—the sense afterwards attached to it, the measure would not have carried. The clergy were soon sorry for what they had been induced to do; but, as the archbishop adds, " it was now too late to recall so solemn an act. Yet some who had a greater kindness for their private opinions than the union of two churches, being ashamed to be thus surprised, if not plainly outwitted, thought to preserve the reputation of their articles and their own, by averring that the articles of England were only received in the sense of, and as they might be expounded by, those of Ireland. And accordingly some few bishops required subscription, for some time, to both confessions."

26 The Irish canons appear to have been first printed and published in the month of September 1635; for Sir George Radcliffe thus writes from Dublin to bishop Bramhall: " The canons are published in print this week; and by occasion of speaking thereof, there is a panic fear risen in this town, as if a new persecution, so they call it, were instantly to be set on foot." Rawd. Pap. p. 22. This trepidation and alarm, which the mere publication of the canons created in Dublin, and which reached the ears of Radcliffe, the master-general of the ordnance, plainly evince the prevalence of non-conforming principles at this period, even in the metropolis.

Bedell on the absurd principle, the application of which had already been so fatal to the progress of the truth,—that the native Irish were a barbarous and degraded people, unworthy and incapable of instruction or civilization. To the honour of the convocation, Bedell so far succeeded, that it was provided in the ninety-fourth canon, that "where most of the people are Irish, the church-warden shall provide a Bible and two Common Prayer-books in the Irish tongue; and where the minister is an Englishman, such a clerk may be chosen as shall be able to read the service in Irish." But they took no steps to have the Bible translated into Irish, or schools established, and ministers provided expressly for the native population. These obvious and indispensable measures being neglected, it was vain to expect any practical advantages to result from this solitary and unsupported enactment.

Wentworth now possessed uncontrolled sway, both in the church and in the state.[27] To render this authority more efficient, soon after the dissolution of the parliament and convocation, he proceeded to erect a high-commission court in Dublin, and to confer upon it the tremendous powers possessed by a similar court in England. By the aid of this unconstitutional tribunal, he was enabled to bring the decision of almost every question of importance, occurring in the courts of law, before himself and his colleagues. The freedom and property of every individual in the kingdom were thus subject to his control; and by the summary pro-

27 Wentworth was fully conscious of the extent of power he possessed as the representative of royalty. In this letter to Laud, already quoted, giving the account of his management of the convocation, he used this remarkable expression:—"So as now I can say, the king is as absolute here as any prince in the whole world can be, and may be still, if it be not spoiled on that side." Happily for the cause of liberty, this despotic system was spoiled in England; and after many painful struggles, during which, by a melancholy coincidence, Wentworth, Laud, and Charles, were all ignominiously beheaded, the royal prerogative, which the former boasted he had rendered so absolute in Ireland, was restrained within constitutional limits.

cesses of this new court, from which there was no appeal, he could at once visit, with exemplary punishment, the slightest opposition to his measures. The prelates found this engine of tyranny peculiarly advantageous for enforcing the observance of the recently enacted canons. It was indeed chiefly with a view to their accommodation that Wentworth had pleaded, both with Laud and Charles, for permission to erect such a court. "I hold it most fit," he writes, "that there were a high-commission settled here in Dublin, conceiving the use of it might be very great to countenance the despised state of the clergy, to support ecclesiastical courts and officers, to provide for the maintenance of the clergy, and for their residence, either by themselves or able curates, to bring the people here to a conformity in religion, and in the way of all these,"—he characteristically concludes, "to raise perhaps a good revenue to the crown."(26) To all these purposes it was in due time applied; and the presbyterians of Ulster were soon made to feel the weight of those new and formidable powers, with which the authorities of both church and state were now invested.

26 Straff. Lett. i. 188.

CHAPTER IV.

Blair's application to Wentworth unsuccessful—Lord Castlestewart interferes—Suspended ministers restored for six months—Deaths of Welsh and Stewart—Conference between Blair and bishop Echlin—Death of Echlin—Is succeeded by Henry Leslie—His visitation sermon—He suspends five other ministers—Public discussion at Belfast—Death of Brice—Ministers embark for New-England—Are driven back—And compelled to fly to Scotland—Their reception there—Deaths of Cunningham and Ridge—Increasing tyranny of Wentworth—His arbitrary proceedings—His attention turned to Scotland—State of the Scottish church—Laud's innovations—Book of Canons—Liturgy—Riot at Edinburgh—General Assembly at Glasgow—Indignation of Charles—He prepares to invade Scotland.

FROM the administration of such a governor as Wentworth, the presbyterians of Ulster had little ground to hope for relief. The course which he designed to pursue towards them was too plainly discovered in his interview with Blair, already described. The haughty deputy, just then entering on his government, treated the humble presbyter with contemptuous disdain; and though Blair produced the king's letter, it only increased his insolence. Instead of acting on his majesty's suggestion of giving the four ministers, unjustly suspended by Echlin, a fair trial, he reproached them for their non-conformity, reviled their parent church of Scotland, and refused to grant them the least indulgence. Disappointed in this quarter, to which they had been for some time anxiously looking for relief, the suspended brethren remained in the country and among their people. They flattered themselves with the hope of the government becoming more tolerant;

and though these expectations were far from being realised, several circumstances, in the mean time, led to a temporary relaxation of their sentence. Wentworth, by rigidly insisting on the fulfilment of the several covenants of plantation under which the northern colonists held their lands, had subjected them to great expense, and had even threatened to proceed to the forfeiture and seizure of their estates. By these measures he had raised, as might be expected, a considerable ferment in Ulster. The landed proprietors, including many of the nobility, were becoming more and more deeply irritated at his harassing proceedings. But lest they might prove intractable members of his first parliament, which he was then preparing to summon, he deemed it necessary to take such steps as, for a time at least, might appease their discontents, and allay their just apprehensions.[1] At this critical conjuncture, Lord Castlestewart, a zealous patron of the northern presbyterians,[2] having visited the deputy, he embraced the opportunity of interceding for the restoration of the suspended ministers. He suggested how acceptable such a measure would be to the Scottish planters, and how likely

[1] Straff. Lett. i. 199, 200. Blair's Life, p. 81.

[2] This was the second Lord Castlestewart. He was a baronet before his father's death, and is better known by the name of Sir Andrew Stewart. "He was a firm patron to all Scotchmen in Ireland, especially of the nonconforming ministers who had left Scotland on account of the articles of the Perth assembly." Lodge, vi. 243. None of his three sons left any male issue; and the title, after lying dormant for many years, was revived in the year 1775, in the descendants of his younger brother, Robert Stewart of the Irry, near Stewartstown, in the county of Tyrone. His presbyterianism afterwards exposed him to the suspicious jealousy of Wentworth, who, in a letter to the king in 1638, thus speaks of his Lordship;—"I shall observe your majesty's directions concerning my Lord Castlestewart. Howbeit, since I was with your majesty, I understand he is an absolute separatist, which moves not me to like him the better, or to judge him further from signing and swearing to their covenant, if he were in place." Straff. Lett. ii. 189. The heir apparent of this ancient title has latterly embraced the Roman Catholic religion;—a sad apostacy from the faith of his Irish ancestors!

it was to soothe their irritated feelings, and give them a more favourable idea of his character and government. Wentworth, anxious to avail himself of every expedient which might ensure a pliant and peaceable parliament, yielded to the request. But as his views extended no farther than to provide for the existing emergency, he consented to restore the ministers for a limited period only. He accordingly wrote, in the month of May 1634, to bishop Echlin, to withdraw, for six months, his sentence of suspension. The command was promptly obeyed. Blair, Livingston, Dunbar, and Welsh, were therefore once more restored to the exercise of their ministry.

"When the news of this unexpected freedom was brought to me," writes the former of these brethren, "I was so astonished, that I slept not for three nights thereafter. The first of these was wholly spent in admiration; the second in thanksgiving to God in fellowship with those of my charge who used solemnly to pray with me; and on the third night, we being now at full liberty to exercise our public ministry, and the ordinary day of my lecture at Bangor following next, I prepared for the work of that day; when I found a large congregation, consisting not only of my own flock, but also of many others from neighbouring congregations, who had come thither without any advertisement. To these I preached on Isaiah xxxviii. 15. 'What shall I say? He hath both spoken unto me, and himself hath done it.' At which time the people were melted down into tears of joy.—When the silenced ministers preached again," adds Blair, "at the monthly meeting, the joy of the people can hardly be expressed. The liberty prolonged to us was, through God's blessing, well improved by all; and the people made more progress in the ways of God than ever before." [3]

This general satisfaction was clouded by the death of two brethren, who had been most laborious and faithful, and who were highly esteemed by all for their work's sake. The for-

[3] Blair's Life, p. 81-2.

mer of these was Mr. Welsh of Templepatrick. During the period of his suspension, he maintained regular worship with his people in his own house; but his audience being too numerous to be accommodated within, he usually preached in the door-way, that he might be heard by those standing without. By this means he contracted a cold, which, terminating in consumption, carried him off after much suffering on Monday, the twenty-third of June, 1634, not more than a month after his restoration to the beloved exercise of the ministry. Both Livingston and Blair, with many other Christian friends, were with him when he died. "He had many gracious and edifying discourses," writes Livingston, "as also some wrestlings; one time when he had said, 'oh! for hypocrisy,' Mr. Blair said to the great company of Christians present, 'See how Satan knibbles at his heel, when he is going over the threshhold of heaven.' A little after, I being at prayer at the bed-side before him, and the word 'victory' coming out of my mouth, he took hold of my hand and desired me to cease a little, and clapped both his hands and cried out, 'victory, victory, victory for evermore!' and then desired me to go on in prayer, and within a short time he expired."[4] He left a son, John Welsh, worthy of the name, who rose to eminence in the Scottish church as minister of Irongray, and was one of those faithful ministers, who, after the Restoration, nobly suffered persecution for the truth's sake.

The other minister, whose death at this time cast a gloom over the brethren, was Mr. Stewart of Donegore. An ample and authentic narrative of the closing scenes of the life of this "grave and eminently godly minister in the church of Ireland," has been fortunately preserved.[5] It is written with such unaffected simplicity, and is so illustrative of the religious feelings and sentiments of this period, that no apology will be required for its insertion.

4 Liv. Life, p. 21.
5 Fleming's Fulf. of the Scrip. i. 444—6.

"Being called to the burial of that excellent man of God, Mr. Josiah Welsh, who was his neighbour minister, Mr. Stewart stood some time at the grave, as a sad observer of such a thing, and to some who were by, said, 'who knows who will be next?' but none answering, he said to them, 'I know,' and thus turned away, and went home to Dunagor on his foot, and entering into the church, did bolt the doors, where he tarried some two hours; and after going to his house, he fell asleep on his bed, with an excess of grief, whence he never in health rose again, but was buried that day month. When his wife returned, whom he had left with Mr. Welsh's widow, she inquired what he had been doing; to whom he said, 'I have been taking my leave of the church of Dunagor, and I was there taking timber and stones to witness, that in my short time I had laboured to be faithful, and that according to my light, I have revealed the whole counsel of God to the people.' How great a testimony of the conscience was this!

"After a fortnight's lying, Mr. Ridge, a choice English minister there, came to visit him and said, 'I hope, sir, you do not rue that ye have been faithful:' he answered, 'I rue nothing, but that I was too long in beginning, (he meant his resisting for several years a call to the ministry, to which he had been much pressed:) and I will tell you a strange thing which hath helped me to be faithful these last seven years;—there hath not one day passed me without thoughts of death, and renewed submission to it; yea, this made me neglect my body, which should have served the Lord, as if it had been the mire in the street, which now troubleth me.'

"That night when he died, several godly and grave Christians were with him, where for a long time he fell in a deep silence, which ended with heavy groanings often reiterated. At last, a Christian there desired to know what troubled him, but he refused to tell. At last, being urged, he said, 'I shall tell you, my hair stands to behold what I see coming on these lands.' And being further pressed, he said, 'The bloody wars of Germany shall never be balanced with the wars of these three kingdoms.' 'What do you speak, sir?' said one of the company; to whom he answered, 'The dead bodies of many thousands, who this day despise the glorious gospel, shall lie upon the earth as dung unburied.' And whilst they asked, 'What then shall become of us and our posterity?' he lifted up his voice and said, 'He that is for the sword, to the sword; he that is for captivity, to captivity; and he that is for famine, to famine; and God shall be avenged on these lands.' And whilst one said, 'Is there no remedy?' he cried thrice, 'No remedy, no remedy, no remedy!' Then he held his peace a little and said, 'I tell you what must be; the broken covenant of Scotland must be renewed, the formality of Ireland must be purged, the prodigality of England removed, and the sons of Saul hung up before the sun.' By these last words, none knew what he meant. Some of his own parish being present, asked what he would say to them; to whom he replied, 'Wo to thee, Dunagor, for the nettles and the long grass shall be in greater plenty in thee, than ever were people to hear the word of God.' This, his son was a witness to three years together, after the rebellion. They asked if he would have his children; he said, no, he had done with them; and whilst they mentioned one of his daughters, he desired to be forborn, and said she should see glorious days after all this. And then he takes his wife by the hand, who, having but a fortnight lain in of a child, crept out of the bed to get and give a long farewell, to whom he said, 'Thou hast in faithfulness suffered many things with me in my pilgrimage, and now wherewith shall I comfort thee, my love?'—think that he left her with four children, much debt contracted whilst he resisted a call to the ministry, and but thirty shillings sterling then, to do all with,—'a father to the fatherless, a judge to the widow, is God in his holy habitation; as God is God, thou shalt never want, nor none of thine, but in all the sad days that are coming, you shall be a wonder of mercy in every place whither you are carried, and not a hair of your head shall fall:' which was, to the edification and conviction of many, fully accomplished." He was buried beside his church in Donegore, where an humble tombstone still preserves the remembrance of this venerable minister. [6]

Scarcely had these faithful men been removed by death, when measures were taken for abridging the liberty which the suspended brethren were now enjoying. In the month of September, bishop Bramhall, always on the alert to suppress nonconformity, remonstrated with Wentworth against continuing the indulgence which he had so recently granted to those ministers, setting forth, no doubt, the necessity of upholding the authority of the church, and of reducing such refractory members to due subordination. In consequence of this interference, Wentworth, though entreated by Lord Castlestewart to extend their liberty for half a year longer, which he had at one time consented to do, now wrote to bishop Echlin to

6 It is worthy of notice, that for two centuries, the descendants of this faithful man have been among the most eminent ministers of the presbyterian church in Ireland. The reader has already learned (Note 18, chap. i.) that Mr. Stewart's son was minister of Donaghadee from the year 1645 to 1671. What became of his descendants I do not know; but his sister Janet, who was only seven years old when their father died, became the wife of the Rev. Thomas Crawford, who succeeded old Mr. Stewart, as minister of Donegore; in which charge he continued from the year 1646 till his death in December 1670. His son, the Rev. Andrew Crawford, was minister of Carnmoney beside Belfast, from 1694, till his death in June 1726. His son, the Rev. Thomas Crawford,—whose wife, by the way, was aunt to the celebrated authoress, Mrs. Elizabeth Hamilton,—was minister of Crumlin from the year 1724 till his death in July 1782. And lastly his son, the Rev. William Crawford, who was consequently great-great-grandson of Mr. Stewart whose death is recorded in the text, was minister first at Strabane and latterly at Holywood from the year 1766, till his death in the year 1801. With him the succession of ministers ceased. He was the author of "Remarks on Lord Chesterfield's Letters," and of a "History of Ireland," in two volumes. He also published two single sermons; and translations from the Latin of the younger Turretine's Dissertations on Natural Theology, in two volumes 8vo. While minister of Donegore I procured the tombstone, alluded to in the text, to be repaired and the letters renewed, that this memorial of my venerable predecessor may be perpetuated through another century.

renew his sentence of suspension on Blair and Dunbar, so soon as their former license should terminate. Accordingly, in the month of November, these brethren were once more compelled to abandon the public exercise of their ministry; "And so," relates Blair, "all hopes of further liberty having been cut off, we closed with celebrating the sacrament of the Lord's supper; and solemnly delivered up our people to the great Bishop of our souls, from whom we had received our charge."(7) They were then cited before the bishop for the third time, and sentence of deposition was formally pronounced against them. On this occasion the following remarkable conference took place between Blair and Echlin. It is now for the first time published from an authentic manuscript,(8) and is eminently entitled to occupy a place in ecclesiastical history, from the striking manner in which it illustrates and contrasts the dastardly spirit of the persecutor, and the unshrinking honesty and intrepidity of the confessor.

"*A conference betwixt the bishop of Down in Ireland, and a preacher there.*

"First at the bishop's house where the pastor, not thinking to meet with the bishop any more, resolved to be free with him, because the bishop had, in pretence of love, formerly given many counsels to him. If ye will follow my advice, said the Bishop, I will also follow yours. Content, said the Pastor, upon condition you will prove yours from Scripture, as I shall do mine.

"*P.* My counsel is, that you, who once had a gift of preaching, but now a long time hath deserted the work and embraced this present world, that you would return to your

7 Blair's Life, p. 82. Rawdon Papers, p. 15.

8 Bibl. Jurid. Edin. MS. Rob. iii. 3. 2. It is evidently written by Blair himself. I have modernized the spelling, as, to most of my readers, the old Scottish orthography would prove very perplexing; while so many specimens of the language of that period occur in other accessible works, that an additional one is not needed for philological purposes.

ministerial charge, especially seeing pulpits are emptied of your painful preachers.

"*B.* Seeing ye have often refused my counsel, I am not bound to follow yours.

"*P.* Goods and money are become your god. The reason why you would forbear us no longer, ye used to say was this, if ye should be questioned for forbearing of us, it would cost you as much as would marry one of your daughters. But now mark, I pray you, so long as ye did hold off from troubling of us, ye had no loss of your worldly estate; but now since ye have wronged God in falling on us his ministers, your god has been lighted upon, and what ye have lost since, ye know.

"*B.* I have indeed lost since, more nor ye trow; but had ye been in my place, I trow ye would have done no better.

"*P.* Your place! I would not be in your place for all the earth; for your place fits you only for ill and no good. And now let me tell you, whereas ye have some pretences against Mr. Livingston and myself, which the Lord knows are groundless, now ye are like to fall against Mr. Cunningham, against whom ye can find scarce any colour of a challenge. If ever ye put hand on his ministry, cast your cap at heaven, never to look for God's mercy. And further, I desire you in making up your accounts, to take notice that your reviling words against me had a great hand in the death of my wife, now in heaven.

"To which the bishop answered little, being astonished: only he said, Think ye to bring thy wife's death upon me? To which was replied, Look ye to it, it is true I tell you, and if I wished not your repentance, I would not thus warn you in private.

"So we parted, thinking never to meet again.

"Yet within a few days, the bishop cited the said preacher to compear before him at Belfast, there to be silenced. The bishop asked him if he could show any reason why he should not be silenced.

"*P.* You always blame us as contemners of lawful authority; now I retort upon you. There is a letter directed from his majesty to try a number of us concerning our doctrine and life, which ye have never yet done. If, therefore, ye proceed against me for not subscribing till ye take that trial as ye are enjoined, you are the contemner of the king's authority.

"*B.* That letter came never into my hands. Have you any more to say for yourself?

"*P.* Ye know well enough in whose hands it is. It is among you, and yet ye wilfully contravene it. Therefore albeit ye have not answered my first, I answer, secondly;—you blame us for violating your canons; this also I retort upon yourself. Ye have twice already sentenced me, and threaten now to do it the third time, without any canons authorizing you to do the same; for this kirk, as yet, has no canons at all.

"*B.* Aye, but I have the civil law for me.

"*P.* The execution of a civil law belongs to another court. You are to be regulated by your canons. Have you proceeded but even according to your own corrupt grounds? Yea, ye present also the civil law contrary to the intention thereof.

"*B.* I pray you, appeal from me.

"*P.* If ye knew that an appellation would be steadable to me, I doubt ye would give that counsel. But I have tried all these fords, and find them passable for whoredom, bloodshed, or any other crime.

"*B.* Have ye any more to say for yourself?

"*P.* I am not well begun yet, albeit ye have answered nothing to what I have said. The main thing that I allege is this, I am not yet convinced of any obstinate persisting in the breach of God's law, or violating the gospel of Jesus Christ.

"*B.* Oh! that is a long field; but I will be short with you. Have ye received the communion kneeling?

"*P.* No, neither ever think I so to do.

"*B.* What needeth more?

"*P.* I pray you, what command of the law or place of the gospel is thereby violated?

"*B.* Register, read the sentence. But yet I pray you over again, appeal from me.

"*P.* Well, seeing ye so much urge upon appellation, I will appeal indeed; and hereby I do appeal indeed to the tribunal of Christ my Lord, to whom I labour to be faithful; and there cite I you to appear, that ye may answer for your ill deeds of this kind, and for what ye are now going to do.

"*B.* I appeal also from justice to mercy, whereof ye have need as well as I.

"*P.* I have indeed great need of it, and am persuaded to find it. But as for you, who come to do such wickedness, see how ye tempt God, and forsake your mercy.

"To which no reply was made, but the sentence read; the pastor coming away rejoicing in the Lord. And the other citation, ere long, took effect, the bishop dying in fearful dumps of conscience."[9]

Echlin died on the 17th of July following, in considerable distress of mind. He was succeeded by Henry Leslie, dean of Down, a native of Scotland, and a man of considerable erudition, but a most violent and bigoted episcopalian. He

[9] Blair in his manuscript life relates the following anecdote respecting the bishop's death:—"Shortly thereafter he sickened; and when the physician, Dr. Maxwell, came to him and inquired what ailed him, he was long silent; and with great difficulty uttered these words, 'It is my conscience, man.' To which the doctor replied, 'I have no cure for that.' This report the doctor made to the old lord viscount of Airds, who discharged him to report the same to any other; but his daughter-in-law (the now lady viscountess of Airds) yet living, being then and there present when the doctor made the report, she replied, 'No man shall get this report suppressed; for I shall bear witness of it to the glory of God, who did smite the bishop for suppressing of Christ's ministers.'" This viscountess of Airds was the Lady Jean Alexander, eldest daughter of the first earl of Stirling mentioned in note (18) chap. iii. After the death of her husband, the second viscount Airds, she married major-general Monro, for several years commander of the Scottish forces in Ulster after the rebellion of 1641. She died in 1670.

was consecrated in Dublin on the fourth of October 1635, and was scarcely in his seat before he commenced the work of persecution. The first person on whom he exercised his newly acquired power was Livingston, who for some reason now unknown, had not been included by the late bishop in the sentence of deposition against the other three brethren, although he had shared with them in their other suspension. He was now, in the month of November, deposed by Leslie, and formally excommunicated by Melvin the minister of Downpatrick. Both he and Blair, however, still continued to discharge in private the duties of the ministry. The latter, it is related, "ordinarily preached in his own house, which was ordered by a discreet old servant, and sometimes in other houses among his friends and acquaintances, especially in Holywood, and sometimes he and his brethren did go into their churches. And as they had done formerly when deposed, so now they prayed with their people, and after one had read a chapter, they discoursed thereon by way of lecture." Livingston pursued a similar course. He resided chiefly at the house of his mother-in-law, Mrs. Stevenson,—"at the iron-furnace at Miloore,[10] twelve miles from Killinchy," where he preached almost every Sabbath. But "perceiving during the winter no appearance of liberty either to preachers or professors, from the bondage of prelacy," the presbyterians of Ulster determined to carry into effect the design of removing to New-England, which they had for some years been meditating. Encouraged by the governor and council of the infant colony, already planted in the new world, they commenced by building a ship, called the Eagle-wing, of one hundred and fifty tons burden,

10 This was Malone, near Belfast, where a Mr. Barr had iron-furnaces. The reader will find him mentioned in the subsequent chapter. Livingston's wife was the eldest daughter of Barth. Fleming, merchant in Edinburgh. Her mother, who was sister to Mr. Blair's first wife, was married secondly to Mr. John Stevenson, who removed with his family to Ireland, and settled at Malone in the end of the year 1633. Liv. Life, p. 22, 3.

at Groomsport on Belfast lough, intending to embark in the spring of the following year. But the preparations necessary for such a voyage, and the delays incident to an undertaking so serious in those days, retarded their departure until late in the season.

In the mean time, the number of their fellow-emigrants was increased by the violent measures of the new bishop of Down and Conner. He held his primary visitation at Lisburn in the month of July; and agreeably to the order of the late convocation, he required from his clergy their subscription of the canons. On this occasion five of the ministers refused to comply, and assigned their reasons. These were Mr. Brice of Broadisland, Mr. Ridge of Antrim, Mr. Cunningham of Holywood, Mr. Colvert of Oldstone, and Mr. Hamilton of Ballywalter. The bishop, impressed with the importance of retaining these men in the church, of which they were among the most zealous and influential ministers, held, on this occasion, a private conference with them, in the hope of inducing them to relinquish their scruples, and promise conformity to the canons. This attempt, however, proving ineffectual, he was urged by bishop Bramhall to proceed forthwith to their deposition. He accordingly summoned his clergy to meet him in the church at Belfast on the tenth of August. The bishop opened the business of this memorable visitation by preaching from the ominous text,—"But if he neglect to hear the church, let him be unto thee as an heathen man and a publican." Matt. xviii. 17.[11]

[11] Soon after this discourse was preached, the bishop committed it to the press, and it was published early in the following year. It is entitled "A Treatise of the Authority of the Church, the summe whereof was delivered in a Sermon preached at Belfast at the visitation of the Diocese of Downe and Conner, the tenth day of August 1636. By Henrie Leslie, bishop of the Diocese; together with an Answer to certain Objections made against the Orders of our Church, especially kneeling at the Communion." Dublin, 1637, 4to. pp. 190. It is dedicated in a strain of fulsome panegyric to Wentworth, and, prefixed to it, is an address in Latin verse, not very complimentary to the presbyterians, by Robert Maxwell, archdeacon of Down. At the recommendation of Dr. George Hicks,

In this elaborate discourse, which is not without distinguished merit as a controversial disquisition, and which contains many undeniable truths forcibly expounded, after illustrating the context, he maintains that by "the church," is not meant, the multitude of believers, nor the Jewish court of elders, nor the civil magistrate, nor the pope, nor a general council, but the prelates. He proceeds to show that the church had power "to keepe and propound the sacred oracles—to ordayne ministers—to decide controversies—to enact ceremonies—and to censure offenders." In the discussion of these topics it is occasionally difficult to believe that the writer is a protestant, or to discover the difference between his reasoning and that of a Jesuit Romanist pleading for the authority of the papal church. He treats the non-conforming portion of his clergy with little ceremony. Speaking of the church's power "to ordain ministers, appoint them their stations, and direct them in the exercises of their function," he indulges in the following rude and disdainful recrimination.—"Hee that will take upon him the office of a minister, not being called by the church, [that is, of course, by the prelates] is an intruder and a thief that commeth not in by the doore, but climbeth up another way. What will you say to some Dominees heere amongst you, who having no ordination to our calling, have taken upon them to preach,—and preach I know not what, even the foolish visions of their owne heart. As they runne when none hath sent them, and runne very swiftly, because like Ahimaaz, they runne by the way of the plaine, so like Ahimaaz when they are come, they have no tydings to tell but doleful news. They think by their puff of preaching to blowe downe the goodly orders of our church, as the walls of Jericho were beaten downe with sheepes hornes. Good God! is not this the sinne of Uzziah, who intruded himselfe into the office of the priest-

this treatise was republished, with a few other tracts, in defence of the English Church, in a volume entitled, "Bibliotheca Scriptorum Ecclesiæ Anglicanæ." London, 1709, 8vo.

hood? And was there ever the like heard amongst Christians, except the Anabaptists, whom some amongst you have matcht in all manner of disordered confusion?"

The principal object of the discourse is to vindicate the power of the church, asserted in the English articles, to make laws and decree ceremonies in the administration of divine worship. The ministers having objected, in particular, to the ceremony of kneeling at the communion, as a most obnoxious relic of popery, and wholly unwarranted by Scripture, he endeavours, at great length, to prove that Christ did not sit at the celebration of his Supper, and that, even if he did, his disciples were not bound to adopt that posture. The presbyterians, on the contrary, maintained the scriptural obligation of using a table-gesture in the observance of the ordinance. In reply, the bishop absurdly reasons that, if they adopted the gesture, they were bound to introduce the other peculiarities, of an ordinary feast; and he thus insolently upbraids them for their alleged inconsistency. "Then why doe yee not receive the Sacrament in your dyning roomes? for the church is not a fit place to eate and drinke in. Why doe you not salute and welcome one another before you sit downe, as the manner is at civill feasts? Why doe you not use trenchers, napkins, knives, as well as stooles? Why doe you not eate a full meale, feede heartily, drinke oftner then once, and pledge one another? For all these doe belong to a liberal and honourable intertainment, such as your authors say must be in the sacrament. I am sure it is as farre from honourable intertainment, and the prerogative of guests, to receive but one bit of bread, and one drop of wine, as it is eyther to stand or to kneele. Why doe you not intertaine discourse one with another? And especially why doe you not keepe on your hats,[12] as at other feasts, that so

[12] It is curious that about ten years after this period, Nye and the other independent teachers insisted on the necessity of all male communicants *keeping on their hats* at the time of participation. *See* Baillie's *Letters*, vol. i. p. 440, and his *Dissuasive*, p. 122. (Lond. 1646.)

you may bee, every man, jacke-fellow-like with Christ in your social communions? I am afraid it will come to this at last, by that time your people have learned all the mysteries of your religion."

In vindicating the power of the church to censure offenders, he thus enumerates the errors maintained by the non-conforming clergy, and thence infers the necessity of cutting them off with the sword of discipline. "Surely as the Lord taxeth the angel of the church of Thyatira, for suffering the woman Jezabel to teach and deceive God's servants; so may hee reprove the governors of our church, for suffering this feminine heresie so long, they of that sexe being the greatest zealots, and chiefe abbettors of the sect, by whom many simple people are deceived, and led from the wholesome pastures of the church to wander in the precipices of schisme.[13] This must

[13] This is a frequent subject of complaint with the bishop. We meet with it in the dedication of his sermon to Wentworth. So extensive was the spread of presbyterianism in his diocese that he thinks it necessary to point out to the deputy the causes of its extraordinary prevalence. Among these he enumerates the exemplary holiness of the ministers, their diligence in preaching, their fidelity in rebuking the vices of the great, &c. The last cause which he assigns is thus stated: "But the special means whereby they have advanced their faction, is by insinuating into the weaker sexe in whom there is least ability of judgment. By this means the serpent overcame mankind; he first tempted the woman, and by her seduced Adam. By this means the Philistines overcame Sampson; they ploughed with his heifer, and so found out his riddle. And this indeed hath been the common practise of all heriticks; as the Jews stirred certaine devout and honourable women to resist Paul. These new Gospellers make use of such instruments to oppose the church, and for the most part their proselytes are of that sexe, as if their generative vertue were so weake that they could beget none but daughters. Now to search a little into the cause of this: Besides the weaknesse of their judgment to discerne between truth and error, and the naturall inclination which is in women to pitty; two things especially make them in love with that religion; one is, it is naturall unto the daughters of Eve to desire knowledge, and those men puff them up with an opinion of science, inabling them to prattle of matters of divinity, which they and their teachers understand much alike: insomuch that albeit St. Paul hath forbidden women to speake in the church, yet they speake of church-matters more than comes to their share.

not be suffered any longer. But you will say, the difference is only about small matters, and it is a pitty to deprive ministers who are paineful and laborious, for a ceremony. For answer, I shall desire you to consider, that they doe not onely oppose the ceremonies, but the whole liturgie of the church, wherein the soul of God's publicke worship doth consist. Besides, their doctrine is not sound: for they have taught that the order of bishops is antichristian, which we know to be apostolicke: that our ceremonies are damnable, which we can prove to bee both lawful and decent: that our service-book is a heap of errors, which we can justify to be the most absolute liturgie that any church in the world hath: that the signe of the cross in baptisme, and kneeling in the act of receiving the communion, is plaine idolatry, then which, hell itself could not have devised a more shamelesse calumnie: that the Eucharist being a supper and a feast, no gesture should be used at it, but a table-gesture, to express our coheirship and equality with Christ, which if it smell not strong of Arianisme, I have lost my sent: that all festivall dayes, besides the Lord's day, and all set fasts are Jewish, and contrary to our Christian liberty; which is the condemned heresie of Aerius. They have cryed downe the most wholesome orders of the church as popish superstitions, namely, confirmation of children, absolution of penitents, private baptisme of children in case of necessity, the communion of the sick, and almost whatsoever hath any conformity with the ancient

The other is, a desire of liberty and fredome from subjection; for these teachers allow them to be at least quarter-masters with their husbands, insomuch that I have not observed that faction to prevaile but where husbands have learned to obey their wives, and where will and affection weare the breeches. There is a civill constitution in the authentickes against women who would not receive the holy and adorable communion, that they should lose their douries or jointures; which if it were in force in this kingdome, I think some of our ladies would not be so stiff-kneed, choosing rather to goe without that blessed sacrament, than receive it kneeling."—The influence of the female sex in promoting the cause of Gospel truth and freedom, in almost all ages and countries, merits a much more extended illustration than it has yet received.

church. If I were not weary to dig in this dung-hill, I could shew you many such *portenta opinionum*, which these new masters have vented to the great scandal of the church, and hinderance of religion, that I may complain with the prophet, *pastores multi*, yea, and *stulti*, many pastors have destroyed my vineyard." The following singular observation, with the exception of a brief exhortation to peace and submission, concludes the bishop's discourse :—" It is said, that when Cain was cast out from the presence of God, that is from his church and the place of his worship, he went and dwelt in the land of Nod. So you, when you are cast out of the church, are preparing to goe and dwell in the land of Noddies, and it is strange if the sides of one ship can contayne them, who cannot be kept within the pale of the church."(14)

This characteristic discourse being ended, the five nonconforming ministers were called forward. The bishop complained that the result of his former confidential conference with them having been misrepresented, and the victory, in point of argument, attributed to them, he would not again converse with them in private. But he now proposed to debate the matter openly in the church on the following day, when he would defend all that was required by the canons. This offer was at once accepted by the brethren; and Mr. Hamilton, who had been a member of the convocation, was appointed by them to conduct the conference in their name. Accordingly, on Thursday, the eleventh of August, this singular and interesting discussion commenced, in the presence of a large assemblage of the nobility, gentry, and clergy of the diocese. It was conducted according to the forms of syllogistic reasoning; and displays great readiness and acuteness on the part of Hamilton, and more moderation on that of the bishop, than could have been anticipated from his sermon. Bramhall was present to encourage his brother pre-

14 Leslie's Treatise, &c., pp. 23. 63, 4. 86, 7, 8. and 106. 'Noddy' is the old word for simpleton, so that the bishop's wretched witticism upon 'the land of noddies,' is not very complimentary to his native country.

late; and he occasionally mingled in the discussion, but in a very arrogant and disorderly manner. As it too often happens in public debates, the controversy merged into the discussion of some of the less important points of difference. It therefore by no means affords a favourable view of the grounds, on which the ministers refused the required conformity. The debate was maintained with good temper and great spirit for several hours. But Bramhall, resenting the liberty afforded the ministers, suddenly interrupted the conference, and Leslie immediately adjourned the meeting, first to the afternoon, and then to the following morning. An ample account of this singular debate, never before published, may be found in the appendix.[15] In the mean time, Leslie was prevailed upon, by the bishop of Derry, not to resume the discussion, but to proceed in a summary way to pass sentence on the ministers. Accordingly, when the meeting was assembled on the morning of Friday, the brethren found themselves deprived of any further opportunity of stating their objections; and as they continued, with unshrinking firmness, to refuse all subscription to the canons, the bishop proceeded to pronounce the sentence of their deposition. The following narrative of the occurrences of this eventful day, appended to the account of the debate already mentioned, is too interesting to be withheld.

"Friday, the 12th day of August, at 9 o'clock in the forenoon, 1636. The bishop called before him Mr. Ridge, &c. and said to this effect,—

"My masters, I thought to have gained you to our church, and was willing to have taken the more pains upon you. But now I am informed, I went further in allowing a public dispute to you than I can justify by law; so that I must not go on in that kind. Yet if you find yourselves satisfied with

15 See Appendix, No. ii. where this account is printed from an accurate collation of three copies, preserved in the Advocates' Library, Edinburgh.

that which is said, so be that ye resolve to subscribe, I am content you write to the full all that ye have to say, and I will answer you, and fully refer what shall be said, to the judgment of any university in Europe. Only it is expedient that we avoid bitterness; and for the present, if ye conform not yourselves to the order of our church, I must and will proceed to read your sentence, sore against my will, God knows. Yet mistake me not. This is for love to your persons, which I so much affect, that I protest my born brother should not have had more favour than ye have gotten. But it is not for love of that cause. My conscience assures me, that your cause is wrong. I wish that all that are here present should know that I love your persons, but hate your cause. What can ye say for yourselves, that I should not pronounce sentence against you?

"Mr. Ridge answered: We acknowledge that you, for your part, did give us a fair hearing yesterday for a space. We were hopeful to have been heard to the full. But since you protest that you cannot do that, I protest that doubts, concerning the matters urged, are so great, that I cannot subscribe unto the same.

"*Bishop.* Mr. Ridge, melancholy causeth many fears. A melancholy man will be afraid of his own shadow; and you are, and have been, a melancholian.

"*Mr. Ridge.* Melancholy is a natural cause, and cannot work spiritual effects; it cannot give light in spiritual things. I am ready to give reasons of abstinence. Besides, I find no fears upon me in any other things. If I were led by fears, methinks the fear of losing my means, my liberty, my estimation, and to be called a contemner of the laws, as we most undeservedly are called, should draw me to conform, and not be run upon these things that are fearful to one who is filled with natural fears.

"The bishop passing him, said to Mr. Hamilton: What say you for yourself, that I may not pass sentence against you?

"Mr. Hamilton answered: I hoped we should have had

a fair proceeding and hearing this day, as we got at your hand in some measure, yesterday.

" *Bishop.* I must not go on in that kind of hearing.

" *Hamilton,* [resuming the subject of debate on the preceding day,] said: Well, since there wants nothing, in kneeling at communion, of perfect idolatry, but the idolatrous intent and the idolatrous opinion, as was confessed yesterday; and seeing never one will confess an idolatrous intent, I think we have little reason to justify it by subscription. For what know we when the intent may change, the heart being so changeable; in the mean time the cause shall stand justifiable by my subscription. And as for the idolatrous opinion; though in the days of King Edward the Sixth, at which time the declaration was made, which was read here yesterday in public audience, they were free from the real presence of the body of Christ in the sacrament; yet the doctrine goes not now, as it did then. For yourself knows, that both in court and country, it is both preached and printed by many, that there is a real presence, which they will not let be discussed, whether it be bodily or spiritual, but people must content themselves with the general. Sure I am, that he that kneels had need to take heed to it, when these opinions are a-stirring, there being a safer course—to receive without kneeling.

" *Bishop.* It is true, indeed, some preach a real presence of the body of Christ, whereby they mean a spiritual presence of the body of Christ; albeit I confess they speak improperly. For the real presence of Christ's body must be bodily, for a thing is said to be present 'secundum esse rei.' Yet they, by real presence, mean, not an opposition to the spiritual and mystical presence; but an imaginary presence, because the papists accuse us, that we acknowledge no further than an imaginary presence of Christ's body.

" *Hamilton.* We all agree upon a spiritual presence; but these late writers will not have it inquired how he is present. But we have need, as we would avoid idolatry, to avoid kneeling; lest with such opinions the idolatrous worship be completed:—I say, when such opinions are stirring, all kneelers had need to beware.

"*Bishop*. Though now ye oppose kneeling, I knew you were once of another mind in Dublin.

"*Hamilton*. I would to God I had leisure to express my mind concerning that which I did at that time. Yet this much shortly:—I take God to witness, that I always desired the reformation of these things which now we oppose. And even then, when I practised kneeling in Dublin, it was the great desire I had to speak for reformation thereof, that made me do as I did.(16) For being called to be a member of that synod, where I hoped to get liberty to speak my mind in these matters, I straited my soul in the beginning, and forced myself to do as I did, (with an assembly that had prejudice of me and the cause,) upon the same intent and ground, as I then conceived, upon which Paul in Acts, xxi. chap. offered an offering and shaved his head, because those that were there assembled had a prejudicate opinion of him and his ministry. And I am sure Paul would not have done it the second time, and no more durst I. Yet when I compared my practices with Paul's, I found that I had done much more unwarrantably than he did, and was sorry for it.

"*Bishop*. Mr. Hamilton, can you say any farther why I should not give sentence against you for not consenting to the orders of our church? They have all the conditions that church constitutions ought to have. They are few and plain, and are significant.

"*Hamilton*. Add, I pray, that they are not scandalous.

"*Bishop*. It is you that takes the scandal: there is none gives you it.

"*Hamilton*. Yea, there is occasion of scandal, because there is an occasion of falling laid in the way, contrary to Rom. xiv. 13.

16 This was on occasion of the convocation publicly receiving the communion kneeling, in the cathedral at Dublin, in 1634.

" *Bishop.* I told you already, that that chapter was made before canons were made, not to stop the power of the church constitutions; for the apostle would not have said so, if the church canons had been made.

" *Hamilton.* If that chapter hinders me to damn myself, and if the 1 Cor. viii. chap. stops me to 'destroy him with my meat for whom Christ died;' then those two chapters were written to that effect, that all Christians might have the benefit of them, and privilege by them, to the end of the world. For it can never be lawful for fulfilling any church constitutions to make a man damn himself, or 'destroy him for whom Christ died.'

" *Bishop.* Do you say, that one for whom Christ died, can be destroyed?

" *Hamilton.* I speak in the phrase of the Holy Ghost; and this I say, that you, by the rigorous pressing of kneeling, may do what in you lies, to destroy him for whom Christ died.

" *Bishop.* Mr. Hamilton, you shall reason no more here at this time. I must not give you way to reason. If you have any thing to say, write your mind, and I shall answer it. What say you to it?

" *Hamilton.* If I may be preserved from peril of law, I will take your offer into consideration. In the mean time, in regard all our desire is to prevent arising idolatry, and that we have pleaded our privilege out of Rom. xiv. and 1 Cor. viii. throughout; and ye do not give us the benefit of our privilege therein contained, alleging that your hands are bound up by church constitutions which ye must see fulfilled, we appeal from your judgment to the first free, lawful, synod of this kingdom.

" *Bishop.* Enter his appeal.

" Then said Thomas Taylor, register, he cannot have the benefit of an appeal, unless he subscribe the first four canons, which he refuses to do.

" *Bishop.* God forbid that he or any man else should be

hindered to appeal, either from a national or general council. If we were stopped from our appealing, then were our Christian liberty taken away indeed. Then was the appeal entered.

"*Bishop.* Hear your sentence. And so he read the five several sentences of perpetual silence within his diocese;—first, against Mr. Brice; secondly, against Mr. Colwart; thirdly, against Mr. Cunningham.

"Then Mr. Hamilton desired to speak one word, which being granted, he said; we are sentenced for not subscribing books which we did never see with our eyes, nor cannot by any means come by. I protest that I myself have been at charges this twelvemonth in seeking them in London and Dublin, and could not, upon any terms, have them. And let any judge if we should be silenced for not subscribing them?

"*Bishop.* What books mean you?

"*Hamilton.* The books of homilies.

"*Bishop.* They are as good books as are in the world, except the Bible.

"*Hamilton.* If I would subscribe any book upon good report, I would subscribe them. But no churchman should subscribe whole books which he did never see, nor peruse, upon report only.

"*Bishop.* Had you alleged this excuse half a year ago, it had been sufficient; I should upon my own charges have gotten them to you. But now this allegation cannot avail you. Hear your sentence. And so he read the like sentence, fourthly, against Mr. Hamilton; and, lastly, against Mr. Ridge.

"After the sentence was read, Mr. Cunningham spake to this effect.—I have now lived these twenty years amongst you in this kingdom, serving the Lord in his holy ministry; and thought so to have spent out the rest of my days (which cannot be long, for my body is very crased) in the same employment. My doctrine and life, for that time, are known to most who are here present. I appeal to all their consciences if they can say any thing against me in either of them. Yea, I ever kept me close to the commission of my Lord; but now I am required to receive impositions upon my ministry which are against my conscience. I rather lay down my ministry at the feet of my Lord and Saviour Christ, of whom I did receive it, than to live with an evil conscience at the free liberty of it.

"At these words, most of them who were present declared the grief of their hearts by their sad countenance; and divers burst out into weeping, not being able to contain themselves.

"But the bishop replied to this purpose:—Mr. Cunningham, I confess your life and doctrine hath both been good. But I must say to you that which was said to a certain man at Rome, who was to be put to death for a mutiny. Some pleaded for his life, alleging that he had done good service to the commonwealth, and could do more afterwards. But one of the council replied, 'non opus est reipublicæ eo cive, qui parere nescit.' And so say I to you, 'the church hath no need of those who cannot tell how to obey.'

"With that he speedily arose and went away, while Mr. Colwart was addressing himself to speak, who much grieved that he was never heard."

In this summary manner were these faithful ministers, sound in doctrine, unblemished in morals, eminent in piety and abundant in labours, deposed from their office, deprived of their support, and ultimately obliged to abandon the kingdom. The other ministers in the diocese who were of similar principles, and who still constituted the majority of the clergy, not possessing the courage or integrity of these brethren, signed the canons, and formally engaged to yield the required conformity. But, in the seclusion of their parishes, they continued to retain the former modes of worship, to which their people were so firmly attached. Oppressive, therefore, as was the conduct of Leslie, it was of little avail, either to advance the cause of prelacy, or to remove the leaven of presbyterianism, with which his diocese was so extensively pervaded. It afforded, however, another instructive proof of the inefficacy of coercive measures to produce more than a mere external and hypocritical conformity.

These severe proceedings hastened the intended voyage to New England. The presbyterian laity were now thoroughly convinced, that it was their duty to abandon this country, in which their religious privileges were so flagrantly violated. In the midst of their preparations for this purpose, one of the silenced brethren was removed by death. Brice of Broad-island scarcely survived his deposition. He returned from the visitation at Belfast, oppressed with the thoughts of being compelled to resign the beloved exercise of his ministry; and before any steps could be taken by Leslie to carry his sentence into effect, this venerable minister resigned both life and office into the hands of the great 'Shepherd and Bishop of souls.' (17)

The number of the intended emigrants, and their preparations for the voyage, were at length completed. This little colony, who were about to settle in the uncultivated wilds of America, for the sake of enjoying liberty of conscience, were one hundred and forty in number. Among them were Mr. Blair, Mr. Livingston, Mr. Robert Hamilton, and Mr. John M'Clelland, afterwards ministers in Scotland, John Stuart, provost of Ayr, captain Andrew Agnew, Charles Campbell, John Sumervil, Hugh Brown, together with many families and single persons, among whom was Andrew Brown, the deaf mute from the parish of Larne, already mentioned.

17 The following is a copy of the inscription on his tomb-stone: "Neare this lyeth the body of that faithful and emenent servant of God, Mr. Edward Brice, who begun preaching of the gospel in this parish, 1613, continuing with quiet success while 1636, in which he dyed, aged 67, and left two sons and two daughters."—His descendants have attained to considerable wealth and eminence. The original family property at Kilroot, between Carrickfergus and Ballycarry, is still possessed by them.

"We had much toil in our preparations," writes Livingston in his graphic narrative of the events of this voyage, "and many hindrances in our outsetting, and both sad and glad hearts in taking leave of our friends. At last, about the ninth of September 1636, we loosed from Loch-Fergus, but were detained sometime with contrary winds in Loch-Ryan in Scotland, and grounded the ship to search some leaks in the keels of the boat. Yet thereafter we set to sea, and for some space had a fair wind, till we were between three and four hundred leagues from Ireland, and so nearer the banks of Newfoundland than any place of Europe. But if ever the Lord spake by his winds and other dispensations, it was made evident to us, that it was not his will that we should go to New England. For we met with a mighty heavy rain out of the north-west, which did break our rudder, which we got mended [by the skill and courage of captain Andrew Agnew, a godly passenger,](18) with much of our gallon-head, and fore-cross-trees, and tore our foresail, five or six of our champlets, a great beam under the gunner-room door broke. Seas came in over the round-house, and broke a plank or two on the deck, and wet all them that were between the decks. We sprung a leak that gave us seven hundred strokes in two pumps in the half-hour glass. Yet we lay at hull a long time to beat out the storm, till the master and company came one morning, and told it was impossible to hold out any longer; and although we beat out that storm, yet we might be sure in that season of the year we would foregather with one or two more of that sort before we could reach New England." After prayer, and much anxious consultation in this emergency, they all agreed to return. "The next morning, so soon as we saw day, we turned and made good way with a main course and a little of a fore-top sail; and after some tossing, we came at last, on the third of November, to an anchor in Loch-Fergus.

18 This clause in brackets, is supplied out of a manuscript life of Mr. Livingston. James Blair says, that the rudder was repaired by a common seaman.

"During all this time, amidst such fears and dangers, the most part of the passengers were very cheerful and confident; yea, some in prayer had expressed such hopes, that rather than the Lord would suffer such a company in such sort to perish, if the ship should break, he should put wings to our shoulders and carry us safe ashore. I never in my days found the day so short as all that time, although I slept some nights not above two hours, and some none at all, but stood most part in the gallery astern the great cabin, where Mr. Blair and I and our families lay. For in the morning, by the time that every one had been some while alone; and then at prayer in their several societies, and then at public prayer in the ship, it was time to go to dinner; and after that, we would visit our friends in the gunner-room, or those between the decks, or any that were sick, and then public prayer would come, and after that, supper and family exercises. Mr. Blair was much of the time sickly, and lay in time of storm. I was sometimes sick, and then my brother, Mr. M'Clelland only performed duty in the ship: several of those between the decks, being throng, were sickly. An aged person and one child died, and were buried in the sea. One woman, the wife of Michael Colvert of Killinchy parish, brought forth a child in the ship; I baptized him on Sabbath following, and called him *Seaborn*. Our outward means were much impaired by this disappointment, for we had put most of our stocks in provision, and somewhat of merchandise, which we behoved to sell at low rates at our return; and had provided ourselves with some servants, for fishing and building of houses, whom we behoved to turn off. That which grieved us most was, that we were like to be a mocking to the wicked; but we found the contrary, that the prelates and their followers were much dismayed and feared at our return.[19] But neither they nor we knew that, within a year,

19 They did not altogether escape being ridiculed and mocked on account of the unsuccessful issue of their voyage. Archdeacon Maxwell, in the

the Lord would root out the prelates out of Scotland, and after that, out of England and Ireland. Mr. Blair went and dwelt at the Stoue in Belfast;[20] others elsewhere. I came back and remained at my mother's house, and preached each Sabbath that winter, as I had done before."

The ministers were not permitted to enjoy their privacy long. "After about four months' continuance in that way, one Frank Hill of Castlereagh, who used to come sometimes to meetings, wherein Mr. Blair and Mr. Livingston preached, went to Dublin and informed the state: whereupon a warrant was issued out against them. But the effect of it was mercifully disappointed thus. One Andrew Young, servant to Mr. Barr, who lived nigh Mr. Livingston's house, being occasionally in Dublin, overheard a pursuivant give orders to provide horses for him and another, who were to set out next day for the north, to bring up two deposed ministers. Upon this he immediately called for his own horse; and continuing his journey homeward with all speed, night and day, gave information of what he had heard; whereby the designs against those ministers were frustrated. For immediately

address prefixed to Leslie's sermon, mentioned in a preceding note, No. (11.) thus insults over their return:—

> En navem* Arcadicâ properantem merce; gravatam
> Mole suâ: miratur onus Neptunus, et undis
> Insolitum prohibet pecus, atque remisit, et unà
> Ruditus veteres, vetus in mendacia virus.
> Et quasi lusa istis divina potentia nugis,
> Majus in opprobrium, velis invexit eisdem
> Quos simulant, ipsos per anomala dogmata, Asellos.†

* Argos puritanica.

† Hæc navis genuinos etiam asinos ex secundo partu è Galliâ nobis effudit.

20 In a manuscript copy which I have seen of Livingstone's life, this place is called "the Strone." The correct word will probably be found to be "the Strand at Belfast." I may add, that the latter part of Livingston's statement in the text, is thus corroborated by Blair;—"They were allowed to live in peace for some time; and did occupy themselves, sometimes in preaching and lecturing privately and exhorting their people, as God gave them opportunity." Life, p. 88.

they went out of the way and came over to Scotland, whither several other deposed ministers came about the same time."

The western parts of Scotland became, at this period, a seasonable asylum for the oppressed people of Ulster. Many attempts were indeed made by the Scottish bishops, now in the plenitude of their power, to prevent this influx of persons whom they knew to be opposed to their arrogant authority, but without success. Numbers removed thither, compelled to abandon Ireland, where fines and other punishments began to be inflicted without mercy on the non-conforming laity. These strangers in their native land, sojourned principally in the shires of Ayr and Galloway, where they were harboured, and many of them kindly entertained by the faithful people of that country. In particular, one Fergus M'Cabbin, of the district of Carrick in Ayrshire, deserves to be noticed for his eminent and seasonable hospitality to the Irish refugees. "Being left a considerable patrimony by his father, and being able, he was at that time a Gaius, and entertained ministers and professors coming from Ireland, as if he had been appointed a public inn for them, and that not for a night or week, but ordinarily; insomuch, that his natural friends said, he would presently exhaust his estate with such dealing. But he professed and found the contrary, that he grew richer, and it always prospered better with him, not only then, but to his dying day. As this was a mercy to him, so it was a special mercy to them who were entertained by him, and encouraged others to do the like."(21) The celebrated David

21 Adair's MS. As this is the first reference I have occasion to make to this valuable manuscript, from which so many important extracts are afterwards made, I may here give the reader some account of it. It is entitled, "A true Narrative of the Rise and Progress of the Presbyterian Government in the North of Ireland; and of the various troubles and afflictions, the ministers and people adhering to that way, did meet with from the adversaries thereof; and of their constant adherence thereunto, notwithstanding. Faithfully collected from the records of the Presbytery." With the exception of one or two Session and Presbytery books of little value to the historian, it is the only record of the Presbyterian church prior to

Dickson, minister at Irvine, afterwards a distinguished ornament and pillar of the church of Scotland, was also conspicuous for his attentions to the exiled brethren. Blair, Livingston, Cunningham, and Ridge, were liberally entertained by him and his people for a considerable time; and though at no little hazard to himself, he occasionally permitted them to preach—a privilege for which they were especially grateful.

The two latter of these brethren died here in the midst of their troubles and privations. Livingston thus narrates the circumstances of the death of that truly good man, Mr. Cunningham. "While we were at Irvine, the Lord called home sweet Mr. Robert Cunningham, minister at Holywood, on March 29th, 1637; for both he and all the rest of the deposed ministers were forced to fly out of Ireland. He had many gracious expressions of the Lord's goodness to him, and his great peace in regard of the cause of his sufferings. Besides many other gracious expressions, he said, 'I see Christ standing over Death's head, and saying, deal warily with my servant, loose now this pin, then that pin, for this tabernacle must be set up again.' The members of the presbytery, [of

the Revolution, existing in Ireland. It extends from the Plantation of Ulster, to the end of the year 1670. Blanks, which were unfortunately never filled up, are left in several places, for the insertion of extracts from the minutes and published papers of the church, now, it is to be feared, irrecoverably lost. It was compiled by the Rev. Patrick Adair, probably son of the Rev. William Adair, minister of Ayr, one of the brethren who administered the covenant to the Presbyterians of Ulster in the year 1644. See chapter x. Patrick Adair was minister first at Cairncastle, near Larne, in the county of Antrim, where he was ordained in the year 1646; and latterly at Belfast, where he died in the early part of the year 1694. During this long period, he was one of the most active and zealous ministers of the Presbyterian church, and enjoyed ample opportunities of obtaining the most correct information. He married the youngest daughter of Sir Robert Adair of Ballymena, by Jane, daughter of Archibald Edmonstone of Redhall; a connexion which also served to enlarge his knowledge of the affairs of Ulster. This manuscript and its author, are noticed at some length in that well-known, but,—so far as historical information is concerned,—most meagre volume, "Presbyterian Loyalty," pp. 165-7.

Irvine,] having made him a visit, he exhorted them to be faithful to God and his cause, and to oppose the service-book which was then urged by the bishops. 'The bishops,' said he, 'have taken my ministry from me, and I may say my life, for my ministry is dearer to me than my life.' A little before his death, his wife sitting on a couch at his bedside, with his hand in hers, he did, by prayer, recommend the whole church, the work of God in Ireland, the parish of Holywood, his suffering brethren in the ministry, and his children, to God. And in the end, he said, 'O Lord, I recommend unto thee this gentlewoman, who is no more my wife;' and with that saying, he softly loosed his hand from hers, and gently thrust her hand a little from him; upon which she, and some others in the company, having fallen a-weeping, he endeavoured, by gracious expressions, to allay their grief, and after a while, he slept in the Lord."(22) Thus was another life sacrificed on the altar of ecclesiastical conformity; nor did its votaries, the prelates, urged on by the despotic deputy, cease to persecute their victims, till the fairest province of the kingdom was almost depopulated, and not Ireland alone, but the whole empire, involved in the miseries of intestine war.

22 Livingston's Life, pp. 29 and 75-6. The following inscription, written by Blair, was engraved on his tomb-stone in the church-yard at Irvine. Life, p. 89.

"Hic Cunninghami recubat Roberti
Corpus. O qualis genius latebat,
Quam divinus fragili involutus,
Pulvere in isto!
Acrius nemo intonuit superbis;
Nemo dejectos magis erigebat;
Sed Dei laudes celebrando, vicit
Seque aliosque."

I have given this epitaph as it stands in the printed "Life." The classical reader will perceive the want of a syllable in the third line. This deficiency, a learned friend suggests, might be supplied by adding *quæ* to the first word of the line, which was probably written *quamq.* and the abbreviated particle omitted by the transcriber.

Wentworth, having obtained from his obsequious parliament the unconditional supplies he demanded, and, from the English court, the extraordinary powers necessary to conduct his administration without domestic control, did not permit his authority to remain long dormant. He immediately commenced the vigorous prosecution of those plans which he had been meditating, for augmenting the revenues, and extending the power, of the crown in Ireland. These favourite objects he pursued in the most arbitrary manner, with a disregard of the acknowledged rights of the subject, scarcely ever equalled by the most imperious or despotic sovereign. In prosecuting the Western plantation, formerly projected, he hesitated not to confiscate the entire province of Connaught, though the proprietors, under patents from the crown, had long enjoyed undisturbed possession of their estates. The ingenuity of the court-lawyers discovered defects in their titles sufficient to render them invalid in the eyes of the rapacious deputy, who lost no time in carrying into effect this daring plan of spoliation. Juries were summoned in the several counties, who pronounced the king's title valid; and the proprietors, either allured by the promises, or intimidated by the threats, of Wentworth, surrendered their estates to his disposal, and were content to re-purchase them, a third-part being reserved for the projected plantation. The county of Galway alone opposed his designs. Its jury refused to find for the crown. For this just and resolute maintenance of their rights, they suffered severely. The sheriff was fined a thousand pounds for returning so intractable a jury. Each juror was fined in the Castle Chamber four thousand pounds, and imprisoned until this exorbitant sum was paid. The entire county was pronounced duly forfeited to the crown; and in the re-granting of the lands, a larger proportion was reserved for the purposes of the plantation, than in any of the other counties of Connaught. He extorted the enormous sum of fifteen thousand pounds from the O'Byrnes of Wicklow, under a similar pretence of defect of title; so that the most powerful nobility in the kingdom, terrified by these arbitrary proceedings, voluntarily surrendered their patents; and, after the payment of heavy fines, were glad to take them out anew at increased rents.

The Ulster colonists did not escape this rapacious inquisition. He subjected their titles to a rigorous and minute examination, and where he found the least default in fulfilling the numerous and expensive conditions of their grants, he compelled them to renew their patents, for which he extorted considerable sums. The corporation of the city of London in particular suffered severely, under this iniquitous system. An action against them had been, for some time, pending in the star-chamber court in England, for the non-fulfilment of the conditions, under which they held the county of Londonderry, and the cities of Derry and Coleraine. This suit was now urged on more vigorously by Wentworth; and in the year 1637, they were sentenced to pay, to the crown, the exorbitant fine of seventy thousand pounds; their patent was revoked; their lands were seized in the name of the king; and bishop Bramhall was appointed receiver-general of all their Irish revenues.

Not only were the rights of property thus outrageously violated, but the personal liberty of the highest subjects was unceremoniously invaded; and even their lives were endangered, when they opposed the views of the ambitious and vindictive deputy. Impatient of contradiction, he inflicted severe and unwarranted punishment on the slightest appearance of resistance to his will, or disregard of his authority. Such was the case with Sir Piers Crosby, a privy counsellor and distinguished soldier; with Loftus the lord chancellor; and with Lord Mountnorris, the vice-treasurer. The latter, a nobleman of unblemished character, for an indiscreet though ambiguous expression, uttered in private, and suspected of conveying an imputation injurious to the character of the deputy, was summarily deprived of his commission in the army, by a court-martial of which

Wentworth, his prosecutor, was president; he was declared incapable of serving his majesty in any capacity; and was sentenced to be beheaded or shot at the option of his accuser!

In the same arbitrary manner Wentworth regulated the commerce of the kingdom; established monopolies; laid heavy duties on the importation of merchandise; prohibited the exportation of many of the valuable products of the country; and crushed the woollen manufactures, which were just beginning to flourish. On the other hand, it is due to his memory to state, that he diverted the trade of the kingdom into new and more profitable channels. He laid the foundation of the linen manufacture, and expended a considerable portion of his private property in its advancement; confidently foretelling the permanent benefit of which it would be productive: (22) a prediction that attests the sagacity of Went-

22 I am inclined to think that Wentworth's exertions, on behalf of the linen manufacture of Ireland, have been much overrated. The manufacture existed and was carried on, in Ireland, long before his time. And, if we are to believe the sworn depositions of Sir John Clotworthy and others upon his trial, his proclamations for regulating the sale and size of yarn, &c., were most vexatious and injurious to the trade; while the ample seizures made by his minions, of yarn alleged to be contrary to his regulations and therefore forfeited, were applied to his private use, and ruined the markets for its sale. A few notices of the early state of this staple manufacture, introduced into Ulster, and long exclusively conducted by the presbyterians, may not be unacceptable. Linen was exported in small quantities from Ireland, so early as the year 1437. The act, 33 Hen. viii. chap. 2. passed by the Irish parliament in 1542, against forestalling, and the private sale of certain commodities, proves that linen yarn was then an article of commerce. But the trade in yarn was very limited until after the plantation of Ulster. It is stated in the year 1670, that the manufacture had originated with the Scots in Ulster, and that within the previous forty years, (i. e. from 1630,) it had grown to a vast extent. Macpherson's Hist. of Com. At the trial of Lord Wentworth in 1641, Sir John Clotworthy deponed, "that yarn was the most native commodity of the kingdom, and paid most part of the May rents, for it is that, the women work on, all the winter season." And Mr. Fitzgarret, a barrister, testified "that yarn and linen cloth was the staple commodity of Ulster—that the merchants bought the yarn and transported it to Lancashire—and that one hundred pounds worth of yarn hath been sold and bought, in a market, in one day."—Rushworth, viii. 419—21.

worth, and that has been amply realized in the industry and wealth which it has been the means of diffusing over Ulster. He repressed with vigour the depredations of pirates, which had become very formidable, even in the Irish channel. He placed the collection of the revenue, under an efficient and salutary control; and thereby saved a considerable sum annually. He reduced the army to a state of strict discipline, and freed the country from the oppressive grievance of an insubordinate soldiery. His administration, therefore, though, in one respect, culpable in the extreme, was, on the whole, productive of many benefits to Ireland, formerly a stranger to commerce or manufactures—to order, or tranquillity.

But from these and other schemes of internal improvement, Wentworth's attention was recalled to more urgent concerns, arising out of the commotions which now began to prevail in Scotland.

The obnoxious measures employed by James for imposing prelacy on the Scottish church, which, at an early period, caused many of her most eminent ministers to seek refuge in Ulster, were renewed by Charles, soon after his accession to the throne, with increased ardour. In these, as in all his other religious schemes, he was incited and directed by Laud, who had accompanied him in his visit to Scotland in the year 1633, and had officiated at his coronation at Edinburgh, according to the unpopular and superstitious forms of the English church.[23] One of the earliest measures of the

23 The following description of the mummery practised at the coronation of Charles, under Laud as master of the ceremonies, is given by a contemporary annalist. "There was a four-nooked tasail in manner of an altar, standing within the kirk, having standing thereon two books, at least, resembling clasped books, called, blind books; with two chandlers, and two wax-candles which were on light, and a bason wherein there was nothing. At the back of the altar, (covered with tapestry) there was a rich tapestry, wherein the crucifix was curiously wrought; and as the bishops, who were in the service, passed by this crucifix, they were seen to bow their knee, and to beck [bow,]; which, with their habit, was noted, and bred great fear of inbringing of popery."—Spalding's Troubles, Glas. edit. p. 16.

king was to obtrude upon the church those innovations in doctrine and worship, which Laud was endeavouring to render predominant in both the sister kingdoms. In Scotland, however, whose national spirit and resources were unaccountably undervalued, the experiment was tried in its most obnoxious form. It was resolved to introduce both a new liturgy, and a new book of canons, in which a closer approximation to the Romish ritual should be made, than in the authorized formularies of the other churches of the empire. In the accomplishment of this object, the older Scottish bishops were studiously overlooked, and the prudent advices of the few, acquainted with the project, were indignantly rejected. The work was intrusted exclusively to four of the younger prelates, who were the creatures of Laud, and ambitious of securing his favour,—the sole avenue to preferment. They were directed by Charles to prepare draughts of the intended publications, and transmit them for correction to the archbishop at Lambeth. Under his auspices, they were successively printed; and, with his own hand, he introduced those deviations from the English standards, which proved so peculiarly offensive to the Scottish nation, and betrayed too palpable a desire to revive some of the grossest abominations of popery. The book of canons was first completed. On the twenty-third of May, 1635, it was ratified by the king in council, and imposed on the nation by virtue of the royal supremacy alone. (24) This publication confirmed the suspicions, which the people of Scotland had long entertained, of the design of Charles to annihilate the little portion of religious freedom, left them by his father.

The enactments, contained in these canons, were of the most obnoxious character, and awakened very general indignation.

24 Brodie, with his characteristic accuracy and research, has corrected Laing's statement of the reasons which led to the introduction, into Scotland, of a distinct liturgy and canons, and not those of the English church. Brodie, ii. 436, 7; and Note B, 559—68; compared with Laing, iii. 116.

The royal supremacy was rendered absolute and unlimited. No assembly of the clergy could be summoned but by the king; and they were even forbidden to hold any private meetings for expounding Scripture. Every ecclesiastical person, dying without issue, was directed to "leave his effects, or a great part of them," to the church. Communicants were compelled to receive the sacrament kneeling; and the remaining portion of the elements was enjoined to be consumed in the church. A font was placed at the entrance, and an altar at the eastern extremity, of the church. Ordination, as if a sacrament, was conferred only at four particular seasons of the year; and the practice of private confession and absolution was permitted and encouraged.(25) But, in addition to these

25 It is curious to mark the progressive inculcation of the popish doctrine of auricular confession. The English canons, established in 1603, are entirely silent on the subject. In the Irish canons, compiled, as the reader is aware, in the year 1634, it is introduced at the end of the 19th canon, the first part of which is precisely the same as the 22d of the English series. It directs the minister to give warning to his parishioners a week before the administration of the communion, "for their better preparation of themselves;" and here the English one very properly ends. But to the Irish canon is added the following direction, which is still in force in the established church of Ireland, and which every minister thereof approves and promises to observe,—"and the minister of every parish—shall, the afternoon before the said administration, give warning by the tolling of the bell, or otherwise, to the intent, that if any have any scruple of conscience, or desire the special ministry of reconciliation, he may afford it to those that need it. And to this end, the people are often to be exhorted to enter into a special examination of the state of their own souls; and that finding themselves either extreme dull, or much troubled in mind, they do resort unto God's ministers, to receive from them, as well advise and counsel for the quickening of their dead hearts, and the subduing of those corruptions whereunto they have been subject; as the benefit of absolution likewise, for the quieting of their consciences, by the power of the keys which Christ hath committed to his ministers for that purpose." Of this objectionable, though insidious enactment, both Laud and Wentworth approved. They were led to notice it by the following incident, which, at the same time, shows the character and bias of the men who enjoyed Laud's patronage. One of his favourites, Mr. James Croxton, had been recommended by the archbishop to Lord Mountnorris as his chaplain, and to Wentworth for preferment. Straff. Lett. i. 58, 82. The deputy soon

objectionable enactments, the Scottish canons contained an absurdity peculiar to themselves, and especially grievous to the church:—they gave an unqualified sanction to the service-book, which was not completed, nor published for above a year afterwards. The second canon excommunicated those "who should affirm that the worship prescribed in the forthcoming book of Common-prayer and administration of the sacraments contained any thing that was repugnant to the Scriptures, or that was corrupt, superstitious, or unlawful in the service and worship of God." By the fifth, every pres-

after presented him to the living of Gowran, in the county of Kilkenny. In a letter to Laud, dated April 1638, Croxton, as a "case most acceptable," thus informs his patron of his proceedings. "To provide the best I could for the more worthy receiving of the holy communion this last Easter, I have (I thanke God for it) beene able in some measure, to do that here, which able men have sufficiently spoken of elsewhere; I have sacramentally heard the confessions of the people committed to my charge in Goran (a certaine throughfare towne in the county of Kilkenye) in the chancell, they kneeling before the altar." Prynne's Cant. Doom. p. 195. This procedure, Croxton himself owns, was "counted a most strange act, without all warrant." Wentworth, however, justified it; "It is very truth, there is something further touching confession in these canons, than are in those of England, and in my poor judgment, much to the better." And Laud observes, in reply, "the Irish canon in that particular is much better than ours; and that which he [Croxton] hath done is, for ought I know, according to it." Straff. Lett. ii. 195. 212. In the Scottish, the last of the series of national, canons, the popish tenets of confession and absolution are less covertly inculcated. The following is a copy of the Scottish canon on this topic, extracted from Wharton's Troubles and Trial of Laud, p. 107. "Canon 9. chap. 18. Albeit sacramental confession and absolution have been in some places very much abused; yet if any of the people be grieved in mind for any delict or offence committed, and for the unburdening of his conscience, confess the same to the bishop or presbyter; they shall, as they are bound, minister to the person so confessing, all spiritual consolations out of the word of God; and shall not deny him the benefit of absolution, after the manner which is prescribed in the visitation of the sick, if the party shew himself truly penitent, and humbly desire to be absolved. And he shall not make known or reveal what hath been opened to him in confession, or to any person whatsoever; except the crime be such, as by the laws of the realm, his own life may be called in question for concealing the same."

byter was bound "to read, or cause divine service to be done according to the form of the book of Scottish Common-prayer before all sermon; and that he should officiate by the said book in all the offices, parts, and rubrics thereof." And by the fifteenth, "no presbyter or reader was permitted to pray extempore, or use any other form in the public service than that prescribed, under the penalty of deprivation." The book concluded with decreeing, "that no person should be admitted to holy orders, nor suffered to preach, catechise, administer the sacraments, or perform any other ecclesiastical function, without first subscribing these canons." Thus were the Scottish clergy, by a most absurd and unprecedented tyranny, compelled to declare their unconditional approbation of an unpublished liturgy, which they had no opportunity of perusing!

The dissatisfaction created by the publication of the canons became more deep and general, when, in the following year, the long-expected liturgy appeared. On examination, it was found to be a transcript of the English service-book, with several important alterations; all of which brought the prescribed worship into still closer conformity to the Romish ritual. These deviations from the English liturgy comprised a benediction or thanksgiving for departed saints, of whom a large number, connected with Scotland, was added to the popish saints of the British calendar. Various transpositions and alterations were introduced into the communion service, which countenanced the doctrine of the real presence of Christ in that ordinance; and the rubric enjoined the officiating minister to stand like the Romish priests, with his back to the congregation, and his arms extended, as if for elevating and adoring the consecrated elements. The sign of the cross was used in baptism, and the water in the font was changed and consecrated twice each month. Additional lessons from the Apocrypha were appointed to be read in public; the use of the ring was enjoined in marriage; and various rubrics were inserted to direct the people in the several gestures of bowing, standing, sitting, and kneeling; due accuracy in these matters being deemed indispensable to the canonical celebration of divine worship.[26]

Much as the people of Scotland would have disrelished the English liturgy, had it been proposed to them, they were still less prepared to adopt that, now not merely offered, but summarily imposed upon them by a royal proclamation, without either the approbation of a parliament, or the sanction of a general assembly.[27] From its obvious and ill-judged assimilation to the Romish ritual, it was believed to be no more than a translation of the mass; while from the arbitrary manner in which it was introduced, it was justly considered to be alike subversive of the rights, as of the religion, of the nation. No wonder then that all ranks cordially united in opposing it; and when, in the month of July 1637, it was, for the first time, used in the celebration of divine worship at Edinburgh, a tumult arose in the church, the service was violently interrupted, and the officiating prelates were with difficulty preserved from the fury of the incensed multitude.[28] The

[26] Collier, Ecc. Hist. ii. 768, 9. Neal, ii. 271. Bramhall, in a letter to Spottiswoode, archbishop of St. Andrews, thus congratulates him on the superiority of the Scottish liturgy, over that of his own church;—"I humbly thank your grace for your high favour, the book of Common-prayer: glad I was to see it; and more glad to see it such as it is, to be envied in some things, perhaps, if one owned." Rawd. Papers, p. 40. This letter is dated on the 13th of August, and it is singular that Bramhall, at Derry, had not then heard of the riot at Edinburgh, mentioned in the text, which had occurred on the 23d of July, three weeks before he wrote: so slow was the transmission of intelligence in those days.

[27] It is worthy of notice, that even in Oxford, influenced and ruled as it was by its chancellor Laud, the alterations in the Scottish liturgy were not popular. One of Wentworth's news-mongers at the English court, in July 1638, informs him, among other articles of intelligence; "They grow foolish at Oxford, for they had a question about the legality of ship-money; as also, whether the *addita* and *alterata* in the Scottish liturgy, did give just cause of scandal: but my Lord's grace of Canterbury hearing of it, forbad them such questions." Straff. Lett. ii. 181.

[28] This riot, so memorable on account of its momentous results, was commenced, it is alleged, by an old woman, called Janet Geddes, flinging

ministers and people, supported by nearly all the nobility of Scotland, found it necessary to unite more closely to defeat the religious innovations of Charles, and to secure themselves against his indignation at their successful opposition to his plans. Deputies from the several parts of the kingdom, and from the various classes of society, assembled at Edinburgh. For their mutual protection and encouragement, they resolved to renew the National Covenant, in which they made a full profession of the reformed faith, abjured the errors of popery, and bound themselves by an oath to defend each other in resisting the recent impositions, on both their civil and religious rights, and to "support the king in the preservation of religion, liberty and law." This covenant was solemnly renewed at Edinburgh, for the third time since the Reformation, on the first day of March 1638.(29) In the course of two months, it was subscribed by all ranks, throughout nearly the entire kingdom, with the utmost alacrity and joy.

These vigorous and well-concerted measures were followed by a general assembly of the church, which Charles, to conciliate the favour of those whom he was not yet able to coerce, permitted to meet at Glasgow in the month of November. It was attended by one hundred and forty ministers, and nearly one hundred elders, as commissioners from the fifty-three presbyteries of which the Scottish church was then compos-

the three-legged stool on which she had been sitting at the head of the dean of Edinburgh, with this exclamation,—"Villain! dost thou say mass at my lug?" Balfour, in his "Stonie-Field Day," quoted by Brodie, ii. p. 454, furnishes the following authentic account. "No less worthy of observation is that renouned Christian valyancie of another godly woman of the same season; for when sche hard a young man behind, sounding forth amen to that new composed comedie, sche quickly turned her about, and after sche had warmed both his cheeks with the weight of her hands, sche thus shot against him the thunderbolt of her zeal: 'false thief,' said sche, 'is there na uther pairt of the churche to sing mess in, but thou must sing it at my luge?'"

29 The reader must not confound this National covenant, with the Solemn league and covenant adopted five years afterwards.

ed.[30] The Marquis of Hamilton was the royal commissioner, and the celebrated Alexander Henderson, then minister at Leuchars in Fifeshire, was unanimously elected moderator. Though the commissioner, on the seventh day of meeting, attempted to dissolve the assembly, and actually retired, when he found it was resolved to bring the prelates to a trial; and though the bishops protested against, and formally declined, its jurisdiction; yet the members were not deterred from the firm and faithful performance of the duties incumbent upon them in this critical emergency. They sat for the long period of thirty days, during which they held twenty-six sessions. They abolished prelacy, deposed the bishops, condemned the liturgy and book of canons, and repealed all the obnoxious regulations imposed upon the church since the commencement of the century. They re-established the presbyterian judicatories, and enacted many salutary laws for preserving the independence of the church, securing the purity of the ministerial character, and promoting piety and godliness throughout the land.

The proceedings of this memorable assembly were received by the Scottish nation with enthusiastic delight. But, by Charles and his advisers, they were beheld with such unmeasured indignation, that nothing less than an immediate appeal to arms was considered sufficient to vindicate his insulted authority. He accordingly prepared to invade his native kingdom. He repaired to York, and, with a considerable force of horse and foot, advanced to the borders. The Scots were not slow to perceive and oppose the hostile designs of the king. They seized the principal fortresses of the kingdom; and marshalling a large army under general Leslie, an experienced soldier, they proceeded to the south, to resist, what had now become, the aggression of a foreign power.

30 Stevenson's Hist. of the Church of Scot. ii. pp. 474—81, where a full list of the Assembly is given.

CHAPTER V.

Wentworth alarmed for the tranquillity of Ulster—Northern Presbyterians disaffected to his government—Settlement of the banished ministers in Scotland—Intercourse between them and their former people in Ulster—Wentworth determines to overawe the Presbyterians—Cuts off their communication with Scotland—Is aided by the prelates—Case of Galbraith—and of Pont—Rigour of Bramhall—and of Leslie—Correspondence between the latter and Wentworth—Leslie's visitation charge—Origin of the Black oath—Is imposed on the Scots in Ulster—Tyrannical proceedings in enforcing it—Lord Claneboy's letters to Wentworth—Sufferings of the Presbyterians—Case of Henry Stewart.

WENTWORTH had been no unconcerned spectator of the progress of the Scottish commotions. Alarmed at the ardour and unanimity with which the National Covenant had been renewed in Scotland, he was apprehensive lest that formidable bond should be introduced into the north of Ireland.

He had good ground for this apprehension. The Scots in Ulster, irritated by his arbitrary and vexatious interference with their patents, and especially by his severities against the London corporation, which embarrassed and aggrieved a very numerous tenantry, were generally disaffected to his government. This disaffection was increased by the violence, with which the northern prelates urged conformity to the ritual of the English church. Their favourite ministers had been grievously oppressed, and ultimately compelled to seek refuge in Scotland. Persecution did not terminate with their banishment. A commission was issued by Wentworth, authorizing the bishop of Down to arrest, in a summary manner, and to imprison during pleasure, the non-conformists in his diocese. This commission, the flagrant illegality of which constituted one of the charges preferred against the deputy on his trial in England, was diligently executed.[1] Numbers were committed to prison, or forced to fly to Scotland; while the great majority of the inhabitants, though yielding a reluctant conformity, were the more firmly attached to the presbyterian church. Suffering under these grievances, both civil and religious, it was not to be expected that the Scots in Ulster would remain indifferent to the events occurring in their native country, which promised to emancipate it from the yoke of prelacy. On the contrary, they sympathised most deeply with their brethren and countrymen in their magnanimous efforts to subvert a system of tyranny and intolerance, similar to that under which they themselves were groaning. This sympathy was sustained by the constant communication which existed with Scotland, and which was kept up especially by means of persons in trade. Several of the landed proprietors too, having estates in both kingdoms, were frequently passing and repassing, and thus maintained a community of feeling between the two countries.

But the opposition of the northern Presbyterians to the administration of Wentworth, was strengthened and increased by the affectionate intercourse which they maintained with their banished ministers, who had survived the storm of persecution. These faithful men, whom they continued to regard with the deepest veneration, were settled in charges in their native country, shortly after their flight from Ireland. Early in the year 1638, Mr. Blair was chosen colleague to Mr. William Annan at Ayr, whence he was subsequently removed to St. Andrews. Mr. Livingston was, in the month of July following, admitted minister of Stranraer, from which charge he was, ten years afterwards, transported to Ancrum in Teviotdale. Mr. James Hamilton was settled at Dum-

[1] Rushworth, viii. 236 et seq.

fries, whence he was removed to Edinburgh. Mr. Dunbar was installed minister at Calder in Lothian; and Mr. Colvert was settled at Paisley. Mr. M'Clelland, who had been admitted to the ministry in Ireland, was ordained in Kirkcudbright; and Mr. John Semple, who had also preached occasionally in Ulster, became minister of Carsphairn in Galloway. Two other banished ministers, whose charges in Ireland cannot now be ascertained, were also admitted at this period to parishes in Scotland. These were Mr. Samuel Row, who was ordained as colleague to Mr. Henry Macgill at Dunfermline; and M ... ho was settled at Ballantrae in A ... isters were zealous promoters of th ... tional Covenant, and of the other measures, ... the triumph of the presbyterian church in Scotland was ultimately secured.[3]

They afforded their countrymen most important aid in that memorable work; and, for this reason, they were especially obnoxious to the prelatical party. Scarcely had they been elected to their respective charges, when the bishops, in a list of grievances and complaints submitted to the king in 1638, represented the settlement of these ministers as a grievous and flagrant contempt of ecclesiastical authority.[4] No fewer than four of them, to wit, Blair, Livingston, M'Clelland, and James Hamilton, were chosen members of the celebrated Assembly at Glasgow, and took a prominent part in its proceedings. The Scottish prelates in their protest against the legality of that Assembly, alleged, as one ground of declining its jurisdiction, that, as these banished ministers were still lying under the censure of the church of Ireland, they

2 Stevenson, ii. 312.

3 The following extract from a letter of the earl of Traquair, dated Holyrood House, May 17, 1638, to the marquis of Hamilton at London, attests their activity. "The pulpits are daily filled with those ministers who were lately put out of Ireland; who, with some of their own, and some such other as come from other places of this kingdom, preach nothing but foolish seditious doctrine." Hardwicke Papers, ii. 107.

4 Burnet's Mem. of the Dukes of Hamilton, p. 41.

could not therefore be qualified to legislate for the sister church of Scotland. So soon as this 'declinature' was presented to the Assembly, the brethren, by desire of the court, vindicated themselves against this aspersion. "The moderator," writes a member of the assembly, who was present throughout all its deliberations, "desired the parties interested in this calumny to clear themselves. Sundry of us could have wished, that for the stopping of the mouths of that party, these had not been chosen commissioners; yet the excellent gifts of the men would not permit the election to pass by them. Mr. Blair, in name of the rest, in a brave extempore harangue, showed at length, that all the censures that had fallen on them, were not only alone for adhering to the discipline of the church of Scotland, but most unjustly inflicted. He gave us all full satisfaction."—"And Mr. Dickson, who, as being settled at Irvine, a port which had frequent intercourse with the Irish, had been at pains to get certain information concerning that point, did likewise attest the same; and in end, the assembly was fully satisfied that the censures inflicted upon these and their brethren, were most unjust, and therefore were of no effect from the beginning; and that the church of Scotland, having no dependence on the church of Ireland, was under no necessity to regard their censures."[5]

Several of these ministers, being settled on the western coast of Scotland, had frequent communication with Ulster; and so great was the veneration in which they were held, that many of their former hearers removed to Scotland, with no other view than to enjoy their ministry. Great numbers usually went over from Ireland at the stated celebration of the communion; and, on one occasion, five hundred persons, principally from the county of Down, visited Stranraer, to receive that ordinance from the hands of Mr. Livingston. The same minister relates that, at another time, he baptized eight and twenty children, brought over for that purpose by their

[5] Baillie, i. 120-1. Stevenson, ii. 578. Balfour's Annals, ii. 304.

parents, unwilling to receive sealing ordinances from the prelatical clergy of Ireland. By means of an intercourse so endearing and reverential, the Irish ministers, notwithstanding their settlement in Scotland, continued to exercise a very powerful influence on the Scots in Ulster. This influence, it may reasonably be conjectured, would be exerted to foster and maintain a spirit, similar to that which had been so long preserved, and at length so successfully manifested, in Scotland. Many of the northern Presbyterians, when visiting their native country, had subscribed the Covenant, and had witnessed with delight the beneficial results of the victory which had been there achieved. They returned to Ulster, more and more dissatisfied with the religious thraldom under which they were compelled to live, and disposed to embrace every proper opportunity, which might offer, to mitigate or escape its oppressive yoke.

Wentworth, therefore, had good reason to be alarmed for the tranquillity of Ulster. His attention was first directed to its condition, by intimations from the English court, of the apprehensions entertained there of the Scottish residents. So early as the month of July 1638, Laud, the most punctual and unreserved of his correspondents, thus wrote to him:—"The Scotish business is extream ill indeed, and what will become of it God knows, but certainly no good, and his majesty hath been notoriously betrayed by some of them. There is a speech here, that they have sent to know the number of Scotchmen in Ulster; and that privately, there hath been a list taken of such as are able to bear arms, and that they are found to be above forty thousand in Ulster only. This is a very private report, and perhaps false, but in such a time as this, I could not think it fit to conceal it from your lordship, coming very casually to my ears."[6] About the same time, Charles, already determined on war, applied to Wentworth to

[6] Straff. Lett. ii. 185.

ascertain what aid could be afforded him in his meditated invasion of Scotland. The vigilant deputy, in reply, apprized his majesty of the unsettled state of the kingdom, and of Ulster in particular; and stated the necessity of reserving the chief part of the Irish forces to overawe the northern Scots:

"Sir George Radcliffe acquaints me your majesty's pleasure is, that I should certify my humble opinion, what strength is to be expected hence, in case these late distempers in Scotland dispose that people to your majesty's trouble; which God avert.

"The army here consists of two thousand foot and six hundred horse, which, in a time better secured, is rather too little than otherwise, to ascertain the peace and tranquillity of this government and subject. For your majesty may be pleased to consider, the settling all the plantations of Connaught, Munster, and other parts of the kingdom, is the great work now upon our hands, and the people more apt, consequently, to stir upon so great an alteration as these will bring amongst them, than at another time; and that there are great numbers of Scotish in Ulster, undoubtedly of the same affections your majesty finds in Scotland, and by so much the more diligently to be attended, by how much the nearer they are to the mutual encouragement and succours they may communicate, the one to the other. So as to draw forth any part of this small army might be a means to raise and spread the flame, to have the fire here also kindled, whilst they find us not in so full power to contain them, as now by God's blessing I conceive we are:——And necessary it will be, however, in case the subjects of Scotland incline not themselves to quietness and obedience, that your majesty give me early instructions what I am to do: especially (as I humbly conceive) that I may speedily draw the greatest part of our little army into Ulster, as near Scotland as can be, and so ready and at hand to incline and bow every motion in their first beginnings to loyalty, safety and obedience: and perchance cause some little diversion on the other side, by reason of our being so close upon them."[7]

Wentworth, thus sensible of the precarious state of Ulster, saw the necessity of acting with the utmost promptitude and vigour. He resolved to cut off all correspondence with Scotland, to repress the northern Scots, and to collect an army in Ulster, either to co-operate with Charles by invading Scotland on the west, or to hold in subjection the Scottish residents at home. On this subject he again wrote, in the month of November, to his Majesty. "The colour I give this levy shall be the putting of a garrison of five hundred men into Carrickfergus, the Derry and Colerane, in regard——I am informed the Scottish in these parts are observed all to ride up and down the country, armed with swords, which formerly they have not been accustomed to do. And, to cover the business the better, I propose so to handle the matter, as the council here shall advise, and avow these preparations for that end, which will be a means, I trust, to effect the service without the least thought of the true intent." And shortly afterwards he avows to Laud the confidence which he felt in the success of his measures;—"if his majesty be pleased still to countenance me in my employment, and honour me with the trust of this army, I say confidently, by the blessing of

7 Straff. Lett. ii. 187—8. The following passage from the same letter is worthy of notice for several reasons. "The earl of Antrim lately writ to me to be furnished of arms, and that the magazine for them might be kept at Coleraine. Communicate this with the council here I durst not, for I am sure they would never advise such strength to be intrusted with a grandchild of the earl of Tyrone. And for myself I hold it unsafe any store of arms should lye so near the great Scotish plantations in those parts; lest if their countrymen grow troublesome, and they partake of the contagion, they might chance to borrow those weapons of his lordship, for a longer time and another purpose, than his Lordship would find cause to thank them for. They are shrewd children, not won much by courtship, especially from a Roman catholick." This was written in July 1638. Could this application of Antrim have any prospective connexion with the rebellion which broke out three years after, and in which the earl acted so conspicuous a part?

Almighty God and the prudent directions of his majesty, I will not only keep all here in peace, bring the Scottish to a conformity in our church-government, but, in case the earl of Rothes or his consorts touch upon Irish ground, send them and their coats home again, as well dusted as ever they had them in all their lives, how high or loud soever their boasts now carry the terror of their looks."[8]

In addition to his military arrangements, Wentworth called in the prelates to his assistance. He directed them to persevere in enforcing conformity; to preach against the covenant, and the rebellion of the Scots;[9] and to exercise a strict vigilance over all who might be suspected of maintaining any intercourse with the covenanters. The presentations to many parishes in Ulster being in the hands of Scottish noblemen possessing estates in the north, they generally conferred these benefices on their countrymen. Wentworth now entreated the bishops to obstruct, so far as they could, the settlement of any more Scottish ministers within their dioceses, unless well recommended for their hostility to the covenant and their adherence to the cause of prelacy. One or two cases will evince the vigilance employed in these affairs.

Mr. Galbraith, a native of Scotland, was presented by a Scottish nobleman, probably the duke of Lennox, to the valuable living of Taughboyne in the county of Donegall, near Derry; and was also appointed archdeacon of the diocese of Raphoe. But Laud, who exercised a patriarchal supremacy over all ecclesiastical matters in the three kingdoms, suspecting him to have subscribed the covenant, directed Wentworth to suspend the appointment until this serious charge should be investigated. The deputy, obsequious in these matters, immediately assures the archbishop, that he may rely on receiving a prompt obedience to his commands: "Your grace may not only undertake for Taboin, but for all that is in my disposal, as oft as you shall be pleased to call

8 Straff. Lett. ii. 233, 273. 9 Ibid. ii. 192.

for it." He assures Laud that Dr. Bruce, his confident and correspondent in Ulster, had also sent him "certain knowledge that Galbraith had signed and sworn the covenant, so we are like to have a brave archdeacon of him; nevertheless if himself may be trusted, all will be well, no doubt, or else there is more ingenuity to confess truth in this gentleman, than I ever yet observed in puritan." After further correspondence relative to this appointment, Laud, though still acting solely on report, and disregarding the solemn disavowal of the individual himself, writes to Wentworth in these decided terms: "Galbreth, that would have your great benefice, is a covenanter, there is certain news of it brought now to the king, and thereupon his majesty hath commanded me to signify unto you that you shall not give him the benefice.—I hear further that this Galbreth hasted out of Scotland for killing a man there; but I am not so certain of this, as I am that he is a covenanter, that is, upon the matter, that he is a traytor."(10)

10 Straff. Lett. ii. 195, 230. Thomas Bruce, D.D. mentioned in the text, was archdeacon of Raphoe, and incumbent of Taughboyne, or Taboin, in the year 1622. See Appendix, No. I. He also enjoyed these dignities in 1641, as appears from a complaint which he then preferred to the Long parliament against the bishop of Raphoe. Com. Journ. July 28, 1641. It is probable that Bruce had been raised about this time (1638) to some higher preferment, and Galbraith appointed to succeed him in Taboin; and when the settlement of the latter was obstructed by Laud, through his interference, that he continued to hold his former dignities; but that Galbraith, having cleared himself from the charge of being a covenanter, had been subsequently inducted by the bishop into his preferment; and that Bruce, unwilling to resign it, had sought the interference of the English commons, disposed, as he well knew, to entertain with favour any complaint against a bishop. This supposition is rendered still more probable by the fact, that Carte makes frequent mention of archdeacon Galbraith as an active negotiator in Ulster in the year 1645 on the royalist side, and gives the following character of him: "Mr. archdeacon Galbraith, a Scot by original, but well affected to episcopacy and monarchy, a man of very good sense and learning, great prudence and full as great resolution, and esteemed by all the British officers and gentlemen in those parts," i. e. the north-west of Ulster. Carte, i. 531. Both Laud and Wentworth had therefore permitted themselves to be imposed on, without inquiry, by Bruce,

In another case, the conduct of Laud and Wentworth was equally unjust and oppressive. Mr. Pont, a minister in the diocese of Raphoe, was noted for declining to use the prescribed ceremonies of the church, and for condemning in his sermons the increasing severities, together with the unscriptural jurisdiction, of the prelates. It appears that he had also held meetings for worship and public preaching, contrary to the canons; and that his wife had, in some way, signalized herself by her opposition to prelacy, and her frequenting of these more private assemblies. He was countenanced by several persons of influence, and among others, by Sir William Stewart, who had expressed a very strong indignation against the oppressions of the ecclesiastical courts. Sir William had also compelled the apparitor of the bishop's court, while it was sitting, to appear before him and other magistrates, probably to answer complaints preferred against his oppressive conduct. The bishop, resenting this procedure as a studied insult to the authority of the church, reported the matter to Wentworth, in conjunction with the sermons of Pont, and the sectarianism of his wife; and, at the same time, he retailed some obsolete scandal respecting Sir William's moral character, to serve as a separate ground of action before the high-commission, should the other charges not be satisfactorily substantiated. On receiving this varied intelligence, Wentworth had immediate recourse to his spiritual adviser; and all these urgent and momentous affairs of state are communicated to Laud, and by him to Charles. The archbishop lost no time in issuing his directions. "These are briefly to let you know that I am so sensible of the business of Pont and his wife in the diocese of Rapho, that I have put it again to his majesty's serious consideration, and thus he hath commanded me to write to your lordship.

"He would have the bishop of Rapho to deprive Pont of his benefice for the wild sermon he made against the bishop's

whose interest it was to misrepresent Galbraith. Thus summarily were the characters and fortunes of men consigned to ruin, at that period, on a bare supposition, supported by interested calumny!

jurisdiction, and to proceed against his wife in such way as her fault deserves, and the laws will bear: and if the crime be not of too old a date, his majesty would have Sir William Stewart questioned for that whoredom and bastardy; but howsoever that fall out, his majesty's command is, that if Sir William Stewart do not give your letters a good answer, and yourself satisfaction in the publick way, you are to remove him from being a counsellor in that state, which he serves no better."[11]

These royal mandates were promptly obeyed by the deputy, who thus replied to Laud;—"As for that business betwixt my Lord of Rapho and Sir William Stewart, it is put into a way of examination, and the cause will have publication this next term; there shall be all care possible taken, and if the bishop make good his charge, as in truth I am persuaded he will, believe me the other shall smart; my eyes are open upon it, as well knowing what the consequences of such beginnings shewing themselves, if not early prevented and stopped. Pont's wife is here in the castle; and for the examination and punishment of that conventicle, I have put it to the high-commission, who will effectually and soundly proceed therein. Pont himself and some other of the principal are got into Scotland;[12] and as for the bastardy, I conceive it will be best to see how Sir William acquits himself in this

11 Straff. Lett. ii. 245. Laud, with some presentiment of the character and results of the General Assembly then sitting at Glasgow, thus dates his letter to Wentworth; "Lambeth, Wednesday, November 21st, 1638, the day of the sitting down of the Assembly in Scotland."

12 It is not improbable that this Mr. Pont was a relative of the Scottish reformer, Robert Pont, who had two sons in the ministry, one of whom was married to a daughter of John Knox. If so, he had been settled in this diocese, through this connexion, under the auspices of the late bishop Knox. Though I have not been able to ascertain his parish, I am inclined to believe that Mr. Pont succeeded Mr. Cunningham at Ramelton, (see note (9) chap ii.) where his name is still preserved by tradition. I find from the following pamphlet, that Sir William Stewart's agent was another Mr. Pont, probably son to this persecuted minister; "Special good news from Ireland, &c. &c. in three letters to Mr. Abraham Pont, solicitor for the said Sir William, in London." Lond. 1643.

business, and thereupon to stir the prosecution, or let it rest, as occasion shall serve."

When this important cause came to be tried at the council-board, Sir William proved he was not aware the bishop's court was sitting, when he compelled its officer to appear before him and his brother justices. He was consequently acquitted of the wilful contempt of the bishop's authority alleged against him; but the vigilant deputy seizing on certain words which he had used, reflecting on the ecclesiastical courts, "gave him a very round and public rebuke for his paine."(13) Mrs. Pont was treated with excessive rigour. She lay in prison for nearly three years, till liberated after the fall of her relentless persecutor, by the interference of the Irish parliament.(14)

Wentworth, conscious that Sir William Stewart was by no means the only one of the northern gentry, tainted with puritanism, resolved to proceed against every one suspected of this heinous offence. Neither rank nor sex escaped his severity. He thus developes his plans to Laud, to whom the intelligence could not fail to be acceptable:—"I have given direction that the Lady Clotworthy and some of the principal nonconformists shall be convened before the high-commission; and e'er it be long, if I may be believed, and but let alone, will bring them under the obedience of their ordinary, [bishops,] or send them back to their fellows in Scotland, placing better subjects in their steads."(15)

In these proceedings the deputy was supported by most of the northern bishops. The zeal and activity of Bramhall

(13) Straff. Lett. ii. 270, 337.

(14) Adair's MS.—I find from the journals of the Irish commons (i. 379, 388-9,) that in May, 1641, Mrs. Pont, who had been recently set at liberty, presented a petition to the house, complaining of the conduct of the bishop of Raphoe in illegally imprisoning her, &c. The house resolved that the bishop "had run into *præmunire* for committing of her by his own authority;" and referred the matter to the house of lords. In these proceedings, Mrs. Pont is styled, "Mrs. Isabel Pont, alias Stewart, widow;" whence it appears that her husband must have died soon after he had fled to Scotland. It is not unlikely she was a relative of Sir William Stewart.

(15) Straff. Lett. ii. 189, 273. See note (7) chap. ii.

drew forth his special commendation;—"Your Lordship's course," writes Wentworth in one of his letters to that prelate, "taken and intended against the two packs of rogues and petty rebels there [about Derry,] I do both well approve of, and desire your lordship it may effectually be pursued, thanking your lordship for the advertisement thereof. And for the clergyman you have committed for his lewd praying for the prosperous success of Scotland in the maintenance of religion; if there be sufficient good witness thereof, as it is likely there may be enow, I desire your lordship that he may be forthwith very safely conveyed up hither, with sufficient proof thereabouts, and examinations, if any be taken therein." (16)

But the deputy's most active supporter was bishop Leslie. His conduct towards the presbyterian ministers in his diocese, already narrated, evinced him to be a fit agent for the work of persecution. He now cordially co-operated with Wentworth in all his arbitrary measures, and displayed much of that mean servility which usually characterises the persecutor. The following letters convey so clear an idea of the state of Ulster at this period, and of the additional severities prepared for the ill-fated non-conformists, that no apology seems necessary for inserting them at length.

"THE LORD BISHOP OF DOWNE TO THE LORD DEPUTY.

"Most honourable my singular good Lord,

"Although it becometh not me to make any address unto your lordship but by petition, yet the matters wherein I am to inform requiring secrecy, I hope your lordship will give me leave to direct them unto your lordship in an enclosed letter. There is one Robert Adaire, (17) a justice of peace in

16 Rawd. Pap. p. 43.

17 The person alluded to by Leslie was Sir Robert Adair, knt. of Kilhill or Kinhilt, in Wigtonshire. His Irish property lay at Ballymena in Antrim, and is still possessed by a lineal descendant of the same name.

the county of Antrim, of five hundred pounds lands a-year, who having some estate in Scotland, both joined himself unto the faction there, signed the covenant, received the oath of rebellion, and now when the Marquis [of Hamilton] was last in Scotland, he was one of the commissioners for the country against the king, and one of them who were appointed to watch the king's castle [at Edinburgh] that no provision should be carried in. I believe that if there were a strict inquiry, there will be found others who have estates in this kingdom have done the like.

"All the puritans in my diocese are confident, that the arms raised against the king in Scotland, will procure them a liberty to set up their own discipline here amongst themselves, insomuch that many whom I had brought to some measure of conformity, have revolted lately; and when I call them in question for it, they scorn my process; if I excommunicate them, they know they will not be apprehended, in regard of the liberty their lords have of excluding all sheriffs. Besides, it grieveth my heart to hear how many who live in Scotland, who coming over hither about matter of trade, do profess openly that they have signed the covenant, and justify what they have done, as if the justice of this kingdom could not overtake them. These things I have presumed to represent unto your lordship. So humbly craving pardon for my boldness, I pray God to bless your lordship with all health and happiness, and to continue long amongst us for the good of

He was sheriff of the county of Antrim in 1630. He escaped the fangs of his prelatical persecutor at this period, and fled to Scotland. But he was nevertheless indicted for treason and his property confiscated. In August 1639, Wentworth thus writes respecting him to Sir Henry Vane, one of the secretaries of state:—"There is one Mr. Adaire, a man of some four hundred pounds land, who went over into Scotland to rebel it there with the rest of that faction, and hath played his part notably and insolently. This fellow I caused to be indicted of treason; but I stay prosecution till I may farther have his majesty's direction therein, which I pray you to procure me; but had his majesty continued at Berwick, within these few days, I should have procured a good confiscation to the crown." Straff. Lett. ii. 426.

this church and kingdom. So prayeth your lordship's most humble servant and daily orator,

"HEN. DUNENSIS."

"*Lisnegarvie*, [*Lisburn*,] *22d of September* 1638."

"THE LORD DEPUTY TO THE LORD BISHOP OF DOWNE.

"My very good Lord,

"This, with your permission, will be an answer to yours of the 22d of September. As concerning Robert Adaire you therein mention, I now send for him, but till his coming up, take not the least notice what the cause is moving me thereunto, and must, in this regard, desire your lordship also to keep the occasion of it to yourself, till you hear again from me, which shortly after his arrival here, you shall not fail to do.

"In my opinion your lordship should do very well privately to enquire out the names of all others that have danced after the same pipe, as also of all such as profess themselves covenanters, and send them hither to me; in the rest of the proceedings your lordship shall not be so much as once touched upon, or heard of.

"If your lordship be pleased to send me, by the bearer, the list of such as have revolted from their conformity, and stand in contempt of your process, as also the places of their abode, I will not fail speedily to send our pursuivants for them, who shall apprehend and render them subject to the ecclesiastical courts, and under the jurisdiction of their ordinary.

"Nor is this a business to be neglected, or faintly to be slipped over, but quickly and roundly to be corrected in the first beginnings, lest dandled over long, the humour grow more churlish and difficult to be directed and disposed to the peace of the church and commonwealth, especially in a time when the assumptions and liberty of this generation of people threaten so much distraction and unquietness to both, and therefore as I much recommend your lordship's zeal therein, so will it be ever becoming your lordship's piety and courage confidentially to oppose and withstand their disobedience and madness, as hitherto you have done, wherein you may be assured of all the assistance that rests in the power of your lordship's very affectionate faithful friend to serve you,

"WENTWORTH."

"*Dublin*, *Oct*. 4, 1638."

"BISHOP LESLIE TO THE LORD DEPUTY.

"Most Noble and Gracious Lord,

"Mr. Adair not being yet returned out of Scotland, I have presumed to take the letter from the messenger, and have adjured him to the like secrecy, as your lordship hath enjoined me, fearing lest he should have inquired after him, the danger would be suspected. And I humbly pray, that your lordship would be pleased to charge Mr. Lindan, now mayor of Carrickfergus, with the delivery of the letters, who being a principal officer of the custom-house, must needs know of his arrival.

"I know there are many in my diocese and other parts of this kingdom, who have joined in this conspiracy, but I am not able to make proof against them, if they should deny it: For of late I have had no intelligence out of Scotland, all letters that come unto me are intercepted. (18) Besides, my

18 One of the intercepted letters, of which Leslie here complains, is in the Advocates' Library, Edinburgh. It is dated March 19, 1638, and is from Mr. David Mitchell, one of the prelatical ministers of Edinburgh, who appears to have been the bishop's chief correspondent. This Mitchell was deposed by the general assembly at Glasgow, in the November following. His character is thus given by Baillie:—"This long time he had delighted to grieve the whole land with the doctrine of the faction, Arminianism in all the heads, and sundry points of popery, proved by sundry witnesses; besides his declining the assembly, which alone, accord-

friends, from whom I had wont to receive my information, live at Edinburgh and Aberdeen, and know not what is done in the west parts of that country, whither only our people do resort; yet I will use all means to discover them. And in the mean time, I dare say that these persons whom I present to your lordship, are guilty; because they are notable non-conformists, and have been lately in Scotland. Robert Barr of Malone, Robert Niven of Belfast, George Martin of the same, and David Kennedy and Robert Rosse, who have fled this kingdom for fear of the high-commission, but have left their land behind them.[19]

ing to the acts of our church, imports deposition:—no man could have kept such a one in our church without serious repentance for his manifold avowed errors."—Baillie, i. 123.

19 Of these persons, specified by the bishop as 'notable non-conformists,' I have been able to glean but few notices. ROBERT BARR was an extensive merchant, and traded, under a special license, between Scotland and Ireland. He also kept extensive iron-works at Malone. He was particularly obnoxious to Wentworth, who, in a letter to Laud in the preceding year, thus bitterly and satirically complains of his officious misrepresentations, "There is one Mr. Barre, a Scotishman by nation, whose person your grace once saw before you at the committee for Irish affairs, at my last being in England. This gentleman that pretends to be a merchant, but indeed is scarce so good as a petty chapman, hath procured a special license under the signet and signature royal of going and coming over without my comptrol, under which he magnifies himself extreamly, as exempt, if not above, any power of mine: And thus leaping like a Jackanapes betwixt two stools, holds on this side very inward intelligence with some here, which wish me ill, blown up by them boldly to calumniate me there, whilst they know my actions here over well, ever to dare to appear in my contrary. There on that side he procures, by some very near his majesty, access to the king; there whispering continually something or another to my prejudice; boasts familiarly how freely he speaks with his majesty, what he saith concerning me,—'*and now,*' *ant pleese your mejesty, et werde mare anent your debuty of Yrland.*" Lett. ii. 107.——GEORGE MARTIN was son of Josiah Martin, who, in the reign of Elizabeth, accompanied Sir Arthur Chichester to Ireland in a military capacity, and received many favours from him; he had a country-seat at Whitehouse near Belfast. His son George, mentioned by Leslie as having fled to Scotland, afterwards returned and settled at Belfast. He was a staunch presbyterian, and, in republican times, like the rest of his brethren, a firm loyalist. On

"As for those who contemn my process, and oppose my jurisdiction, they are more in number than would fill all the gaols in Ireland; but the church-wardens are the deepest in that guilt, who will present none, who are disobedient to the government, and to that purpose they are chosen. As in Scotland they are entered into a bond to defend one another by arms, so it seems that in my diocese they have joined in a bond to defend one another by their oaths. I have therefore, in obedience to your lordship's commands, sent a list of these church-wardens, extracted out of my registry: If it may so please your good lordship to make all or some of them examples, it will strike a terror in the rest of that faction.

"Since his majesty hath been pleased to condescend so far unto them in Scotland by his last proclamation, against which, notwithstanding, they have protested; a copy of both I have sent to my Lord of Derry, there is such insulting amongst them here, that they make me weary of my life. And, as I am informed, they are now drawing a petition to his majesty, that they may have the like favour in Ireland, as is granted to their fellows in Scotland, which I hope your lordship in your deep wisdom will prevent. My officers have been beaten in open court. I have sent a warrant for apprehending of the parties, by virtue of a writ of assistance from your lordship, whereof I never made use before, and if I apprehend them, I will keep them in restraint, till your lordship's pleasure be known. They do threaten me for my

the seizure of Belfast by Venables in 1649, he happened to be sovereign, or chief municipal officer of the town, and refused to billet the republican troops; on which they pillaged his house, seized his goods and chattels at Whitehouse, and he and his family with difficulty escaped their vengeance. From him are descended the present family of Martins, baronets of Lockinge, Berkshire. Edmon. Baron. iv. 210. David Kennedy was minister at Newtonards in the county of Down: And Robert Rosse was of the parish of Bangor, in the same county. Both were afterwards excommunicated by the high-commission court for their non-conformity. Robert Niven of Belfast I have not seen elsewhere mentioned.

life; but, by the grace of God, all their brags shall never make me faint in doing service to God and the king. I crave your lordship's humble pardon for this tedious letter; and pray God to increase and multiply all his blessings upon your lordship. This is the constant prayer of your lordship's most humble servant and daily orator,

"HEN. DUNENSIS." [20]

"*October* 18, 1638."

These letters of the bishop were regularly transmitted to Laud, to whom, from the intelligence they contained, they would not fail to prove deeply interesting, if not, in some degree, alarming. The intimation of a petition from the northern Scots, praying the king to indulge them in the free exercise of their religious worship and government in Ulster, as he had granted to their countrymen in Scotland, was peculiarly offensive to the archbishop. For he immediately wrote to Wentworth on the subject, in these decided terms: "Whereas the bishop writes, he is informed that some Scots in Ireland are drawing a petition to his majesty, that they may have the like favour in Ireland, which is granted to them in Scotland. To this his majesty says, you may make this answer, That whatsoever he hath indulged to Scotland, is because they have there had sometime a church-government, such as it was, confused enough, without bishops; but for Ireland it hath been ever reformed by and to the church of England; and your lordship, his majesty hopes, will keep the people steady to that; and the Scotishmen which will live there, your lordship must see that they conform themselves to it, or if they will not, they may return into Scotland, and leave honester men to fill the plantations." [21]

Leslie, not content with stirring up the civil power against the non-conformists, resolved to try the force of threats and invectives, now especially formidable in consequence of the

[20] Straff. Lett. ii. 219, 20, and 226, 7.
[21] Ibid. ii. 231.

promised support of the deputy. Accordingly, at his annual visitation, held at Lisburn during the interval between the two letters which he addressed to Wentworth, he delivered to his clergy and to the laity there assembled, a long and elaborate charge. His principal object in this discourse is, to condemn the conduct of the Scottish people in resisting the religious innovations of Laud, and the tyrannical attempts of the court to impose them on the nation. This he does in the bitterest terms. He labours to show the unlawfulness of the covenant lately sworn in that kingdom, and attributes the conduct of its adherents to the most dishonourable motives. At the same time, he complains of the prevalence of non-conforming principles in his diocese, and warns his auditors, both lay and clerical, of the danger which may accrue from persisting any longer in their disobedience to his ecclesiastical authority.[22] A few extracts from this charge are necessary to complete the view, of the religious condition of a large portion of Ulster, already given in his correspondence with Wentworth.

"And now, my brethren of the clergy, and all you gentlemen of the laity, I entreat your attention, while I shall express myself in some things that concern my pastoral charge. Some things I have to say that concern the clergie onely, some things that concern the church-wardens, and somewhat that doth concern both the clergie and the laity.

22 This charge was soon after printed with the following title: "A full confutation of the covenant, lately sworne and subscribed by many in Scotland; delivered in a speech at the visitation of Down and Connor, held in Lissegarvy [Lisburn] the 26th of September, 1638. Published by authority." London, 1639, 4to. pp. 38. So anxious was Leslie for the preservation and circulation of this production, that, at his own request, one of his chaplains shortly after published a Latin translation of it, thus entitled: "Examen conjurationis Scoticæ: Sive oratio habita Lisnegarvæ, in visitatione Diœceseos, Dunensis et Connorensis, 26 Septem. 1638. In qua, ad convincendos quos ecclesia nostra habet non conformes, fœdus, confessio et juramentum mutuæ tutelæ, quibus apud Scotos hodie subscribitur, enucleantur et penitus convelluntur: per Rev. in Ch. P. Hen. Dunensem. Latinitate donavit, Jacobus Portussus, dicto Rev. P. ex sacris domesticis." Dubl. 1639. 4to.

"As for you of the clergie, there is generally a great fault in you in the neglect of catechising.(23) You know that you are bound to it by the canons of the church, bound by an act in my first visitation, and though ye regard neither of these, as I know many of you do not, yet consider, I beseech you, that ye are bound to it in consciences. It is milk for babes, whereas preaching is meat for men that are of age, who have their wits exercised 'to discern both good and evil.' But you cannot abide to give milk, and are all for strong meat, albeit there are many of you who are not well able to chew it. Preaching amongst you is grown to that esteem that it hath shuffled out of the church, both the publique prayers which is the immediate worship of God, and this duty of catechising; and is now accounted the sole and onely service of God, the very *consummatum est* of all Christianity, as if all religion consisted in the hearing of a sermon. Unto whom I may say in the words of the apostle, 'What? Is all hearing? Is the whole body an eare?'(24) Or, tell you in the words of a most

[23] By the presbyterian ministers neglecting to catechise, as here charged against them by the bishop, is meant solely their refusing to use the catechism of the episcopal church, especially at the time prescribed in the rubric, that is, as a part of the public service of the church. No class of ministers have been so uniformly faithful and laborious in teaching and catechising both the old and young of their charges, as the presbyterian clergy have been, wherever settled.

[24] This quotation, with others in the bishop's writings, is taken from the Geneva translation, in use prior to the present authorised version of the Bible, which was completed and published in 1611. The Scottish divines, of all parties, adhered to the Geneva Bible, until about the year 1640, when the present translation, originally designed only for the English church and too partial to prelacy, was at length silently established in general use.—Memorial for the Bible Societies in Scotland, p. 87, et seq. Much exceedingly curious and most valuable information respecting the progress of printing in Scotland, the earlier editions of the Scriptures, and other collateral topics of considerable interest to the general reader, is to be found in this 'Memorial,' which, though anonymous, was written by the Rev. John Lee, D.D. F.R.S.E., one of the ministers of Edinburgh, and principal clerk to the General Assembly. No one who has the happiness of being acquainted with Dr. Lee, but must join in the regret express-

reverend prelate, 'That if you be the sheep of Christ, you have no mark of his sheep, but the eare-mark.' And therefore, to conclude this point, if you will not hereafter make conscience of this duty of catechising, then the conscience of my duty will inforce me to proceed against you according to the canons of the church.

"As for the church-wardens, I have a double complaint against them. One, That whereas by their place, they are to look unto the fabrick of the church; the greatest part of your temples are kept no better than hog-styes. I know that it is one of the mysteries of their religion, that God is most purely served, when he is worshipped slovenly in a poor and homely cottage, and that any cost is too much to be bestowed upon God's service. They are much like unto the officers of Julian the apostate, who when they saw the stately vessels of the temple, cried out, '*En qualibus vasis ministratur Mariæ filio?*' What stately plate is this for the carpenter's sonne?

"But my second complaint is yet greater. They are bound by their oath to present all known disorders within their parish, especially them who do not repair unto the church to hear divine service, and to receive the sacrament according to the orders of this church; yet they present none at all. And indeed, the church-wardens, especially in the Ards and Claneboyes, are of all others the most disorderly men, the very ring-leaders of the separation; and it is for that cause they are chosen, that others may not be presented. So that it seems unto me, that too many of them in Scotland have entered in a mutual bond to defend one another by arms; so their fellows in this diocesse, have entered in a mutual bond to defend one another by their oathes. But, here I tell them plainly, that I will proceed against them; first, for the neglect of the repair of their churches; next, for their own nonconformity; thirdly, for not presenting notorious offenders;

ed by my friend Dr. M'Crie, (preface to Life of Melville,) that his eminent historical acquirements have not been employed in illustrating some portion of the literary or eccleiastical history of Scotland.

and lastly, for their perjury. And if they think my authority too weak to overtake them, in regard of the great patronage and countenance they have, I will deliver them over unto a court that is able to deal with them.

"My last complaint will hold me longer. It strikes both against the clergy and the laity, for their general non-conformity, and disobedience unto the orders of this church. You of the clergy have all sworn, subscribed and promised absolute conformity. And yet, when you come amongst your people, you slide back, and for a colour of obedience, read some part of the service, it may be the lessons and a few collects, as if it were left unto your power to mince the service of God, cutting and carving upon it as you please. I must tell you that those who will not be tyed, neither by oaths, subscriptions nor promises, there is nothing will tye them but a coercive power.

"But, they of the laity are yet worse, they will hear no prayer at all. While divine service is reading, they walke in the church-yard, and when prayer is ended, they come rushing into the church, as it were into a play-house, to hear a sermon. But, ere it be long, I hope a course shall be taken, that they who will hear no prayers, shall hear no sermon.

"I know that the thing which doth encourage you in this your disobedience, is the present insurrection in Scotland. You think, and some of you do not stick for to speak it, that they will inforce the king for to yeeld unto all their demands, and amongst the rest, procure unto you a liberty to live here as you list. But deceive not yourselves. For howsoever, in Scotland, some think themselves strong enough to resist their prince, yet, (I thanke God,) you are not so many here, but the king's laws and authority is well able to overtake you. And be assured, that their insolent opposition against our most pious prince, will make you, that are of their faction, to be more narrowly looked unto here, than otherwise you would have been. For now, that our neighbour's house is on fire, it is high time to look to our own."

The facts contained in these extracts from the correspondence and visitation charge of Leslie, are highly instructive. They prove the continued existence of a very general disobedience to the ceremonies of the church, throughout a most extensive and populous diocese. They justify the inference, that if nonconformity was so prevalent under this most vigilant and active prelate, it must have been still more prevalent under less intolerant bishops, in other parts of the province. They corroborate, in the amplest manner, the statements already made, respecting the numbers of the northern clergy who were in principle presbyterian, and who, though coerced into the promise of conformity to save themselves from persecution, adhered, in the seclusion of their parishes, to the presbyterian ritual. They testify the conscientious aversion of the great mass of the population to the liturgy and common-prayer of the episcopal church, the use of which they refused to countenance by their presence, while they punctually attended during the preaching of the sermon, which was usually preceded and concluded with extempore prayer. And above all, they furnish another unquestionable proof, of the total inefficacy of compulsory measures to ensure a cordial or absolute conformity in religious matters.

Wentworth, in pursuance of his precautionary plans for preventing the Scots in Ulster from joining in the covenant, or opposing, in any way, the designs of the king, had recourse to an expedient more illegal in its character, and more oppressive in its effects, than any which he had yet adopted. This was the imposition, on all the northern Scots, of an oath, styled, from the dismal calamities which it occasioned, THE BLACK OATH, in which they were compelled to swear, never to oppose any of the king's commands, and to abjure all covenants and oaths, contrary to the tenor of this unconditional engagement.

The first idea of this measure originated with Charles. In the month of January 1639, he suggested it to Wentworth as likely to furnish an additional security to his cause in Ulster, against the apprehended machinations of the Scottish covenanters.[25] The deputy approved of the plan, and thus wrote to Charles for instructions. "In case any Scottish refuse to take the oath of abjuration, what is your pleasure we should do with them? Shall we *lege talionis* here, as there, imprison the parties delinquent, and seize their lands and holdings to your majesty for the use of the public?[26] Shortly after, he summoned several of the Scottish noblemen, clergy, and gentry, on whose cordial co-operation he could rely, to meet him in Dublin on business, as he alleged, of especial importance to his majesty's service. When assembled in the latter end of April, in the apartments of the lord viscount Ards, Wentworth opened to them his design. He apprized them of the disorders which had occurred in Scotland; of the surmises entertained of the Scots in Ulster favouring these seditious proceedings; and of the propriety of their vindicating themselves from such injurious suspicions. He concluded by reminding them how much more acceptable and becoming it would be for them, to enter into a voluntary declaration of their fidelity and obedience to the king, than delay the tender of their loyalty, till extorted from them by the increasing dangers of the state. This suggestion of the deputy was hailed with acclamations by the bishops who were present. It was not opposed by the noblemen and other gentlemen, who appear to have been very passive instruments in the hands of Wentworth and the prelates.

The bishop of Raphoe immediately framed a petition to the deputy and council, in the name of the Ulster Scots, praying to be permitted, by oath or otherwise, to vindicate themselves

25 Rushworth, viii. 504. It is more than probable, however, that the scheme was entirely Wentworth's; and that the letter from Charles, which he produced on his trial, directing him to frame and administer the oath in question, was afterwards procured for his justification, when called to answer this charge.

26 Straff. Lett. ii. 324.

from approving the proceedings of their countrymen in Scotland. This petition was in due form presented to the council. It was signed by Hamilton, Lord Claneboy, and Montgomery, lord of Ards; by the bishops of Clogher, Raphoe, and Down; by the archdeacons of Armagh and of Down; by ten knights, and by twenty-four individuals, the majority of whom were clergymen. The form of the intended oath was submitted by the council to the consideration of the petitioners.[27] Objections were made, by some of the laymen present, to the unconditional manner in which they were required to swear never to oppose, nor even to 'protest against any of his royal commands.' They entreated that the qualifying phrase of 'just commands,' or 'commands according to law,' might be inserted. But Wentworth would admit of no alteration, and they silently, though reluctantly, acquiesced. As a rebuke to their scrupulosity, the bishop of Raphoe lamented that that part of the oath, which appeared so obnoxious, had not been rendered more strong and explicit; and in a spirit of affected disappointment at the moderation with which the doctrine of passive obedience and non-resistance was expressed therein, he exclaimed, 'that the oath was so mean, he would not come from his house to take it.'[28] Yet

[27] The following is a copy of this celebrated oath, as set forth in the proclamation:—" I, ——— do faithfully swear, profess and promise, that I will honour and obey my sovereign lord King Charles, and will bear faith and true allegiance unto him, and defend and maintain his royal power and authority, and that I will not bear arms, or do any rebellious or hostile act against him, or protest against any his royal commands, but submit myself in all due obedience thereunto: and that I will not enter into any covenant, oath, or band of mutual defence and assistance against all sorts of persons whatsoever, or into any covenant, oath, or band of mutual defence and assistance against any persons whatsoever by force, without his majesty's sovereign and regal authority. And I do renounce and abjure all covenants, oaths, and bands whatsoever, contrary to what I have herein sworn, professed and promised. So help me God, in Christ Jesus." Straff. Lett. ii. 345.

[28] Rushw. viii. 492.

it is scarcely possible to conceive a more objectionable oath, or one more directly at variance with the ordinary principles of civil liberty, and the acknowledged rights of subjects.

By a proclamation from the deputy and council, dated the twenty-first of May, and containing a copy of the petition, all the Scottish residents in Ulster above the age of sixteen years, were required to take this oath, "upon the holy evangelists, and that upon pain of his majesty's high displeasure, and the uttermost and most severe punishments which may be inflicted, according to the laws of this realm, on contemners of sovereign authority." Commissions were issued to the northern magistracy to administer the oath in their respective districts. And as there had been, about the same time, "a foolish discourse to surprise the castle of Carrickfergus, therefore to provoke the Scottish here to take arms, and to call in the covenanters to their support,"[29] Wentworth resolved to secure this important fortress, and to support the magis-

29 Straff. Lett. ii. 342. This was a mere sham plot, fomented by spies, the danger of which was purposely aggravated to justify the imposition of the oath, and the augmentation of the army in Ulster. Sir John Clotworthy, who happened to be on the bench during the trial of Trueman for this plot, at the Carrickfergus summer assizes, 1639, gave the following testimony on Wentworth's trial:—"That Trueman was an Englishman, that dwelt not far from Knockfergus, and one that was sent about the country, but by whom Sir John could not tell; but, there were vehement suspicions that he was employed to find out those that would engage in discourse concerning the Scotch business; he spake with one Captain Giles, who feigned himself a great friend of the Scotch nation; and said, that he conceived they were greatly distressed, and wished that he could use means whereby they might be eased. Hence he discoursed with Trueman, who was but a silly man, and got from him words whereby he discovered a good will to the Scotch nation, and some discourse about the castle of Knockfergus; insomuch that he got Trueman's letter to recommend him into Scotland, whither he pretended a desire to go, to serve under that command: Upon this he [Giles] produced the letter, and that was given in evidence against him, and so he [Trueman] was condemned and executed." Rushworth, viii. 511. Baillie adds,—"For this confession he is hanged, and quartered half quick, after the English fashion, as a traitor." Lett. i. 170.

trates in the execution of their commissions, by despatching thither a large military force. On these subjects the deputy thus expressed himself in his letters to the English court:

"Considering the distemper of these times, and of their countrymen, it was judged fit by this state to gain a renunciation of the Scottish on this, of the frantick covenant of some of their countrymen on the other, side. To which intent the act of state enclosed was framed, and themselves procured to be petitioners, it might be so, according as you will find therein contained; whereunto very chearfully they conformed, and all the principal of them took the oath before this council, and the rest in the country will, without all peradventure, follow, as they have begun unto them: Commissioners are going down, and in the execution thereof, we take such a course without being discerned, as will, I trust, enable us to guess very near, what the number of the natives of that kingdom are here inhabiting amongst us."—"Yet to prevent all accidents which might happen to hinder the good proceeding of so necessary a service, my patents are gone to all the troops and companies in Leinster and Ulster, to march forthwith to Knockfergus, to be there by the thirtieth of this month, [May,] thence to be disposed and garrisoned in such places of Ulster as may not only contain the Scots on this side in their duty and obedience, but also prevent the landing of any more of them upon us from the other side. These troops and companies I put under the command of the master of the ordnance, [Sir George Radcliffe,] making in all one thousand foot and five hundred horse, which shall also attentively look on, whilst the oath is given by the commissioners, and taken by the Scots; and if there be an occasion, as indeed I am confident there will not, I am ready, on a day's warning, to march up to them myself with the other half of this army." (30)

30 Straff. Lett. ii. 342 and 337.

The commissioners were directed to proceed in the most summary manner. The ministers and church-wardens were required to make a return of all the Scots resident in their respective parishes. The oath was publicly read by the commissioners, and then taken by the people on their knees; but from the persons called on to swear, the privilege, of a deliberate perusal of it for themselves, was studiously withheld. It was imposed equally on women as on men. The only exception made, was in favour of those Scots who professed to be Roman catholics; these alone were not required to take the oath. The names of those who scrupled to swear, were immediately forwarded to Dublin; whence the deputy despatched his officers to execute his pleasure on the recusants.

Contrary to the expectations of Wentworth, great numbers refused to take the oath in the unqualified form in which it was proposed. None of them had the least hesitation to swear in the terms of the former part, expressive of bearing true and faithful allegiance to his majesty. But they conscientiously and firmly refused to take the latter part, by which they would have been bound to yield an unconditional obedience to all his royal commands, whether civil or religious—just or unjust—constitutional or unconstitutional. On these individuals, the highest penalties of the law, short of death, were unsparingly inflicted, frequently under circumstances of extreme cruelty. Thus, pregnant women were forced to travel considerable distances to the places appointed by the commissioners. If they hesitated to attend, and still more, if they scrupled to swear, they were treated in a barbarous manner; so that crowds of defenceless females fled to the woods, and concealed themselves in caves to escape their merciless persecutors. Respectable persons, untainted with crime, were bound together with chains, and immured in dungeons. Several were dragged to Dublin, and fined in exorbitant sums; while multitudes fled to Scotland, leaving their houses and properties to certain ruin; and so many of the labouring population abandoned the country, that it was scarcely possible to carry forward the necessary work of the harvest. The following letter, addressed to Wentworth by Hamilton, lord Claneboy, now converted from the generous patron to the keen persecutor of his presbyterian countrymen, will convey some idea of the manner in which this obnoxious oath was enforced, and of the opposition which it very generally encountered.

"The Lord Viscount Claneboye to the Lord Deputy.

"My much observed Lord,

"May it please your lordship to know, that the master of the ordnance, when he had his meeting at Bangor with the lord Montgomery, lord Chichester, and myself, for taking order according to your lordship's directions for such as refused to take the oath, he had then the view of the books which were given up to us by the preachers and church-wardens of the parishes in the Claneboyes and Ards, of such of the Scots as were to take the oath. And we are hopeful that he both saw by our progress upon the said books, and hath showed to your lordship the willingness of the people, and our diligence in the work, although by the greatness thereof and paucity of the commissioners, who are to be at least three at every swearing, sundry of the parishes were then remaining uncalled, of which the people, as we are able to come at them, are since come in, and have taken their oaths, except the gleanings everywhere of sick or absent persons, who are remitted and directed upon their recovery or return home, to come to Killileagh, where the oath is to be given to them of the territory of Dufferin, and of the adjoining parishes, which is to be the last sitting for this service, and is to make the perclose of our books, and what we may say upon the whole matter. For which purpose I am come to Killileagh, where, contrary to my expectation, I find the people much altered in my absence from what I left them, and to be made apprehend much unlawfulness in the oath, and much danger of soul to take it.

Insomuch, that upon notice of my coming hither, many are fled out of the country, and especially servants, that their masters are doubtful to find sufficient to reap their corn; for whose apprehension, as they may be found, I have sent out warrants.

"It is conceived, that some aspersions, lyingly cast upon the oath, and a suggestion that it is greatly disliked in Scotland, (for which I can find no author to lay hold on, albeit this might have operated with them in part,) hath been the cause of this averseness. But, indeed, I do apprehend, that the chief, if not the only cause, is proceeded from Mr. John Bole, the preacher at Killileagh,[31] the old blind man that was once with your lordship; who, instead of obviating such aspersions, and satisfying the people in their doubts, hath very presumptuously and perversely, both in his common conferences, and in his public sermons upon the Sabbath-day to the people in the church, taxed the oath to be without any ground, to be unnecessary, uncertain, doubtful, and in the branches of it, unlawful, and contrary to all former oaths.

"I have herein taken the examinations of sundry persons of respect, which, tested with their own hands, I herewith send to your lordship, that by them, he may be presented to your lordship in his own words. I lay not my hand upon any clergyman, especially a preacher, without direction, otherwise I had sent him myself.

"I altered also, upon this rub, for a short time, the day of calling the people to the oath, that there might be opportunity to settle the minds of the people to their true duty. Wherein I doubt not but your lordship shall find the faithful endeavours of him, who, leaving all to your lordship's wisdom, is ever your lordship's most humble, and most obliged servant,

"J. Claneboye."

"*Killileagh, Aug.* 23, 1639."

31 The reader will find this minister settled in the parish of Killileagh, in the year 1622. See Appendix, No. 1.

"THE LORD VISCOUNT CLANEBOYE TO THE LORD DEPUTY.

"My much honoured Lord,

"Your lordship's noble favours to me at all times, and especially by your last letters of the 27th of August, do bind me to a continual loving and honouring of your lordship, and expression of the same, as any your lordship's service shall require; which I hereby profess.

"If Mr. Bole, who is now carried up by a pursuivant, shall deny any of the things charged against him, which is too usual with him, boldly to speak, and more boldly to deny it, the witnesses who have, under their hands, tested the same, are of credit, and if required, shall repair thither, and upon their oaths, make it good in his hearing.

"Since my last to your lordship, I made intimation to the people of the parishes hereabout, who especially were possessed with a prejudice of the oath, that if any were doubtful of any thing contained in it, they should freely repair to me, and that I would satisfy them to the full, before they should be put to take it. Very many came in, of whom some had been misled by foul reproaches cast upon it, others by misconstructions of it, and some by their apprehended doubts of what might be required of them hereafter, if they should take it. But, in a short debating, they had all contentment, and were sorry of their shunning. Amongst the rest, Mr. Bole came to me, hearing that his speeches had been revealed to me, and made profession of his bounden duty to his majesty, and of his respect to the oath. But I told him I was sorry to hear of his much miscarriage against both, of which he desired to hear the particulars. I said he would hear of them soon enough in another place, and willed him to remember himself what he had said. And not long thereafter, upon that day which we had appointed for the people to come in for taking the oath, I sent to him, and required him to be there; for that was the form, that the minister and church-wardens, and chief men of the parish, were made leaders to the people in taking the oath. I did likewise direct the provost of the town to be with him. But he desired that, (in respect it fell out, that the same day was the day of the week, upon which he ordinarily used to have weekly an exhortation to the people,) he might be heard in his sermon first, and to declare himself concerning the oath in hand, wherein he hoped to give satisfaction to us and the people, which we thought not amiss to afford him, to see how he would amend himself.

" His text he took out of the sixth chapter of the prophet Daniel, the 6, 7, 8, 9, and 10th verses. [32] Your lordship will see how pertinent that text was to such a purpose; and he indeed accordingly handled it so, as none I think could tell what he was seeking, or in what or how he gave any satisfaction to the people for the matter of the oath. Much he taxed the princes of Persia for abusing the king, and destroying his soul, by leading him upon a false decree to destroy Daniel; and, by the way, some admonitions he gave us the commissioners, to take heed that we did nothing that might give us cause of grief hereafter. But for the oath nothing expressly, but that some had reported to him, that he had made the oath doubtful and unlawful, wherein he said they

[32] The following is the text from which Mr. Bole preached;

" 6. Then these presidents and princes assembled together to the king, and said thus unto him, king Darius, live for ever.

" 7. All the presidents of the kingdom, the governors, and the princes, the counsellors, and the captains, have consulted together to establish a royal statute, and to make a firm decree, that whosoever shall ask a petition of any god or man for thirty days, save of thee, O king, he shall be cast into the den of lions.

" 8. Now, O king, establish the decree, and sign the writing, that it be not changed, according to the law of the Medes and Persians, which altereth not.

" 9. Wherefore king Darius signed the writing and the decree.

" 10. Now when Daniel knew that the writing was signed, he went into his house; and his windows being open in his chamber towards Jerusalem, he kneeled upon his knees three times a-day, and prayed, and gave thanks before his God, as he did aforetime."

had done him wrong, and that therefore they should see him then take it in the pulpit of himself. And without more, he swore and protested generally, his loyalty and fidelity to his majesty, and concluded with an exhortation to me, to explain the oath to the people before they took it; and so ended with the usual form.

"Thereupon I called him and the people unto me, and told them, that according to Mr. Bole's desires I was ready, if they would show me their doubts, to explain the oath for the same, and to give them satisfaction. But, for that I believed that the doubts were made by Mr. Bole himself, I would first address me to him, who was best able to move them, and to discern of the answer I should give to them. In effect, there was nothing propounded but their misconstructions, fears and surmises of what hereafter might be drawn upon them by the power of the oath; and having heard him and the people, in all they could say, I gave them so full satisfaction, that they all confessed the oath was rightful to be taken. Whereupon I willed Mr. Bole, the provost of the town of Killileagh, and the church-wardens, and some of the aldermen to kneel down and I would give it them. Mr. Bole told me, that he had taken it already. I asked him, where? he said he had taken it in my hearing in the pulpit. I told him that shuffling would not serve his turn, he should take it in the express words of the prescribed oath, following me as others did. And after two or three bouts in the hearing of the people, I required him either to kneel with the rest, and to take it in the ordinary form, or if he refused, he should instantly hear me in another sort; and then indeed he did kneel and take it with the rest.

"I pray your Lordship to excuse this prolix narration, which is drawn on to show your lordship, that he hath taken the oath, and by what degrees he was brought to it. And since, as I hear, he did persuade the people to it, who nevertheless come nothing so chearfully in, as they did in other parts. But nothing shall be undone of my part to forward and finish the business, and to pray for the increase of all happiness to your lordship, which is the affectionate desire of your lordship's most humble and most obliged servant,

"J. CLANEBOYE." (33)

"*Killileagh*, *Sept.* 2, 1639."

Throughout Ulster, the BLACK oath was rigorously enforced; and this descriptive epithet was too amply justified in the persecutions which it occasioned, not only to the conscientious presbyterians, but to every one attached to the principles, or zealous for the maintenance, of civil and religious freedom. The following detail of the grievances endured by those Christian patriots who refused to take it, though never before published, must not be withheld.

"This oath, a generality did take, who were not bound with a conscience; others hid themselves or fled, leaving their houses and goods; and divers were imprisoned and kept in divers gaols for a considerable time. This proved the hottest piece of persecution this poor infant church did meet with, and the strongest wind to separate between the wheat and the chaff. However, God strengthened many to hazard all before they would swallow it.

"In the county of Down, not only divers lost their habitations, and most of their goods, and followed to Scotland; but others were apprehended and long imprisoned, amongst whom, as an encouragement of the rest, was one Margaret Stewart, a woman eminent for piety and zeal for God, not without Christian discretion. They were kept long in the prison, till thereafter Wentworth was executed in England.

33 Straff. Lett. ii. 382-3, and 384-5. One cannot read this letter without feeling deeply for the hardships to which this aged and venerable minister was exposed. How cruel to dragoon the old and blind man into the swearing of this obnoxious oath! And yet how adroitly he endeavoured to evade it himself, and indirectly to warn his people against its ensnaring obligations! What became of him, when dragged up to Dublin, I have no means of ascertaining.

In the county of Antrim likewise, many were necessitated to flee, wherein they sustained great loss in the goods they left behind them; and yet were provided for and lived sparingly in Scotland under the gospel; and those men who were fit for war were made use of in the levies of Scotland about that time. One Fulk Ellis, an English gentleman, had the most considerable company of soldiers under his command, which was in the whole army, consisting of above one hundred men, who were both resolute and religious, all banished out of Ireland. (34)

"The like sufferings befell those of the Scottish nation who were godly in the counties of Tyrone and Londonderry;

34 Captain Fulk Ellis was eldest son of Edmond Ellis of Carrickfergus, an English colonist. He and his company joined the Scottish forces in resisting the arms of Charles in 1640, and were at the battle of Newburn. He shared in the supplies forwarded to the different companies of the army from their respective parishes in Scotland, as appears from the following interesting anecdote recorded by Livingston: "In November 1640, I returned back, [from the army] to Stranraer. All the rest of the parishes of the country had, before that, contributed money to send to buy clothes for the soldiers whom they had sent out. This was not yet done in Stranraer, by reason of my absence. Therefore at our meeting on Saturday I propounded unto them the condition of the army, and desired that they would prepare their contributions to be given to-morrow after sermon: At which time we got L.45, sterling, whereof we sent L.15, sterling to our own soldiers, and L.15, to Captain Ellis's company, who were all Irishmen, and so had no parish in Scotland to provide for them, and L.15 to the commissary-general, to be distributed by public order. The reason that we got so much was, that there were sundry families of Irish people dwelling in that town. One Margaret James, the wife of William Scott, a maltman, who had fled out of Ireland, and were but in a mean condition, gave seven twenty-two shilling sterling pieces, and one eleven pound piece. When the day after, I inquired at her, how she came to give so much? She answered, 'I was gathering, and had laid up this to be a part of a portion to a young daughter I had; and as the Lord hath lately been pleased to take my daughter to himself, I thought I would give him her portion also.'"—Captain Ellis returned to Ireland after the rebellion; he was captain and major in Sir John Clotworthy's regiment of foot, and is believed to have fallen in action near Desertmartin in the county of Derry, in September 1643. His descendants, of the same name, still reside at Carrickfergus.

fewer of them going at first to Scotland, they were subject to the more suffering. Upon refusing the oath, they had their names returned to Dublin, from whence pursuivants were sent to apprehend those who were refractory. Divers were apprehended and taken prisoners to Dublin; amongst whom was worthy Mrs. Pont, who remained prisoner nigh three years, and her husband escaping, was forced to flee the country. Others, though sent for, yet by special and very remarkable providences, escaped the pursuivants who were most earnest to apprehend them.

"John Semple, afterwards an honest zealous minister in the church of Scotland for many years; and Mr. Campbell of Duket-hall,[35] and the laird of Leckie were so nigh to be taken by the pursuivants divers times, that it appeared to be more than ordinary providence that they escaped. Particularly one time John Semple met a pursuivant by the way, who was sent to take him, and of John Semple inquired the way. Yet the man, having formerly a description of him, did not know him. Another time, the laird of Leckie, with major Stewart and John Semple, came to Newton-Stewart together about their affairs. While the former were taking a drink, it was presently told them that three pursuivants were at the door; upon which major Stewart mounted John Semple on his horse, and gave him his hat; who being mounted, and riding by the pursuivants, inquired, 'whom they were seeking?' They said, 'if you will tell us where they are whom we are seeking, we will give you a reward.' He answered, 'it may be I will.' Then said they, 'we are seeking the laird of Leckie and John Semple.' Then putting spurs to his horse, he answered, 'I am John Semple, you rogues!' While they were calling others to help them to follow him, the laird took his horse and escaped, and major Stewart also. The pursuivants being disappointed, said, 'all the devils in hell will not catch these rogues.'

"Mr. John M'Clelland being excommunicated by the

[35] See note (4) chap. ii.

court in Down, retired up the country to Strabane, and being lodged one night in a house where the woman was a non-conformist, and it being noticed thereafter, her husband, called William Kennah, was fined in five pounds for lodging an excommunicated person one night. There being a young man, a merchant in Strabane, a non-conformist, the bishop of Derry, Bramhall, coming to that place, inquired of the provost, 'what a man he was?' The provost answered, 'he was a young man, a merchant of the town.' The bishop answered, 'a young man! he is a young devil.' Thus that spirit raged amongst them [the prelatists] before the rebellion, persecuting and imprisoning all who would not conform and take the black oath; amongst whom were divers women eminent in suffering with patience and constancy, which become the godly."[36]

One case of peculiar hardship, arising out of the imposition of this oath, demands especial notice, from the importance afterwards attached to it on the trial of Wentworth. Among those who refused to swear in the unconditional terms in which the oath was designedly framed, were Henry Stewart, a gentleman of considerable property, his wife and family consisting of two daughters, and a domestic named James Gray. These persons were, on their refusal, carried up to Dublin by a sergeant at arms, and placed in close and rigorous confinement. They were separately interrogated on oath by the attorney general, and their examinations taken as evidence against them. On the tenth of September they were brought to trial in the star-chamber, a court in which the substance, as well as the forms, of law and justice were equally despised. The majority of the lords, including several prelates, pronounced all the individuals guilty of treason for refusing to take the oath. Among these judges was Bramhall, never absent when a presbyterian is to be persecuted, and when present, always concurring in the harshest measures, and sanctioning the severest punishments. The unhappy prisoners

36 Adair's MS.

were, at the same time, mocked with the assurance, that the utmost leniency had been displayed in favouring them with a trial, before the star-chamber which could not inflict a capital punishment, and not before the ordinary courts of law, which must, of necessity, as it was alleged, have sentenced them to death, for their traitorous disobedience to royal authority. Primate Ussher, who also sat on the bench on this occasion, and whom every protestant must lament to find employed in such an office, was somewhat more moderate than his prelatical brethren. While he admitted that a refusal of the former part of the oath was treason, he protested against the doctrine, laid down by the other judges, that a refusal of the latter part, involving obedience to ecclesiastical injunctions, amounted to treason. But the resolute deputy boldly told the venerable primate he was mistaken; and, as might be anticipated, he expressed his cordial concurrence with Bramhall and the other lords in finding the prisoners guilty of treason. Mr. Stewart, being permitted to speak in his defence, declared before the court, that he had no objection whatever to take the former part of the oath, promising civil allegiance to his majesty; but as he conceived the latter part bound those who took it, to yield ecclesiastical obedience to every thing which the king might choose, at any time, to enjoin, he durst not, in conscience, enter into so extensive and unconditional an engagement. Wentworth, in reply, assured him he was quite right in his interpretation of the oath; that it was intended to bind the Scots to conform to every doctrine and rite, which were either then authorized, or which might, at any time, be afterwards enjoined by royal authority; and that he would prosecute all who refused to take it 'to the blood,' and drive them 'root and branch' out of the kingdom. He concluded by pronouncing the sentence of the court; Mr. Stewart was fined in five thousand pounds, and his wife in a similar sum; his daughters, two thousand pounds each; and Gray, though only a servant, two thousand pounds,—a sum of sixteen thousand pounds off one family! To complete the hardship of the case, they were imprisoned in Dublin, at their own charges, until all these exorbitant fines should be paid.[37]

Thus did the despotic deputy tyrannize over the presbyterian non-conformists in Ulster, by the imposition of an oath, unconstitutional in its origin, because unauthorized by parliament, illegal in its nature, and ensnaring in its construction; and enforced on one class of subjects, of all ages, ranks and sexes, with unrelenting rigour and unfeeling cruelty.

37 Rushworth, viii. 496, et seq. Baillie, i. 281-2.

CHAPTER VI.

Wentworth in the zenith of his power—Case of Archibald Adair, bishop of Killala—He is deposed—Conduct of Bedell thereon—Wentworth created earl of Strafford—Collects a Roman Catholic army—and joins the king in England—Proposes to transport the Scots out of Ulster—His plans frustrated—Loses the confidence of the Irish parliament—Their Remonstrance—Commissioners sent to England—State of affairs there—General discontent—The Long Parliament meet—Strafford impeached and imprisoned—Ulster Presbyterians petition the English parliament—Copy of their petition—and list of grievances—Trial and execution of Strafford—Redress of Irish grievances—Archibald Adair released and made bishop of Waterford—Applications of Henry Stewart and Robert Adair to the Scottish Parliament—English Parliament restore the county of Derry to the corporation of London—Irish Parliament abolish the High Commission Court—and rescind its sentences against the Ulster Presbyterians—Petitioned by Mrs. Pont—Commence the reformation of Trinity College—Irish army disbanded.

WENTWORTH was now in the zenith of his power. His administration had been conducted with a vigour and success, hitherto unprecedented. No one dared to oppose his most oppressive measures. The highest nobility in the kingdom quailed before him. The least opposition to his plans, and above all, the slightest manifestation of sympathy for the Scottish covenanters, marked out the offender, however elevated in rank or station, for certain ruin. This was strikingly exemplified in the case of the bishop of Killala, who, by a few casual expressions in favour of his countrymen the Scots, drew down upon himself, at this inauspicious crisis, the formidable indignation of the deputy.

Among the ministers whom the late ecclesiastical changes in Scotland rendered uncomfortable at home, was Mr. John Corbet, minister of Bonhill, near Dumbarton. He had been an adherent and advocate of the prelatical party, and had joined with the bishops in their protest against the legality of the General Assembly at Glasgow. He afterwards withdrew his name from that protest, and subscribed the national covenant. But his attachment to the reformed church of Scotland being suspected by some of his vigilant and zealous brethren in the presbytery of Dumbarton, he was required to subscribe the assembly's declaration against the bishops and prelacy. Refusing to comply, he fled to Ireland and made his case known to Bramhall, from whom he was certain of receiving protection and support. The bishop recommended him to Wentworth; and he accordingly removed to Dublin in the early part of the year 1639, where he employed his pen in vilifying the Scots and reprobating their proceedings, as in the highest degree seditious and treasonable. He published, writes Baillie from Glasgow, "a refutation of Mr. Henderson's Instructions,[1] with so little matter, and so much spiteful venom, as no man would have ever conceived to have been lurking in his heart, against all our proceedings. We had thought him unworthy of a reply, and are content of our advantage, that my lord deputy permits to go out, under his patronage, that desperate doctrine of absolute submission to princes; that notwithstanding of all our laws, yet our whole estate may no more oppose the prince's deed, if he should play all the pranks of Nero, than the poorest slave at Constantinople may resist the tyranny of the great Turk."[2]

1 This paper was published by authority of the Scottish estates, but was drawn up by the Rev. A. Henderson. It was entitled, "Instructions for defensive arms," and is printed in Stevenson's History, ii. 686—95.

2 Baillie, i. 152—3. Corbet's tract in answer to Henderson was entitled, "The ungirding of the Scottish armour, or an answer to the Informations for defensive armes against the king's majestie, which were drawn up at Edenburgh by the common help and industrie of the three Tables of the rigid Covenanters of the Nobility, Barons, Ministry, and Burgesses, and

The inculcation of such doctrines as these secured to him the cordial and powerful patronage of Wentworth, who resolved to provide, for so seasonable an advocate, in the Irish church. A valuable living in the gift of Archibald Adair, bishop of Killala, (3) becoming soon after vacant, the deputy recommended him to the bishop, and calculated on the weight of his recommendation, supported also by that of Bramhall, as amply sufficient to ensure him the benefice. The bishop, a native of Scotland, had been apprized of Corbet's virulent abuse of the Scottish covenanters; and though he himself condemned their rejection of prelacy, yet out of a pardonable regard for his countrymen, he disliked to see them so malevolently traduced, as they had recently been, by this candidate for his patronage. He accordingly received Corbet very coldly. He hesitated not to reproach him for the rancour which he had displayed towards the Scots, and for the discredit which he had been labouring to cast on his native kingdom. Punning on his name, Corbet or 'Corbey,' which, in the provincial dialect of Scotland, signifies a 'raven,' he observed, 'it was an ill bird that defiled its own nest;' and added, that 'he was a corbey that had fled out of the ark, and that he should not have where to set his foot in his diocese.' (4) The termination and results of this singular interview are thus narrated by one, not likely to be prejudiced in favour of the bishop. "And whereas Corbet had said in his book, that he had hardly escaped with his own life, but had left his wife

ordered to be read out of Pulpit by each Minister, and pressed upon the people, to draw them to take up armes to resist the *Lords anointed* throughout the whole kingdome of Scotland." Dublin, 1639, 4to. Pp. 56. It is dedicated to the lord deputy Wentworth; and was licensed on the 6th of May 1639, by Ed. Parry, chaplain to the Archbishop of Dublin.

3 He had been dean of Raphoe, and was elevated to the see of Killala in May 1630. The reader will find him in the former office in the year 1622. See appendix, No. I.

4 The latter of these sayings is taken from Vesey's Life of Bramhall, prefixed to his works. Bramhall also reported Adair's conduct at this interview to Wentworth in the most unfavourable light, and urged the necessity of punishing severely his brother prelate.

behind him to try the humanity of the Scots; he told him, he had left his wife to a very base office. Several other things the bishop said, which in themselves amounted to nothing, but only expressed an inclination to lessen the fault of the Scots, and to aggravate some provocations that had been given them. Corbet came up [to Dublin] full of wrath, and brought with him many informations against the bishop, which, at any other time, would not have been much considered. But it being then thought necessary to make examples of all that seemed favourable to the covenanters, it was resolved to turn him out of his bishoprick." (5)

Corbet was soon after provided for elsewhere. In the mean time, he published in Dublin, but without affixing his name, another small treatise against the Scots, more severe and malicious than his former tract. (6) It was written in the

5 Burnet's Bedell, pp. 109—10. Let the reader contrast with bishop Burnet's account of this transaction, the following version of it by Leland, who, let it be observed, possessed no additional information on the subject. "Archibald Adair, a native of Scotland, had been tempted to conformity by the prospect of gain, and advanced to the bishoprick of Killala, a station little suited to his puritanic principles. The wretch was not so guarded or confirmed in his hypocrisy, as to suppress his indignation at a clergyman of his own country, who had written with severity against the covenanters; he reproached him for his conduct, and was even provoked to justify their conduct, with a warmth and acrimony utterly indecent." Hist. iii. 52. The 'utter indecency' of the 'warmth and acrimony' of the historian in this passage against the calumniated bishop, is surely much more obvious and culpable than that of Adair's reproaches of Corbet.

6 It is entitled, "The Epistle congratulatorie of Lysimachus Nicanor of the Societie of Jesu, to the Covenanters in Scotland. Wherein is parallelled our sweet harmony and correspondency in divers materiall points of Doctrine and Practice." Anno Domini, M.DC.XL. 4to. pp. 84. No place of printing is given, but it was evidently Dublin; at the conclusion it is dated, 'From my study at Basileopolis, the first of January, 1640.' The Scottish divines were greatly at a loss to whom to ascribe it. Principal Baillie, at the end of his 'Canterburian Self-conviction,' adds, "A postscript for the personate Jesuite, Lysimachus Nicanor," extending to 37 pages 4to. in which he is uncertain whether to assign it to Bramhall, or Leslie, or Maxwell bishop of Ross, or Mitchell, mentioned in note (18) chap. v. In another tract he afterwards thus writes: "In that most scurrilous and

character of a jesuit, addressing the Scottish covenanters, and expressing satisfaction at observing in their late proceedings, 'their begun returne from their former errors and heresies.' A parallel is drawn between the jesuits and the covenanters; and no less than sixteen points of resemblance and approximation are illustrated with singular ingenuity and learning, and corroborated by the most apt quotations from the writings of popish canonists and protestant reformers. The conduct of Charles and the cause of prelacy are defended with great plausibility, but little regard to truth; while the tenets and practices of the presbyterians are reviled and satirized in a strain of the most bitter sarcasm. This witty and anonymous pasquil proved much more provoking to the covenanters, than the elaborate attacks of their more serious and formidable antagonists.

Wentworth, provoked by the refusal of Adair to promote Corbet, determined on punishing the obnoxious prelate as a favourer of the covenant. He took this resolution the more readily, as Charles had just been applying to him to promote Maxwell, formerly bishop of Ross in Scotland, but now deposed by his own church, and forced to fly for refuge to England. The deputy, therefore, entered with the greater alacrity on a measure, which served at once to punish a disaffected, and reward a loyal and suffering, bishop; and at the same time to gratify the express wishes of his royal master. The following communication to the king shows that, in the beginning of September, he had already determined on no less a punishment than the deposition of Adair. "The satisfac-

invenomed satyre *Lysimachus Nicanor*, his [Maxwell's] pen was thought to be principall; for this he got a warning from heaven so distinct and loud as any uses to be given on earth, to reclaime him from his former errours: with his eyes did he see the miserable man John Corbet, who took upon him the shame of penning that rable of contumelious lies against his mother-church, hewed in pieces in the very armes of his poore wife; this prelate himself in the meane time was striken down, and left with many wounds, as dead by the hand of the Irish, with whom he had been but too familiar." Hist. Vind. of the Church of Scotland, p. 2.

tion of the bishop of Ross shall be the only thing I shall attend in the next place, and have found even already the means to effect it, by depriving, and that deservedly, the bishop of Killala, and substituting the other in his place. This is one of the best bishopricks in the kingdom, worth at least one thousand pounds a-year. The way how to effect it, and the cause wherefore, I now write to my lord's grace of Canterbury, which, if approved by your majesty, shall forthwith be accomplished, as also quench the venom of that rebellious humour, at least among us in this kingdom, and preserve it still, I hope, the freest from the evil of it, of any part perchance of your majesty's dominions." (7)

Shortly after this communication, Wentworth had occasion to repair to England; but he urged forward the measure he had propounded to Charles, with his characteristic promptitude and vigour. In the latter end of September, only two days after he reached London, (8) he thus wrote to his confidant, Sir George Radcliffe: "The particular haste of this dispatch is only to advertise you, that my lord's grace of Canterbury having already represented to the king the examination of Corbet transmitted hither, touching the bishop of Killala; his majesty thereupon was very sensible of that bishop's apparent ill-affections, as unworthily as unseasonably expressed, to the violation of those due regards a person of his eminency and place ought, more especially as the times now go, to have preserved and paid to the peace and settlement of his affairs. And therefore commands that thereupon he be forthwith proceeded against, and deservedly avoided out of his bishoprick, if it may be, which you will acquaint my cousin Wandesford withal, and take present course therein accordingly." (9) Wandesforde, who had charge of the go-

7 Straff. Lett. ii. 383.

8 Wentworth reached London on the 21st (Rushw. viii. 506,) and his letter to Radcliffe is dated on the 23d of September 1639.

9 Life and original correspondence of Sir George Radcliffe, Knt. pp. 181, 2. Dr. Whittaker, an English divine, editor of this showy but

vernment during the deputy's absence, was probably remiss in discharging so irksome a duty; Wentworth, accordingly, two months later, again urges Radcliffe to push forward this vindictive prosecution. "The bishop of Killala's papers are herewith restored; you must proceed with effect, either to degrade him, or at least deprive him of his bishoprick: the sooner you dispatch it the better. The bishop of Ross is destined to succeed him, who is ready to take it with thanks." (10)

After these repeated applications, proceedings were at length commenced against the unfortunate bishop. A pursuivant was despatched to bring him up to Dublin. He was committed to prison; and tried before the high-commission court for being a favourer of the covenant. As might be expected from the constitution of this court and the servility of its presiding judges, he was without hesitation found guilty. None of these judges were so hostile to him as some of his brother prelates. Adderton, bishop of Waterford, was especially severe upon him, for the language he had used in his interview with Corbet; and Bramhall, the indefatigable persecutor of all who differed from him, in the exuberance of his zeal, declared in another place, that on account of that language, 'he deserved to be thrown into the sea in a sack, neither to see nor enjoy the air!' (11) He was, accordingly, deprived of his see, fined two thousand pounds, and ordered to be imprisoned during pleasure; and directions were issued to the convocation, about to meet at the opening of a new parliament, to take the necessary steps for effecting his deposition. Archbishop Ussher endeavoured to procure a mitigation of this iniquitous sentence, but without success. The archbishop of Tuam was directed by the convocation to proceed forthwith to execute the sentence on his suffragan

meagre volume, makes the following apposite remark on this transaction; "Under Strafford's administration the bishops of Ireland were displaced with little more ceremony than excisemen."

10 Ibid. p. 190.

11 Lords' Journals, i. 112.

bishop;[12] and at length, on the eighteenth of May, 1640, Adair was formally deposed from the ministerial office, in the cathedral church of St. Patrick's, Dublin.[13]

The conduct of bishop Bedell, on the trial of Adair, is too honourable to be passed over in silence. The reader has already seen, and no doubt admired, the firmness and fidelity of this venerable prelate in reforming ecclesiastical abuses, and his zeal and assiduity in promoting the spiritual interests of the people committed to his charge. He will now behold him worthy, perhaps, of higher admiration, in boldly withstanding the tide of popular clamour, opposing the despotic power of the state, and, at the hazard of incurring the indignation of an implacable ruler, generously befriending an injured and calumniated brother. His biographer thus narrates his conduct on this trying occasion. "Bishop Adair was accused before the high-commission court for those things that Corbet objected to him; and every man being ready to push a man down that is fallen into disgrace, many designed to merit by aggravating his faults. But when it came to bishop Bedell's turn to give his sentence in the court, he that was afraid of nothing but sinning against God, did not stick to venture against the stream. He first read over all that was objected to the bishop at the bar; then he fetched his argument from the qualifications of a bishop set down by St. Paul in his epistles to Timothy and Titus; and assumed that he found nothing in those articles contrary to these qualifications, nothing that touched either his life or doctrine. He fortified this by showing in what manner they proceeded against bishops, both in the Greek and Latin churches, and so concluded in the bishop's favour. This put many out of countenance who had considered nothing in his sentence but the consequences that were drawn from the bishop's expressions, from which they gathered the ill dispositions of his

12 Radcliffe's Life and Corresp. p. 252.

13 Ware's Bishops.

mind, so that they had gone high in their censures, without examining the canons of the church in such cases. But though those that gave their votes after our bishop were more moderate than those that had gone before him had been; yet the current run so strong that none durst plainly acquit him, as our bishop had done. So he was deprived, fined and imprisoned, and his bishoprick was given to Maxwell —— that had been bishop of Ross in Scotland, and was indeed a man of eminent parts and an excellent preacher; but by his forwardness and aspiring had been the unhappy instrument of that which brought on all the disorders in Scotland."(14)

14 Burnet's Bedell, pp. 110-11. John Maxwell, the successor of bishop Adair in the see of Killala, was a native of Dumfries-shire, and minister at Mortlick in Banffshire, whence he was removed in 1620 to Edinburgh. He was made bishop of Ross by Charles in 1633; and afterwards a privy counsellor, and an extraordinary Lord of Session. He was a most violent supporter of prelacy, an instigator of the persecutions against the Irish presbyterian ministers; and was employed by Laud in the compilation of the Scottish canons and liturgy: he possessed a considerable share of learning, and proved himself an acute antagonist of the presbyterian polity. He was the author of the treatise entitled, "Sacro-Sancta Regum Majestas," which called forth Rutherford's celebrated reply, "Lex, Rex; or the Law and the Prince." After escaping the fury of the Irish rebels, mentioned in a preceding note, (6) he retired to Oxford, and died in 1646. The following incident, the immediate cause of Maxwell's departure from Scotland, is illustrative of the prevailing spirit of the times, which so soon after issued in the overthrow of prelacy. "On the 11th of March 1638, being Sunday, he causes, as his custom was, lay down a service-book upon the reader's desk, [in his church at Ross,] and upon some other gentlemen's desks who used the same, about the ringing of the first bell to the preaching. But before the last bell was rung, certain scholars came in pertly to the kirk, and took up the whole service-books, and carried them down to the Ness, with a coal of fire, there to have burnt them altogether. But there fell out such a sudden shower, that before they could win to the Ness, the coal was drowned out. The scholars seeing this, tore them all in pieces, and threw them all into the sea. The bishop hearing of this, miskens [overlooks] all wisely, comes to church, and preaches wanting service-books. He had soon done with sermon, and therefore hastily goes to horse, —— and privately disguised, he rode south, and to the king goes he directly; a very busy man thought to be, in bringing in this service-book, and therefore

By these vigorous, but tyrannical measures, Wentworth succeeded in preserving Ulster in apparent tranquillity. But the embarrassments which were now crowding around the king, in consequence of his unpopular and insincere pacification with the Scots, and their determination to remain on the defensive, soon led to important changes in the administration of Irish affairs, and in the temper and disposition of the nation.

Charles had early resolved to seize the first pretext to renew the war with the Scots, which had been hastily terminated by treaty in the month of June 1639. But his finances being exhausted, and the majority of the nation either indifferent or averse to the renewal of hostilities, he had recourse to Wentworth for counsel in this emergency. To secure his more cordial co-operation, Charles appointed him lord lieutenant, instead of lord deputy of Ireland, elevated him to the rank of an earl by the title of Strafford, and conferred upon him other flattering marks of approbation and confidence. In return for these honours, Wentworth, who must now be designated by his new and more memorable title of STRAFFORD, entered with ardour into the royal plans. He contributed largely, out of his private fortune, to the loan raised by the chief officers of the court to provide for the urgent necessities of the state, and to enable the king to execute his designs without having recourse to parliaments. He summoned the Irish parliament to meet in the month of March 1640; and by his paramount influence, he obtained from them most liberal supplies, coupled with ardent declarations of loyalty to the king, and flattering encomiums on the excellence of his own administration;—declarations, which soon after proved to be as insincere on the part of the parliament, as they were undeserved on that of Strafford. The necessary grants being obtained, he issued immediate orders for raising a new army

durst not, for fear of his life, return to Scotland again." Spalding's Troubles, &c. p. 47.

to occupy the north-eastern parts of Ulster. Having completed these important arrangements, and committed the government of the kingdom to Sir Christopher Wandesford, as his deputy, on the fourth of April he set out for London, never again to return to Ireland.

The army, under the direction of the earl of Ormond, was speedily raised and equipped. It amounted to eight thousand foot and one thousand horse, of whom a very inconsiderable portion were protestants. It was, in effect, a Roman catholic army, arrayed to crush the rising cause of freedom, and to support Charles in his arbitrary measures.[15] For these reasons it was most obnoxious to the protestant patriots in both kingdoms, whose first uncontrolled efforts were directed to procure its disbanding. These forces assembled at Carrickfergus in the month of July, where, by incessant training, they were soon brought into a state of complete discipline. They were stationed at various points along the coast, operating as a formidable check upon any movements in Ulster favourable to the popular, or hostile to the royal, cause; and prepared, at a few hours notice, to be transported into Scotland, should Charles resolve to invade that kingdom.

But notwithstanding these successful and unresisted efforts to preserve the northern province in peace and submission, and to secure it against the danger either of internal commotion or of invasion from Scotland, Strafford was by no means satisfied with its state. He experienced the just retribution of all despotic governors, whose feelings of insecurity increase in proportion as their tyrannical oppressions appear to have placed them beyond the apprehension of danger. Although he had rigorously repressed, and had punished with the utmost severity, every symptom of disaffection to his government; although he had compelled the Scots, of whom alone he was apprehensive, to swear never on any pretext to resist the sovereign authority of the king, yet, since his removal to

15 Brodie, iii. 160-1. See addition to this note at the end of the chapter

England, he was more alarmed than ever for the tranquillity of Ulster. He had tried every expedient, short of extirpation—oaths, fines, forfeitures, imprisonments, with ecclesiastical as well as civil penalties, to prevent the possibility of danger from that quarter. But the sturdy presbyterians, though as yet suffering in silence under grievous oppressions, refused to be tranquillized so long as these grievances, which pressed so heavily on conscience, liberty and right, remained unredressed. Strafford, fully aware of this state of things, as his last resource, took the daring resolution of removing the Scottish residents out of Ulster, and of banishing them altogether from the kingdom. His plan, as developed to Radcliffe, was, that the Irish parliament, at its re-assembling, should be dealt with to recommend to him the transportation of the Scots, lest they might be induced to join with their covenanted countrymen in Scotland, or lest Argyle should invade Ireland, and placing himself at their head, organize a formidable insurrection in the north. On this recommendation of parliament, which he confidently expected to obtain, Strafford proposed to issue a proclamation commanding their departure, under the usual penalties, within a prescribed period; but exempting from its operation the more considerable proprietors, and declaring the banishment to be merely conditional, until peace be restored between the king and his Scottish subjects, or the circumstances of the kingdom be such as to warrant him to permit their return. Transports were to be provided at the public expense; and every facility afforded for getting rid, as speedily and effectually as possible, of these intractable colonists. But though daring enough to propose this iniquitous measure, he was too sagacious not to perceive the objections which would be urged against its execution. The more formidable of these he thus proposed to obviate.

"Happily it will be objected, that the Scots in Ulster, took the [Black] oath in implicit abjuration of the Covenant, that they are the king's subjects, not yet convinced of actual rebellion, that it will be a hard case to banish the king's people upon supposition and conjecture, and that, by this course, the major part of all the north will be untenanted.

"To this I answer, that many thousands in the north never took the oath; and as I am certainly made believe, they now publicly avouch it as an unlawful oath; and for aught I see, they will shortly return, to any that dares question them, such an answer as Robert Bruce, earl of Carrick, made to sir John Comyn, who, charging him with breach of oath, taken at Westminster to king Edward, replies, with cleaving his head in two. None is so dim-sighted, but sees the general inclination of the Ulster Scots to the covenant: and God forbid they should tarry there till the earl of Argyle brings them armies [arms?] to cut our throats, to our apparent disturbance, if not certain ruin. And what commonwealth will not give way, that a few landlords, and they are but a few, should receive some small prejudice, where the public safety, and certain peace of the whole is concerned?

"It will be objected that the Scots are many in number, every ordinary fellow still carrying his sword and pistol; and therefore, unsafe to be too far provoked. I answer,—'tis more unsafe to deal with an enemy by halves; and that, I fear, will fall out to be our case, if resolutely this design be not put in execution; for, who sees not, if the now standing army be not able, without any manner of danger or difficulty, without any danger to give them the law, and send them forthwith pacqueing—I say, who sees not that, upon Argyle's landing and arming of them, we shall be exposed to a most assured scorn, and certain ruin?"(16)

Had this nefarious project succeeded, it would not only have overturned the foundations on which the presbyterian church chiefly rested for support in Ireland, but it must have terminated in the ruin of protestantism, and the desolation of the

16 Radcliffe's Life and Corresp. pp. 209-10. The document from which these extracts are made, is dated October 8, 1640, and is endorsed by Radcliffe, "Proposition—Scotts—rejected by me and crossed."

northern province. Destitute of the powerful aid of the numerous and resolute presbyterian population, the few and scattered protestants who would have remained in the kingdom, could never have withstood the exterminating fury of the Roman catholics, during the rebellion which, in twelve months after, broke out in Ulster. Happily, however, the Irish parliament reassembled under such an alteration of views and circumstances, that Radcliffe, in the absence of Strafford, dared not venture to submit the proposal to their consideration. It accordingly fell abortive to the ground, and remains only as a record of the despotic dispositions of that audacious and unprincipled governor.

Whilst Strafford was maturing his plans at the British court, and completing his arrangements for maintaining the royal cause triumphant in Ireland, the national temper and dispositions had been silently but rapidly changing. Scarcely had he retired to England, and intrusted his government to the hands of a deputy, than a spirit of resolute opposition to the court began to manifest itself. Freed from the restraints of his presence, all parties began to complain of the burden of the subsidies imposed by parliament. Discontent spread quickly through the kingdom. The people no longer suffered in silence. The intolerable grievances of his administration were freely exposed and denounced; and the popular demand for a relief from its oppressions, and a reform of its abuses, became loud and general.

Both houses of parliament participated in the general feeling. At the opening of the second session, in the month of June, a signal alteration in their temper was immediately discernible. During their recess, Charles had summoned the English parliament; and in disgust at their preferring the consideration of national grievances to the voting of supplies, not unlikely to be employed in crushing the popular cause, he had wantonly and precipitately dissolved them. This injudicious step increased the discontent already prevalent throughout that kingdom. Its effects were felt in Ireland. The urgent dangers which were now gathering round the cause of freedom, compelled its friends to be more than usually vigilant and active. The English patriots found it necessary to open a communication with Ireland, where they met with many congenial spirits who, oppressed by the tyranny of Strafford and the severities of the prelates, appreciated the value of civil and religious liberty, and were prepared to stand forward in its defence. To these, the distinguishing epithet of Puritans had been, at an early period, applied. In both kingdoms, they formed the only party, who, at this time, entertained correct views of constitutional liberty; and though they have been grossly maligned, even their bitterest enemies have been forced to acknowledge, that whatever measure of freedom the empire now enjoys, is, in a great measure, to be attributed to their generous and disinterested patriotism.[17] In Ireland they were numerous, and were to be found among the members of both houses of parliament; and in Ulster, though many had abandoned the country and retired to Scotland, they still constituted the predominant party. The overbearing power of Strafford had depressed them for a time. But emancipated from this restraint, and encouraged by their brethren in England, and their countrymen in Scotland, they now manifested a determination to seek a thorough redress of the grievances under which the country had been groaning.

In this determination, they were at first joined by the Roman catholic party—a singular coalition, which did not exist in either of the sister kingdoms. But in Ireland, both presbyterian and papist had equally felt the severities of Strafford's administration; both were equally indignant at the usurpations of the bishops and the ecclesiastical courts; and both could unite, to a certain length, in resisting and removing these oppressions. But as the one party sought only a reformation of the church, while the other aimed at effecting

17 The following is Hume's remarkable admission:—"The precious spark of liberty had been kindled and was preserved by the Puritans alone; and it was to this sect that the English owe the whole freedom of their constitution."

its overthrow, and, with it, the demolition of protestantism, the period soon arrived when they could no longer co-operate. In the mean time, while united, they constituted a formidable party; and, even in the second session, their influence proved predominant in both houses of parliament. They reduced the subsidies which they had, a few months before, voted with a lavish generosity and with extraordinary declarations of loyalty, to a fourth part of the original grant; and, at the same time, they presented a spirited address to Wandesford, complaining of the abuses of the church-courts, and the exorbitant exactions of the established clergy.

On the reassembling of parliament, in the beginning of October, they ventured on still bolder measures. In opposition to the court-party, the commons proceeded to draw up a Remonstrance, detailing, in fifteen articles, the grievances imposed upon the kingdom during the government of Strafford. The following articles show that the case of the northern Scots was not overlooked.

"8. The extream and cruel usage by certain late commissioners and others, of the inhabitants of the city and county of Londonderry, by means whereof the worthy plantation of that county is almost destroyed, and the said inhabitants are reduced to great poverty, and many of them forced to forsake the country; the same being the first and most useful plantation in the large province of Ulster, to the great weakening of the kingdom in this time of danger, the said plantation being the principal strength of those parts.

"9. The late erection of the court of high-commission, for causes ecclesiastical in those necessitous times; the proceedings of the said court in many causes without legal warrant, and yet so supported, that prohibitions have not been obtained, though legally sought for; and the excessive fees exacted by the ministers thereof: and the encroaching of the same upon the jurisdiction of the ecclesiastical courts."[18]

18 Commons' Journals, i. 281.

Not content with adopting this celebrated remonstrance, the commons appointed a committee to repair with it to England, for the purpose of presenting it to the king in person, and claiming an immediate redress of the enumerated grievances. This committee consisted of three members from each province, all of whom belonged either to the Roman catholic or the puritan party. Those from Ulster were, Sir James Montgomery, member for the county of Down, Sir William Cole, member for the county of Fermanagh, and Edward Rowley, Esq., member for the county of Londonderry.(19) Though charged by the deputy on their allegiance not to leave Dublin, they set out privately on the twelfth of November. On their arrival in London, they found the oppressor of their country, once so formidable, stripped of his power, impeached by the commons of England, and imprisoned under the charge of high treason!

The circumstances which led to this unexpected vicissitude are well known. The pressing necessities of the king had at length compelled him reluctantly to summon another parliament, which from its unusual duration, has been styled the Long parliament.(20) It assembled at one of the most critical periods in the history of the nation. The tyrannical conduct of Charles—his arbitrary encroachments on the rights of the people—his avowed contempt of parliaments, and his determination to rule, if possible, independently of their control—the glaring abuses in the administration of justice—the cruelty and oppression of illegal courts—the decay of trade by monopolies and impositions—and, above all, the corruption of religion—the insolence and violence of the clergy, and the gradual assimilation of the church, under the auspices of Laud, to the Romish superstition;—these grievances, affecting every class, and involving matters of the deepest interest to every individual, had justly excited so general a discontent

19 Commons' Journal, i. 286.

20 This parliament sat, with little interruption, about twelve years and a half, until violently dissolved by Cromwell.

throughout the kingdom, and roused so resolute a spirit of hostility to the court, as could no longer be subdued or repressed.

Under these circumstances, an unusual number of representatives, pledged to prosecute the redress of grievances, and to support the cause of popular privileges and rights against the encroachments of the prerogative, were returned as members of this parliament—the most memorable in the annals of Britain. On the third of November 1640, it was opened by the king in person. The commons, inflexibly resolved to prosecute, as their primary object, the thorough examination and redress of the national grievances, immediately proceeded to appoint committees for that purpose. And on the third day of meeting, Mr. Pym, in a speech of great force and eloquence, moved for a committee of the whole house to take into consideration the affairs of Ireland. This motion was seconded by Sir John Clotworthy of Antrim, who had, a short time before, settled in England to escape the vindictive hostility of Strafford; and had been returned to parliament for the borough of Malden in Essex.(21) Sir John continued to be the same in England as he had been in Ireland—a firm patriot and a staunch presbyterian. While at Antrim, his patriotism, no less than his non-conformity, had rendered him peculiarly obnoxious to Strafford, whose fall he now accelerated by his zeal and courage, but especially by his accurate knowledge of Irish affairs. On the eleventh of November, the commons adopted the bold and hazardous resolution of impeaching Strafford of high treason. A committee, of whom

21 Sir John had been a member of the Irish house of commons in 1634. In 1636, he appears to have first rendered himself obnoxious to Strafford, by refusing to support his plans for establishing a monopoly of linen yarn. Rush. viii. 418. He was in Dublin in August 1639; (Rawd. Papers, 62.) but he shortly after removed to England. His was one of the few double returns to the long parliament, a circumstance which shows the value attached by the popular party to his services. He was elected for the borough of Bossiney in Cornwall, as well as for Malden; but he preferred taking his seat for the latter. Hansard's Parl. Hist. See also Note 2, chap. ii.

Sir John Clotworthy was one, was appointed to prepare the charges against him. The same day he was formally impeached at the bar of the house of Lords, and immediately sequestered from his seat, and committed to the Tower:—a reverse of fortune which, for its extent and rapidity, has been seldom paralleled.(22)

The committee from the Irish parliament, arriving at this critical conjuncture, were received in London with every mark of respect. On the twentieth of November, their Remonstrance was presented to the house of commons, and produced

22 Principal Baillie, who was at this period in London, a commissioner for concluding the treaty between the Scots and Charles begun at Ripon, gives the following graphic sketch of the proceedings of this day, so eventful in its consequences both to Strafford and to the empire at large. "All things go here as our hearts could wish. The Lieutenant of Ireland came but on Monday to town late, on Tuesday rested, on Wednesday came to parliament; but ere night he was caged. Intolerable pride and oppression cries to heaven for a vengeance. The lower house closed their doors, the Speaker kept the keys till his accusation was concluded. Thereafter Mr. Pym went up, with a number at his back, to the higher house; and, in a pretty short speech, did, in name of the lower house, and in the name of the commons of all England, accuse Thomas earl of Strafford, Lord lieutenant of Ireland, of high treason; and required his person to be arrested till probation might be heard: so Mr. Pym and his back were removed. The lords began to consult on that strange and unexpected motion. The word goes in haste to the Lord lieutenant, where he was with the king: with speed he comes to the house; he calls rudely at the door; James Maxwell, keeper of the black rod, opens: his lordship, with a proud gloomy countenance, makes towards his place at the board head: but at once many bid him void the house: so he is forced, in confusion, to go to the door till he was called. After consultation, being called in, he stands, but is commanded to kneel; and on his knees to hear the sentence. Being on his knees, he is delivered to the keeper of the black rod, to be prisoner till he was cleared of these crimes the house of commons had charged him with. He offered to speak, but was commanded to be gone, without a word. In the outer room, James Maxwell required him, as prisoner, to deliver his sword. When he had got it, he cries, with a loud voice, for his man to carry my Lord lieutenant's sword. This done, he makes through a number of people towards his coach, all gazing, no man capping to him, before whom that morning the greatest of England would have stood discovered." Baillie, i. 217.

an impression most unfavourable to Strafford. This application was the first ever made by the Irish to the English parliament,[23] and formed, at this period, an important precedent in favour of the people of Ireland. Their own parliament had been suddenly prorogued by Wandesford, with the view of checking the spirit of opposition to the court which had been growing daily more formidable. The only channel, therefore, through which they could make known their grievances, or seek for redress, lay in the parliament of England. The way having been once opened to this tribunal, their petitions were favourably received; and many of the Irish nobility and commoners having repaired to London to assist in bringing to justice their impeached governor, every facility was thereby enjoyed by the oppressed in Ireland for submitting their respective grievances to the notice of parliament.

The suffering non-conformists in Ulster were not slow to embrace this method of making known their grievances to their brethren in England. All the efforts of Strafford had not weakened their attachment to the presbyterian faith and order. Notwithstanding the dangers to which they were exposed, those who continued to reside in Ulster held private meetings for religious worship among themselves, most frequently in the night season. After their ministers had been forced to fly to Scotland, and the more timid who remained were afraid to attend these proscribed assemblies, the more eminent among the laity conducted the worship, and usually expounded scripture for their mutual comfort and edification.[24] By these means, the

23 Carte, i. 115.

24 These practices of private meetings and lay preaching, abundantly justifiable in a time of persecution, were introduced into Scotland by several of the Ulster refugees; and being continued, sometimes to the prejudice of the parochial ministry, complaint was made against them to the general assembly in 1640 by Guthrie, minister of Stirling, who conceived himself injured by some expressions used at these private assemblies, where the laird of Leckie, who had fled from Ireland, usually presided. The keen controversies excited by the efforts of a party, to put an end to these practices as irregular and inexpedient in a settled church,

knowledge and love of the truth were preserved among multitudes, who might otherwise have conformed to prelacy; so that when a favourable opportunity was at length presented for making an effort to regain their religious freedom, it was eagerly embraced by a large majority of the protestant population of Ulster. Encouraged by the overthrow of Strafford and the countenance of the English commons, they drew up a Petition, which was most numerously signed, detailing their grievances, both civil and religious, and praying for the enjoyment of liberty of conscience. In particular, they apply for the restoration of their banished pastors, and the endowment of an adequate ministry, as essential to the welfare and security of the kingdom. This petition, the first which emanated from the Irish presbyterians, was presented to the long parliament by their steady friend, Sir John Clotworthy,[25] who had himself experienced the evils

may be seen in Baillie's Letters, i. 196—202, 301, 2. The laird of Leckie, or as he was styled in Scotland, Leckie of that ilk, was originally from Stirlingshire, and had suffered much in Ireland for his attachment to presbytery. He was settled somewhere in the neighbourhood of Derry, as we learn from the following observation of Vesey in his life of Bramhall. Speaking of the bishop's assiduity, he says, "Nor was his labour wanting among the lay gentry, reducing some that had strayed, and confirming some that staggered, their blood being apt to take infection from the neighbour kingdom, as the laird of Lacquey and others brought to his lordship by Dr. Walker, to whom he gave full satisfaction in their scruples." Either the bishop or his biographer miscalculated the success of these efforts, for Leckie's scruples were far from being removed, as subsequent events soon evinced. Several highly respectable families of the same name with this staunch presbyterian, and probably descended from him, still exist in the vicinity of Derry.

25 I cannot ascertain the date of this petition being presented to parliament. It could not have been before the end of April, 1641, as appears from the following letter, written on the 26th of that month, by Bramhall to Ussher then in London, misrepresenting, in the spirit of party still displayed on similar occasions, the method of obtaining the numerous signatures attached to it. "I send your grace the copy of a petition enclosed as was sent me. The solicitor who gets the hands is one Gray, censured in the star-chamber in one Steward's case. I hear he has got L.300 by it, and that the most of the subscribers did not know what they subscribed,

therein deplored, and who had now become one of the most popular and influential members in that assembly. It breathes the same attachment to gospel truth and civil liberty, and the same spirit of firm and inflexible resistance to tyranny, by which, as a body of people, they have been uniformly distinguished. It proves how numerous they continued to be, and how decided they were in their non-conformity, in despite of all the persecutions they had endured on that account; and together with the list of grievances which, according to the custom of those days, was annexed, it presents so instructive and authentic a picture of the religious condition of Ulster, while under the uncontrolled influence of prelacy, that its insertion is indispensable to corroborate the statements already submitted to the reader.

"The humble Petition of some Protestant Inhabitants of the Counties of Antrim, Downe, Derry, Tyrone, &c., part of the Province of Ulster, in the Kingdom of Ireland,

"Humbly representeth unto your grave wisdomes and judicious considerations, that your petitioners, having translated themselves out of the several parts of his majestie's kingdoms of England and Scotland, to promote the infant plantation of Ireland; wherein your petitioners, by their great labour and industry, so much contributed to the settlement of that kingdom, as they were in a most hopeful way of a comforta-

but in general that it was for the purity of religion, and the honour of their nation. They say he has gathered a rabble of 1500 hands, all obscure persons. It were no difficult task, if that were thought the way, to get half of those hands to a contrary petition, and 5000 more of a better rank." Life of Vesey. Bramhall attempted to get up such a petition as he here alludes to; but from the following reply of Ussher to him it seems he was far from meeting with the success he anticipated. "Sir John Clotworthy hath presented a far larger petition to the house of commons here, for the abolishing of episcopacy in Ireland, than that which you sent unto me, and signed with a huge number of hands." Rawdon Papers, p. 82.

ble abode, and when they expected to reape the fruit of their great and long labour, partly by the cruel severity and arbitrary proceedings of the civil magistrate; but principally through the unblest way of the prelacy with their faction, our souls are starved, our estates undone, our families impoverished, and many lives among us cut off and destroyed.

"The prelates have by their canons of late, their fines, fees, and imprisonments at their pleasure; their silencing, suspending, banishing and excommunicating of our learned and conscionable ministers; their obtruding upon us ignorant, erroneous and profane persons to be our teachers; their censuring of many hundreds, even to excommunication, for matters acknowledged by all to be indifferent and not necessary; their favouring popery, in this kingdom a double fault; their persecuting of purity, and endeavouring to bring all to a lifeless formality; divers of them being notorious incendiaries of the unquietness and unsettled estate between these kingdoms: with many the like too tedious to relate, as more fully in our ensuing grievances doth appear. These our cruel task-masters have made of us who were once a people, to become, as it were, no people, an astonishment to ourselves, the object of pity and amazement to others, and hopeless of remedy, unless 'He with whom are bowels of compassion,' work in you an heart to interpose for your petitioners' relief.

"They therefore most humbly pray that such a course may be laid down, as to your great wisdoms shall seem meet, for reparation, in some measure, of our unutterable damages; your petitioners settled in a way whereby their persecuted ministers may have leave to return from exile, and be freed from the unjust censure imposed upon them, and an open door continued unto us, for provision of a powerful and able ministry, the only best way to promote plantation, and settle the kingdom in the possession and practice of true religion. Which, as it is the earnest expectation, so it shall be the dayly prayer of many thousands besides your petitioners, who will ever entreat the Lord for your direction herein, and in all other your weighty and important affairs; as becometh your poor petitioners, &c.

"A particular of manifold evils and heavy pressures, caused and occasioned by the prelacie and their dependants.

"1. Before they had so much as a pretended canon for their warrant, the prelates urged their ceremonies with such vehemency, that divers of our most learned and painfull ministers, for not obeying them, were silenced, and many of us for the like oppressed in their courts.

"2. In the year 1634, they made such 'canons and constitutions ecclesiastical' as enjoined many corruptions in the worship of God, and government of the church, which exceedingly retarded the work of reformation, animated papists, and made way for many popish superstitions.

"3. Our most painfull, godly and learned ministers, were by the bishops and their commissaries, silenced and deprived for not conforming and subscribing to the said unlawful canon; yea, through the hotness of their persecution, forced to flee the land, and afterward excommunicated, to the danger of all, and loss of some of their lives.

"4. In their places others were obtruded, not only ignorant, lazy and lukewarm, but many of them unsound in doctrine, profane in life, and cruel in persecution.

"5. Many, though sufficiently furnished, were not admitted to the ministry, only for not swallowing down their groundless innovations: yea, some though conforme, yet for appearing strict in life, were likewise kept out.

"6. Good and painful ministers are not suffered to exercise the function which God hath raised them unto, nor suffered to enjoy any living; whereas the bishops do hold by commendam, besides those proper to their bishoprics, many livings; and do conferr livings upon their children and retainers, 'studendi gratia,' as is pretended, and divers benefices, as four, five, six, or more, upon their favourites.

"7. Hence the care of souls is committed to hirelings, who receive five, six, eight, ten pounds by year for their cures, divers of which are put together, to the charge of some illiterate curate; by which means the people perish for want of food, though the parson or vicar, through connivance of the bishop, is utterly non-resident, and by each one of the many benefices he enjoyeth, hath a competent allowance for a moderate minded man, to maintain himself and family upon.

"8. Whereas the bishops should give all good example by painfull preaching and holy conversation, they preach very rarely themselves; and like those in the gospel who will neither enter themselves, nor suffer others to enter, they have supprest divers others from preaching, both on the afternoon, on the Lord's day, and in many places where weekly lectures were maintained, either by the free-will of the minister, or cost of the people, they have utterly forbidden the same, and thrown all manner of discountenance to those who were forward therein; so that a lecturing minister appeared before them, under more prejudice than a popish priest, or undermining Jesuit.

"9. Lest those who could not be admitted into the ministry, undertaking to teach school, should there lay impressions of piety and good learning; they urge on the very school-masters a subscription beyond what is enjoyned by their own canon, and punish by excommunication and otherwise the refusers thereof: so as the schools formerly much frequented, are now utterly desolate to the spoyle of youth, and promoting of prophaneness and ignorance.

"10. Thus whiles they proceed so severely and unjustly in punishing the refusers of their unlawful commands, though otherwise never so honest and able men, they favour popery to the continuance and great increase thereof. Hence,

"11. Titular bishops are by them winked at in the exercise of jurisdiction from foreign power, mass-priests are frequent, and pretend a title to every parish in the kingdom, masses publickly celebrated without controulment, to the great grief of God's people, and increase of idolatry and superstition.

"12. They permit frieries and nunneries to be within their dioceses, whereby they continue and increase of late in many places; yea, divers of them suffered to remain in the very places where some of the bishops have their special residence.

"13. In many places of the land where protestants are forbidden and restrained, papists are permitted to keep schools; unto some whereof such multitudes of children and young men do resort, that they may be esteemed rather universities, teaching therein not only the tongues, but likewise the liberal arts and sciences.

"14. They set forth and suffer to be published wicked libels and ungodly pamphlets, tending to sedition, faction, and disunion of the British inhabitants, such as, 'Examen Conjurationis Scoticae,'—'Lysimachus Nicanor,' &c. And in their sermons, prayers and ordinary table-talk, divers of the bishops in matters quite beside their calling, have not desisted to raile, curse, and most bitterly inveigh against the kingdom of Scotland, and all their proceedings; labouring to make them odious, thereby proving themselves firebrands of sedition between the two nations, proclaiming their profanity by drinking healths to the confusion of that nation.

"15. The most learned and seemingly moderate and pious of prelates publickly in sermons at Dublin, exclaimed against and condemned the Scotish covenant and religion profest in that kingdom, with most invictive terms: and in the Starchamber in Dublin, at the censure of Henry Steward, Esquire, his wife, and two daughters, and James Gray, for refusing to take an oath, for which there was no other ground than the Earl of Strafford's command, and which was against the covenant of Scotland, uttered these words, viz. 'These people, with Corah, Dathan, and Abiram, do withstand the ordinance of God; and therefore I leave them to the judgment of Corah, Dathan, and Abiram, and agree to their censure though deeper.'

"16. They have frequently made symoniacal pactions and bargains in the conferring of benefices, and ordinarily permit ministers to exchange their leases of tythes, which the former incumbent ministers have set at certain rates.

"17. The prelates have usually appointed such men to be their commissaries, officials, and registers, who altogether neglecting the punishment of vices cognizable in their courts, look only to their gain.

"18. Though they pretend themselves the advancers of virtue and punishers of vice, yet they usually, without farther satisfaction, absolve the most scandalous persons for a summe of money, and often question not at all such, from whom before hand they receive such a summe; which is a cause that many wickednesses do more and more abound.

"19. If any be presented by their apparitors, who are usually papists, if it be but for non-payment of the clerk's groate, or not observing some one of their frivolous injunctions, yea, though the party be not found culpable, yet they require most excessive and unjust fees. And if their demands be not satisfied, though never so great poverty might plead for mercy, they presently proceed to the censure of excommunication; thus vainly and blasphemously abusing the high ordinance of God, so many hundreds of us remain under that censure, and multitudes constrained to run out of the land, to the undoing of them and theirs.

"20. The prelates, that they might manage Peter's sword as well as his keys, have, some of them, procured that most unlawful writ of assistance, whereby his majestie's officers and ministers are required to yield assistance unto the bishop, his official, or any deputed by him: which writ is by their officers most notoriously abused, and many times put into the hands of their apparitors, who, under colour thereof, apprehend honest men and women, casting them into prison, untill they be forced to free themselves by a heavy composition.

"21. They charge church-wardens with articles far beyond their understandings, to every particular whereof, if they refuse to answer or present, then are they bound to answer for it at council-table, or high-commission court, or both; and though there acquitted, yet no remedy left them for their great dammages.

"22. They swore church-wardens to attend all their visitations and circular courts; and these, for their articles, oaths, admissions, and discharges, they make them pay most excessive and undue fees never before practised or required.

"23. The commutations for penance, which either should not be at all, or, if exacted, then set apart for the poor and other pious uses, cometh either to the prelates' kitchen, the commissarie's purse, or both.

"24. The prelates and their faction, as they inherit the superstition of the papacy, so of late they exact, with all severity, the obsolete customs of St. Mary-Gallons, mortuaries, portions, &c. which, as they were given by superstition and used to idolatry, so now they are taken by oppression and applied to riotousness.

"25. They have also constantly practised and suffered the buying and selling of the sacraments, which is an heavy burden. And where the poor have not to pay the minister's and clerk's fees, they will not marry them, nor suffer their dead to be buried.

"26. In the high-commission court, against all law and equity, they sit judges in their own cause, and take cognizance of the highest and smallest matters, going therein without controul. Hence,

"27. In the said court they usurp with an high hand the judicature of civil causes, impose fines beyond all bounds, and imprison at their pleasure, whereby many have been utterly undone.

"28. They proceed in the said court by way of most cruel and lawless inquisition, not only into men's actions and words, but reaching even to their very thoughts, in imposing the most unlawful oath ex-officio, to force accuse, not only others, but likewise their own selves, contrary to law and the very maxims of nature. And if any refuse to take this oath, then are they imprisoned and fined beyond measure, to the ruin of all that fall under their indignation.

"29. Divers of the prelates did jointly frame, and wickedly contrive, with the earl of Strafford, that most lawless and scandalous oath, imposed upon the Scottish-British among us, who were protestants, for receiving all commands indefinitely. And some of the prelates were the occasion, that women and maids should be forced thereunto. Hence commissions issuing to all places for the exacting of it, they were prosecuted with so much rigour, that very many, as if they had been traitors in the highest degree, were searched for, apprehended, examined, reviled, threatened, imprisoned, fettered, by threes and fours in iron yoakes; some carried up to Dublin in chains, and fined in the star-chamber in thousands beyond ability, and condemned to perpetuall imprisonment. Divers, before delivring of children, were apprehended, threatened and terrifyed. Others of them, two or three days after child-birth, so narrowly searched for, that they were fain to fly out of all harbour into woods, mountains, caves, and corn-fields, and many days and nights together absent themselves, to the impairing the health of very many, and to the death of divers and loss of their goods, which the enemy at their pleasure made havock of. These, with many more inexpressible, have been the woefull effects of the oath, drawn up by the advice of the prelates, and so unjustly pressed by the authority of the earl of Strafford.

"30. The prelates with their faction, have been injurious not only to the spiritual, but also to the temporal estates of most men; for, under the colour of church-lands, they have injuriously seized into their hands much of the best lands in every county, so that there is scarce a gentleman of any worth, whom they have not bereaved of some part of his inheritance; few daring to oppose their unjust commands, and if any did, there is none able to maintain their just titles against their power and oppression.

"31. By these ways have they ruinated and undone many families, destroyed and cast away thousands of souls, and moreover, in their own persons, have been a scandal to the gospel, and a stumbling-block, even unto the common enemy, by their swearing, cursing, drunkenness, Sabbath-breaking, &c., having such servants usually in their families as are the most profane in the kingdom, few others countenanced by them but such; and if any seem to be of an holy life, he is scorned and persecuted by them.

"Thus, they publishing and proclaiming themselves the children of Ishmael and Esau, we must humbly beseech you, as the true sons of Israel, to take order with them as God shall direct, whom we shall ever pray to be aiding and assistant unto you in this great and glorious work of reformation."[26]

The representations contained in this petition, which the reader has seen were but too well-founded, were followed by others equally strong against the conduct of Strafford in the administration of the civil affairs of the kingdom. Meanwhile the commons proceeded leisurely but steadily with their impeachment. And the Irish commons, following the example

[26] This valuable document was published immediately after it had been presented to parliament, in the form of a tract, entitled, "The humble Petition of the Protestant inhabitants of the counties of Antrim, Downe, Tyrone, &c., part of the province of Ulster, in the kingdom of Ireland, concerning bishops. Expressed in thirtie-one heads of grievances, by reason of their over ruling lordly power. As it was presented to the Right honourable assembly, the knights, citizens, and burgesses of the house of commons in this present parliament. And accepted of that honourable house." London, 1641, 4to. pp. 12. It is inserted at length by Prynne, in his "Antipathy of Lordly Prelacy to Monarchy." Lond. 1641, 4to. part ii. pp. 369, et seq. And it was reprinted in the beginning of the last century, in a rare controversial tract, in defence of presbyterians, bearing the quaint but apposite title,—"A sample of Jet-black Prelatic Calumny." Glasgow, 1713, 4to. pp. 133, et seq.

set them in England, at their reassembling in March 1641, impeached four of the confidants of Strafford, among whom was bishop Bramhall, as participators in his treason.

Sixteen of the charges against Strafford, related to his government of Ireland, the more important of which were fully substantiated. Among these, his issuing of the warrant to bishop Leslie, empowering him to imprison at pleasure the nonconformists of his diocese; and his imposing of the black oath without authority of parliament, held a prominent place. In the investigation of the latter charge, the case of Henry Stewart and his family, already detailed, was particularly dwelt on, and produced a strong impression on the house. Sir John Clotworthy and sir James Montgomery, appeared as witnesses on several of the articles; and their testimony was of great importance in bringing home to him the general charge of an arbitrary and tyrannical violation of the fundamental laws of the kingdom. His trial commenced in Westminster Hall on the twenty-first of March, and after seventeen sessions, closed on the thirteenth of April. The judicial was then exchanged for the legislative mode of procedure, and a bill of attainder, founded on the evidence produced upon the impeachment, was introduced into the commons, and speedily passed, only fifty-nine voting against it. On the sixth of May, the judges, being referred to, gave it as their opinion that Strafford deserved to undergo the penalties of the law against high treason. Two days afterwards, the bill was passed by the lords, only nineteen voting in the minority;[27] and the king having given the royal assent to it,—an act of inexcusable perfidy,—the unfortunate but guilty Strafford, was beheaded on Tower-hill, on the twelfth of May, in the forty-ninth year of his age—a memorable example to all ambitious and unprincipled statesmen!

The deputy Wandesford, shocked and alarmed by the im-

27 The bishops were not present, the canons forbidding them to take part in any measure involving a capital punishment.

peachment of Strafford, and the intractable turbulence of the Irish parliament, took seriously ill, and died suddenly on the third of December. The government of Ireland, after some changes, was ultimately committed, in the beginning of the year 1641, to two lords justices, sir John Parsons and sir John Borlase. Both of these belonged to the puritan party; but the latter being a military officer, the chief burden and responsibility of the government rested on the former. They laboured to repair the evils of Strafford's administration; and cordially co-operated with the Romanist party in prosecuting the redress of those grievances which had been so long the subject of general complaint. The several individuals, who had suffered under the arbitrary proceedings of the late deputy, were now freed from the penalties wantonly imposed on them. Archibald Adair, the deposed bishop of Killala, was released from his cruel imprisonment, and elevated to the bishopric of Waterford, which was vacant by the death of his former enemy, Adderton, who was publicly executed for gross and horrible immorality.[28]

Henry Stewart and his family were also liberated from their unjust confinement in Dublin. But their property having been, in the mean time, confiscated, they were reduced to a state of abject poverty. Mr. Stewart retired to Scotland, and as he was a native of that kingdom, he applied, in the month of September, to the parliament sitting at Edinburgh, to aid him in obtaining the restitution of his property. He thus submitted his case to their notice:—" Petition exhibited to the house, by Henry Stewart, Esquire, who was imprisoned in Ireland, a year and three months, for not taking the unlawful oath, and his goods taken from him, whereby his wife and children are utterly impoverished; humbly beseeching the king and parliament for their recommendation to the parliament of England for his restitution." On this representation,

28 Adair's appointment to Waterford took place, July 13th. At the rebellion, he retired to England, and died at Bristol in 1647. For the case of Adderton, see Ware's Bishops.

"the house ordains the lord chancellor and the earl of Dunfermline, seriously to recommend this petition from them to the English commissioners."[29]

A second application was shortly afterwards made to the same court by another aggrieved subject of Ireland, whose case has been already related. Mr. Adair of Ballymena, whom Strafford and bishop Leslie were so anxious to seize, but who, by escaping to Scotland, had eluded their vigilance, had, during his absence, been condemned as a traitor, and his property in Ireland confiscated. He continued, however, to reside unmolested on his paternal inheritance in his native country. Here he possessed considerable influence, and had been returned to sit in the Scottish parliament as laird of Kilhill, and member for the shire of Galloway. He applied to the house to recommend his case to Charles, then at Edinburgh, in order that the sentence of the Irish courts, pronouncing him a traitor, might be reversed. The following minute shows the favourable manner in which they received his application:—"November 5th, 1641. The house, all in one voice, does seriously recommend Kilhill's business to his majesty, anent the cancelling some records in Ireland, and taking them off the file; whereby he was cited by the late deputy there, and adjudged as a traitor, in respect that he, in the late troubles, had adjoined himself to his own native country."[30] When this unanimous recommendation was laid before Charles, he engaged to have it carried into effect, which was subsequently accomplished. The sentence was rescinded, and its penalties removed; and, it may be added, a lineal descendant of the same name still enjoys the restored property.

The English parliament also contributed its powerful aid to the redress of Irish grievances. In the month of August,

29 Balfour's Annals, iii. 93. I have not been able to ascertain the result of this recommendation to the long parliament.

30 Balfour, iii. 138.

by a unanimous vote of the house, they rescinded the sentence of the Star-Chamber court in England, by which the county of Londonderry, with the towns of Derry and Coleraine, had been forfeited to the crown. This extensive confiscation was one of the most impolitic, as it was one of the most unjust, measures of Strafford's administration. For not only did it, by endangering the property, rouse the indignation, of all who held by patent from the crown,—a very numerous and influential class in Ireland; but by wresting this valuable plantation from the corporation of London, so deep a resentment was excited in the city against him, that his fall was thereby greatly accelerated. Their property was now restored to the corporation, to the great joy of the whole city, and to the manifest prosperity of this important portion of Ulster. Nor ought it to be forgotten, that, in less than half a century afterwards, the safety of the empire at large, and its deliverance from popish tyranny and misrule, were, in a great measure, owing to the performance of this act of justice by the English commons. Had this extensive plantation, with its important towns and cities, continued under the immediate patronage and direct influence of the subsequent kings of England, in all human probability, James II. would never have been defeated under the walls of Derry.

The Irish parliament, following in the train of the sister judicatories in both kingdoms, engaged still more vigorously in remedying the evils of Strafford's government. One act of theirs deserves to be specially noticed. The high-commission court, the chief engine of his cruel and arbitrary impositions, was summarily abolished, as an intolerable grievance, and contrary to the fundamental laws of the nation. The following minute, entered on their journals upon that occasion, shows the light in which the proceedings of that court were then contemplated. "It is voted upon question, that all the proceedings in the court, called the high-commission court, and the several pretended sentences of excommunication in the said court against Robert Rosse of the parish of Bangor;

James Hamilton of the parish of Ballywalter, clerk; Robert Bleare of Bangor, clerk; David Kennedy of the parish of Newton, clerk; and Robert Wilson of Killeghie, [Killileagh,] all of the diocese of Down respectively, were from the beginning, and are void in law and null, as if they had never been pronounced against them, or any of them; and that all the said several sentences shall be taken off the file of the registry, and out of the registry of the said court: as also, all the original proceedings there, that there may remain no records of those illegal and extrajudicial proceedings which are voted for a general grievance by this house: And that a copy of this order shall be read in the several parish churches, where the said persons lately dwelt, by the ministers, that so all persons may take notice." [31]

The parliament also took steps to redress the several grievances, arising out of the oppressions of the ecclesiastical courts, and the illegal severities of the prelates. Petitions poured in during this session, extending from May to August, against the bishops; particularly against those of Derry, Down, and Raphoe. Mrs. Pont, with whose case the reader is already acquainted, now a widow, presented a petition against the latter, for committing her to prison, and charging her with high treason, solely on his own authority. Her petition was referred to a select committee, who reported that the bishop, by his illegal conduct in this case, had involved himself in the penalties of the statute of *Præmunire*. Their report was sustained by the house, and formally communicated to the lords, but no further proceedings appear to have been taken against the guilty prelate. [32] Chappell, bishop of Ross, was called to account for his oppressive conduct while provost of Trinity College; and "all and every his proceedings— during his continuance in the said office," were unanimously voted to be "great grievances, and fit to receive redress." [33] Steps were subsequently taken by the parliament to alter the

31 Commons' Journals, i. 526. 32 Ibid. i. 379, 453, 5. 33 Ibid. i. 414

constitution of the college, as regulated by the intolerant canons established under the auspices of Laud, and to place it upon its original foundation; but this important reformation was interrupted by the Rebellion, and never afterwards resumed.

During these legislative proceedings, the army which Strafford had stationed on the eastern coast of Antrim remained inactive. Their only employment had been that of raising a fort of earth at Olderfleet, to preserve the shipping in the harbour of Larne; and constructing an encampment with trenches and parapets, that, when called on actual service, they might be experienced in the formation of such temporary fortifications.[34] Charles having, in the mean time, acceded to the demands of his Scottish subjects, and relinquished the design of invading that kingdom—the object for which these forces had been raised—they were thus rendered useless, nor was there any pretext for maintaining any longer this expensive establishment. The English parliament, accordingly, urged Charles to disband this army; but he evinced the utmost anxiety to keep it on foot. The former began to be apprehensive, that, consisting chiefly of Romanists,[35] and commanded by the creatures of Strafford, it might be transported to England to support, by force of arms, the royal, against the popular, party. They therefore urged their applications with greater earnestness. Charles was at length compelled to

34 Carte, i. 104.

35 See note 15 of this chapter, p. 269.—In corroboration of what Mr. Brodie has urged to prove the army raised by Strafford in 1640 to have been almost entirely composed of Roman catholics, I subjoin the following testimony of a Romanist writer, which I recently met with in a Latin work, entitled, "Descriptio Regni Hiberniæ, Sanctorum insulæ, et de prima origine Miseriarum et motuum in Angliâ, Scotiâ et Hiberniâ regnante Carolo primo rege. Per R. P. F. Antonium Prodinum, Hibernum Lectorem Jubilatum, &c." 4to. pp. 111. Published at Rome in 1721, and dedicated by "O'Neill" to Cardinal Pamphilus. In page 44, the writer says, "Thomas Comes Straffordiæ, Hiberniæ pro-rex, vir magni concilii et authoritatis, decem millia Catholicorum Hibernorum militum, à multis antea mensibus in armis habuit in Ultonia."

yield to their importunity; and these obnoxious forces were disbanded in the month of August, and their arms and ammunition deposited in the castle at Dublin.

But though dissolved as an Irish army, Charles was anxious that, in conjunction with additional levies, they might, under the sanction of the Irish parliament, be permitted to enter into the service of his ally, the king of Spain, in Flanders. But all parties in the commons united in opposing this design. The puritans were against it, on the ground that these forces would be as conveniently placed there, as in Ireland, for the invasion of England, should Charles be led to adopt this desperate measure, of which they were becoming more and more apprehensive. The Roman catholic party affected to clamour against their removal, lest they might be sent back by the Spanish monarch, whose ancestors had often meditated the invasion of Ireland, for the purposes of rebellion or of conquest. Subsequent events render it probable that the leaders of the latter party opposed the removal of this disciplined soldiery, actuated by the same religious prejudices and antipathies as themselves, as the view of retaining them to aid in the rebellion, which, there is reason to believe, was even then meditated. The English concurred with the Irish parliament in opposing the removal of these troops; and thus thousands of an idle restless soldiery, hostile to the English power, full of hatred against the puritans, and ready to be engaged in any enterprise, however desperate, were detained in the country to aggravate the horrors of the rebellion, which, in a few weeks afterwards, broke out, and deluged the kingdom with seas of blood.

CHAPTER VII.

The kingdom peaceful and prosperous—Rebellion projected by the native Irish—Incited by religious antipathies—Hastened by the state of affairs in England—Irish conspirators actuated by different views—Secret intrigues of the king—The day appointed for the insurrection—Plot discovered—Progress of the rebellion in Ulster—Seizure of Charlemont, Dungannon, Newry, &c.—Enniskillen, Derry, Coleraine, &c. preserved—Proceedings at Carrickfergus—And in the county of Antrim—Belfast and Lisburn secured—Proceedings in the county of Down—Success of the Romanists—Their subsequent cruelties—Retaliated by the protestants—Massacre at Island-Magee—Followed by famine and pestilence—Sufferings of the clergy—Death of bishop Bedell—Number of protestants massacred—Ulster Scots partially preserved.

IRELAND was now in a state of universal tranquillity. At no former period had the country enjoyed so much real prosperity, and so long internal peace. The evils of Strafford's administration had been, in a great measure, remedied; and that obnoxious and formidable governor had paid the penalty of his delinquencies. Charles had confirmed to all parties the privileges for which they had so long petitioned, and fully redressed the grievances of which they had so repeatedly complained. All dissatisfaction or anxiety with respect to defective titles, had been removed by the confirmation of the graces, and by other conciliatory acts of the sovereign and the English parliament. The Roman catholic party enjoyed ample toleration. Their nobility were unrestricted in their privileges, and shared in the titles and dignities conferred on the peers of Ireland by James and Charles. Their gentry were members of parliament, judges, magistrates and sheriffs.

Their lawyers occupied the same station at the bar as protestants, and practised as freely in the courts of law. Their clergy were unmolested in the performance of their religious rites, and their other ecclesiastical functions.[1] In obtaining the redress of national grievances, both protestants and Romanists cordially co-operated. The constitutional administration of the lords justices was universally popular; and a new era of national improvement and civilization appeared to be opening on this long-distracted country.

But these anticipations were awfully disappointed. "The hopes conceived from a peace of forty years, from the gradual improvement of the nation, from the activity of its parliament, from the favourable disposition of the king, from the temper of the English parliament, were in an instant confounded; and the calamities of former times revived in all their bitterness."[2]

The causes of the memorable Rebellion which occurred at this period, are very variously stated by historians. The scheme of an insurrection for the overthrow of the British power, the recovery of the forfeited estates, and the re-establishment of popery, undoubtedly originated with the descendants of the northern chieftains, who had been banished from Ireland and whose properties had been confiscated, in the beginning of the century. They had lived in favour at the courts of Rome and Madrid, where they enjoyed splendid allowances, and held high military rank.[3] They maintained almost uninterrupted communication with their relatives in Ulster, whose antipathies against the English as invaders and usurpers on the one hand, and heretics and persecutors on the other, were studiously inflamed by those most bigoted emissaries—the foreign educated priests.[4] Conscious that the occupiers of their former

1 Cox, ii. 72. O'Connor, Hist. Add. part ii. 254.

2 Leland, iii. 86.

3 O'Connor's Hist. Add. ii. 314.

4 The following is the remarkable language of lord Castlehaven, a Roman catholic nobleman, attached to the royalist party. "True it is, that forty years continual and flourishing peace, from the last of queen Eliza-

properties could not be dispossessed, except by the total subversion of the British power, these plotting exiles assured their countrymen of an invasion, supported by continental succours, which would rescue them from their fancied bondage, and restore them to their territories, and the nation to her independence. This alluring proposal was eagerly embraced by the leaders of that party, denominated the old or native Irish. This portion of the population still brooded over the wrongs inflicted on their ancestors by the English; and their aversion to the British government had been latterly increased by the insincerity of Charles in the matter of the graces, and the tyranny of Strafford in that of defective titles; though these causes of complaint had been recently removed under the administration of the lords justices.

But it was on the ground of religious grievances that the native Irish were most readily incited to rebellion. They were the adherents of popery in its grossest form. The reformed faith, as the reader has seen, had been presented to them under all the disadvantages of being the religion professed and propagated by those whom they were artfully taught to consider as invaders and oppressors. No adequate means, except in a few insulated cases, had been employed for their conversion; even the use of their native language, as a medium of instruction, had been unaccountably and perversely neglected. With not many exceptions, the reformed clergy had been either indolent or careless on the one hand; or bigoted and intolerant on the other, despising the Irish as mere barbarians, unworthy as well as incapable of being educated or reformed. The prejudices and ignorance of the people at-

beth to 1641, seemed to carry a fair outside, as if all those national former animosities had been extinguished. But, alas! the earls of Tyrone and Tyrconnal, and the councils of Spain and Rome, and the Irish monasteries and seminaries in so many countries of Europe, and very many of the churchmen returning home out of them, and chiefly the titular bishops, together with the superiors of regular orders, took an effectual course, under the specious colour of religion, to add continually more fuel to the burning coals." Memoirs, p. 22.

tached them the more firmly to their ancient superstition; while, by their own clergy, they were taught to hate and abhor both the persons and religion of the British. Although, since the commencement of the century, the penal statutes had been seldom enforced, and that only in extreme cases, on political rather than on religious grounds, and although they had been for some time virtually repealed; yet the exasperating cry of persecution continued to be rung in their ears, till the multitude were fully prepared for the work of extirpation. These embittered feelings were studiously fostered by the priesthood, who were more anxious for an insurrection, that they might regain the ecclesiastical property of the kingdom, than even the gentry were, that they might recover their forfeited estates.(5) The priesthood, in their turn, were instigated by the emissaries of the pope, ambitious of signalizing his pontificate by re-establishing his supremacy over this 'island of saints,' still regarded as the especial patrimony of the Romish see. The destruction of protestantism was accordingly a prominent object of the contemplated rebellion; and the necessity of such a measure, for their own safety and the security of their religion, was assiduously urged upon the people, by alarming but unfounded reports of the persecuting dispositions of the English puritans.(6) The late successful struggles, too, of the Scots, in defence of their national faith and independence, against the arbitrary impositions of the king and his ecclesiastical advisers, contributed not a little to encourage the Irish in their design. But the former had vindicated their religious liberties in a manner far different from that in which

5 Sir William Petty says, "the cause of the rebellion was a desire of the Romists to recover the church revenues, worth about L.110,000 per annum." Pol. Anat. p. 317, apud "Tracts relating to Ireland." Dub. 1769.

6 Sir John Clotworthy was absurdly reported to have said in a speech in the English parliament, "that the conversion of the papists in Ireland was only to be effected by the Bible in one hand, and the sword in the other." Nalson, ii. 536. This was a royalist calumny, totally at variance with the whole tenor of his character and actions.

the latter were preparing to proceed. The one revolution had been effected by a firm, open, and unanimous expression of the national will, without secret conspiracy or open violence; while the other was about to be accomplished by the most criminal means—already employed with success in France—the merciless extirpation of the adherents of the reformed faith.[7]

The leaders of the native Irish and the more adventurous of their clergy, had held frequent consultations, even during Strafford's administration, on the projected insurrection. But the scheme of so extensive and perilous an enterprise, as the subversion of the British power, was not easily perfected. And it is highly probable their plans would not have been matured, even so soon as they eventually were, had it not been for the posture of affairs at this period in England. Charles, indignant at the noble efforts of the long parliament to rescue the kingdom from his arbitrary encroachments on constitutional rights, had early resolved to crush it, if possible, by force. For this purpose, he had secretly endeavoured to induce the English army to declare for the royal prerogative, in opposition to the parliament, that, with their aid, he might disperse that dreaded and now formidable assembly.[8] It was in the prosecution of the same design that he had laboured to prevent the disbanding of the Irish army, relying on them as assured and faithful auxiliaries, when the proper time might arrive for openly opposing the parliament. He had already, under Strafford, received aid from Ireland in his first attempts to overawe and repress the Scottish nation,

7 The Bartholomew massacre—that unparalleled scene of perfidy and bloodshed—commenced at Paris, August the 24th, 1572; when the protestants, caressed and lulled asleep by royal oaths, were inhumanly butchered, with a view to their entire extirpation out of France. In eight days, according to Sully, 70,000 were massacred. The pope declared his approbation of it by appointing a day of jubilee, and causing magnificent paintings to be drawn, and medals cast, to commemorate the glorious and joyful event!

8 Brodie, iii. 108—14.

and he now again looked for assistance from the same quarter.

With the Roman catholics of the committee, deputed from the Irish parliament to represent the grievances of the nation, it is believed both Charles and his queen intrigued, with the view of detaching them from the puritans, with whom they had hitherto co-operated, and of inducing them to form a party in their native kingdom and parliament, in support of the falling cause of prerogative. In return for this seasonable assistance, ample immunities, both civil and religious, were freely promised; extending, it is alleged, even to the legal establishment of the Romish faith.[9] The Irish deputies readily listened to the royal suggestions, and at once espoused the cause of Charles. The marquisses of Ormond and of Antrim, the most influential noblemen at this time in Ireland, had already been separately enlisted in the same cause.

The plan on which these several partizans of the king were required to act was, to take measures for the simultaneous seizure of Dublin and the principal forts and castles throughout the kingdom, and for disarming and securing those who would not join in the project—even the lords justices themselves, in case they offered any opposition. They were then to organize the disbanded soldiery, and augment their number to twenty thousand. And having thus secured the power, and assumed the authority, of the government in the king's name, they were finally to call a parliament, which, circumstanced as the country would then be, would be necessarily devoted to the royal cause. With the resources of the entire kingdom thus placed at his disposal, Charles, with his bigoted and overbearing consort, calculated on obtaining a speedy and final triumph over the obnoxious parliament.

While these plans for inducing Ireland to espouse his cause were under consideration, Charles resolved to visit Scotland, in the hope that, either by ample concessions, or, should these fail, by secret stratagems, he might secure the

[9] Brodie, iii. 173—6.

co-operation of that kingdom also in his favourite enterprise against the national liberties, so vigilantly protected by the English commons. He set out for Edinburgh in the month of August; and in his train was lord Dillon, a Roman catholic nobleman, a member of the Irish committee, who accompanied him to receive his latest instructions. The other Roman catholic members of that committee returned, about the same time, to Ireland, and urged forward the projected enterprise with zeal and caution. The Romanists of the pale, who constituted the more liberal portion of the catholic population, entered readily enough into the scheme; and on communicating it, through the officers employed in raising forces for Spain, to the Ulster Irish, of whose long-meditated project for the total subversion of the British power they appear to have been ignorant, the agents of Charles met with a still more cheerful concurrence in their views. The northern partisans, however, concealed from their new and less violent associates the plans of spoliation which they had been secretly maturing in conjunction with their expatriated relatives. But, at the same time, they hesitated not to embrace with ardour the proposed co-operation, in order to gain one step, and that the most material in their original scheme—the wresting of the kingdom out of the hands of the puritans, then predominant both in the parliament and the government.

Up to this point, the views of both parties among the conspirators were perfectly coincident; beyond it, they were quite opposite.[10] The primary projectors of the rebellion, such as lord Maguire, Roger Moore, Plunket, sir Phelim O'Neil, &c., looked upon the seizure of Dublin and the re-organization of the army, merely as preliminary steps to the overthrow

10 These two different schemes may be considered as embodied in lord Maguire's 'Relation,' and in lord Antrim's 'Information.' The former, printed in Nalson, ii. 543—54, and in Borlase, App. No. ii. and abridged by Carte, i. 158—64, gives an outline of the plot as projected by the native Irish. The latter printed in Cox, App. No. xlix. 206—11, presents the plot as advised by Charles, and adopted by the royalist party. Neither of these noblemen, it is apparent, told the *whole* truth.

of the British power, the separation of the kingdom from England, the recovery of the forfeited estates, and the expulsion of the protestants:—on the accomplishment of these objects, they might then, as an independent catholic nation, support Charles against his refractory parliament. On the other hand, the king's confidential friends, such as the earls of Ormond and Antrim, lord Gormanstown, and perhaps the other gentry of the pale, sir James Dillon, &c., do not appear to have contemplated, in their scheme of insurrection, any unnecessary violence to the persons or properties of the British. Their grand aim was to remove the puritan party from the government of the kingdom, and to place it and its resources at the disposal of the king. Until the rebellion broke out, however, both parties cordially co-operated, and conducted their negociations without division or apparent distrust.

At length Charles, conceiving himself on the point of inducing Scotland to espouse his cause, granted commissions under the great seal of that kingdom, dated at Edinburgh on the first day of October, empowering the Irish leaders, to whom they were addressed, to take up arms on his behalf, to seize in his name the chief places of strength, and to disarm and arrest the Irish protestants, who, as a body, were of the puritan party, and were therefore, as a matter of course, assumed to be hostile to the royalist cause. But, at the same time, his partizans were specially instructed not to disturb or molest the Ulster Scots, whom he describes as his "loyal and loving subjects," and whom he then hoped to see united with their countrymen in Scotland, in one common cause against his rebellious parliament. (11) These commis-

11 A copy of this commission was first published by sir Phelim O'Neill in his proclamation from Newry, in November 1641; but I believe it is not now extant in that form. It was next printed in an important pamphlet, entitled, "The Mysterie of Iniquity," pp. 34-6, published in 1643; and was reprinted by Viccars, in the third part of his Parliamentary Chronicle, p. 70, published in 1646, from which it was copied into the folio edition of Mil-

sions, it is conjectured, were carried to Ireland by lord Dillon, and accelerated the breaking out of the insurrection.[12]

ton's prose works, (ii. 528,) printed at Amsterdam in 1698. Viccar's copy, with the exception of a few verbal alterations, agrees with that afterwards published by Rushworth, iv. 400, 2d pagination. On the margin of the former copy it is stated that the word 'protestant,' is, in another copy, 'Puritan' [party in Ireland.]

12 I have been led to take the view stated in the text, especially of the participation of Charles, to a certain extent, in the insurrection, and of the genuineness of the commission produced by the rebels, from an attentive consideration of what has been recently urged on this subject by Brodie, iii. 190—9., and by Godwin, i. 225—30. Preceding writers, such as Harris, in his 'History of Charles I.' pp. 336—51., and Mrs. Macaulay in her 'History of England,' iii. 89—98, had rendered it probable that Charles, urged on by his bigoted queen, had encouraged his partizans in Ireland to take up arms against the Irish puritans. But the former historians, I conceive, have so strengthened this probability, as to give it almost the certainty of an historical fact. Though so far approving their view, I am not insensible to some plausible things which might be urged against it. But this is not the place for examining them. This curious and interesting subject demands an ampler discussion, and a more minute and detailed investigation, than it has yet received. An 'INQUIRY' into it, after the manner of Birch's satisfactory Inquiry into the kindred topic of Charles's intrigues with Glamorgan, would be another valuable accession to British history. It is right to add, that neither in the text, nor in any of the works above referred to, is it at all designed to implicate Charles in the guilt of the massacre, in which the insurrection so soon issued. That result of his imprudent negotiations with the Irish leaders was as unexpected, and doubtless as deplorable to him, as to all sincere protestants.

Since this portion of the work was completed, I have met with a small volume entitled, "Ireland's case briefly stated; or a summary account of the most remarkable transactions of that kingdom since the reformation," (Lond. 1693,) which has been since repeatedly reprinted under the title of "The impartial," and sometimes "The genuine history of Ireland," by Hugh Reilly. This 'impartial' history, the production of a Romanist, is of course strongly in favour of his own party; and though I am ignorant of the character of the book, or what credit is to be attached to its statements, I am induced to extract from it the following account of the origin of the rebellion, as corroborating, to a certain length, the view given in the text. At all events, it shows what was the Roman catholic version of the plot in the end of the seventeenth century, when all inducements to suppress the name of the king had been removed. The author represents the scheme of the insurrection as originating with Charles, who sent instructions to

The day originally fixed for the simultaneous seizure of Dublin, and the other castles in the kingdom, was the fifth of October. But owing to the reluctance of the more moderate party to have recourse so suddenly to arms, and their desire of first endeavouring to accomplish their object in the parliament, which had been summoned to meet in the beginning of November, the attempt was postponed to a future day. This procrastination was highly resented by the original conspirators, who, alarmed by this appearance of indifference, if not of defection, on the part of their associates, urged forward their project with redoubled vigour. At length, the twenty-

Antrim and Ormond to seize the lords justices, the castle, &c., and that the matter being concerted with a select number both of catholics and protestants, the day of the meeting of the Irish parliament in November was appointed for putting it in execution. He then proceeds, "But the design taking wind and coming to the knowledge of those they call the old Irish, from whom Ormond earnestly desired it should be kept secret, Sir Phelim O'Neill, with several others of Ulster, resolving to be beforehand with his lordship, against whom they were highly incensed for offering to conceal this secret from them, as if they were less zealous than others for his majesty's service, entered for the same end into a conspiracy, persuading themselves that if they succeeded they should not only be indulged in point of religion, as the presbyterian covenanters, but also be restored to their forfeited estates, out of which they had been dispossessed but about thirty years before, by the English and Scottish protestants, who now were generally bent for the parliament against the king.——This is the naked truth of the rise and original of the Irish insurrection in winter 1641, as I have been often assured by men of sense and known integrity in that kingdom, particularly by a very honest gentleman now in France, who, above ten years ago, affirmed to me he had it even from Ormond's own mouth some years before: and I am fully persuaded it is the most rational and likely account that has been yet given of that matter: and for a further confirmation of it, the marchioness of Antrim, still living, and always a very zealous protestant, and therefore, in this case, a witness beyond exception, owned to some friends in London in the year 1683, that she had often heard the marquis, her husband, give much the same relation of this particular; and withal to affirm, that Ormond had no other ground or motive for the great persecution he raised against him upon the late king's restoration, but that he suspected him, (and that very wrongfully, as the marquis solemnly protested to herself and others,) to have discovered the secret aforesaid to Sir Phelim O'Neill."

third of October was definitely fixed for commencing this hazardous enterprise, soon to issue in as atrocious and extensive a massacre as history has recorded. The plan agreed upon, after repeated conferences, was, that two hundred men, under pretence of being levies intended for Spain, should by different routes meet in Dublin on the day appointed, which was Saturday; and, headed by Roger Moore, Maguire, and others, surprise the castle in the afternoon, and take possession of its valuable stores of artillery, arms and ammunition: Sir Phelim O'Neill of Kinnard, not far from Caledon in the county of Tyrone, engaged to commence the insurrection in Ulster on the same Saturday, by the seizure of its chief places of strength. He was especially charged with the capture of Derry; his relative, Sir Henry O'Neill,[13] was to be urged to surprise Carrickfergus; and Sir Con Magennis, his brother-in-law, to seize Newry. The protestants were to be taken and imprisoned with as little violence as possible; and agreeably to the king's commission, the Scots were to remain unmolested.

Throughout all these negotiations the utmost secrecy had been observed, although rumours occasionally transpired of some approaching convulsion. So early as the month of March, Charles informed the lords justices he had received intelligence, by his ambassador in Spain, that an unusual

13 There were two Sir Henry O'Neills at this period; one of whom was the ancestor of the present noble family of O'Neill. It does not appear that he entered into the plot; for his house of Edenduffcarrick,—better known by its modern name of Shanescastle,—was an asylum for the protestants after the breaking out of the rebellion. See page 319. I am inclined to believe this Sir Henry was a protestant; and this conjecture is strengthened by the statement of the Roman catholic historian in the preceding note, that the marchioness of Antrim,—who was Sir Henry's daughter and sole heir, Rose O'Neill,—had been "always a very zealous protestant." This lady died at Shanescastle on the 27th of April 1695, aged 64 years, and was buried in the church at Carrickfergus. Her funeral sermon was preached by the archdeacon of Down. M'Skimin, p. 141.

number of Irish priests were returning home under suspicious circumstances; and that reports were prevalent in that country of an expected rebellion in Ireland. He accordingly directed them to use their best efforts to discover whether such a design was meditated by the native Irish. This intimation was given by Charles before the trial of Strafford, when "nothing could have been more baneful to the interest of the monarch, and of his devoted minister, than a rebellion."(14) But the original conspirators, to whose schemes this letter referred, conducted their proceedings with such consummate dissimulation, that no traces of such a plot could be discovered. On the eleventh of October, Sir William Cole of Enniskillen informed the lords justices that many suspicious persons had of late resorted to Sir Phelim O'Neill's house in Tyrone, and to lord Maguire's in Fermanagh; and that the latter had been carrying on a very extensive correspondence with certain of the native Irish, and of the lords of the Pale.(15) But this information was so vague, that they could do no more than direct Sir William to use increased vigilance, and to communicate the result without delay.

It was from a different quarter that the lords justices received the first distinct intelligence of the plot. Owen O'Connolly, by birth a native Irishman and a Romanist, had, when a boy, been taken into the family of Sir Hugh Clotworthy at Antrim. In this religious household, he had been carefully instructed in the principles of the reformed faith; and under this training, he became a zealous presbyterian. He had now left the service of Sir John Clotworthy, probably at the removal of that excellent family to England; and had settled at Moneymore in the county of Derry, where James Clotworthy, brother to Sir John, resided. M'Mahon, one of the conspirators, being intimately acquainted with O'Connolly, whom he knew to be a native, but probably not to be a protestant, entreated him to meet him at his residence in the

14 Brodie, iii. 177. 15 Carte, iii. 35.

county of Monaghan, on business of importance. O'Connolly complied with this urgent request; and finding his friend had proceeded to Dublin, followed him thither. They met on the afternoon of Friday, the twenty-second of October, when M'Mahon cautiously confided to him the scheme of the projected insurrection. O'Connolly endeavoured, but without success, to dissuade his friend from this hazardous project; and escaping with difficulty from the alarmed and suspecting conspirator, he, that night, communicated the astounding intelligence to the lords justices. At first they could scarcely credit him; but at length being convinced of his veracity, and of the imminent danger which impended, they seized the chief conspirators, put the castle in a posture of defence, and took such judicious measures as preserved the metropolis, and secured the peace of the neighbouring districts. By this seasonable disclosure of O'Connolly, a presbyterian, the seizure of the castle,—the principal aim of the conspirators, and involving the main success of their enterprise,—was providentially defeated; and their associates of the Pale were so disheartened by the disappointment, and so awed by the vigilance of the executive, that they appear to have abandoned the cause, until the successful progress of the northern rebels encouraged them to resume it, a few months afterwards.

In Ulster, the rebellion broke out at the appointed time; and owing to the defenceless state of the protestants, [16] and their consternation at so sudden and simultaneous an attack, it met, for a time, with no effectual resistance. On the same

16 Strafford had, in the year 1639, disarmed the Scots and the puritan party generally through Ulster, to prevent them from assisting their brethren in Scotland against the king. They were strictly forbidden to sell or keep in their houses either powder or arms, except what might be allowed them out of the king's stores in Dublin. Powder they were compelled to buy of the king at two shillings, equal to above half a guinea present currency, per pound; and they were prevented from having a larger quantity at one time than five pounds weight.

night, on which the first intelligence of the plot had been communicated to the lords justices, Sir Phelim O'Neill, according to his engagement, surprised the castle of Charlemont. Accompanied by a larger retinue than usual, he on that day paid a visit of hospitality to the aged Lord Caulfield, and was kindly entertained; when, on a sudden, protesting he had due authority for what he was doing, he seized on his unsuspecting host and family; and his followers, at the same moment, made prisoners of the garrison, who had laid aside their arms amidst the general festivity of the castle.

Having secured this post, at that time one of considerable importance, as it commanded the pass of the Blackwater on the great road from Dublin to the North, Sir Phelim lost no time. That same night he proceeded to Dungannon, which he also surprised early in the morning of Saturday, the twenty-third; and on the same day one of his officers took the strong castle of Moneymore (17) in the county

17 Cox, ii. 98.—The following account of the seizure of Moneymore castle, extracted from the Examination of Neil Oge O'Quin, of the parish of Lissan adjoining that town, taken before the commissioners at Coleraine, on the 17th of March, 1652, will show the manner in which the plot, kept secret to the last moment, was transmitted from one to another among the insurgents, as well as the comparative moderation with which the enterprise was commenced. It also establishes how intimately connected the pretended levies for Spain were with the purposes of the rebellion; and how early O'Neill,—even before the outbreaking of the insurrection,—pleaded the authority of Charles for his proceedings. 'The examinant stated, that upon Thursday or Friday, the 21st and 22d of October, 1641, Cormack O'Hagan sent to this examinant to his house, about three miles from Moneymore, desiring his company there, for that his son, Shane O'Hagan, with his company of foot, which he had raised by the king's authority, and had licensed to transport for Spain, were ready, and would, on the said Friday, rendezvous at Moneymore—that he went to Moneymore with two boys to wait upon him, on Saturday, the 23d of October, in the afternoon—that he met James Young, a Scottishman, who dwelt in Moneymore, and who told him that O'Hagan's company were quarrelling with the English and Scotch in Moneymore, because the Irish would not pay for their drink—that Cormack O'Hagan showed examinant an order from Sir Philemy Roe O'Neill, whereby this examinant was re-

of Derry, and seized on the houses and effects of the surrounding protestants. At the same time, the sept of the O'Quins took the castle of Mountjoy in the county of Tyrone, where they made prisoners of captain Blayney and his company of soldiers; and the sept of the O'Hanlons surprised Tandragee, in the county of Armagh, where a troop of lord Grandison's horse, under the command of captain St. John, were quartered. The captain and a few of the dragoons escaped with difficulty, leaving the remainder with their horses, arms and accoutrements, a prey to the insurgents. On the same eventful day, Sir Con Magennis, at the head of the Magennisses and the M'Cartans, and assisted by the Roman catholic inhabitants led on by a father Crelly, surprised the town and castle of Newry. The governor, Sir Arthur Tyringham, very narrowly escaped; but the entire garrison were captured and disarmed, and fifteen of the towns-people hanged.[18] The rebels found in the castle a considerable supply of arms, and, what was still more seasonable, a large quantity of gunpowder.

In every direction through Ulster, the work proceeded simultaneously. The MacMahons and other septs gained, almost without opposition, the castles of Monaghan, Castleblayney, and Carrickmacross, in the county of Monaghan; the O'Reillys and others seized Cloughouter, the chief place of

quired to take and guard Sir Thomas Staples's house at Lissan, and to keep Sir Thomas's family safe from pillaging; and when he (O'Hagan) gave this examinant the said order, he told him there was further business in hand than he, the said examinant, knew of, and that if all the Irish did not presently rise in arms for the king, they would be killed and undone,—that at that very instant Cormack O'Hagan, with about twenty men, entered and surprised the castle of Moneymore for the king's use—that examinant took, as required, Sir Thomas Staples's house, who was absent at Cookstown, two miles off, but his lady and children in the house—that Sir Philemy Roe O'Neill made an inventory, about a month after, of the goods—that examinant employed the forgeman in making of iron at Sir Thomas's iron-works, and the British carpenters and smiths who dwelt there in making pikes and pike-heads; &c. &c.' MS. Dep. Trin. Coll. Dub.

18 MS. Dep. Trin. Coll. Dub.

strength in Cavan; the Maguires took the field in Fermanagh; and the open towns throughout the counties of Derry and Donegall were immediately taken possession of by the rebels.[19]

A few towns and castles were happily preserved in the midst of this general and extended insurrection. Enniskillen was secured by the activity of Sir William Cole, who had succeeded in obtaining precise intelligence of the intended rising so early as Thursday, the twenty-first of October. Information to this effect he had forwarded to the lords justices; but his letters were intercepted at Lough Ramar, near the town of Kells. At the same time, he despatched messengers to Derry, Clogher, Glasslough, and to as many of the neighbouring towns and castles as lay within his reach.[20] Sir Frederick Hamilton, then at Derry, received this seasonable notice on Friday, so that this important city, and the town of Newtonlimavady, were secured from surprise, together with a few insulated castles in the immediate vicinity of these places.[21]

When the rebellion did break out, the tidings spread so rapidly in some directions, that several places received notice in time to act upon the defensive, and thereby defeat the plans of the insurgents. Thus, Mr. William Rowley, alarmed by the seizure of Moneymore near his residence, on the afternoon of Saturday, fled to Coleraine, where he arrived about eight o'clock on the morning of Sunday. The unexpected intelligence which he brought was soon too amply confirmed, by the multitudes of pillaged people from the counties of Derry and Antrim, who fled thither for pro-

19 Carte, i. 172, 3.

20 See a pamphlet, containing much curious local information, entitled, "The Information of Sir Frederick Hamilton, Knt. and Col. given to the Committees of both kingdoms, concerning Sir William Cole, Knt. and Col. With the scandalous answer of the said Sir William Cole, together with the replication of Sir Frederick Hamilton, &c." Lond. 1645, pp. 91, 4to.

21 Such as the castles of Culmore, Bellaghy, Ballycastle near Newtonlimavady, Dungiven, &c.

tection during the course of that eventful Sabbath.[22] By this timely notice, Coleraine, then a port of considerable importance, was also secured. Though frequently attacked, it was gallantly defended by the inhabitants under colonel Edward Rowley of Castleroe, until relieved by aid from Scotland; and, during the early period of the rebellion, it proved a seasonable asylum for many protestants, including no less than twenty ministers.[23] The city of Armagh was, in the first instance, left unmolested; and Sir William Brownlow, having received early intelligence, was enabled to put his castle at Lurgan in the county of Armagh, in a posture of defence.

Carrickfergus, the only fortified town on the eastern coast of Ulster, was likewise providentially preserved from the intended attack, which, according to previous arrangement, was to be conducted by one of the Macdonnells. The alarming news of the insurrection reached this place at ten o'clock on the night of Saturday, the twenty-third of October. The governor, colonel Arthur Chichester, immediately took the requisite measures to secure the town and castle; and by the beating of drums, and lighting of fires on the hills, he warned the country of the impending danger. On the Sabbath day, the protestants from the surrounding districts rushed into the town in considerable numbers, in a state of great consternation; most of them equipped with no better arms than pitchforks, and attended with crowds of affrighted women and children. The able-bodied men were quickly furnished with such arms and supplies of ammunition as the stores in the castle could

22 Cox, ii. 98.

23 MSS. Trin. Coll. Dub. F. 4. 16. The following intelligence was communicated to the Irish house of commons on Tuesday, Nov. 16th. " Robert Wallback came from the north and informed the house as follows; 1. That Londonderry and Knockfergus are safe, and that the rebels are not come to Coleraine, [nor] within six or seven miles of it. 2. That the people of Coleraine, some two hundred in number, fought with 1000 of the rebels, and slew six of them, and not one of themselves hurt." App. to Com. Jour. i. 15,

afford; and were marshalled in companies under the command of the principal gentlemen of the county, who had also fled to Carrickfergus, and were increasing in number every hour. In the afternoon of the same day, colonel Arthur Hill arrived, having escaped with difficulty from his castle at Hillsborough in the county of Down. At first the insurrection was considered to be no more than a local quarrel between particular parties of the English and Irish. But scouts having been sent out, during this anxious Sabbath, to ascertain the real nature of the disturbance, it was soon discovered to be a general and simultaneous rising of the Irish Romanists against the British power and people. On receiving this information, lord Chichester at Belfast, immediately despatched intelligence thereof to the king at Edinburgh. It reached him on Thursday the twenty-eighth of October, and was the earliest news of this deplorable event received in Scotland. The gentlemen and military officers, assembled at Carrickfergus, were at first uncertain whether they should remain within the walls for the defence of the town and castle; or march out in search of the insurgents. Having communicated an account of their state by letter to Montgomery, lord of Ards, in the county of Down, they were directed by his lordship to meet him, with whatever forces they could muster, at Lisburn, on the following day.

The town and castle of Antrim were early secured against any sudden attack of the rebels by the zeal of colonel James Clotworthy, in the absence of his brother, Sir John, who was attending his parliamentary duties in London. Castle-Norton, at Templepatrick in the vicinity of Antrim, was also put in a defensive state by captain Henry Upton. The town of Larne, remote from any large body of the insurgents, was maintained and fortified by the inhabitants of the adjoining districts, under the command of captain Agnew: and the neighbouring castle of Ballygelly was held by Mr. James Shaw; and on his retiring with his family to Scotland, it was garrisoned by part of his tenantry under the command of Mr. James Cromie.[24] At the same time, a considerable portion of the lower part of the county of Antrim, from the town of Ballymena, northward to Ballintoy, was preserved by the exertions of Archibald Stewart, Esq. This gentleman, the most influential protestant in that extensive district, received early intelligence of the rebellion from Coleraine; and on the memorable Sabbath so often referred to, he came to the church at Dervock, and communicated to the congregation the unwelcome tidings. He immediately raised a force of nearly eight hundred men from among his own tenantry and those of the earl of Antrim. He placed garrisons, composed principally of Scots, in the house and church of Ballintoy, under Mr. Fullerton and Mr. Archibald Boyd; in the castle of Oldstone near Clough, under Mr. Walter Kennedy; and in such other posts, through the open country, as might most effectually check the incursions of the rebels.[25]

To detach the surrounding Roman catholics from the insurrection, he appointed one of the chiefs of that party, Alexander, or Alaster Macdonnell, better known in history by his Irish name, Colkittagh,[26] to be one of the captains of his own regiment: and when, in consequence of information received by the governor, a party of horse were despatched from Carrickfergus to apprehend this influential Romanist, Mr. Stewart interfered in his behalf, and entered into engagements for his loyalty and good behaviour. This generous confidence was repaid by Macdonnell immediately joining the Antrim Roman catholics, and becoming the cruel and implacable enemy of the surrounding protestants. The castles of Dunluce and Glenarm were held for the earl of Antrim, who, at this

[24] MS. Trin. Coll. Dub. [25] Ibid.—Carte, i. 188.

[26] Colkittagh, or Colkitto, that is 'Col the left handed,' was more properly his father's *soubriquet*, who was at this time a prisoner in Scotland, where he was not long after executed. His son Alaster, was styled Mac-Colkittagh, but the English and Scottish historians almost universally drop the Mac; and some, trying to anglicise the name, have absurdly converted him into Colonel Kittagh.

crisis, was resident in Dublin; and the house of Ballycastle was occupied by his mother, the countess dowager of Antrim; but none of these fortified places afforded any protection to the protestants.[27]

The towns of Belfast and Lisburn owed their preservation, in a great measure, to the courage and promptitude of a single individual, Mr. Robert Lawson, a merchant of the city of Derry, and son-in-law of Mr. Barr of Malone, already mentioned as a staunch presbyterian. Mr., afterwards captain Lawson, thus narrates his proceedings at this eventful crisis. "About the sixteenth of October, before any notice of an insurrection, having occasion to take a journey from Londonderry to Dublin, and to travel by way of Belfast to the iron-works within two miles thereof, wherein he had some stock and interest, he took his journey from thence to go to Dublin upon the twenty-first." His progress was stopped at Newry, by the news of the rebellion; and, together with several fugitives from that town, he returned by Dundrum and Downpatrick, which he reached on the Sabbath day, and "where they stayed to hear a sermon, all the town being in a great affright.——After which they went forwards, and came that night to Killileagh, to the Lord Hamilton's, where Sir Thomas Lucas and the rest stayed. And captain Lawson thereupon, that night, procured a man with him, and came in the night by Comber, through the lord of Ards' country, about by Little Belfast, and came to Great Belfast, and up to the iron-works near thereunto, about three o'clock in the morning, where his wife was then resident, who had sent several messengers before to inquire after him, all of whom were either taken or robbed. But captain Lawson, not having rest there above two hours, arose, calling two horsemen with him. And in the morning, being Monday, went down back again to Great Belfast, where they found most

27 MS. Trin. Coll. Dub.—This dowager countess of Antrim, was Alice O'Neill, sister to Hugh, the last earl of Tyrone. Lodge, i. 207, 8.

part of the inhabitants fled and flying, and carrying away their goods to Carrickfergus; and the old lord Chichester [26] shipped aboard in a ship. So captain Lawson went throughout the town, and blamed them much for offering to leave the town, and entreated for some arms, either by buying or lending, but could not prevail. At last he found, in Master Lesquire's house, seven musquets and eight halberds, ready in the streets to be shipped for Carrickfergus: which arms he took, and bought a drum, and beating the same throughout the town, raised about twenty men, who came with him again up to the iron-works, having Mr. Forbes and some number with him, joined with captain Lawson, where also he gathered in all about one hundred and sixty horse and foot, who, about two of the clock, upon the same Monday in the afternoon, being the twenty-fifth of October, the second day after the rebellion, marched into Lisnegarvey, and there entered the town about four of the clock the same day, all the people, with the troops there engarrisoned, having left the town to the enemy's mercy the Sunday before.

"They quartered all night in the house the bishop of Down lived in, and put many candles in the market-house, and sentries out in every quarter of the town, making show of six or seven lighted matches for every piece, to astonish the enemy, who came to the sentries that night, intending to have burned the town. But our show and carriage was more than our force, the enemy being strong and many in number, by which means they were affrighted and beat off that night. The next morning, being Tuesday, the enemy appeared above the town's end, and drove before them about four hundred cows. Whereupon captain Lawson, with forty-five horse, issued forth, leaving the rest to guard the town; and it pleased God, by their good labour and industry, they took the prey of cows

26 This was Edward, the second lord Chichester, brother and heir to the great lord deputy Chichester. Colonel Arthur Chichester, governor of Carrickfergus, was his son and heir, and afterwards became the first earl of Donegall. Lodge, i. 328.

and some prisoners, and killing others of the enemy; and got seventeen of their mantles. After sending the prey into the town, they adventured three miles farther, and brought in before night as many more cows, and kept them within the town-wall of the bishop's house; and all the next night also, they secured the town, Sir Con Magennis threatening and sending word he would burn the town that night. But it pleased God they were prevented and beaten off, and the town kept in safety. They often issued forth amongst the enemy to prevent their gathering to a great head; until at length, upon the next day, being Wednesday, the troop and townsmen that had fled the Sabbath before, came in again to the town, hearing and understanding what service captain Lawson and his small company of men had done there in securing the same; the preservation whereof, under God, was a means of the safety not only of Lisnegarvey and Belfast, but of most of those parts thereabouts, being the first that opposed the enemy in those parts."[29]

While captain Lawson was thus seasonably and gallantly protecting Lisburn, colonel Chichester had been endeavouring to effect the proposed junction with the lord of Ards, at that town. On Monday he mustered his forces in a field adjoining Carrickfergus; and having left a sufficient garrison in the castle, he marched with the remainder, amounting to about three hundred horse and foot, towards the appointed rendezvous. They arrived at Belfast in the afternoon, where they were joined by a reinforcement of one hundred and fifty men from Antrim. On their march, they met with one of lord Antrim's domestics hastening from Dublin to inform his lordship's friends in the north of the state of affairs there. From him they obtained the welcome intelligence of the preserva-

29 This extract is from a pamphlet, in the British Museum, entitled, "A true relation of several acts, passages and proceedings, done, undertaken, suffered and performed, by captain Robert Lawson, now one of the sheriff's of the city and county of Londonderry, upon and since the first beginning of the great and general rebellion in Ireland, &c." Lond. 1643, 4to. pp. 15.

tion of the metropolis, and the seizure of the principal conspirators. They remained on Monday night at Belfast; but receiving information in the morning, that the rebels, in considerable strength, were marching behind the mountains to the north of the town to attack Carrickfergus, colonel Chichester, on Tuesday, fell back for the defence of that important post. The information, however, proved incorrect. A small party of the insurgents had indeed on that day attacked the house of a Mr. Spencer in Kilultagh, beside Lough Neagh; but he had succeeded in driving them off, and had afterwards retired in safety to Glenavy. At length, in the afternoon of Wednesday, colonel Chichester and the lord of Ards, who had advanced by Drumbo, effected the desired junction at Lisburn. They were joined by lord Claneboy, Sir Thomas Lucas, Sir Arthur Tyringham, Sir James Montgomery of Greyabbey, Mr. Arthur Hill of Hillsborough, captains Blunt, Armstrong, and Edmonstone of Broadisland, with several other experienced officers.[30] They commended Mr. Lawson for his "good care and service in the town, and offered him a commission, which he was very unwilling to accept of, in regard of his calling, being a merchant, but which he at length accepted."[31] The united forces of the protestants, now assembled at Lisburn, amounted to about fifteen hundred horse and foot, though as yet neither adequately armed nor duly disciplined.

The protestants, in the southern portion of the county of Antrim, were thus supplied with several places of security, to which they were soon compelled to fly for refuge from the cruelties of the insurgents. A contemporary document gives the following description of their melancholy state at this crisis. "On the twenty-third of October, 1641, and within a few days after, the Irish rebels made slaughter of all men, women, and children which they could lay hands on, within the county of Antrim, that were protestants, burning their houses

30 Carte, i. 185. 31 Lawson's "True Relation," &c.

and corn; and such as escaped their fury, took sanctuary in the towns of Carrickfergus, Belfast, Lisnegarvey, Antrim and Larne, and the two houses of Templepatrick and Edendough-carrick; all the said towns and houses lying near the one to the other. The rebels had the command of all the rest of the country, and within musket-shot of the towns, and to the very walls of the two houses, until the middle of June, 1642."[32]

While the protestants in the county of Antrim were thus occupied in providing for their security, their brethren in the county of Down were not inactive. The lords Claneboy and Ards—the former resident at his castle in Killileagh, which the rebels had attempted to surprise but without success; and the latter at Newtonards,—stood upon the defensive, and effectually checked the progress of the insurrection in the adjoining districts. From Newry, however, the insurgents under Sir Con Magennis, advanced in a northerly direction towards the town of Dromore. The news of the rebellion had reached the latter place on the afternoon of Saturday; and on the following morning, colonel Matthews, the governor, with as many men as he could muster, marched in the direction of Newry, to ascertain the state of the country, and the precise nature of the disturbance which had so suddenly arisen. Having reached the river Bann, he perceived on the opposite side a large body of the insurgents amounting to five hundred, who, upon being demanded what their purpose was, boldly avowed it was to "fire all the protestants out of the country." As the colonel's escort consisted of only about twenty men, he was compelled to fall back to Dromore. On his return, he found the inhabitants had received certain intelligence of the nature of the rebellion, and were hastily preparing to abandon the town. After many entreaties, he succeeded in inducing the bishop, Dr. Buckworth, to remain for the encouragement of the rest;

32 Extracted from a paper entitled, "State of the county of Antrim in 1641-2." Published in the Rawdon Papers, pp. 91-2.

and on Monday, having collected about one hundred horse and eighty foot, he boldly attacked the rebels, who had now advanced to the vicinity of Dromore; and without losing a man, he defeated and dispersed them with the loss of some hundreds. But, during his absence, the timorous bishop, with the principal part of the inhabitants, finally deserted the town; and although on Thursday, colonel Chichester at the head of two hundred infantry, with his own and lord Conway's troop of horse, and one of light cavalry under captain Edmonstone, marched to the relief of the town still held by Matthews, they found it so defenceless and untenable, that, on the following day, they returned to their quarters at Lisburn.

Sir Con Magennis immediately took possession of Dromore, and treated with wanton and unprovoked cruelty the few protestants who had ventured to remain. Having burned the town, he fell back to Newry, where he effected a junction with Sir Phelim O'Neill. From this place, on the fourth of November, they published a proclamation thus addressed:— "To all Catholiques of the Roman Partie, both English and Irish, within the Kingdome of Ireland, we wish all Happinesse, Freedome of conscience, and Victory over the English hereticks, who have for a long time tyrannized over our bodies, and usurped by Extortion, our Estates." In this document, they set forth a copy of the king's commission from Edinburgh, authorizing them to take up arms in support of the royal power and authority; which copy, they say, "we have here sent unto you, to be published with all speed, in all parts of this kingdome, that you may be assured of our sufficient warrant and authority herein."[33] These proclamations were diligently dispersed, and contributed no little to augment the number, and increase the confidence, of the insurgents. At this time, though scarcely a fortnight had elapsed from the commencement of the rebellion, they were masters of the greater part of the province of Ulster, together with the

33 Myst. of Iniq. p. 34—6.

counties of Longford in Leinster, and Leitrim in Connaught. Nearly thirty thousand men had already joined the standard of revolt—all actuated with the deadliest hatred against the English, whom they detested as conquerors, and execrated as heretics; so that the moment they obtained a manifest and decided superiority, they commenced to wreak their vengeance on the defenceless protestants.

From this period, the comparative moderation with which the Irish commenced the insurrection was abandoned. They had hitherto contented themselves with seizing the houses of the English, despoiling them of their goods, and turning them out naked and defenceless. They had at first spared the lives of their victims, except where local or personal animosities impelled them to the work of blood; and they left the Scottish residents in a great measure unmolested. So far, Sir Phelim and his partizans had acted in accordance with the directions and stipulations of the royal commission. But perceiving his more timid and humane associates, especially those of the Pale, withdrawing from the enterprise, in consequence of the failure of the attempt on Dublin; and finding himself placed, without control, at the head of a much more formidable force than he had ever anticipated, he immediately abandoned what may be called the royal, and prosecuted the original, scheme of the insurrection; and henceforth openly aimed at the extirpation of the entire protestant population, whether of English or Scottish descent. He, therefore, encouraged his infuriated followers to give free vent to the direful passions of hatred and revenge, which the Romish priesthood had for years been fostering in the breast of their people, against their protestant neighbours. The insurrection was speedily converted into a religious war, carried on with a vindictive fury and a savage ferocity, which have been seldom exceeded. Though the enterprise was now formally disowned by Charles, and though Sir Phelim, by his brutal excesses, had disgusted some of the more ardent of his original associates, yet urged on by Ever M'Mahon, Romish bishop of Down, he plunged into the deepest atrocities.

The shocking tale of the cruelties perpetrated by the undisciplined and blood-thirsty levies of O'Neill, during several months, has been often told; by none more affectingly than by the female historian of England. "An universal massacre ensued; nor age, nor sex, nor infancy were spared; all conditions were involved in the general ruin. In vain did the unhappy victim appeal to the sacred ties of humanity, hospitality, family connexion, and all the tender obligations of social commerce; companions, friends, relatives, not only denied protection, but dealt with their own hands the fatal blow. In vain did the pious son plead for his devoted parent; himself was doomed to suffer a more premature mortality. In vain did the tender mother attempt to soften the obdurate heart of the assassin in behalf of her helpless children; she was reserved to see them cruelly butchered, and then to undergo a like fate. The weeping wife, lamenting over the mangled carcase of her husband, experienced a death no less horrid than that which she deplored. This scene of blood received yet a deeper stain from the wanton exercise of more execrable cruelty than had ever yet occurred to the warm and fertile imagination of eastern barbarians. Women, whose feeble minds received a yet stronger impression of religious frenzy, were more ferocious than the men; and children, excited by the example and exhortation of their parents, stained their innocent age with the blackest deeds of human butchery.

"The persons of the English were not the only victims to the general rage: their commodious houses and magnificent buildings were either consumed with fire, or laid level with the ground. Their cattle, though now part of the possession of their murderers, because they had belonged to abhorred heretics, were either killed outright, or, covered with wounds, were turned loose into the woods and deserts, there to abide a lingering, painful end. This amazing, unexpected scene of horror, was yet heightened by the bitter revilings, imprecations, threats and insults which everywhere resounded in the ears of the astonished English. Their sighs, groans, shrieks, cries and bitter lamentations, were answered with—'Spare neither man, woman nor child; the English are meat for dogs; there shall not be one drop of English blood left within the kingdom.' Nor did there want the most barbarous insults and exultation on beholding those expressions of agonizing pain which a variety of torments extorted."[34]

These dreadful massacres were no doubt retaliated, to a certain extent, by the exasperated British. Suffering under the treachery and revenge of the Romanists, who declared they would be satisfied with nothing short of the utter extirpation of the heretics, it was scarcely possible for the protestants to provide for their security, without inflicting summary punishment on such perfidious and implacable enemies. The violence of the protestant soldiery was in some degree justified, as well by the authority of the state, as by the circumstances of the country, and a due regard to self-preservation. In many instances they doubtless exceeded their orders, and acted with unnecessary and culpable cruelty. But their severities have been grossly exaggerated by Romanist, and even by protestant writers, who not only shut their eyes to the awful provocations previously received, but endeavour to fix upon the British the guilt of being the foremost in the work of blood. Thus, the murder of several Roman catholic inhabitants of the district of Island-Magee, near Carrickfergus, in the beginning of the month of January, has not only been egregiously exaggerated, and attributed to parties wholly innocent of it; but it has been placed early in November, and averred to have been the first blood shed in this unhappy contest.

34 Macaulay's Hist. of England, iii. 70-4. 4to. I refrain from inserting the note, annexed by Mrs. Macaulay to the above extract, which furnishes a detail of suffering too revolting to be dwelt upon but with intense horror; and yet too amply borne out by the original depositions to be denied. While the truth of history will not permit these atrocities to be either disguised or extenuated, yet party feelings alone could be gratified by any minuter specification of them, than that given in the text.

This deed of cruelty, however, though deeply to be deplored, and incapable of any justification, cannot in justice be confounded with those extensive and unprovoked massacres which, during the two preceding months, had deluged Ulster with seas of blood. It resulted out of certain barbarous murders which had been perpetrated only a few days before, on the protestant inhabitants of the northern parts of the county of Antrim. On the morning of Monday the third of January, a party of Irish rebels, from both sides of the river Bann, headed by Alaster M'Coll Macdonnell, (Colkittagh,) surprised a detachment of the British stationed at Portna, near Kilrea, under the command of captains Fergus M'Dougall, Peebles and Glover, and massacred between sixty and eighty of them in their beds.[35] From this place they crossed the Bann, and marched through the extensive district of the ROUTE, "with fire and sword, murdering men, women and children of the British, all along in their march to Ballintoy." Thence they proceeded to Oldstone castle, near Clough, which was surrendered to them by Mr. Kennedy on Thursday, upon the solemn assurance of Colkittagh that "none in the place should suffer in body or goods." Yet notwithstanding this assurance, "about twenty women with children upon their backs and in their hands, were knocked down and murdered under the castle wall; and about three score old men, women and children, who had licence to go unto Larne or Carrickfergus, were that day or the next, murdered by the O'Hara's party, within a mile and a half of the said castle."[36]

These outrages could not fail to exasperate the protestants of the adjoining districts, and lead to violent retaliation. Accord-

[35] From the examination of Gilduff O'Cahan of Dunseveric, it appears that the other leaders in this murder were James M'Coll Macdonnell, Patrick M'Henry, Manus Roe O'Cahan, John Mortimer, and examinant's son, Tirlagh O'Cahan. MS. Dep. Trin. Coll. Dub.

[36] Examinations of Alice, countess dowager of Antrim,—Fergus Fullerton of Billy, maltman,—John Blair of Coleraine, &c. &c. MS. Dep. ut supra.

ingly, on the following Sabbath, a number of persons from beyond the river Bann, and from the neighbourhood of Ballymena, "all strangers, met at the village of Ballycarry about sermon time;"[37] and being joined by a few soldiers from Carrickfergus, then garrisoned by raw and undisciplined levies, and not by the regular troops, they proceeded to Island-Magee, and unhappily retaliated on the Roman catholic inhabitants of that district, who had hitherto lived unmolested, the barbarous murders committed on their countrymen and relatives during the preceding week.

Such are the well authenticated circumstances of this disastrous event, which occurred on Sunday the ninth of January 1642, and by which not more than thirty individuals—though still too large a number—lost their lives. Yet many writers, repeating even to the present day the thrice refuted tale, assert that this was a deliberate and authorized massacre, of all the inhabitants, men, women and children, of the territory of Island-Magee, to the number of three thousand and upwards, perpetrated by the Scottish puritan soldiery of Carrickfergus,[38] regularly marshalled under their officers, and led to the field of slaughter; and at a time, too, it is gravely added, when no blood had as yet been shed in Ireland![39]

37 Examination of James Marshall, who saw these persons at Ballycarry on Sabbath forenoon. MS. Dep. ut supra.

38 The Scottish forces, to whom this murder is attributed by some of the popish writers, were not at Carrickfergus until the month of April following.

39 The Rev. Dr. O'Connor, a Roman catholic ecclesiastic, to whom I have had occasion already to refer, (see note 68, Intro.) calls this "the pretended massacre of Island-Magee;" and after clearly proving the ordinary accounts of it to be destitute of evidence, he adds, "yet so credulous are our Irish writers, that they have hitherto taken this pretended massacre upon trust as an *historical fact!*" Hist. Add. Part ii. 234.—I may add, that the Doctor, like every candid and enlightened Romanist, viewed the transactions of this period in their proper light; for, speaking of them, he says, "our ancestors were guilty of abominations, atrocious crimes, to which the present generation, thank God, look back with all the horror and indignation they deserve." Ibid. p. 223.

Ulster was now converted into 'a field of blood.' The cruelties of the Romanists drew down upon them severe retaliation on the part of the betrayed and exasperated protestants; by which the former were incited to still deeper atrocities. Seldom was any quarter given by the rebels to those who fell into their hands; so that, during the winter season, the greater part of all the northern counties exhibited appalling scenes of 'horrid cruelty.'

The evils inseparable from such an exterminating contest were aggravated by the severity of the season, which was more than usually inclement; and were succeeded by the ordinary attendants of civil war—famine and pestilence. Owing to the reckless malice which the Irish bore against every thing British, the valuable stores of corn and cattle belonging to the latter were wantonly squandered and destroyed; while, owing to the scarcity of food thus occasioned, and the refusal of the rebels in many parts to bury the mangled corpses of their victims, a pestilential fever broke out, which, during the spring, carried off thousands of those who, by flying to the towns, had escaped the fury of their enemies. The following account of its ravages, in the county of Antrim alone, has been preserved; and, though probably exaggerated, will convey some idea of its malignity. "The Lord sent a pestilential fever which swept away innumerable people; insomuch that in Coleraine there died in four months by computation six thousand; in Carrickfergus, two thousand five hundred; in Belfast and Malone, above two thousand; in Lisnegarvey, eight hundred; and in Antrim and other places, a proportionable number."[40]

Coleraine appears to have suffered more severely under this malady than any of the other towns. A minister who resided in it during the whole course of the rebellion says,—"In four months, the mortality beginning with the spring,

40 Hist. Coll. of Belfast, p. 15, where the authority quoted is, "An original manuscript formerly in the possession of the Moira family."

there died an hundred a week constantly, and sometimes an hundred and fifty, by just account taken by Henry Beresford, gentleman, one of the last that closed that black list.—So that two thousand died in a short space."[41]

Though all classes of British protestants, whether of English or Scottish descent, were equally exposed to the sufferings now detailed, yet on no class did they fall more heavily than on the clergy. They were marked out for persecution by the priestly instigators of the insurrection, so that, wherever they could be found, they became almost the first victims of the infuriated rage of their enemies. When they fell into the hands of the rebels, they seldom met with any quarter. Many, whose lives were spared, were plundered of their goods, and speedily sank under their grievous privations; while others were committed to rigorous confinement, and a few reserved to be exchanged for the more noted rebels captured by the protestant forces.

Nor was the rage of the rebels confined to the unoffending protestant clergy. Every thing which could be considered in any way identified with protestantism was wantonly destroyed. The Bible, in a particular manner, was an object on which the Romanists vented their detestation of the truth. "They have torn it in pieces," say the commissioners in their remonstrance presented, by the agent for the Irish clergy, to the English commons, scarcely four months after the breaking out of the rebellion, "they have kicked it up and down, treading it under foot, with leaping thereon, they causing a

41 MSS. Trin. Coll. Dub. F. 4. 16. This statement is corroborated by the following deposition printed in Temple, p. 138.—"James Redferne, of the county of Londonderry, deposeth, That in the town of Coleraine, since the rebellion began, there died of robbed and stripped people that fled thither for succour, many hundreds, besides those of the town who had antiently dwelt there; and that the mortality there was such, and so great, as many thousands died there in two days; and that the living, though scarce able to do it, laid the carcases of those dead persons in great ranks, into vast and wide holes, laying them so close and thick as if they had packed up herrings together."

bag-pipe to play the while: laying also the leaves in the kennel, leaping and trampling thereupon; saying, 'a plague on it, this book hath bred all the quarrel,' hoping within three weeks all the Bibles in Ireland should be so used or worse, and that none should be left in the kingdom: and while two Bibles were in burning, saying that it was hell-fire that was burning, and wishing they had all the Bibles in Christendom, that they might use them so."[42]

An authentic statement of the sufferings of the protestant clergy at this dreadful crisis, taken by authority, has been preserved.[43] The writer, one of the commissioners appointed for the examination of protestant grievances, relates that about thirty ministers were massacred in a small part of Ulster alone, while a still larger number died in circumstances of extreme wretchedness.

Of those who were murdered he enumerates the following:—"Mr. Mather of Donoughmore, [in Tyrone,] cut to pieces and left unburied; Mr. Blythe, minister of Dungannon, hanged; Mr. Fullarton of Loughgall, to whom Sir Phelim O'Neill owed at least six hundred pounds upon mort-

42 On the 23d of December the lords justices issued a commission, which was renewed and extended on the 18th of January, to seven clergymen to investigate the losses, &c. occasioned by the rebellion, and to report to the English parliament. Their first report is embodied in a pamphlet, the title of which I subjoin, which was ordered by the House to be printed on the 21st of March, 1642. It of course includes those examinations only which were taken up to that date, and which amount to no more than forty, relating chiefly to the counties of Monaghan and Armagh. It is entitled, "A Remonstrance of divers remarkable passages concerning the church and kingdom of Ireland; recommended by letters from the Right Honourable the Lords Justices and Council of Ireland, and presented by Henry Jones, D. D. and agent for the ministers of the gospel in that kingdom; to the honourable House of Commons in England." London, 4to, 1642.

43 This was in consequence of a second commission issued soon after the commissioners, mentioned in the preceding note, had given in and printed their report. It is dated April 6, 1642, and was confined to Ulster. The commissioners specified are, Nath. Draiton, Daniel Harcourt, William Hammond, Simon Chichester, &c.

gages, and though he had a pass, was stripped and murdered; Mr. Matchett, minister of Magherafelt, after long imprisonment, was murdered at lieutenant Thursbie's in the county of Londonderry; Mr. Hudson, minister of Desertmartin, taken between two feather beds out of Mrs. Chappel's house, where he had been long fed and concealed, was discovered and murdered; Mr. Campion of Killowen, [beside Coleraine,] being at the battle of Ballymoney, which the English, in regard of the fatability of the day, called Black Friday, was killed, the rebels commanded by Colkitto's sons; at the same battle was slain a Scottish minister under the command of colonel Archibald Stewart, late agent to the earl of Antrim; [44] Mr. Tudge, minister of Newry, after long imprisonment and many perfidious promises, was, with thirteen more, cruelly put to death; of which none but one Greene, a tapster to Mr. Butterfield of the Newry, escaped, ransoming his life for forty shillings. This Greene brought me this relation in May 1642. [45] Mr. Hastings, minister, endowed into a living of Mr. Fairfax, but being schoolmaster in Ballysegart, a house belonging to my honoured friend, the virtuous Mrs. Clotworthy: him they caused to swim in the lough [Neagh] till he was drowned; Mr. Darragh, my lord Caulfield's chaplain, killed; Mr. Fleming, minister of Clonfeckle, Mr. Mercer, minister of Mullabrack, and Mr. Burns, curate of Loughgilly, murdered; Mr. Bradley's curate of Ardtrea, Mr. New, killed; Mr. Wilkinson of Clones, killed at the Cavan; Mr. Thomas Crauford, killed by the rebels after quarter was promised; Mr. Montgomery of Dunamain parish,

44 This battle was fought on Friday, February 11, 1642. The British, under Archibald Stewart, already mentioned, had marched out of Coleraine with six hundred Scots and three hundred English. They were met at the Lainy, near the town of Ballymoney, by a large body of rebels under Alaster Macdonnell, who routed them; and, no quarter being given, six hundred of the protestant fugitives were massacred. MS. Dep. ut supra. Cox, ii. 98.

45 For a full account of this cold-blooded murder, which was perpetrated early in January, see Harris's Down, p. 93.

hanged; Mr. Paulmaster, that once lived at Carrickfergus, minister there, was, as his wife informed me, hanged at his church-door; Mr. Flack of Fermanagh, a minister of special note, was, with two of his sons, taken out of Castle-Crevenish, and also offered up to God as a sacrifice; Mr. Michael Berket of Salter's-town, flying for safety with his wife and seven small children to Carrickfergus; where his wife and all his poor children died most miserably for want of ordinary nourishment, himself being famished to the point of death, finding the pangs strong upon him, got leave to go into the church at Carrickfergus, where he had not long stayed, did there depart this life; Mr. Griffin, Mr. Bartley, Mr. Starkey, curate, all of Armagh, murdered on the sixth of May; Mr. Beveridge of Killaman and Mr. Robison of Kilmore, ministers of the same county, were sufferers at the same time; Mr. Lightfoot of Castleblayney, cruelly murdered. (46)

"Besides these thus massacred, there died of the pestilential fever, Bedel, bishop of Kilmore; Mr. Pierce, minister of the Lurgan, at Carrickfergus; Mr. Simon Chichester, minister of Belfast; Mr. Duckett of Lisnegarvey; Mr. Redshaw, minister of Coleraine; Mr. Collins, minister of Kilrea,

46 Besides these ministers, the depositions in Temple and Borlase supply the names of several others who were murdered in Ulster; such as Mr. Middleton of Castle-Balfour, Mr. Morgan Aubrey, Mr. Robison of Caledon, Mr. John Matthew, Mr. Smith and Mr. Birge in the counties of Armagh and Tyrone, and Mr. Akin in Donegall. Of the murder of this last-mentioned minister, which is referred to both by Temple and Borlase, I subjoin an account, from an original deposition, as a sample of the proceedings of the Romanists at this unhappy period:—"Mulrony Carroll, late of Castledoe, gentleman, deposed that Manus Bane, of Doe, and his three sons, hanged and murdered Robert Akins, a protestant minister who had often relieved and kindly entertained them in his house; and two of his brothers, viz. John and Marcus Akins, in their own barn at Cloudevadock; also three women and eight more protestants in Doe: which murders were done chiefly by the command of Mulmory MacSwyne, grandchild to Sir Mulmory MacSwyne, those septs being the most cruel and bloody-minded people of any other in that county of Donegall." Harl. MSS. apud Mus. Brit. No. 5999.

and three ministers more, whose names I cannot learn, all died in Coleraine; Mr. Taylor of Carlingford; Mr. Chesman of Moneymore, minister; Mr. Winter of Astra, [Ardstraw] minister; Mr. Luke Astrie, minister of Ballykelly; Mr. Farwood, dean of Dromore; Mr. Edward Stanhope, archdeacon; Mr. Baxter died in Castle-Craig [in Fermanagh]; Mr. Edward Livesly; Mr. Erskine of Fermanagh, who took his sickness in Derry, but died in Scotland; the son of captain John Kilmer of Faughanvale, [beside Derry] being a minister, died of fatigue and sickness; Mr. Newcome, minister of Fawne [near Derry] at Fawne; Mr. Richard Walker, minister of Lifford, at Lifford." (47)

While recording the sufferings of the protestant clergy, the case of bishop Bedell must not be omitted. The notices of this venerable prelate, already presented to the reader, cannot fail to have imparted so much interest to his history, as to justify a brief detail of the closing scenes of his useful and exemplary life. Although no man had laboured more earnestly for the conversion of the native Irish than he did, yet his zeal was tempered with so much affection and forbear-

47 The above extracts are from a tract entitled, "A New Remonstrance from Ireland, &c." It is dated July 24, 1643, and appears to have been twice republished; first, under the title of "The Levites' Lamentation, &c.;" and again, under that of "The Clergie's Lamentation, &c. By Daniel Harcourt, one of the commissioners for the examination of the protestant grievances in Ulster." Lond. 1644. pp. 23. 4to. Besides specifying those who had perished in the rebellion, Harcourt gives the names of the ministers who were held in custody by the rebels; and also of those who were living in the garrison towns in a state of great penury. "I come now," he says, "to render an account of such as I left in Carrickfergus, Belfast, Newry, Lisnegarvy and the neighbouring parts, in so unfathomed misery as my plum and line is too light and short to express their indigencies." Out of a large catalogue of these ministers I select the following, as their parishes are also given:—Mr. Wilson of Larne, Mr. Durry of Ballymena, Mr. James Tracy of Templepatrick, Mr. Forrest of Donegore, Mr. James Stewart of Garvagh, Mr. David Rowan of Red-bay, Mr. John Mitchell of Anaghlone, and Mr. James Melvin of Downpatrick.

ance, that instead of rendering them hostile to him on that account, he secured the respect of even the most bigoted Romanists in his diocese. They admired his humility, disinterestedness and hospitality; but the chief ground of their attachment to him was his generous and unwearied assiduity in reviving and extending the use of their native language, so long proscribed, but so dearly beloved. These services, to the credit of the Irish, were remembered at this critical period. "The rebels," observes his biographer, "expressed their esteem for him in such a manner that he had reason to ascribe it wholly to that over-ruling power that stills the raging of the seas, and the tumult of the people; they seemed to be overcome with his exemplary conversation among them, and with the tenderness and charity that he had upon all occasions expressed for them, and they often said, he should be the last Englishman that should be put out of Ireland. He was the only Englishman in the whole county of Cavan, that was suffered to live in his own house without disturbance. Not only his house and all the out-buildings, but the church and church-yard were full of people; and many that, a few days before, lived in great ease and much plenty, were now glad of a heap of straw or hay to lie upon, and of some boiled wheat to support nature; and were every day expecting when those swords that had, according to the prophetick phrase, 'drunk up so much blood,' should likewise be satiated with theirs." (48)

For eight weeks after the breaking out of the rebellion, he and his family were permitted to remain in their house in this state of anxiety, but of comparative security. (49)

48 Burnet's Bedell, p. 140.

49 During this alarming period, Swiney, the popish bishop of Kilmore, wished to be permitted to live in bishop Bedell's house, under the pretence of protecting him and his family from violence. But Bedell declined the offer in a letter written in Latin, which was the last of that excellent man's productions, and which displays Christian meekness, discretion and firmness

When more violent measures were resorted to by the Irish leaders, they were forced to remove. "On the eighteenth of December, the rebels came and seized on him, and on all that belonged to him, and carried him and his two sons and Mr. Clogy [50] prisoners to the castle of Lochwater, [Clough-

of the highest order. I am confident many of my readers will feel gratified by inserting here the following translation of it, taken from his 'Life by Burnet.

"REVEREND BROTHER,

"I am sensible of your civility in offering to protect me by your presence in the midst of this tumult; and upon the like occasion I would not be wanting to do the like charitable office to you: But there are many things that hinder me from making use of the favour you now offer me. My house is strait, and there is a great number of miserable people of all ranks, ages, and of both sexes, that have fled hither as to a sanctuary; besides that some of them are sick, among whom my own son is one. But that which is beyond all the rest, is the difference of our way of worship: I do not say of our religion, for I have ever thought and published it in my writings, that we have one common Christian religion. Under our present miseries we comfort ourselves with the reading of the Holy Scriptures, with daily prayers, which we offer up to God in our vulgar tongue, and with the singing of psalms; and since we find so little truth among men, we rely on the truth of God and on his assistance. These things would offend your company, if not yourself; nor could others be hindered, who would pretend that they came to see you, if you were among us; and under that colour, those murderers [circumcelliones] would break in upon us, who, after they have robbed us of all that belongs to us, would, in conclusion, think they did God good service by our slaughter. For my own part, I am resolved to trust to the divine protection. To a Christian and a bishop, that is now almost seventy, no death for the cause of Christ can be bitter: On the contrary, nothing is more desirable. And though I ask nothing for myself alone, yet, if you will require the people, under an *anathema*, not to do any other acts of violence to those whom they have so often beaten, spoiled and stript, it will be both acceptable to God, honourable to yourself, and happy to the people, if they obey you: But if not, consider that God will remember all that is now done. To whom, reverend brother, I do heartily commend you. Yours in Christ,

"*November* 2d, [11,] 1641. WILLIAM KILMORE."

50 Mr. Clogy was a minister, and married to the bishop's step-daughter. It was from materials furnished by him, that bishop Burnet compiled his 'Life of Bedell.'—See Life, p. 136, and Preface.

ovter,] the only place of strength in the whole county. They suffered the prisoners to carry nothing with them; for the titular bishop took possession of all that belonged to the bishop, and said mass the next Lord's day in the church. All but the bishop were at first clapt into irons, for the Irish, that were perpetually drunk, were afraid lest they should seize both on them and on the castle. Yet it pleased God so far to abate their fury, that they took off their irons, and gave them no disturbance in the worship of God, which was now all the comfort that was left them." After three weeks' imprisonment in this wretched tower, situated in the middle of a lake, and scarcely sufficient to protect them from the inclemency of the weather, an exchange of prisoners was effected; and on the seventh of January, the bishop and his family were released. They were not permitted, however, to leave the county, but were compelled to reside at the house of a protestant minister, who was originally of Irish extraction. "Here the bishop spent the few remaining days of his pilgrimage, having his latter end so full in view, that he seemed dead to the world and every thing in it, and to be hasting for the coming of the day of God. During the last Sabbaths of his life, though there were three ministers present, he read all the prayers and lessons himself, and preached on all those days."(51)

In the beginning of February he was seized with an ague which soon became so violent as to leave no hopes of recovery to a frame worn out, "by the sad weight of sorrow that lay upon his mind, and his ill usage in his imprisonment."—— "As his sickness increased, his speech failed, and he slumbered out most of the time; only between hands it appeared, that he was cheerfully waiting for his change, which at last came about midnight, on the seventh of February, that he fell asleep in the Lord, and entered into his rest." He had, before his death, expressed a desire to be buried beside his

51 Burnet's Bedell, pp. 156, 7. 160.

wife in the church-yard of Kilmore; but this privilege could be obtained only by an application to the Romish bishop, who continued to reside at the episcopal house. To him, therefore, the friends of the deceased prelate immediately applied. "They found the bishop lying in his own vomit, and saw a sad change in that house which was before a house of prayer and of good works; but was now a den of thieves and a nest of uncleanness. The bishop, when he was awakened out of his drunkenness, excepted a little to it, and said, the church-yard was holy ground, and was no more to be defiled with hereticks' bodies: yet he consented to it at last. So on the ninth of February, he was buried, according to the direction himself had given, next his wife's coffin. The Irish did him unusual honours at his burial; for the chief of the rebels gathered their forces together, and with them accompanied his body to the church-yard of Kilmore in great solemnity. The Irish discharged a volley of shot at his interment, and cried out in Latin, 'Requiescat in pace ultimus Anglorum,'—may the last of the English rest in peace; for they had often said, that as they esteemed him the best of the English bishops, so he should be the last that should be left among them." [52]

The devastation produced in Ulster by the exterminating warfare, carried on between the opposing parties for several months, was most deplorable. The northern province was the principal scene of rapine and of bloodshed. In the other parts of the kingdom, to which the rebellion soon extended, the confederated Roman catholics acted with more humanity and moderation; while many of them denounced in strong

[52] Burnet's Bedell, pp. 168, 9. It is right to add, that owing to the humanity of Philip O'Reilly, representative in parliament for Cavan, fewer cruelties were perpetrated by the Irish in this county, than in any other part of Ulster. Carte, i. 173, 4. I have seen it stated as another occurrence at the interment of Bedell, that 'Edmund Farilly, a popish priest, exclaimed at the same time, O, sit anima mea cum Bedello! Would to God that my soul were with Bedell!' But this fact is not noticed in my edition of Burnet, Dub. 1736.

terms the barbarous massacre which had almost depopulated Ulster.

The number of protestants who perished during the early part of the rebellion has been variously estimated. While Roman catholic writers have not hesitated to aver, in the face of the most indubitable testimony, that there was no massacre, save of their innocent and unoffending party, by the vindictive and blood-thirsty protestants; (53) on the other hand, several protestant historians have run into the opposite extreme of exaggerating the extent of the slaughter to several hundreds of thousands. (54) From the impossibility of preserv-

53 For the Roman catholic version of the massacre, see Curry's 'Historical Review of the Civil wars of Ireland,' pp. 178—81; and Lingard's 'History of England,' x. 154, and note, p. 483. The latter historian "omits all mention of the massacre, and endeavours, in a note at the end of the volume, to disprove by mere scraps of quotation, an event of such notoriety, that we must abandon all faith in public fame if it were really unfounded." Hallam's Const. Hist. ii. 752. Of the former work, Hallam justly observes, that "the catholics themselves might better leave their cause to Carte and Leland, than excite prejudices instead of allaying them, by such a tissue of misrepresentation and disingenuousness, as Curry's Historical Account of the Civil Wars in Ireland." According to the testimony of the Rev. Dr. Maxwell, afterwards bishop of Kilmore, the rebels boasted to him, while in their custody, that by the month of March, they had slain 154,000 protestants; and O'Mahony, an Irish Jesuit, in his "Disputatio Apologetica," published in 1645, confesses, that his party had cut off 150,000 heretics in four years. Harris's Fiction Unmasked, p. 196. The most curious work on the Romish side of the controversy which I have met with, is one published in Philadelphia, so recently as the year 1819. I have not seen it referred to by any late writer on this part of Irish history, although it discusses at great length, and with an imposing air of research, accuracy, and impartiality, all the controverted topics connected with both the rebellion and the massacre. I allude to "Vindiciae Hibernicae, or Ireland vindicated, &c. By M. Carey." Phil. 1819. 8vo. pp. 504. I notice it here only on account of its flagrant demerits as a work of historical inquiry. It is, in its results, little more than an echo of Curry; but the American, is much more partial and disingenuous than the Irish, writer, while his abuse of the protestants is more violent and rancorous.

54 The following is a brief summary of the calculations of the more eminent protestant writers. May (p. 81) estimates the number slain at 200,000 in the first month. Temple makes it 150,000 in the first two

ing any exact details of so promiscuous a massacre, as well as from the vagueness of the testimony, and the insufficiency of the statistics, on which any calculations could now be founded, it is altogether impossible to arrive at a satisfactory conclusion. The partiality and violence, too, with which the conflicting disputants have discussed the subject, and the confidence with which they insist upon the most opposite results, have tended still more to perplex and obscure it: so that it is equally vain and presumptuous, at the present day, to hope, by any renewal of the investigation, to discover the exact number of protestant sufferers during the first or earliest stage of the rebellion. Suffice it to say, that the lowest probable computation [55] presents an awful sacrifice of human life, and

months, or 300,000 in two years. Rapin (ix. 343.) gives 150,000 in about four months. Lord Clarendon (i. 299.) says, that above 40,000 were murdered at the first outbreak before any danger was apprehended; and he is followed by Hume. Sir William Petty, a very expert and accurate calculator, computes that 37,000 perished within the first year; (Pol. Anat. p. 313.) and this estimate is adopted by Carte. I feel quite incompetent to add any thing which could enable the reader to decide between these conflicting accounts, except to say that, in my opinion, the first three estimates are decided exaggerations.

55 The 'lowest probable computation,' by a protestant writer, is that given by the Rev. Dr. Warner, in his "History of the Rebellion and Civil War in Ireland," published in the year 1768. After a minute scrutiny, as he informs us, of the original depositions preserved in thirty-two folio volumes, in the library of Trinity college, Dublin, an authentic copy of a part of which was in his own possession, and after assuring us that 'it is easy enough to demonstrate the falsehood of the relation of every protestant historian of this rebellion,' who had written before himself, he comes to the conclusion that the number of protestants who lost their lives in the first two years of the rebellion, '*out of war*,' could not have been more than 12,000, and of these, he calculates that 4000 were murdered. In stating the grounds of his computation, he makes the following observation, which has thrown considerable discredit on the authenticity of the depositions above referred to:—' There is one circumstance in these books, not taken notice of as I perceived by any body before me, that though all the examinations signed by the commissioners are said to be upon oath, yet in infinitely the greater number of them, the words "BEING DULY SWORN," have the pen drawn through them, with the same ink with which the ex-

a fearful proof of the implacable spirit of the Romish faith in those days of ignorance and bigotry.

After these lengthened details of the progress and extent of this memorable rebellion, during its earlier stage, it is

aminations are written; and in several of those where such words remain, many parts of the examinations are crossed out. This is a circumstance which shows, that the bulk of this immense collection is parole evidence, and upon report of common fame.' Hist. ii. 7. Entertaining some doubts of the accuracy of this sweeping assertion, I consulted the 'books' of depositions in the college library; and, assisted by a friend, examined a good many of the volumes, time not permitting me to go over the whole, with the view of determining this point, which was readily done by referring to the beginning of each deposition; but we could not find a single one in which the words "being duly sworn," were crossed with the pen, or otherwise obliterated. It is probable some such cases do occur; but to assert, as Warner has done, that they occur 'in infinitely the greater number of them,' is a very incorrect and exaggerated statement. It is also to be remarked, that Warner's computation is founded, not on the depositions whose authority he thus rashly impugned, but upon a copy of a part of them in his own possession, all of which were 'duly sworn,' and authenticated by the signatures of the commissioners. A duplicate of this copy, he states, was deposited among the manuscripts in the British Museum. This volume I found out, and carefully examined. It is No. 5999, vol. iii. of the Harleian MSS. It is marked, "*Original. Received at the Board, 10th November*, 1643;" and corresponds with the description given by Warner of his own copy. But I found it to contain only 'extracts' from no more than about two hundred depositions. Among these, there are only four from the county of Down, all relating to one occurrence; four from Tyrone; three from Donegall, two of which refer to one occurrence; three from Derry; and not a single deposition relating to Antrim. It is quite impossible, therefore, that a correct enumeration of the number who perished, could be formed from any examination, however minute, of these extracts. They could furnish the inquirer with only a portion of the murders perpetrated, the full catalogue of which was not completed till ten years afterwards, when the republican authorities renewed the inquiry, by appointing commissioners for the purpose. These commissioners took a vast number of additional and most important depositions; and they bound over the several deponents to appear at the subsequent assizes for each county, in order to prosecute such of the more noted of the murderers as could then be found,—a circumstance which renders these depositions, taken with the view of being afterwards repeated on a public trial for a capital offence, and at a time when party-feeling had in a great measure subsided, of more value than the depositions contained in the Harleian and Warner's MS.

scarcely necessary to add, that the presbyterian interest in Ulster was thereby almost entirely destroyed. Protestant prelates had commenced the work by compelling the greater part of the presbyterians to flee to Scotland. But what appeared to be the ruin, proved to be the preservation of the church; while they who had been the foremost to persecute, were the first to suffer. For, on the bishops and other dignified clergy, the Roman catholics early vented their rage and indignation; and while the Scots were, in the first instance, spared, their episcopal persecutors were, in their turn, compelled to abandon their properties, and fly for refuge to England.

As a body, the presbyterians suffered less by the ravages of the rebellion than any other class. The more influential of their ministers, and the principal part of their gentry, had previously retired to Scotland to escape the tyranny of Strafford and the severities of the bishops, and were thus providentially preserved. Those who remained in the country, were at first unmolested by the Irish, in conformity with the royal commission. This temporary preservation gave them time to procure arms, and to take other necessary measures to protect themselves against the storm which they saw approaching. When the rebels, therefore, abandoned their professed neutrality, and fell upon them, as furiously as upon the English, they were prepared for the attack. Where they associated to-

which were taken privately, at the very hottest period of the rebellion, and without any view of being subjected to the ordeal of examination on a public trial. The greater part of the thirty-two volumes in Trinity college, is composed of these valuable supplementary depositions. I perused with some care, the entire volume marked 'Co. Antrim;' and all the depositions contained in it, relative to the rebellion, were taken before the parliamentary commissioners in 1653; by whom too, let it be observed,—a fact not generally known,—the retaliatory murders alleged to have been committed by the protestants on the Irish, at Island Magee and other places, are as closely and impartially investigated as the original massacres by the Roman catholics. The latter were pretty extensive in this populous protestant county; yet not one of them is included in Warner's computation; which, it is therefore quite evident, must be considered as falling short of the truth; but how far short, I am not qualified to give an opinion.

gether in sufficient numbers, they were generally enabled to maintain their ground, and frequently repulsed the assailants with loss. But when, trusting to the professions of their Irish neighbours, they relaxed their vigilance and continued unarmed, they seldom failed to suffer the penalty of their misplaced confidence. One instance may suffice to prove the truth of this observation. Mr. Robert Stewart of the Irry, near Stewartstown, in the county of Tyrone, a relative of the Castlestewart family, and married to the grand-daughter of the outlawed earl of Tyrone, had, on the first alarm of the rebellion, collected and armed about six hundred Scots. With this force, he could easily have defended the whole of the surrounding country. Being assured, however, by his Irish relatives, that none of the Scots should suffer any molestation, he was induced, in a few days, to dismiss his followers, and take back their arms. But the very night on which they reached their homes, the greater number of them were murdered by their perfidious enemies.[98]

The presbyterians who were preserved amidst the surrounding carnage and devastation, were in a great measure destitute of the public ordinances of religion. The clergy had been murdered, or had fled to the towns for safety; and the churches which had not been seized by the Roman catholics, were garrisoned, and converted into places of refuge. But neither the restraints to which they were subjected under the bishops, nor their present destitution, had weakened their attachment to their church. They maintained their religious principles as firmly and successfully as they did their lives and properties; until the arrival of succours from Scotland, and the return of their banished brethren after peace had been restored, enabled them to revive their church in Ulster, under more favourable circumstances than at its first plantation.

98 Cox, ii. 98. Cox makes a slight mistake in the name of Mr. Stewart, calling him William. That Robert was his name, is evident from Lodge, vi. 258.

CHAPTER VIII.

Proceedings of the lords justices—The king sends commissions to the protestant leaders in Ulster—O'Neill reduces Lurgan—His unsuccessful attack upon Lisburn—Is defeated in Tyrone by Sir William and Sir Robert Stewart—Their services in Donegal—State of Derry—English and Scottish parliaments negotiate for the relief of Ireland—Arrival of Scottish forces under Monro—They march to Newry—and Armagh—Return to Carrickfergus—Letter to Monro from Derry—Movements of the Lagan forces—Conduct of the earl of Antrim—Is taken prisoner by Monro—Proceedings in Armagh—and on Lough Neagh—Peace restored—State of the church in Ulster—Revival of presbytery—Army chaplains—First Presbytery meets—Its proceedings—Congregations erected by it—First petition to the General Assembly in Scotland—Assembly's reply—Ministers appointed to visit Ulster.

The lords justices, having taken the necessary steps for the security of the metropolis, immediately despatched intelligence of the rebellion, both to the king at Edinburgh, and to the houses of parliament in London. They also sent commissions by sea to Ulster, the communication by land being interrupted by the rebels, empowering captain Arthur Chichester and Sir Arthur Tyringham to take the command of all the forces in the county of Antrim; and urging the lords Chichester, Claneboy and Ards, with several knights and gentlemen, to use their best efforts for the suppression of the rebellion.[1]

These despatches were followed by others from the king at Edinburgh, received on the seventh of November, assuring

[1] Carte, i. 187.

the northern protestants of speedy and efficient support. Shortly after, he forwarded commissions, dated the sixteenth of the same month, to the lord of Ards and Sir James Montgomery in the county of Down, and to Sir William and Sir Robert Stewart in the counties of Derry and Donegall, authorising each of them to raise a regiment of one thousand foot and a troop of horse. Sir William Cole of Enniskillen, and Sir Ralph Gore of Magherabeg in Donegall, also received commissions to raise five hundred men each for the defence of the kingdom. In the following month the English parliament ordered two more regiments to be raised, and placed them under the command of lord Conway and Sir John Clotworthy. For the purpose of accelerating the levy and taking the command of his regiment, Sir John returned to Antrim in the end of the year, and shared with his countrymen in the subsequent perils and fatigues of the war. These forces, however, were in great want of arms. The lords justices had sent four hundred muskets, with a due proportion of ammunition, to the lords Claneboy and Ards;[2] but this supply was insufficient, as the former nobleman soon after sent to Scotland, to purchase an additional quantity of arms.[3] The lord Chichester also, with his son captain Arthur Chichester, Sir Arthur Tyringham and captain Arthur Hill, despatched Mr. Edmonstone of Broadisland to Edinburgh, who purchased a supply of muskets, swords and pikes for the newly raised regiments.[4] Assisted by these seasonable supplies, and encouraged by these promises of succour, the protestant leaders

[2] Borlase, 23. Temple, 91.

[3] MSS. Gen. Reg. House, Edinb. This application was made, Jan. 21, 1642. by "Robert Tweedie, servitor to the Lord Claneboy."

[4] For the gratification of the curious in these matters, I have inserted, in the Appendix, an extract from the state records of Scotland, deposited in the Register Office, Edinburgh, containing the minute of the committee of estates for the delivery of the arms required; and reciting the power of attorney granted, on that occasion, to Mr. Edmonstone by lord Claneboy and the other applicants. See Appendix, No. III.

in Ulster were soon enabled to repel the incursions of the rebels.

Meanwhile Sir Phelim O'Neill succeeded in reducing the town and castle of Lurgan, which he had for some time closely besieged. In consequence of the supply of arms and ammunition which Sir William Brownlow had received, he had gallantly resisted the assaults of the insurgents for above a fortnight. At length, on the fifteenth of November, he capitulated, on condition of being permitted to retire with his family and property unmolested. But though these terms were agreed to by the besiegers, yet the moment possession was obtained of the castle, they were flagrantly violated. Sir William, his lady and children were cast into prison; his house was rifled; his servants were stripped and plundered, and many of them inhumanly butchered; while the inhabitants of the town were treated with similar unprovoked cruelty.(5)

Encouraged by the reduction of this post, O'Neill shortly after renewed his attempt upon Lisburn, the occupation of which was indispensable to the success of his designs against Belfast and Carrickfergus—two important posts which he was most anxious to possess. Accordingly, on Sunday the twenty-eighth of November, at the head of four thousand men, and assisted by Sir Con Magennis and major-general Plunket, he made a furious assault upon Lisburn. His forces succeeded in setting fire to the town; but they were ultimately repulsed, with considerable loss, by the steady courage of the protestant soldiery and inhabitants, under the command of Sir Arthur Tyringham and Sir George Rawdon of Moira. Towards the close of the contest, which was prolonged till night, they were assisted by a seasonable reinforcement of horse and foot from Belfast under the command of captain Boyd, who "was unhappily slain after his first entrance into the town."(6) This spirited and successful defence deterred O'Neill from attempting any further inroads on the

5 Carte, i. 188. 6 Carte, i. 189. Hist. Coll. of Belfast, p. 20.

protestants in this quarter. He soon after led his insurgent troops to the north-western parts of the province, which he hoped to find less efficiently protected.

In this expectation he was happily disappointed. His success in those parts was confined to the capture of a few places of little importance. In the beginning of December he succeeded in taking the town of Strabane, which he plundered and burned. He also obtained possession of the castle which had been held by the relict of Claude, first lord Strabane. Here he remained with his forces for several weeks, making occasional incursions through the adjoining country; but becoming enamoured of his fair captive, the lady Strabane, he carried her with him to his castle in Tyrone, where they were afterwards married.[7] Besides the taking of this town and castle, he obtained no other advantage in that part of the province.

For, shortly after the breaking out of the rebellion, Sir William and Sir Robert Stewart, acting upon the commissions received from the king, had embodied about a thousand men in the counties of Donegall and Tyrone, who were afterwards known by the name of the "LAGAN FORCES."[8] With this body they were enabled not only to hold the insurgents in check, but to succour several towns and castles which were closely besieged, and in danger of falling into the hands of the enemy. Though unable to protect Strabane, they garrisoned the castles of Newtonstewart and Omagh; both of which were seasonable asylums for the plundered and defenceless protestants of Tyrone. To the former of these places, the inhabitants of the barony of Dungannon repaired in a body, under the command of Sir Thomas Staples and colo-

7 Sir Phelim said to lady Strabane, as he carried her off, that 'he would never leave off the work he had begun, until mass should be sung or said in every church in Ireland; and that a protestant should not live in Ireland, be he of what nation he would.' Lodge, v. 114.

8 The 'LAGAN' is the name of a large district in the county of Donegall, lying between the Foyle and the Swilly.

nel Saunderson. "They marched forth of that barony to Newton, nigh twenty miles through the barbarous mountains of Munterlony, one of the greatest fastnesses of Ireland, to join Sir William Stewart's forces there, where they were joyfully entertained."[9] The castle of Augher in Tyrone was held by the Rev. Archibald Areskine, son and heir to Sir James Areskine, assisted by a company of soldiers, and by Archibald Hamilton, Esquire, and his tenants, who, at the first alarm of the rebellion, had fled thither for protection. The rebels, to the amount of two thousand, having burned the small town of Augher, laid close siege to the castle for a considerable time, but were repulsed in all their attempts to take it, and ultimately compelled by Sir William Stewart to abandon the siege. Irritated at the gallant defence of this post, Sir Phelim O'Neill, in conjunction with colonel Rory Maguire of Fermanagh, marched against it, and again invested the castle with nearly four thousand men. "They planted a small field-piece to batter; and in a dark night stormed the gate and bawn upon all parts. Yet by the resolution of Master Areskine, and the ready fire of Sir Henry Tichborne's old company, they beat them from their walls and scaling-ladders with the loss of two hundred men."

Sir William Stewart, apprized of this renewed and more formidable attack, despatched colonel Saunderson, major James Galbraith and captain Audley Mervyn from Newton, with all his disposable force, to the relief of Augher. The rebels, being once more compelled by the approach of this body to raise the siege, next invested Castle Derg in the same county; from which also they were repulsed by Sir Robert Stewart, who "thence marched over against Glenfin,—burnt that

9 See "An Exact Relation of all such occurrences as have happened in the several counties of Donegall, Londonderry, Tyrone and Fermanagh, in the north of Ireland, since the beginning of this horrid, bloody and unparalleled rebellion there begun in October last. Presented to the House of Commons in England by Colonel Audley Mervyn, June 4, 1642." Lond. 1642. 4to. pp. 14.

country and killed divers,—afterwards fell over in the night upon the rebels' quarters above Strabane, and killed above eighty men."(10)

Meanwhile Sir William Stewart, with another portion of the Lagan forces, proceeded into the barony of Kilmacrenan in Donegall, where the rebels had early taken possession of the castles upon his estate, plundered his towns, and scattered the protestant inhabitants. "Captain Maxwell and captain George Stewart marched towards Ramelton with one hundred and fifty men, and killed ninety of the rebels, and brought home eighteen hundred cows. Captain Basill, about the same time, being New-Year's day, marched over into the enemy's country with sixty men, and encountered four hundred men and killed thirty-six." They regained possession of Ramelton and the castle there; and, supported by the neighbouring garrison of Derry, they effectually checked the further incursions of the Romanists in that quarter.

The city of Derry was securely placed under the command of the governor, Sir John Vaughan, knt. So early as the fourth of November, the lords justices issued a commission to alderman Henry Finch, to raise a company of foot for the defence of the city. Not long afterwards, captain Lawson, having received intelligence that one of his vessels, freighted with butter for France, had been detained at Derry, obtained permission from Sir Arthur Tyringham to place his newly-raised regiment at Lisburn, under the charge of his two lieutenants, Clugston and Hanna, and of his quarter-master Stewart; and having considerable property embarked in trade at this critical period, he proceeded to Derry to attend to his mercantile concerns. He found the cargo of his ship had been laid up for the use of the inhabitants, then apprehensive of being besieged by the rebels; and that the vessel itself was "employed to carry away into Scotland about five hundred poor souls which would have perished, if that occasion had

10 Mervyn's Exact Relation, &c.

not offered; no other shipping being there resident for the space of six months before."[11] Having obtained another commission to raise a company for the defence of the town, Mr. Lawson remained at Derry, where the principal part of his property lay. His brother-in-law, alderman Henry Osborne, and several other gentlemen, were also commissioned to raise soldiers, so that the city was soon fully garrisoned with seven companies of foot, commanded by the following captains:— Robert Thornton, who was also mayor, Simon Pitt, Henry Finch, Henry Osborne, John Kilmer, Robert Lawson, and Hewit Finch, whose company was subsequently placed under the command of the governor's son, captain Henry Vaughan.

These commanders took prompt and efficient measures for the defence of this important post. They entered into a mutual 'league' or agreement for 'the keeping thereof, and the country adjoining.'[12] They repaired the gates and

11 Lawson's "True Relation," &c.

12 As no history of this 'maiden city,' so full of interest to the northern protestant, has yet appeared, I am tempted to lay before the reader, throughout this work, ampler gleanings respecting its early state than I might otherwise have done. I accordingly subjoin a copy of the 'League,' noticed in the text, taken from a very rare and curious pamphlet, entitled, "A true copy of a letter sent from Doe Castle, in Ireland, from an Irish rebel, to Dunkirke," &c. Lond. 1643. 4to, pp. 5.

"The League of the captains of Londonderry for the keeping thereof, and country adjoining.

"1. It is concluded by us, whose names are subscribed, that we will, from this time forward, stand together for the safe keeping of this city of Londonderry and country adjoining, and be helpful in all things concerning the same. 2. It is agreed, that on the morrow morning, we will all join together, with a competent number of our men, to expel all such Irish out of the city, as we shall conceive to be needful for the safety of this city. 3. That after this is done, that a proclamation be made, that no man or woman so expelled the city shall, upon pain of death, return into this city, or make their abode within two miles of the same. 4. That the morrow morning we take the advice of Sir John Vaughan, and captain Henry Vaughan; that we survey the suburbs of this city, and conclude what houses are to be pulled down, and what gardens and orchards to be cut for annoying the enemy's approach, and that the same be speedily put in execution. 5. That forty men be spared every watch-night to guard the ramparts, and erected temporary houses of wood within the walls for the accommodation of the soldiery, who were principally landholders from the surrounding districts.(13) They

ordnance and the gates the next day, that twenty men of the main guard, and twenty men of the bye guard, out of the two hundred watches every night. 6. It is thought fit all our companies be drawn forth into the fields, and that the captains and officers shall take a voluntary oath to be true to the king and state, and to keep the city to the expense of his life, and to leave it to the rest of the companies to do the like if they pleased.

"The division of the walls for each captain's quarter to make good.

"7. Captain Pitts to make good the king's bulwark to the Ferrigate. 8. Captain Thornton from the Ferrigate to master Wabion's bulwark; and they two to make good the Ferrigate. 9. Captain Kilmer from Master Wabion's bulwark to Chichester's bulwark, and make good the Shipkey-gate. 10. Captain Finch from the end of Chichester bulwark to the Butchersgate. 11. Captain Osborne from the end of Chichester bulwark to the Butchersgate. 12. Captain Lawson to make good the Prince's bulwark, and the Bishopsgate to the King's bulwark. 13. Whoever hath the town-guard, captain Lawson is to make good his quarter, and the captain of the town's guard to make good captain Lawson's quarter. 14. Sir John Vaughan and Sir Robert Stewart to make good the main-guard, and all the inhabitants or residents within the said city, not under the captain's commands, to repair to the main-guard, for the better strengthening thereof, and issuing of supplies as occasion shall require. 15. All women and children to keep within doors, and hang out lights in their several houses. 16. Every captain to allow so many men to the cannoneers as shall be requisite, and to give them their names the morrow morning. 17. Every captain to take the oversight of his own quarter, for the repairing of the defects of their several quarters, or other fortifications, with the gabions for the cannoneers, which is to be done at the general charge.

"The names of the captains,—Robert Thornton, Simon Pitt, Henry Finch, Henry Osborne, John Kilmer, Robert Lawson, Hew Finch.

"Since, the honourable city of London hath sent us fifteen pieces of ordnance, and four we had before, in all nineteen pieces, for which, amongst other their goodness towards us, we pray the Lord reward them, and preserve them, and continue his mercy with them, and direct his judgments in these evil times from them, that it may still continue a city flowing with plenty for ever."

13 In captain Lawson's "True Relation," it is certified, on his behalf, that he "hath issued and delivered out about 4000 deal-boards to make several houses, with timber, planks and nails, to receive the soldiers, their wives and children in the dead of winter, most of them having been men of good ability and householders; neither hath he been wanting on his part

sent intelligence of their situation to the king in Scotland; to their landlords, the corporation of the city of London, who sent them several pieces of ordnance; and also to the lords justices at Dublin, who despatched thirty barrels of powder and a supply of arms, which reached the city in the beginning of December.(14) Assisted by these seasonable supplies, they held possession of Derry; but, though unmolested by the enemy, the inhabitants and soldiers, during the winter season, suffered many severe privations.

The eyes of the whole empire were now intently directed to the progress of these events in Ulster. So soon as the Scottish parliament were informed by Charles, on Thursday the twenty-eighth of October, of the breaking out of the rebellion, they ordered immediate inquiry to be made into the quantity of shipping on the western coast, and the number of disposable men who could be transported to Ulster. When more accurate intelligence was received, on the first of November, of the extent of the insurrection and the dangerous situation of the northern protestants, they offered a supply of three thousand stand of arms, and ten thousand men for the

for and towards the repairing of the decayed walls, gates, and ramparts of the city, and doing other necessary works there, and hath begun a trench without the walls of the city of good consequence, intended to be perfected; for all which he cannot have expended less than L.5000 sterling."

14 The manner in which this intelligence of the state of Derry was conveyed to Dublin, and the relief sent thither, are thus stated by captain Lawson:—"Having a ship come into Carrickfergus, at the first of the rebellion, which was laden with eighty-five tuns of salmon for the accompt of him, [captain Lawson,] captain Finch, and captain Osborne, with other goods from Derry and bound for France, he caused the same to transport from thence to Dublin, Sir Thomas Lucas, and captain Charles Boulton, where being landed, and the ship intending forwards to France, was presently after cast away, worth L.2000 sterling, occasioned by the same. And by that conveyance, captain Boulton getting to Dublin, shortly afterwards brought back from thence to Londonderry thirty barrels of powder, with other arms and munition, being the first relief and supply which came thither for the supplies of the regiments and soldiers there, without which they had been utterly lost and perished, as being destitute before of any powder or arms."

relief of Ireland.[15] But as their own resources were insufficient for raising and supporting such an army, and as Ireland was a dependency of England, it was obviously necessary that the authorities of the latter kingdom should not only previously give their sanction to the introduction of Scottish forces into that part of their realm, but should also engage to support them, when employed in their service.

A negociation to this effect was accordingly opened with the English parliament, on the return of Charles to London, in the latter end of November. The commons had already, on the first of that month, when O'Connolly communicated to them the intelligence of the rebellion, voted a liberal supply of money, and a considerable levy of men, for the relief of Ireland.[16] When they received fuller information of the dangerous state of the kingdom, they voted, ten days afterwards, a much larger supply; and, at the same time, they agreed to negociate with the Scottish parliament for the proposed aid of ten thousand men. On the tenth of December, the first conference on this subject took place in London, between a committee from the two houses of parliament on the one hand, and commissioners sent up from Scotland, on the other.

15 The entry on the journals of the Scottish parliament, relative to this offer, is as follows:—The committee reported to the house, "That they had found it expedient, how soon ever the parliament of England should approve the conveniency of their aid and assistance in this business, that eight regiments of foot should, with all diligence, be levied, consisting of 10,000 men, whereof 2500 to be highland men, and 7500 to be levied out of the lowland shires, with ammunition to them. They made report likewise, that they could supply their brethren in Ireland with arms out of the common magazine for 3000 men, two part muskets, and the third part pikes: England giving assurance for redelivery and payment of the same." Balfour, iii. 134.

16 The state of the distressed protestants in Ireland very soon excited the commiseration of the English; as appears from a discourse, which I have met with, entitled, "Ireland's Advocate, or a Sermon preached upon November 14th, 1641, to promote the contributions by way of lending, for the present relief of the protestant party in Ireland. In the parish church of St. Stephens, Coleman Street, London, by the pastor there." Lond. 1641. Pp. 36.

But the jealousies which existed between Charles and the commons, and which were now rapidly ripening into an open rupture, unhappily retarded the issue of this negociation. The king, in the first instance, wished to cast upon the parliament the whole weight of conducting the affairs of Ireland at this critical period; with the view of drawing off their attention from his proceedings at home, and enfeebling their growing opposition to his arbitrary measures. [17] He was, therefore, secretly averse to the employment of any Scottish auxiliaries. The commons, on their part, were afraid of weakening the resources, necessary for the conflict which they saw approaching between them and their sovereign, by granting too liberal a supply for the reduction of the Irish rebels. They were also afraid—and subsequent events proved the justness of their apprehensions—that the premature pacification of Ireland would afford Charles, in the coming hour of need, a reinforcement of troops from that country, hostile to the cause of truth and freedom. Charles, on the other hand, taking advantage of their apparent indifference to the fate of Ireland, suddenly changed his policy, and proposed to raise a body of ten thousand volunteers, and to go over in person to chastise the rebels. But the parliament utterly refused to listen to a proposal, the effect of which would have been, to place the king at the head of a force entirely subject to his authority alone, and ready to be employed, at a moment's warning, against themselves.

This offer of Charles, however, quickened the parliament in their negociation with the Scottish commissioners. After several ineffectual attempts on the part of the house of lords, where the royal influence was predominant, to retard its successful issue, the terms upon which the Scots offered their aid were agreed to, on the twenty-fourth of January. When these proposals were, two days afterwards, submitted to the king, he objected to the third article, by which it was stipu-

17 Laing, i. 224.

lated that the Scottish forces were to be put in possession of the castle of Carrickfergus. At length, however, he reluctantly acquiesced; and on the eighth of February he finally issued his commission for their transportation to Ulster. [18] Two thousand five hundred men were, in the first instance, to be embodied and sent forward to occupy Carrickfergus; and the remainder of the stipulated supply of ten thousand were to follow, at their earliest convenience; and on their arrival, to be put in possession of the town and castle of Coleraine. [19]

Though great exertions were made to raise and embody these forces with despatch, it was the middle of March before they had reached the appointed rendezvous on the western coast of Scotland. Detachments from seven regiments, viz. Glencairn's, Argyle's, Eglinton's, Sinclair's, Home's formerly Cochrane's, Monro's and Lindsay's, formed this first draft of two thousand five hundred men, under the command of major-general Robert Monro,—an officer of considerable experience and great military skill. They lay, for more than a fortnight, in the towns of Irvine, Ayr and Kilmarnock, waiting for a favourable wind. In the beginning of the following month they put to sea, under convoy of an English frigate; but were soon after driven into Lamlash, in the island of Arran. After being detained another fortnight in this secluded harbour, they again set sail on the evening of the fourteenth of April. The following day, they reached Carrickfergus; and before night were securely established in the possession of the town and castle. The regiments of lords Conway and Chichester, who previously formed the garrison, having surrendered their quarters, marched to Belfast; and, with the other British regiments in Ulster, placed themselves under the command of Monro, agreeably to the terms of the treaty with the English parliament.

The Scottish general did not long remain inactive. Leav-

18 Rymer, vol. ix. part iii. p. 83.

19 Rushworth, iv. 501-2.

ing a garrison of eight hundred men in Carrickfergus, upon the twenty-seventh of April he marched with the remainder to Belfast, where he was joined by the regiments of lords Conway and Chichester. On the following day, he formed a junction at Lisburn with the forces from the county of Down under the command of the lords Claneboy and Ards.

Monro had now at his disposal, an effective body of, at least, three thousand five hundred men, and eight troops of horse. With the one-half of this force he proceeded to attack the rebels in the woods of Kilwarlin; where, under the command of Magennis the lord Iveagh, and to the number of near three thousand, they occupied an important pass on the road to Newry. After a short skirmish, the rebels were put to flight; and the British, following the example which the Irish had too often set in previous encounters,—of refusing quarter, cruelly and unjustifiably put to death all who fell into their hands. (20) On Saturday, the thirtieth of April, both divisions of the army met at this pass; and having defeated another body of the rebels at Loughbrickland, they marched to Newry, which had been in possession of the Irish above half-a-year. The town, being imperfectly fortified, was immediately taken by Monro; and, with the exception of a few houses, given up to plunder. The castle held out for two days; but on the third of May it was surrendered to the British. The garrison were treated with shocking severity, —they were immediately put to death; and many of the inhabitants, who had fled for refuge to the castle, and some women, (21) lost their lives in this indiscriminate slaughter.

20 Livingston, who, as one of the chaplains to the Scottish army, was present at this skirmish, gives us the following curious piece of information, respecting the rebels who were killed:—" They were so fat, that one might have hid their fingers in the lirks of their breasts." Life, p. 37.

21 The Irish women were so obnoxious to the English and Scots, on account of their well known cruelties to the protestants, who fell into the hands of the rebels in the beginning of the insurrection, that the soldiery could scarcely be refrained from cutting them off whenever they met with them. This was the case at Newry. An eye-witness relates that the

These severities, though amply merited, and designed to strike terror into the insurgents, were as impolitic, as they were disgraceful and unjustifiable. For, by this means, the rebels were inflamed to greater fury against those who were yet in their power, while too good ground was afforded to their partizans to reprobate the cruelty of the protestant forces.

After resting his troops at Newry for two days, Monro left the detachment of lord Sinclair's regiment, which had come from Scotland, with an additional force of two hundred men, in command of the town and castle. This garrison he placed under the command of lieutenant-colonel Sinclair, and of major, afterwards the well-known Sir James Turner, who became so notorious, during the subsequent reign, as the barbarous persecutor of his presbyterian countrymen in the south of Scotland. On Friday, the sixth of May, Monro marched to Armagh, hoping to take Sir Phelim O'Neill by surprise.

soldiers there, without any authority from Monro or their officers, took "some eighteen of the Irish women of the town, and stript them naked, and threw them into the river, and drowned them, shooting some in the water. More had suffered, but that some of the common soldiers were made examples on and punished." Taken from a small tract of only seven pages, bearing the following lengthy title, which, however, serves as an index to its contents: "A true Relation of the proceedings of the Scots and English forces in the North of Ireland, sent in a letter to Mr. Tobias Sedgwicke, living in London, relating these particulars, viz. 1. Their meeting at Drumbo in the county of Antrim; 2. The manner of their march towards the Newry, with the taking of a fort near Kilwarlin Woods; 3. The taking of the town and castle of the Newry, and the releasing of divers prisoners of note; 4. The great spoil they took in those parts, with great terror to the rebels, and their flight from those parts; 5. Divers skirmishes with the rebels in M'Cartan's Woods; 6. The desires of the earl of Antrim to be received into the English army. With divers other things worthy your observation." The letter or tract is signed, Roger Pike; and is dated from Carrickfergus, May 30th, 1642. The statement of this writer, given above, I find corroborated, though in a somewhat exaggerated strain, by Sir James Turner, in his valuable "Memoirs," lately published. But Turner, writing from memory above forty years after the event, cannot be expected to be so accurate as Pike, who wrote within a few days of it.

But the latter having notice of his approach, and being exasperated at the loss of Newry, set fire to this ancient city, not sparing even the venerable cathedral, though dedicated to the patron-saint of Ireland; and having murdered a vast number of protestants, partly inhabitants of Armagh and partly prisoners, he retired to the strong fort of Charlemont, and the greater part of his troops betook themselves to the fastnesses of the bogs and mountains of Tyrone.

From Armagh, the British and Scottish forces returned to Carrickfergus, where they arrived on the twelfth of May. On their march, during the night of Sunday, the eighth of the month, they encountered a storm of unusual severity at that season of the year, as they lay encamped in the open country. Its extraordinary violence is thus described by Turner. "I do remember that there we suffered one of the most stormy and tempestuous nights for hail, rain, cold and excessive wind, though it was the beginning of May, that ever I yet saw. All the tents were in a trice blown over. It was not possible for any match to keep fire, or any soldier to handle his musket, or yet to stand; yea, severals of them died that night of mere cold. So that if the rebels, whereof there were five hundred not far from us, had offered to beat up our quarters with such weapons as they had, which were half-pikes, swords, and daggers which they call skeens, they would undoubtedly have had a cheap market of us."[22] This officer was returning with Monro to Carrickfergus, for the purpose of conducting to Newry a reinforcement for his regiment, which had just arrived from Scotland. His proceedings on this occasion, thus narrated by himself, point out the hardships which the Scottish troops had already begun to encounter in Ulster.

22 "Memoirs," &c. Edin. 1829, 4to. Turner's account of this storm is thus confirmed by Pike in his letter to Sedgwicke, mentioned in the preceding note:—"Sunday, May 8. At night was such stormy weather, that some thirty of the soldiers and others which followed the camp, perished with mere cold; and no wonder, for it killed some fifteen horses which were found dead the next morning."

"I found about five hundred of my lord Sinclair's regiment lately arrived at Carrickfergus. These I shipped, and having obtained some wheat from the major-general, but very sparingly, and some lead, whereof we had none at the Newry, I went aboard, and the wind being fair, next morning I cast anchor at Carlingford, where I found that man-of-war who had convoyed us out of Scotland. In the afternoon, I marched into the Newry: pitiful quarters we had, and when the rest of the regiment came over, which that summer they did, we found we had not houses for the half of them; for we were necessitated to take down a great many houses to make the circumference of our walls the less. Our own preservation taught us to work almost day and night, till we had finished the irregular fortification begun by the rebels. This great fatigue and toil, a very spare diet, lying on the ground, little sleep, constant watching, Sir Philemy being for most part always within a day's march of us; all these, I say, added to the change of the air, made most, or rather indeed, all our officers and soldiers fall sick of Irish agues, fluxes, and other diseases, of which very many died. Those who recovered, being inured to hardships and well-trained, became excellent soldiers and good firemen."

On Monro's return to Carrickfergus, he found waiting his arrival, a messenger sent by sea from Derry, to acquaint him with the distressed situation of that city, and to entreat supplies of arms and ammunition. The following letter, presented on this occasion to the Scottish general, gives so interesting a sketch of the hardships, which the protestants in that town and neighbourhood had already suffered, during the six months which had elapsed from the commencement of the rebellion, as to justify its insertion.

"We of this city of Londonderry and other parts, have either been forgotten, or given over for lost as we conceive; for all other parts of the kingdom are plentifully supplied, and yet though we have made our wants and miseries known divers times to Dublin, and to England, and to Scotland, yet no relief ever came to us, but only thirty barrels of powder, brought by captain Boulton from Dublin,[23] long before Christmas, which was partly upon the arrival thereof, disposed to all needful parts; and want of powder and arms here hath been our ruin. It is the great providence and goodness of God, that we are hitherto preserved, having been so ill armed and provided for; all the arms within his majesty's store here were shipped to Dublin last summer, and nothing left here but old decayed calivers which we have hitherto made a shift with, and trimmed them up to our great charges.

"We have raised seven hundred men for the defence of this city, and keep them hitherto at our own charges, in expectation of money and other supplies, but there is not one hundred good swords amongst them, and their arms but mean. Sir William Stewart, Sir Robert Stewart, and Sir Ralph Gore, had commissions from his majesty out of Scotland in November, for raising three regiments, and two horse troops. They lie in the county of Tyrone and thereabout, and so have done all this winter, to oppose the enemy; but being unprovided for, and not one penny to pay them, they could never attempt any great service. It is much that they keep the enemies from our walls to this hour; now our powder is gone, our victuals beginning to fail, and these three regiments had been starved long since, if we of this city had not relieved them with beef, butter, herrings and other necessaries, to a great value. But this will hold out no longer, for we have not now victuals enough for our own men in the city. And if a ship of Bristol had not arrived here with some peas, meal, and wheat, we could not have shifted longer; and all that will not last the regiments fourteen days. For the provision of the country is destroyed by the enemy, or devoured by our own men; and we are enforced to feed multitudes of unser-

23 This corroborates Lawson's statement given in note 14 of this chapter.

viceable people that are fled hither for relief; so if the enemy's sword spare us, famine will despatch us, except God in mercy provide for us. But this is not all; for now at this very hour, Sir Phelim O'Neill having gathered from all parts what forces he can make, is with a very great army of horse and foot at Strabane, within ten or twelve miles of this city, intending (by all the intelligence we can get,) to set up his rest, and desperately to break in upon us, where all the forces we can make are ready to bid him welcome.

"Sir Phelim on the one side of the river, and ours on the other, in sight one of the other, so as we of this city were enforced not only to send a great part of our men out of the city to join with them, but also unfurnished and parted with what little powder was left us, which with a little we got out of the Bristol ship, we have sent to encounter the Irish rebels. And now to relieve our fainting spirits, God hath provided for our relief, and sent this bearer captain Strange into Lough Foyle, who being in his majesty's service, and sent for the comfort of his majesty's distressed subjects, into those parts, we have made a true relation to him of our desperate estate, and the great danger we are in for want of powder and other provision, that we have not only prevailed with him to lend us, for the present, six barrels of powder, but also to set sail for us to Carrickfergus, to present our wants and dangers we are in to your honourable consideration, most earnestly praying that for the love of God, and honour of our king, and the safety of this place and people, ye will dispatch him back again to us with a good and large proportion of powder, match and lead, muskets, swords, pikes, some spades and shovels, whereof we have not any; and of these or what else may be had, as much as ye can possibly spare us; for we want all things fit to defend a distressed country and offend a desperate enemy.

"We also pray that you will restore the captain the six barrels of powder we have borrowed of him; and if there be any biscuit, cheese, or any other victuals to be spared, to send us some good proportion thereof. So being at present in great haste and perplexity, with our service presented to your honour, we remain your humble servants, &c." [24]

The situation of Derry, as well as of Coleraine and the other British garrisons in the north-west of Ulster, had become extremely critical. For no sooner had Sir Phelim ascertained that the Scottish forces had returned to Carrickfergus, than again collecting his scattered followers, he set out from Charlemont to occupy his former quarters at Strabane; with the view of expelling the protestants from Donegall and Tyrone, and if possible obtaining possession of Derry. But he was so vigorously opposed by Sir William and Sir Robert Stewart, that he was not only compelled to retire, but the castle of Strabane was re-taken, and several important places, which had for some time been closely besieged in the county of Derry, were relieved by these active and enterprising commanders. The services of the Lagan forces in that district, during the month of May, will be best narrated in the words of one of their own officers.

"Sir Phelim O'Neill drew down to Strabane about five thousand men, intending to burn Raphoe, and to raise Enishowen; and we being, as he absolutely conceived, defeated, to draw the other forces to the contrary side of Lough Foyle, and so assault the Derry. Our regiments assisted by two strong companies of captain Pitt's and captain Lawson's of the city of Londonderry, —— by break of day, were upon march an unusual way to Strabane, thinking to have beset him and his forces which quartered there visibly. But Sir Phelim was newly departed with his forces; only the castle

24 This letter is copied from a small pamphlet, entitled, "A true relation of the proceedings of the Scottish armie now in Ireland, by three letters," &c. Lond. 1642, pp. 9. It is dated 'Londonderry, the 27th April 1642;' and is signed, 'Robert Thornton, mayor, Henry Osborne, John Vaughan.'

he committed to captain Hugh Murragh O'Devin, a bloody fellow, and a hundred of his choice musketeers, and a hundred pikes to guard much of his own baggage and my lady Strabane's goods. But we easily forced the castle, and put the men to the sword; only captain O'Devin's life respited, who is now in the Derry gaol. The castle we left a garrison in, commanded by captain Wisher, a discreet gentleman, under the command of Sir William Hamilton.

"From Strabane we marched up on the O'Cahan's country, on the other side of Lough Foyle; and coming over against Derry, four companies of the Derry joined with us to relieve Lymavaddy castle and Ballycastle, which had been, ten weeks before, strongly beleaguered by great forces; and yet had sallied forth and killed many hundreds of the enemies, being commanded by a resolute young gentleman, captain Thomas Philips; his elder brother, Mr. Dudley Philips, being gone about with three boats to bring provision from Derry. That night we were welcome guests to the two castles who despaired of all succour;—next morning we advanced our march into the enemy's country, where at Magilligan, we encountered the enemy, the O'Cahans, the Magilligans, the O'Hagans, and the O'Neals; we killed upwards of five hundred of them, and scattered the rest.

"Having received late letters from Coleraine of their miserable wants and narrow beleaguer, we continued our march towards the mountains, that we might find some prey, that we might be the welcomer to almost famished Coleraine." They accordingly encountered a large body of the enemy in these mountains of the county of Derry, whom they routed, and from whom they recovered a considerable booty which had been carried off, not long before, from the neighbourhood of Coleraine and the river Bann. "Then with our prey and abundance of horse, &c., we marched to Dungiven castle, one of the king's houses, which was kept by colonel Manus MacGuy Ballagh MacRichard O'Kane. He, upon parley, delivered up the castle. Hence we marched to Coleraine, every regiment bestowed some [of their plunder] upon the town; the soldiers at easy rates sold the rest, but such as were delivered to the right owners. At Castle Roe, a mile from Coleraine, were lodged seven colours of the enemy to secure the Bann fishing to themselves. We took the colours, put many to the sword; and the town of Coleraine hath a garrison there now, and enjoys the fishing to themselves, being the greatest salmon fishing in Christendom." [25]

By the zeal and courage of these forces, the power of the rebels, in the north-west of Ulster, was in a great measure subdued; and the chief places of strength were in the occupation of the protestants. "We have at present," concludes the officer, already quoted, writing in the end of May, "these garrisons, castle of Strabane, Lifford, Raphoe, Drumboe castle, Letterkenny, Ramelton, Lymavaddy, Ballycastle, Ballyshannon, Donegall, Castle Rahin, [near Donegall,] being places of great consequence by situation and strength."

These proceedings were regularly communicated to the Scottish general at Carrickfergus, who was looked upon by the British regiments throughout Ulster, as their chief ally and protector. Urgent applications were also made to him for supplies of provisions and military stores; but he was wholly unable to afford them any assistance. From his despatches to general Leslie at Edinburgh, dated the day after his return from Newry and Armagh, it appears that so far from being in a capacity to afford aid to others, his own troops had already begun to feel a deficiency in their supplies —a want, by which the activity and usefulness of the Scottish forces were impaired, during the entire period of their stay in Ireland. The English parliament, who had engaged to support them, were soon compelled to provide for hostilities at home; and while they accused Charles of converting to his own use the supplies intended by them for their Irish forces, he, in his turn, justly condemned a vote of the com-

25 Colonel Audley Mervyn's "Exact Relation," &c.

mons, by which one hundred thousand pounds were appropriated, under the pretext of a loan, to the equipping of the parliamentary army, out of the fund raised for the relief of Ireland. The state of affairs, therefore, in this country, became a subordinate matter in the eyes of the English commons; the immediate result of which was a deficiency both in the pay and provisions promised for the support of their Scottish auxiliaries in Ulster. Monro was consequently compelled, even at this early period in the campaign, to quarter some of his forces upon the country. "Lord Lindsay's men," he writes to general Leslie, "I have quartered in Broadisland and Isle-Magee, where they have houses and no victuals; and if all should be trusted to the mayor of Carrickfergus's furnishing, a thousand must live on a hundred men's allowance a-day."[26]

Together with these despatches, he forwarded to Edinburgh the copy of a letter which he had received from the earl of Antrim, and which was dated from Dunluce on the last day of April. This wary and perfidious nobleman had no sooner learned the failure of the attack upon Dublin, and seen the precipitancy and cruelty of O'Neill, than he withdrew from the enterprise. The original conspirators having gone far beyond the scheme of the insurrection laid down by himself and Ormond, he cautiously forbore co-operating with them. "The fools," as he afterwards stated in his celebrated INFORMATION, "well liking the business, would not expect our time or manner for ordering the work; but fell upon it without us, and sooner, and *otherwise* than *we* should have done, taking to themselves and in their own way, the managing of the work, and so spoiled it."[27] But notwithstanding this disappointment, he was far from being an unconcerned spectator of the progress of the insurrection. He remained in the vicinity of Dublin until the month of April. He

26 "A true relation of the proceedings of the Scottish armie," &c. *ut supra.*

27 Cox, ii. App. 208.

then removed to Ulster, and took up his residence in his castle at Dunluce, which had been held by captain Digby for the king from the beginning of the rebellion. Here he acted with the utmost duplicity, and endeavoured to acquire an ascendancy over both the conflicting parties. While he encouraged and directed the Romanists, so far as was consistent with his not identifying himself with that party; he employed every artifice to induce the protestants to confide in him as their ally and protector. On the one hand, he held secret interviews with O'Neill, and occasionally mingled with the insurgents, among whom his brother Alexander, afterwards the third earl of Antrim, was a most influential leader; on the other, he professed sympathy for the plundered British, and officiously sought to alleviate their distresses.

In accordance with this policy, so soon as Antrim heard of the arrival of the Scottish forces at Carrickfergus, he endeavoured to conciliate the favour of Monro, and induce him to accept of his services in restoring peace to the country. Such was the purport of the letter which he now addressed to the Scottish commander. He apologized for some acts of hostility which his followers had committed upon the Scots shortly after their arrival; he professed the warmest friendship for Monro, and concluded with inviting him to a confidential interview at his castle at Glenarm.[28] But the vigilant general was not to be so easily duped. He already possessed abundant evidence of the insincerity of Antrim, and of his enmity to the protestant cause. At the same time that he sent the earl's letter to Leslie, he stated in his own despatch,—" he is joyned strong with the rebels, making a pretext of laying downe of armes, in the meantime doth what he can to cut our throats."[29] Accordingly, early in June,

28 Pike, in his letter to Sedgwicke from Carrickfergus, already quoted, writes under date of May 30th,—" The earl of Antrim is now at Glenarm, a place twelve miles off Carrickfergus, and would fain be received into this towne."

29 " A true relation of the proceedings of the Scottish armie," &c. *ut supra*, p. 6.

Monro re-assembled his forces, and, being joined by Sir John Clotworthy and his regiment, set out to meet the earl. Having reached Glenarm, he found Antrim had retired to Dunluce; and probably meeting with opposition here, he burned the town, and proceeded towards the north of the county. Here he was joined by additional levies from Scotland, belonging principally to Argyle's regiment. Aided by this reinforcement, he invested Dunluce, and forced the earl to surrender himself and castle into his hands.[30] Monro confined his noble prisoner in Carrickfergus, and placed his lieutenant-colonel in charge of that important post—the castle of Dunluce. At the same time, he garrisoned the other fortified places belonging to Antrim with the regiment of Argyle—the hereditary foe of the house of the Macdonnells. The rebels, who had hitherto possessed and ravaged the northern part of the county, having fled before him across the Bann, he immediately returned, with a considerable booty of cows, to his head-quarters at Carrickfergus.

Meanwhile, those fugitives from the county of Antrim under the command of Alaster Macdonnell, or Colkittagh, effected a junction with Sir Phelim O'Neill, who was still lurking among the fastnesses of the county of Derry. O'Neill, being apprized of the distressed state of the Lagan forces, through want of provisions and ammunition, and encouraged by this unexpected reinforcement, resolved to make another desperate effort to retrieve his sinking cause in that part of the province. He accordingly collected all the levies which could be raised in the adjoining counties, and marched into Donegall, to meet Sir William and Sir Robert Stewart.

[30] Cox, ii. 114. Carte (i. 310.) gives a different account of the capture of Antrim. He states that the earl received Monro hospitably at Dunluce, "and provided for him a great entertainment;"—not a very likely way to greet the destroyer of his town and castle of Glenarm, the fires of which were scarcely extinguished,—and that after the feast, Monro treacherously seized on Antrim, and thus secured possession of the castle. But Cox's account ought to be preferred to that of Carte, who was most violently prejudiced against the Scots, and sought every opportunity of rendering them odious, even at the expense of truth.

On Thursday, the sixteenth of June, both parties met at Glenmackwin, beside Raphoe; and after the severest conflict which had yet taken place in Ulster, the rebels were totally routed, with the loss, according to some, of five hundred men. The victorious commanders, however, were prevented, by their want of supplies, from pursuing the fugitives. [31]

Shortly after this decisive victory, Monro, in conjunction with the lords Conway, Ards and Claneboy, made a second descent upon the rebels in the county of Armagh. They took the fort of Dungannon—re-entered Armagh—burned Sir Phelim O'Neill's house near Caledon—and invested Charlemont, the only place of strength possessed by the rebels in this part of the province. But owing to the want of ammunition, and the scarcity of provisions, Monro was forced to abandon the siege, and returned again, by way of Newry, to his quarters at Carrickfergus.

About the same time, Sir John Clotworthy defeated the rebels in several skirmishes on Lough Neagh, the command of which had been intrusted to him by a special resolution of the English commons. [32] They authorized him to provide vessels for the defence of the Lough, and its extensive line of

31 Carte, i. 310. Cox, ii. 115. The latter estimates the number of the rebels slain in this battle at two hundred.

32 The following is the resolution of the parliament alluded to in the text. "27 January, 1641-2. Resolved, upon the question, that this house holds it fit that Sir John Clotworthy (as his father before had) shall have the command of the bark, and the boats to be provided for the defence and safety of the lough in Ireland, called Lough Neagh, alias Lough Sydney; and that he shall have the like wages as his father had: And he is to build the hulls of the bark and the boats, and to maintain them at his own charge: But he is to have so much monies presently allowed him as shall be necessary for their rigging, according to the note agreed upon by the committee for the Irish affairs.

"Sir John Clotworthy is to have for this service as captain, 15 shillings per diem, his lieutenant 4 shillings per day, the master 4 shillings per day, master's mate 2 shillings per day, master-gunner 18 pence per day, two gunners 12 pence a-piece per day, and 40 common men 18 pence a-piece per diem." Commons' Journals.

coast; and to man them with a competent force, who were to be in the pay of the parliament. He accordingly built a large vessel, called the Sydney, of about twenty tons burden, and furnished with six brass guns; and about a dozen smaller boats, carrying sixty men each, and capable of transporting a thousand men to any part of the Lough. These he placed under the command of his relative, captain Langford, and of the celebrated Owen O'Connolly, who had returned with him from London, and on whom he had also conferred the command of a company in his regiment of foot. James Clotworthy, the brother of Sir John, was lieutenant-colonel of this regiment, and held the fort of Mountjoy in Tyrone, on the opposite side of the lough from Antrim, with which, by means of the boats, he maintained constant intercourse.

While in this post, Colonel Clotworthy gained several important advantages over the rebels; driving them from certain entrenchments which they had formed upon that side of the Lough; routing Sir Phelim O'Neill in the beginning of July, with the loss of his lieutenant-colonel, one of the O'Quins, several officers, and about sixty men; and breaking up an encampment of the rebels at Moneymore, where he saved the lives of one hundred and twenty English and Scottish prisoners, whom they were just preparing to murder. Sir John also erected a fort at Toome upon the Bann, which gave him the command of that river, and enabled his regiment to make incursions, at their pleasure, into the county of Derry. To retaliate these inroads, the Irish garrison at Charlemont also built several boats, in which they sailed down the river Blackwater into the Lough, and plundered the coast in various directions. Several skirmishes occurred between these boats and those of Sir John Clotworthy, until the beginning of July, when the rebels were at length entirely routed, with the loss of above sixty men; and their boats, with a large number of prisoners, were conveyed in triumph to Antrim.[33]

[33] Cox, ii. 115. See also a small but curious tract entitled,—" A relation from Belfast in Ireland sent to a friend, mentioning some late

These vigorous proceedings contributed to restore partial peace to Ulster. The Romanist party, defeated in so many quarters, despaired of being able to offer any further opposition to the Scottish and British forces; and the insurgent leaders came to the resolution of disbanding their followers, and retiring for safety either to the continent, or to the highlands of Scotland.

This cessation of hostilities, though partial and temporary, paved the way for the re-establishment of religion. The episcopal church, which had been so intolerant in the hour of her prosperity, was now overthrown and desolate, and out of her ruins speedily arose the simpler fabric of presbyterianism. Few of her clergy, and not one of her prelates, remained in the province. The last of the bishops, who left the country, was Leslie of Raphoe. After gallantly defending the episcopal castle, which he had erected at Raphoe, against the repeated assaults of the rebels, and relieving several besieged castles in that district, [34] he retired to Scotland in the latter end of June, and thence to England, where he joined the royalist party. Of the protestant laity who escaped the fury of the insurgents, few were conscientiously attached to prelacy. Even under the despotic sway of Strafford and the northern bishops, the reader has seen that little more than a reluctant and insincere conformity was effected by all their severities. When this oppressive constraint was removed, the majority hesitated not to declare their approbation of the scriptural forms of the Scottish church; while many who were in principle episcopalians, were, at this critical conjuncture, disposed to abandon that church, when they

successes against the rebels by colonel Clotworthy, about Mountjoy, in the county of Tyrone. Dated 28 July 1642." Lond. 1642. 4to.

34 In particular, he relieved Sir Ralph Gore of Magherabeg, in Donegal, who was reduced to great extremities; and this, too, after the Lagan forces had refused to hazard themselves in the attempt. Borlase, Pref. p. xiii. Lodge, iii. 281. The gallant bishop lived many years, and was advanced to the see of Clogher, after the Restoration.

beheld its prelates and higher clergy in the sister kingdom, opposed to the great cause of civil liberty. The number of those attached to presbytery, was still farther increased by the return of the original Scottish settlers or their descendants. This portion of the population had been greatly reduced by the continual emigration to Scotland, which had been going on during the last four years. But though peace was only partially restored, they had begun to revisit, in considerable numbers, this land of their adoption; and they returned still more firmly attached to their national church, which, during their sojourn in Scotland, they saw restored to her genuine character, and blessed with an eminent degree of purity and efficiency.

Owing to these circumstances, a preponderating majority of the protestants in Ulster were now decidedly in favour of presbyterianism, and desirous that the re-edification of the protestant church in Ulster might proceed upon that scriptural foundation.

The opportune arrival of the Scottish forces was happily instrumental in promoting this desired reformation. According to the salutary practice of the church and nation of Scotland, at this period, most of the regiments were accompanied by chaplains, who were ordained ministers, and firmly attached to the doctrine, worship, and government of their national church. By these prudent and zealous men, the foundations of the presbyterian church were once more laid in Ulster, in exact conformity with the parent establishment in Scotland. The effects of their labours remain to this day. By their agency, the Scottish church in Ulster assumed that regular and organized form which she still retains; and from this period, the history of her ministers, her congregations, and her ecclesiastical courts, as they now exist, can be traced in uninterrupted succession. The doctrines taught by these brethren, she still zealously inculcates and upholds; the forms of worship they introduced, continue to be strictly observed; and the government and discipline they founded, remain in all essential points unaltered at the present time. The benefits conferred by these venerable ministers, on the church and province of Ulster, entitle them to especial notice.

THE REV. HUGH CUNNINGHAM was chaplain to the earl of Glencairn's regiment; and having received a call from a congregation here, he remained in the country, after the return of his regiment to Scotland. He was ordained, about the year 1646, to the charge of the parish and congregation of Ray, near Letterkenny, in the county of Donegall. He was silenced at the Restoration, by Robert Leslie, bishop of Raphoe, who had succeeded his uncle in that see. It is uncertain whether he then fled to Scotland, or remained in privacy with his people till his death. Another minister was in charge of this congregation in the year 1680. THE REV. THOMAS PEEBLES was chaplain to the earl of Eglinton's regiment, which was quartered at Newtonards in the county of Down. He preached not only at the head-quarters of the regiment, but in all the neighbouring towns, as he had opportunity; and two years afterwards he received a call to become minister of the united parishes of Dundonald and Holywood, situated between Newtonards and Belfast. To this charge he was ordained in the year 1645, and continued in it, through all the subsequent vicissitudes of those unsettled times, till his death in the year 1670. THE REV. JOHN BAIRD was chaplain to the earl of Argyle's regiment. In the year 1646, he was ordained to the charge of a congregation, probably Dervock, in the Route, a district of country in the north of the county of Antrim.[35] It is uncertain how long he continued in Ulster, or what afterwards became of him. THE REV. JAMES SIMPSON was chaplain to the Lord Sinclair's regiment. He appears to have settled in the charge of a congregation in Ulster; perhaps at Newry, which was

35 I have said that Dervock was 'probably' the congregation in the Route, in which Mr. Baird was settled. My reason for fixing on this old established congregation is, that shortly after this date, I find all the other congregations in this district supplied with ministers.

the head-quarters of his regiment for several years.[36] THE REV. JOHN SCOTT was chaplain, most likely, to Lord Home's regiment. No record remains of his settlement in Ireland, and it is probable he returned with his regiment to Scotland. He was afterwards settled as minister of Oxnam, in the presbytery of Jedburgh. THE REV. JOHN AIRD was chaplain either to Lord Lindsay's, or to Monroe's regiment. Of him likewise nothing farther is known, except he be the same who was afterwards minister of Newbattle, in the presbytery of Dalkeith. The only other minister who accompanied the army, of whom any record remains, is one, with whose life and character the reader is already familiar,—THE REV. JOHN LIVINGSTON. He has left the following notices of his proceedings, and of the religious state of Ulster at this period.

"In April 1642, I was sent by order of the council of Scotland to Ireland, to wait on the Scottish army, that went over with major-general Monro; and staid for six weeks, part in Carrickfergus, where the head-quarters were; and for other six weeks most part at Antrim, with Sir John Clotworthy and his regiment, who had obtained an order from the council for me so to do. I preached for the most part in these two places; but sometimes in other parishes of the coast-side about; and before I left Antrim, we had the communion celebrated there, where sundry that had taken the [black] oath did willingly, and with great expressions of grief, publickly confess the same. I found a great alteration in Ireland, many of those who had been civil before, were become many ways exceeding loose; yea, sundry who, as could be conceived, had true grace, were declined much in tenderness; so as it would seem the sword opens a gap, and makes every body worse than before, an inward plague coming with the outward; yet some few were in a very lively condition."[37]

36 He was still in his charge in Ireland in 1650, in which year I find the Rev. Hugh Binning, minister of Govan, was married to his daughter. Scots Worthies, i. 208.

37 Livingston's Life, pp. 36, 7.

The first duty of these ministers, when the army returned to Carrickfergus after the taking of Newry, and were in some measure settled in quarters, was to erect sessions or elderships in each of the regiments of which they had the charge. These elderships were erected with the concurrence of the general and of the several colonels; and were composed of such of the officers as were pious and godly men; many of whom were, at this period, to be found in the Scottish army. Having constituted sessions in four of the regiments then at head-quarters, viz. in Argyle's, Eglinton's, Glencairn's and Home's, the ministers found themselves in a capacity to hold a meeting of presbytery, in accordance with the discipline of the church of Scotland.

This meeting, memorable as the first regularly constituted presbytery held in Ireland, took place at Carrickfergus, on Friday the tenth of June 1642.[38] It was attended by five ministers, viz. the Rev. Messrs. Cunningham, Baird, Peebles, Scott and Aird, Mr. Simpson being at Newry with his regiment, and Mr. Livingston at Antrim; and by four ruling elders from the four sessions already erected. The Rev. Mr. Baird, by previous appointment, preached on the latter part of the 51st Psalm; "Do good in thy good pleasure unto Zion: build thou up the walls of Jerusalem," &c. A moderator was appointed, and the Rev. Mr. Peebles was chosen clerk of the presbytery,—an office which he held through every vicissitude till his death, a period of near thirty years. Each minister produced his act of admission to his charge or regiment, in virtue of which he sat as a member of presbytery; and the ruling elders, in like manner, submitted their commissions from their respective sessions. They authorized some of the brethren to confer with the colonels of those regiments in which there were as yet no sessions, in order that

38 The date of this meeting is erroneously placed a month later by the author of "Presbyterian Loyalty," p. 253. There are several other mistakes in names and dates throughout this work, all of them probably errors of the press, for the book is wretchedly printed.

these courts might be forthwith constituted. They enjoined each minister to commence a regular course of examination and catechetical instruction in his regimental charge; they resolved to hold, for a time at least, weekly meetings, and to open each meeting with a discourse by one of the brethren, choosing, as the subject of these presbyterial exercises, the book of Isaiah; and they concluded with appointing a fast to be observed the following week,—"wherein they were to sympathize with the case of the churches abroad in Germany and Bohemia—the present distraction of England and hazard of God's work there at that time, through the difference beginning between the king and parliament—and the case of this poor land who were as brands scarce plucked out of the fire, yet security and profanity remaining among many both in country and army—and that God should be cried unto to bless the country with a spiritual ministry—and for a blessing to the going out of the army against the Irish," &c.(39)

At this meeting they also wrote to the lords Claneboy and Ards, to whose regiments two presbyterian ministers, though unordained, had been for some time officiating as chaplains, acquainting them with their proceedings, and requesting permission for their chaplains to attend the meetings of presbytery, and assist in renovating and re-establishing the protestant church in Ulster. The answers returned by these noblemen—formerly the strenuous supporters of prelacy, and the pliant tools of Strafford—were most favourable to the views of the presbytery.(40) On the 19th inst. the lord of Ards sent a respectful message by captain Magill, one of his officers, not only assuring them of his regard, but promising "to join them in discipline." The same day lord Claneboy wrote to the same effect, and gave a similar assurance that he

39 Adair's MS.

40 The reader has seen both of these noblemen taking part in preparing and pressing the black oath. See chapter v. pages 243-4. They did not long survive their junction with the presbytery. The lord of Ards died in November 1642, and the lord Claneboy in the following year.

would support the presbytery in their measures. And both noblemen expressed their willingness to have their chaplains regularly tried and admitted as ministers to their respective regiments; which was soon after done by the presbytery, agreeably to the discipline of the church of Scotland.[41]

No sooner had intelligence gone abroad respecting the formation of a presbytery among the army ministers at Carrickfergus, than applications poured in from the adjoining parishes, to be received into their communion, and to obtain from them the preaching of the gospel. "Upon which the presbytery moved that there should be elderships erected with the consent of the congregations, and that, by their help, a present supply might be procured, and in due time ministers be settled among them. This motion of the presbytery was very acceptable to these congregations, as appeared by their immediate and earnest address to the presbytery for ministers to be sent for that effect; which also was readily done by the presbytery, who sent ministers to divers congregations who were first in a case for eldership, viz. Ballymena, Antrim, Cairncastle, Templepatrick, Carrickfergus, Larne and Belfast in the county of Antrim: Ballywalter, Portaferry, Newtonards, Donaghadee, Killileagh, Comber, Holywood and Bangor in the county of Down. And the elderships being erected in these places, there began a little appearance of a formed church in the country."[42] It was soon found, however, that without assistance from the parent church, it was impossible to afford all these places adequate supplies of preaching. Accordingly the people, being most anxious for the enjoyment of divine ordinances, agreed to petition the General Assembly for a supply of ministers; and several of the parishes, where the brethren, now alive in Scotland, had officiated before the persecutions of Strafford and Leslie, desirous of obtaining once more the services of their beloved

41 Presbyterian Loyalty, p. 253, confirmed by Adair's MS.

42 Adair's MS.

pastors, resolved to make special application to the Assembly to permit these ministers to accept of calls from Ireland.

With this view, the parishes of Bangor and Ballywalter drew up petitions to the General Assembly, appointed to meet at St. Andrews, on the last Wednesday of July, the one signed by sixty-three, and the other by forty-one heads of families, praying for the restoration of Mr. Blair and Mr. Hamilton to their former charges. At the same time the presbyterians of the counties of Down and Antrim drew up a large and general petition, to which, in a short time, two hundred and twenty-five signatures were attached. In this petition, which has been fortunately preserved,—though now scarcely known to the descendants of its venerable subscribers,—they set forth their distressed condition in such affecting terms, and describe so feelingly their destitution of divine ordinances, and the value which they attached to the enjoyment of the gospel upon the scriptural basis of their parent church, as to entitle it to a place in these pages. It is thus addressed :—

"To the reverend and right honourable the moderator and remanent members of the General Assembly of Scotland, convened at St. Andrews, July 1642.

"The humble petition of the most part of the Scottish nation in the north of Ireland, in their own names, and in the name of the rest of the protestants there, humbly sheweth,—

"That where your petitioners, by the great blessing of the Lord, enjoyed for a little while, a peaceable and fruitful ministry of the gospel; yet through our own abuse of so rich a mercy, and through the tyranny of the prelates, we have been a long time spoiled of our ministers, (a yoke to many of us heavier than death,) who being chased into Scotland, were not altogether unuseful in the day of your need: and we having been since oppressed and scattered, as sheep who have no shepherd, now at last the wise and righteous hand of the Lord, by the sword of the rebels, hath bereft us of our friends, and spoiled us of our goods, and left us but a few, and that a poor handful of many, and hath chased from us the rest that were called our ministers; the greater part whereof we could scarce esteem as such, being rather officers to put the prelates' injunctions in execution, than feeders of our souls. So that now being visited with sword and sickness, and under some apprehension of famine, if withal we shall taste of the sorest of all plagues, to be altogether deprived of the ministry of the word, we shall become in so much a worse condition than any pagans, as that once we enjoyed a better. Neither know we what hand to turn us to for help, but to the land so far obliged by the Lord's late rare mercies, and so far enriched to furnish help of that kind,—a land whence many of us drew our blood and breath, and where (pardon the necessary boldness) some of our own ministers now are, who were so violently plucked from us, so sore against both their own and our wills:—yea, the land that so tenderly in their bosoms received our poor outcasts, and that hath already sent us so rich a supply of able and prosperous soldiers to revenge our wrong.

"Therefore, although we know that your zeal and brotherly affection would urge you to take notice without our advertisement, yet give us leave in the bowels of our Lord Jesus Christ, to intreat, if there be any consolation in Christ, if any comfort of love, if any fellowship of the Spirit, if any bowels of mercy, that now, in this nick of time, when the sword of the enemy, making way for a more profitable entertaining the gospel, having also banished the prelates and their followers, when our extremity of distress, and the fair hopes of speedy settling of peace hath opened so fair a door to the gospel,—you would take the case of 'your younger sister that hath no breasts,' [43] to your serious consideration, and pity poor Macedonians, crying to you that ye would come over and help us, being the servants of the God of your fathers, and claim-

[43] Solomon's Song, viii. 8.

ing interest with you in a common covenant, that, according to the good hand of God upon us, ye may send us ministers for the house of our God. We do not take upon us to prescribe to you the way or the number; but, in the view of all, the finger of the Lord points at these, whom, though persecution of the prelates drew from us, yet our interest in them could not be taken away; wherein we trust, in regard of several of them, called home by death, your bounty will superadd some able men of your own, that may help to lay the foundation of God's house, according to the pattern. But for these, so unjustly reft from us, not only our necessity, but equity pleads, that either you would send them all over, which were a work to be paralleled to the glories of the primitive times; or, at least, that you would declare them transportable, that when invitators shall be sent to any of them, wherein they may discern a call from God, there may be no difficulty in their loosing from thence, but they may come back to perfect what they began, and may get praise and fame in the land, where they were put to shame. Neither are you to question your power over us so to do, or crave a precedent of your own practice in that kind, for our extraordinary need calling on you, furnisheth you with a power to make this a precedent for the like cases hereafter: Herein if you shall lay aside the particular concernment of some few places, which you may easily, out of your rich nurseries, plant again, and make use of your public spirits, which are not spent, but increase by your so many noble designs; you shall leave upon us and our posterity the stamp of an obligation that cannot be delete, or that cannot be expressed,—you shall send to all the neighbouring churches a pattern, and erect for after ages a monument of self-denying tender zeal;—you shall disburden the land of the many outcasts, who will follow over their ministers,—and you shall make it appear, that the churlish bounty of the prelates, which at first cast some of these men over to us, is not comparable with the cheerful liberality of a rightly constituted General Assembly, to whom, we are persuaded, the Lord will give seed for the loan which you bestow on the Lord: yea, the day may come, when a General Assembly in this land, may return to you the first fruits of thanks, for the plants of your free gift. And although you were scant of furniture of this kind yourselves, or might apprehend more need than formerly, yet, doubtless your bowels of compassion would make your deep poverty, even in a great trial of affliction, abound to the riches of your liberality. But now seeing you abound in all things, and have formerly given so ample a proof of your large bestowing on churches abroad in Germany and France, and knowing that you are not wearied in well-doing, we confidently promise to ourselves in your name, that you will abound in this grace also, following the example of our Lord and the primitive churches who always sent out disciples in pairs. But if herein our hopes shall fail us, we shall not know whether to wish that we had died with our brethren by the enemies' hands, for we shall be if it were said unto us, 'Go, serve other gods.' Yet looking for another kind of answer at your hands—for in this you are to us as an angel of God—we have sent these bearers, M. John Gordon and M. Hugh Campbell, our brethren,(44) who may more particularly inform you of our case, and desire that, at their return, they may refresh the bowels of

"Your most instant and earnest supplicants."(45)

44 From the prefix of M. for master, characteristic of ministers in those days, being placed before the names of these commissioners, it would appear that they were ministers. If so, we have no record of where they were settled. They had probably remained in the country during the rebellion.

45 Copies of this petition, and of those from Bangor and Ballywalter, are preserved among the records of the church of Scotland, to which free access was afforded me, in the kindest manner, by the principal clerk of Assembly, the Rev. Dr. Lee. I have since discovered that the general petition, given in the text, was printed in the form of a pamphlet in London shortly after it was presented to the Assembly, with this title;—"The humble Petition of the Scottish and many others, the inhabitants of the province of Ulster, in the kingdom of Ireland. To the Right Reverend

This petition was presented to the General Assembly on Friday the thirtieth of July. Principal Baillie, who was an active member of this Assembly, describes it as "a very well penned letter by sundry noblemen and gentlemen, for help of ministers in Ireland." It was very favourably received, and the following commission, in reply, was drawn out by a committee, and unanimously passed the Assembly a few days after:—

"COMMISSION TO SOME MINISTERS TO GO TO IRELAND.

"The Assembly having received a petition, subscribed by a considerable number in the north of Ireland, intimating their deplorable condition, through want of the ministry of the gospel, occasioned by the tyranny of the prelates, and the sword of the rebels, and desiring some ministers, especially such as had been chased from them, by the persecution of the prelates, and some others to be added, either to be sent presently over to reside amongst them, or declared transportable, that upon invitation from them, they might go and settle there; together with some particular petitions, desiring the return of some particular ministers who had laboured there before: All which the Assembly hath taken to their serious consideration, being most heartily willing to sympathize with every member of Christ's body, although never so remote; much more with that plantation there, which, for the most part, was a branch of the Lord's vine, planted in this land. In which solicitude, as they would be loath to usurp without their own bounds, or stretch themselves beyond their own measure; so they dare not be wanting to the enlargement of Christ's kingdom, where so loud a cry of so extreme necessity, could not but stir up the bowels of Christian compassion.

and Right Honourable the Moderator and remanent members of the General Assembly of Scotland, convened at St. Andrews in July 1642." Lond. 4to, pp. 5.

And although they conceive, that the present unsettled condition both of church and state and land, will not suffer them, as yet, to loose any to make constant abode there, yet they have resolved to send over some for the present exigent till the next General Assembly, by courses to stay there four months allanerly (only): And therefore do thereby authorize and give commission to the persons following, to wit, M. Robert Blair, minister at St. Andrews, and M. James Hamilton, minister at Dumfries, for the first four months: M. Robert Ramsay, minister at Glasgow, and M. John Maclelland, minister at Kirkcudbright, for the next four months; and to M. Robert Baillie, professor of divinity in the university of Glasgow, and M. John Livingston, minister of Stranraer, for the last four months: To repair into the north of Ireland, and there to visit, comfort, instruct and encourage the scattered flocks of Christ, to employ themselves to their uttermost, with all faithfulness and singleness of heart, in planting and watering, according to the direction of Jesus Christ, and according to the doctrine and discipline of this church in all things: And, if need be, (with concurrence of such of the ministers of the army as are there,) to try and ordain such, as shall be found qualified for the ministry; giving charge to the persons aforesaid, that in doctrine, in worship, in discipline and in their daily conversation, they study to approve themselves as the ministers of Jesus Christ, and that they be comptable to the General Assembly of this kirk, in all things. And in case, if any of the above-mentioned ministers be impeded by sickness, or otherwise necessarily detained from this service, the Assembly ordains the commissioners residing at Edinburgh, for the public affairs of the church, to nominate, in their place, well-qualified men, who hereby are authorized to undertake the foresaid employment, as if they had been expressly nominate in the face of the Assembly. And this, although possibly it shall not fully satisfy the large expectation of the brethren in Ireland, yet the Assembly is confident they will take in good part, at this time, that which is judged most convenient for their present condition—even a lent mite out of their own, not very great, plenty—to supply the present necessity; requiring of them no other recompense, but that they, in all cheerfulness, may embrace and make use of salvation, and promising to enlarge their indebted bounty at the next Assembly, as they shall find the work of the Lord there to require. In the meanwhile, wishing that these who are sent may come with the full blessing of the gospel of peace, and recommending them, their labours, and those to whom they are sent, to the rich blessing of the great Shepherd of the flock." [46]

[46] Acts of General Assembly. Printed 1682. Pp. 148—53.

CHAPTER IX.

Arrival of the ministers appointed by the General Assembly—Rapid extension of the church—Proceedings of the Scottish ministers—Several of the episcopal clergy join the presbytery—Mode of receiving them—Discipline strictly enforced by the presbytery—Fast observed, with its causes—Two ministers ordained—Livingston pays a second visit to Ulster—The presbytery send a second petition to the General Assembly—Assembly's proceedings—Ministers again appointed to visit the church in Ulster—State of affairs in the mean time in England—Civil war commenced—Ecclesiastical changes—Growing opposition to prelacy—English parliament open a correspondence with the General Assembly—Afterwards abolish prelacy—Westminster Assembly called—Commissioners from the Parliament sent to Scotland—Solemn League and Covenant—Taken in London—And in Edinburgh—Explained and vindicated—Forwarded to Ireland.

Agreeably to the appointment of the General Assembly, the Rev. Robert Blair, formerly minister of Bangor, and the Rev. James Hamilton, cousin to the then lord Claneboy, and formerly minister of Ballywalter, visited Ulster in the beginning of September. At the first meeting of the presbytery held after their arrival, they produced the Assembly's commission, which was most thankfully received by the brethren; and as a mark of their respect and gratitude, was ordered to be inserted in their minutes, and preserved among their presbyterial records.

Guided by these experienced ministers, who were intimately acquainted with the circumstances of the country, and who had already proved themselves skilful and successful missionaries, the church in Ulster rapidly revived, and 'broke forth on the right hand and on the left.' The seed which had been sown in faith by these eminent men and their persecuted brethren, prior to the rebellion, though long checked in its growth by the chilling severities of the prelates, now began to spring up with renovated vigour, and to gladden the wilderness with its verdure and fertility. The fruit of their labour appeared in the numbers who had preserved their principles uncorrupted, and their attachment to scriptural truth and freedom unabated, notwithstanding the discouragements of ecclesiastical bondage and the ravages of civil war. Multitudes, from all quarters, hastened to declare themselves in favour of the presbyterian church, and expressed the strongest desires for her establishment in Ulster. They were most anxious to be permitted to join her standard and partake of her privileges.

But neither the importunity of the people to be received into communion, nor the desire, so natural to men in their circumstances, of speedily securing to their church the ascendancy in Ulster, induced the presbytery to deviate from the strict rules of discipline, characteristic of the parent, and, it may be added, of the primitive, church. No person was admitted to the privileges, or recognised as enjoying the fellowship, of the church, who did not possess a competent degree of religious knowledge, or who did not fully approve of her constitution and discipline, or who was unable to state the grounds of that approbation. Neither were any received into communion who had either willingly conformed to prelacy, or taken the black oath, or been immoral in their conduct, until they publicly renounced their errors, and professed repentance for their irregularities. "Any persons who at that time were under scandals of any kind, and not properly under the ministry of any in the presbytery, were received, upon their own free offer, to public repentance; but were not compelled, till they became members of some formed congregation; except in case that they required the benefit of sealing ordinances.—The presbytery did also impose public evidences of repentance upon scandalous persons in their parishes, and where elderships were erected, with as great severity as had been done at any time in the church of Scotland: And these persons did submit themselves thereunto, though the most part were not properly formed into congregations as yet, nor under the inspection of ministers." [1]

The chief duty of the delegates from the Scottish church was to organize congregations throughout the country in accordance with these principles; and to cement the union of the people associated in their newly-formed churches, by the administration of the Lord's Supper. In the performance of these duties of "planting and watering according to the direction of Jesus Christ," they were, everywhere, received with the utmost respect and gratitude. The parish churches were again crowded with worshippers, and once more resounded with the voice of prayer and thanksgiving. The people rejoiced in the restoration of their church and the recovery of their religious rights. They truly "came to Zion with songs, and joy upon their heads." Their worship could be now conducted without the slavish restrictions of the service-book, and their ecclesiastical concerns regulated, not by the statutes of parliament, or the ordinances of civil rulers, but by the deliberations of church officers guided by the dictates of the word of God. At the same time, they bewailed their former compliances with prelacy; and those who had been induced to take the black oath, professed deep sorrow for having been ensnared into that engagement.

The following narrative of Mr. Blair's proceedings during this visit, has been happily preserved. "During all the three months he was in Ireland, he generally preached once every day and twice on the Sabbath, and frequently in the fields; the auditories being so large that no house could contain them; and in some of these he administered the sacrament of the Lord's Supper.

"But because many of the people had formerly through

1 Adair's MS.

constraint, taken an oath imposed by the lord deputy, abjuring the national covenant of Scotland, Mr. Blair, after a pathetic discourse, laying out the guilt of that black oath, charged all whose conscience accused and condemned them, to separate themselves from amongst those who were not involved in that grievous provocation. And they having willingly done so, and stood in a body on his left hand, he as a son, first of thunder and then of consolation, did with great vehemency, energy and warmth, set before them, the awful threatenings held forth by the holy law against such transgressors; and then endeavoured to display the exceeding greatness of God's mercy and grace, exhorting them to fly to God for reconciliation and pardon through Christ. And after the guilty had willingly, and with great expressions of grief and sorrow, confessed their sin, they were received as sincere penitents, and admitted to the holy communion.

"Of that solemnity, several old experienced Christians declared that they never saw the like, nor ever heard the gospel so powerfully preached and pertinently applied, with such variety of threatenings, promises, exhortations, motives, comforts and cordials; and that they never saw such commotion and heart-melting among hearers, both guilty and innocent: so that it might be truly said, that 'they gathered together' to that place, 'and drew water and poured it out before the Lord, and said, we have sinned against the Lord.' 1 Sam. vii. 6. During this short visit to Ireland, both ministers and professors had many sweet and soul-refreshing days of the gospel, and some solemn high Sabbaths, the like of which Mr. Blair seldom enjoyed in St. Andrews."(2)

His colleague, Mr. Hamilton, was engaged in similar labours. Both ministers extended their missionary journies as far as the army could afford them protection from the Roman catholics,—a circuit embracing the greater part of the counties of Down and Antrim. They sat with the presbytery when

2 Blair's Life, pp. 96—7.

assembled as a church-court, and aided them in extending to all parts of the country which desired it, the enjoyment of divine ordinances, in connexion with the presbyterian church. They do not appear to have obtruded their government or mode of worship, on those who were conscientiously opposed to its adoption. But they certainly insisted on as many as had voluntarily joined the presbytery, to abide by its discipline, and "to walk by the same rule." Several of the episcopal clergy who had survived the ravages of the rebellion, continued to perform divine worship according to the common-prayer. But the presbytery, while they interfered not with the duties or emoluments of such ministers, could not be expected to countenance their proceedings, so long as they opposed the discipline of the presbyterian church. Accordingly, by an act published in all the churches of their communion, they warned their people not to hear those ministers, or in any other way testify an approbation of the prelatic government or worship.

Many of the episcopal clergy, however, now came forward and joined the presbytery. They were received into communion, but not until they professed repentance for their former courses; some, for taking the black oath; others, for having imposed it upon the people; some, for having been persecutors of the non-conformists; and all, for having departed from scriptural truth by their submission to prelacy.(3) These con-

3 The same rules of discipline were observed by the church of Scotland, where several Irish ministers and many of the people after the rebellion, applied to be received into communion. I find the following entries, originally extracted from the session records of Ayr, in Wodrow's life of Mr. John Fergushill, minister of Ayr, preserved among his manuscript collections in Glasgow college. "March 7, 1642. Compeared before the session, Mr. Adam Ritchy, sometime minister in Ireland, and for using superstitious rites and ceremonies in the sacraments there, and in marrying people with a ring; all which he confesseth to have been against the light of his own conscience. The session ordains him to appear next Sunday.

"The same day, Robert Coupar, free of the Irish oath, but troubled in mind for his countenancing superstitious ceremonies and the service-book;

fessions and acknowledgments they made in public; a few before the presbytery, and others before their respective parishes, in presence of some of the brethren. They were then received as preachers of the gospel; but they were not recognized as members of the presbytery, until they had been regularly called and ordained to the charge of congregations. "Divers ministers and others who had taken the black oath, and been instrumental in ensnaring others in it, and had gone on in a course of conformity and defection, upon an intimation from the presbytery, did come and own their sinful defection, and made the same acknowledgments in those places where they had been particularly scandalous; as Mr. Nevin at Donaghadee,[4] &c. &c. Divers of them gave satisfaction, some before Mr. Blair in Bangor, Donaghadee, and Killileagh; and others before Mr. Hamilton. In this the hand of the Lord is to be observed, that these men, who, a few years before, were deposed and driven out of the country for refusing conformity, shall be the first who shall receive the acknowledgments and repentance of conformists."[5]

This circumstance constituted another of those singular vicissitudes with which the history of these brethren abounded—all involving the welfare and extension of the presbyterian church. Restrained by the Scottish prelates from the exercise of the ministry in their native country, they removed to Ireland, and were the means of introducing here the presbyterian discipline. Banished from this country, they returned to Scotland, where they were the chief instruments

allowed to make his public repentance. Both these are done by order of the presbytery." Very many are publicly admitted to declare their repentance for taking the Irish, that is the black, oath.

[4] Among these ought perhaps to be noticed, Mr. James Melvin, minister at Downpatrick. In 1635, he published the bishop's sentence of excommunication against Livingston, and was a violent prelatist. See page 187. But when Livingston came to Ireland in 1642, he says, "Mr. Melvin was the first that welcomed me ashore, and professed his grief that he had a hand in such a wicked act." Life, p. 24.

[5] Adair's MS.

in overthrowing prelacy, and restoring the presbyterian church to her former ascendency in their native kingdom. And now, the more violent of their persecutors being driven away by the sword of the rebels, they revisit Ireland in peace and honour, and are successfully employed, for a third time, in reconstructing their church on the ruins of prelacy. This duty they discharged, in a manner becoming their Christian character. They received the submission of their former opponents and persecutors, not contemptuously triumphing over them, as the prelatists did over the presbyterians at the Restoration; but meekly rejoicing in the spread of truth and purity, and grateful that they were the witnesses and the honoured instruments of its extension.

These converts from prelacy were not at first very observant of the stricter rules of discipline in force in the presbyterian church. Some continued to administer in private the ordinance of baptism; marriage was also privately solemnized by others; and a few were disposed to celebrate the Lord's supper, as they had been accustomed to do, in a kneeling posture. But these practices were discountenanced by the presbytery, and requested to be relinquished.—"The presbytery being informed of a minister's practice who had been a conformist before in the country, and now had taken the covenant, that he used to baptize privately, brought him to acknowledge his fault, which, he said, he knew not was so, and promised to forbear that practice.——And whereas some ministers who had been conformists, and had come and submitted to the presbytery, did use private baptism and private marriage, the presbytery discharged such practices in these ministers, which they promise to forbear.——At this time, there being one Mr. Black, preacher in Belfast, who intended to give the sacrament after the way of the common prayer, the presbytery informed of it, sent to colonel Chichester, afterwards earl of Donegall, desiring forbearance of that way, in order to prevent scandal and inconveniences among the people. The said colonel Chichester interfered with him to forbear.

They also appointed Mr. Baird to preach every third sabbath in Belfast, there being the third part of a regiment under his charge quartered there."(6) This exercise of authority on the part of the presbytery, let it be observed, was confined to those ministers who had voluntarily joined their communion, and adopted the presbyterian name and discipline. They only desired that, so long as their brethren professed to be presbyterians, they should act consistently with that profession. But with those who adhered to their former profession of episcopacy, they do not appear to have in any way interfered.

The attention of the presbytery was next directed to check the progress of certain errors originating in the same quarter, from which the church had been troubled nearly twenty years before. Two baptist preachers at Antrim, where a few separatists still lingered,(7) began to vent their peculiar principles condemnatory of infant baptism, and of a regular ministry or government in the church, and verging towards, if not altogether favouring, antinomianism. They were countenanced by several persons, with whom they held separate assemblies on the exclusive principles characteristic of that denomination. The proceedings of the brethren, assisted by Blair and Hamilton, on this occasion, are thus narrated :—" In this time also, with the assistance of these two worthy men, the presbytery, upon information of the danger of separation, and the beginnings of some heterodox opinions spreading about Antrim, by one Thomas Cornwall and Verner ;(8) they did order Mr. Blair in his visiting these places, to obviate these dangers, by warning the people and publickly declaring against them. As also all the ministers are appointed in public to give

6 Adair's MS. 7 See note 14, chap. ii.

8 There was at this time a celebrated baptist preacher in England of the name of Francis Cornwall, who wrote several works in favour of the peculiarities of that sect. See Ivimey's Eng. Baptists, i. 167, 205. In 1653, I find a baptist minister in Dublin of the name of Vernon, perhaps the Verner of the text. Ibid. i. 240.

warning to the people against those snares. They also summoned the said persons to appear before the presbytery to give a confession of their faith; but none did appear. Thomas said he was not subject to the presbytery, was a stranger and ready to depart. Others, in private conference, did give satisfaction; some were otherwise hindered. However, these opinions did not spread."[9]

In the latter end of November, the presbytery ordered a second fast to be observed. The following reasons for this appointment illustrate the state of the country, and the difficulties with which they were obliged to contend. "There was at this time another fast appointed to be kept on the Lord's day, November the twenty-seventh and the Thursday thereafter, for the troubles of the churches abroad;—the sad distractions in England, whence help only could be expected to this country, under God;—the discouragement of soldiers through want of necessary supplies, and of the country through their poverty and oppression;—the enemy's strength and cruelty yet much remaining;—general carelessness and security, with little life and zeal among people;—many gross sins breaking forth among some;—want of faithful ministers residing in the country to encourage the people and stir them up;—and the sinfulness of the army who should be instruments of deliverance. These days were accordingly kept."[10]

The last duty performed by Blair and Hamilton, before their return to Scotland, was the ordination of two of the army ministers, the Rev. Messrs. John Drysdale and James Baty, to pastoral charges in the county of Down. These ministers had officiated as chaplains to the regiments of the lord Claneboy and the lord of Ards; and after due examination, had been admitted as members of the presbytery. They were now presented with unanimous calls from the parishes of Portaferry and Ballywalter, near which their regiments had been stationed; and having passed through the usual course

9 Adair's MS. 10 Ibid.

of second trials, they were solemnly ordained by the presbytery to their respective charges. Mr. Blair presided at the ordination of Mr. Drysdale at Portaferry; and Mr. Hamilton at that of Mr. Baty, as his own successor, at Ballywalter; "only in Ballywalter there was a reservation of Mr. Hamilton's interest there, if God should clear his return to that place." These two ministers, having now completed their prescribed term of four months, and having laboured most assiduously in erecting congregations, admitting members, and establishing the presbyterian discipline through the greater part of the counties of Down and Antrim, returned in the end of December to Scotland, carrying with them letters to the standing commission of the church, urging the despatch of the ministers appointed by the Assembly for the next supply.[11]

The Scottish army having been increased in August by a reinforcement of near four thousand men under general Leslie, earl of Leven, who returned in November without having performed any service of consequence against the rebels,[12] an additional number of chaplains was required.

11 One of these brethren, Mr. John Maclelland, it appears from Baillie, (i. 384.) was prevented from filling his appointment by ill health, and was consequently excused by the next General Assembly. He came over as a supply two years afterwards.

12 Spalding (p. 298) says 3600 men. From the same authority (p. 313) we learn, that Leven arrived at Edinburgh, on his return, on the last day of November. Sir James Turner, in his "Memoirs," gives the following account of Leven's visit to Ulster:—"About Lammas, in this year 1642, came general Leven over to Ireland, and with him the earl of Eglintoun, who had one of these ten regiments, my lord Sinclair, and Hamilton, general of the artillery, better known by the name of dear Sandie. (Baillie gives him the same *soubriquet*, and calls him brother to the earl of Haddington, i. 392.) Great matters were expected from so famous a captain as Leven was; but he did not answer expectation. One cavalcade he made, which I joined with him with 300 men, in which I could not see what he intended, or what he proposed to himself. Sure I am, he returned to Carrickfergus without doing any thing. And the same game he played over again, at his second march, except that he visited the Newry, for which we were but little obliged to him, being forced thereby

The presbytery were therefore "earnest with the regiments, who yet wanted ministers, to supply themselves" as soon as possible. This recommendation was duly attended to, and several ministers were invited from Scotland to officiate as chaplains; "and according as they were presented to the presbytery, they were put on their trials, and some rejected and some admitted."

Among these chaplains was Mr. James Houston, whose case may be noticed as illustrative of the state of discipline, at this time, in the Scottish church. He had been minister at Glasford, in the presbytery of Hamilton, and was esteemed "a pious and very zealous young man;" but having fallen into a flagrant sin, he was, soon after his settlement there, deposed by the presbytery. Being invited over here as chaplain to one of the Scottish regiments, he was, with that view, permitted to preach by the presbytery of Paisley, who probably conceived him good enough for Ireland, and the army. But his former parishioners, hearing of his restoration to the ministry, earnestly supplicated the presbytery of Hamilton to permit his return to them, which that presbytery peremptorily refused. They then brought their case before the provincial synod of Glasgow, who, viewing the matter in a more favourable light than the presbytery, ordered him to be restored to the pastoral charge of Glasford. The presbytery, however, appealed to the General Assembly in 1643, who sustained their appeal, reproved the synod for restoring, in so summary a way, a deposed minister to his charge, and finally removed Houston from the ministerial office.(13)

In the month of May, the indefatigable Mr. Livingston, pursuant to the appointment of the Assembly, came over as a supply for three months, accompanied by the Rev. James Blair, minister at Portpatrick, in room of professor Baillie. The former appears to have followed the same course of preach-

to part with our hay, wine, beer, and bread, of which we were not very well stored."

13 Baillie's Letters, i. 387, 8.

ing, visiting, and administering ordinances which the preceding ministers had done. "For the most part of all these three months," writes Livingston, "I preached every day once, and twice on the Sabbath; the destitute parishes were many; the hunger of the people was become great, and the Lord was pleased to furnish otherwise than usually I wont to get at home. I came ordinarily the night before to the place where I was to preach, and commonly lodged in some religious person's house, where we were often well refreshed at family exercise: Usually I desired no more before I went to bed, but to make sure the place of scripture I was to preach on the next day. And rising in the morning, I had four or five hours myself alone, either in a chamber, or in the fields; after that we went to church, and then dined, and then rode five or six miles, more or less, to another parish. Sometimes there would be four or five communions in several places, in the three months time."[14] During his stay, the presbytery held another fast on the twenty-fourth of May, "for the former causes; and especially, the sinfulness of the army and country continuing, notwithstanding the great distresses on both; and that God would bless the expedition of the army, going to the field this summer."

After the departure of Livingston and James Blair, the presbytery prepared another petition to the General Assembly, appointed to meet at Edinburgh on the first Wednesday of August. A short time before, the presbyterians of Derry and its vicinity had applied to the presbytery to send them a minister, naming, in particular, a Mr. John Kemp, as one whom they desired might be deputed to visit them, with a view to his settlement as their stated pastor. But in consequence of the scarcity of ministers, this application was referred to the consideration of the Assembly. The presbytery also resolved to send over one of their number as a commissioner to that meeting; who, on his arrival, was duly recognised and

14 Livingston's Life, pp. 37, 8.

admitted as a member of the court.[15] The lord viscount Ards[16] also wrote at the same time to the Assembly, thanking them for their former supplies of ministers, and recom-

15 Baillie's Letters, i. 376. The Rev. John Scott was the commissioner on this occasion. Stevenson, iii. 1082.

16 This was Hugh Montgomery, the third viscount, who succeeded his father in November 1642. He afterwards deserted the presbyterian church, and became the persecutor of the ministers, whom he now patronized. As it became convenient, after the Restoration, to represent this nobleman as having uniformly opposed the presbyterian church in Ulster, I subjoin a copy of his lordship's letter, on this occasion, to the General Assembly, extracted from the manuscript records of the church of Scotland, that it may be seen what his real sentiments were at this period.

" To my right honourable and reverend friends, the moderator and remanent members of the General Assembly in Scotland.

" Right honourable and reverend friends,

" The necessity whereunto this part of the kingdom of Ireland is driven for want of a lively ministry, together with our sense of that want, partly occasioned by the violent acts of prelates in driving away some of our best ministers out of the same, partly through the devastation of this land, by the cruel hand of the murthering rebel, which hath made all our churches void of ministers. So as, though there be a remnant of well-disposed Christians yet preserved alive by the mercy of God in these parts, yet the outward means of their salvation is altogether wanting: And the by-past experience of your care and love toward us in supplying our wants, in sending pastors to this place by turns, (for which, your care, we are infinitely bound unto you,) together with the assured hopes of the continuance of your tender care and love towards us, and my true and earnest desires to have this part of the country planted with good and able ministers, sets me forward to second the petition out from the inhabitants of this desolate land, earnestly entreating, that out of your grave and considerate wisdoms and Christian respects to us, you will be pleased to return such a favourable answer to that petition, as our necessity calls for at your hands, and the wants of this land requires. And withal, that you will be pleased to make choice of some two grave and learned ministers of good and holy lives and conversations, and them recommend, and send over to this country, the one for the parish church of Newton, and the other for my regiment, and by the assistance of God, they shall not want competent stipends. In doing whereof, your care to advance God's glory, and to settle his church in these parts will appear to the world, and you shall engage me for ever to be your true and real friend and servant,

" MONTGOMERIE."

" *Mount-Alexander, the 20th July* 1643.

mending this second petition "of the Scots in Ulster," to their favourable consideration.

This petition, like the former one, was "subscribed by very many hands." It was intrusted to Sir Robert Adair of Kinhilt, knt., with whom the reader is already acquainted, as a sufferer, under Strafford, for the presbyterian cause,(17) and to Mr. William Mackenna, of Belfast, merchant; and, with the accompanying papers, was presented to the Assembly on Friday the fourth of August.(18) In this petition, they thus feelingly express their gratitude for the Assembly's former attention to their wants:—

"Whereas you were pleased the last year to take notice of our petition, and conceived so favourable an act in our behalf, from our hearts we bless the Lord God of our fathers, who put such a thing as this in your heart, to begin in any sort to beautify the house of the Lord amongst us. Doubtless you have brought upon yourselves the blessing of them who consider the poor; the Lord will certainly deliver you in time of trouble. We trust no distance of place, no length of time, no pressure of affliction, yea nor smiling of prosperity, shall delete out of our thankful memories, the humble acknowledgment of your so motherly care, in drawing out your breasts, yea, your souls to satisfy the hungry. Although we have been beaten with the sword, bitten with famine, our own wickedness correcting us, our back-slidings reproving us, yet we have not so far forgotten the Lord's ancient love, but that our

17 Note 17, chap. v. and chap. vi. page 291.

18 In Lightfoot's Journal of the proceedings of the Westminster Assembly, I find the following entry of the same date with the petition in the text. "Friday, August 4, 1643. Before the Assembly sat, a petition was read directed to the parliament, by the poor ministers of Ireland, but first brought in amongst us to desire that we would forward the promoting of it." I have no means of knowing whether this petition was from the presbyterian ministers of Ulster, or from distressed ministers in other parts of the kingdom. I find that on the 18th September following, the parliament made an ordinance for a collection for the clergy of Ireland, (Cox, ii. 136.) probably in consequence of this petition.

hearts were brought to a little reviving in the midst of our bondage, by the ministry of those, who, at your direction, made a short visit amongst us."

After setting forth their destitute condition, and stating that they trusted to the Assembly alone, as their parent church, to supply their spiritual wants, they conclude with this renewed and affecting appeal, that their former ministers might be permitted to settle among them :—"It is therefore our humble and earnest desire, that you would yet again look on our former petition, and your own obligatory act, and at least declare your consent, that a competent number of our own ministers may be loosed to settle here, and break bread to the children that lie fainting at the head of all streets; which, although it may be accounted but a restoring of what *we* lost and *you* have found, yet we shall esteem it as the most precious gift that earth can afford. When they are so loosed, if they find not all things concurring to clear God's calling, it will be in their hand to forbear, and you have testified your bounty. But oh! for the Lord's sake, do not kill our dying souls, by denying these our necessary desires. There are about twelve or fourteen waste congregations on this nearest coast; let us have at least a competent number that may erect Christ's throne of discipline, and may help to bring in others, and then shall we sing, that the people who were left of the sword, have found grace in the wilderness."

This petition, with the application from the presbyterians of Derry, and the letter of the lord of Ards, were referred by the Assembly to a committee, to consider what course ought to be pursued. As Ireland was a dependency of England, it became necessary to obtain the sanction of the English parliament for the ecclesiastical changes which had been effected in Ulster, under the preaching of the Scottish ministers. Accordingly, at the suggestion of the committee, the state of the church in the north of Ireland, was recommended to the commissioners from the English parliament who were present at this Assembly. The standing commission of the church were authorized to provide suitable ministers for the lord viscount Ards, and for the presbyterians of Derry. They were also empowered to send over to Ulster such expectants or probationers, as they might find, upon trial, qualified to discharge the arduous duties of the ministry in so desolate a land.(19)

19 The following extracts from the "Report of Committee appointed to consider of the petitions from the distressed people of Ireland," are necessary to illustrate the statements in the text.—"7. Further, this committee hath represented to the honourable commissioners from England, that these ministers who are sought for Ireland can hardly be removed from their particular flocks, and are of special steadableness to this kirk; wherefore the said committee hath desired the said honourable commissioners from both houses of parliament to express what certainty of continuance there, our brethren may have; not so much for maintenance, as for liberty of adhering to the doctrine and discipline of this kirk of Scotland, and not to be ejected for unconformity as heretofore they were. Which the said honourable commissioners have determined to make known to the parliament of England, and have promised to advertise the commissioners of this kirk, of their answer, when it shall be sent to them. 8. Moreover, the said petitioners from Ireland have acquainted us that where they dwell, divers prelatical, ignorant and scandalous preachers, (especially such as took and urged the oath against our covenant,) engyre [ingratiate] themselves upon the people, and disturb the present good work in hand. For remedy whereof, they do earnestly desire that the commissioners from England be consulted with, by such as this Assembly shall appoint. 9. The matter anent the lord of Ard's letter for two ministers be recommended both to the commissioners of the General Assembly, and to such as are sent to Ireland, and the presbytery there, with special advice of Mr. James Blair, to be taken thereanent. And the Scottishmen of Derry's petition for a minister, in general it is approven and recommended as the former: But Mr. John Kemp, in special, is not thought fit for them, by special knowledge of divers upon the committee. 12. Messrs. Robert Blair and James Hamilton, who were four months in Ireland, and Messrs. James Blair and John Livingston, for the time they were there, did very painfully and fruitfully labour in their ministry, as is evident to us by the reading and considering the register of the presbytery of the Scottish forces there, so that they have deserved the General Assembly's approbation.

David Lindsay, *Moderator to the Committee.*"

The following is the minute of Assembly relative to the sending of probationers to Ulster:—"The Assembly considering that there will be necessity to send some expectants to the kingdom of Ireland for satisfaction of the desires of the petitions given to the Assembly from the distressed

At the same time, a reply to the general petition presented by Sir Robert Adair, was drawn up and approved, in which the Assembly still declined to loose any of their ministers from their present charges, with a view to their settlement in Ireland. But they very cheerfully appointed the following ministers to visit Ulster in rotation, and to supply the province with preaching until the next annual meeting of the Assembly:—"Master William Cockburne, minister at Kirkmichael, and Master Matthew Mackaill, minister at Carmanoch, for the first three months, beginning upon the eighth of September next. Master George Hutchison, minister at Colmonel, and Master Hugh Henderson, minister at Dailly, for the next three months, beginning the eighth of December. Master William Adair, minister at Ayr, and Master John Weir, minister at Dalserf, for the third three months, beginning the eighth of March, 1644. And Master James Hamilton, minister at Dumfries, and Master John Maclelland, minister at Kirkcudbright, for the last three months, beginning the eighth of June, in the said year 1644; to repair unto the north of Ireland, and there to visit, instruct, comfort and encourage the scattered flocks of Christ." [20]

The General Assembly, whose proceedings in relation to Ireland have now been narrated, is most memorable in the annals, not merely of the church of Scotland, but of the empire at large. For at this meeting, was concluded that civil and religious league between the two kingdoms, which produced so signal a change in the national affairs, as to render this period the most interesting and remarkable in the history of Britain.

people in Ireland; therefore gives power to the commissioners to be appointed by this Assembly for the public affairs of the kirk to sit at Edinburgh to consider of the fittest expectants to go to the said kingdom, to try and examine them; and being fit and qualified for that employment, to give them calling and commission to go unto the said kingdom, to do and perform such things as they shall find necessary and answerable to the desires of the said petitions." MSS. Arch. Ecc. Scot.

[20] Acts of General Assembly. Printed 1682. Pp. 160, 1.—190, 1.

In England, Charles had at length come to an open rupture with his parliament; and on the twenty-fifth of August 1642, had erected his standard at Nottingham, and declared his resolution of appealing to arms in defence of his prerogative. The parliament had, in some measure, provided for this emergency, by securing possession of several principal towns and forts in various parts of the kingdom. They placed their troops under the command of the earl of Essex, and resolved to resist, at all hazards, in the field as well as in their House, with their swords as well as their votes, the hostile attempts of the king. In the first campaign, which was terminated by the approach of winter, neither party gained any material advantages over the other. On the renewal of hostilities, however, in the spring of 1643, the royal arms were decidedly triumphant, both in the north and west. The parliament was placed in a very precarious, if not desperate situation; and the civil and religious liberties of the kingdom were apparently at the mercy of a victorious and indignant despot. In this critical emergency, the fraternal assistance of the Scots was anxiously solicited. They were implored to aid the parliament in defence of constitutional freedom against a sovereign, who had already attempted to trample on their own rights, and who only awaited the hour of victory over his English subjects, to avenge upon themselves their late successful opposition to his designs. As a more persuasive inducement, the prospect that the sister kingdom would adopt their ecclesiastical polity was distinctly held out; and they were invited to co-operate in establishing a uniformity of doctrine, government and worship throughout the entire empire.

The ecclesiastical changes which had, in the mean time, occurred in England, had prepared the way for this inviting proposal. The meeting of the long parliament was no less favourable to the vindication of civil liberty, than to the removal of the religious thraldom, under which the nation had been long groaning. The execution of Strafford and the impeachment and imprisonment of Laud were early and decisive indications of the spirit of the parliament on the subject of religion ; while the subsequent conduct of the prelates accelerated the crisis which was slowly though certainly approaching. Their determined hostility to constitutional freedom,—their support of all the arbitrary proceedings of Charles,—their unmitigated persecution of the puritans, and their manifest leaning to popery, in advocating several of its doctrinal errors, and introducing some of its superstitious ceremonies,—exposed them equally to the indignation of the patriot, and the reprobation of the Christian. They were considered as the chief, if not sole, impediments in the way of the civil and religious reformation of the kingdom. Petitions against the hierarchy poured into the house of commons from all quarters, pointing out the evil consequences resulting from episcopal government ; praying that it might be either abolished, or at least greatly modified ; and especially entreating that the prelates might be no longer permitted to interfere in civil affairs, but be confined to the discharge of their spiritual functions. Accordingly, early in the year 1641, the commons pledged themselves to proceed, in due time, with the ecclesiastical reform so much desired. About the same time, they passed resolutions against the legislative and judicial power of the bishops, and generally against the clerical order being employed in any civil or temporal office. But the bill founded on these resolutions was thrown out by the Lords.

Various plans were subsequently suggested for re-modelling the government of the church, which, it was apparent, could be no longer tolerated, as it then stood. Of these, the most remarkable was that by archbishop Ussher, now resident in England, by which he proposed to unite the two schemes of prelacy and presbytery, and reduce them to what he styled " the form of synodical government received in the ancient church."(21) But the king and the great body of the bishops

21 Ussher's " model of church government" was summed up in the four following propositions, which I give in an abridged form :—

obstinately resisted every concession. The absence of Charles in Scotland during the remainder of the year, and the interruption occasioned by the Irish rebellion, retarded, for some time, the consideration of ecclesiastical affairs. In the month of February 1642, however, both houses passed a bill for disabling persons in holy orders from exercising temporal jurisdiction, and by consequence depriving the bishops of their seats in parliament. The royal assent was, with some difficulty, procured for this bill on the fourteenth of the same month; and thus sanctioned, it formed the first decided prognostication of the approaching downfall of prelacy. In the following month, the commons declared their intention of speedily calling an assembly of divines to assist them in reforming abuses in the church; and in the month of June, both houses concurred in passing a bill to that effect.

Encouraged by these proceedings in parliament, the public mind continued to be steadily directed to the subject of ecclesiastical reform. The conduct of the prelates had weakened the attachment of the great bulk of the people to episcopacy, and led many to long for its reform; and the greater number

"I. The incumbent with the church-wardens and sides-men to exercise discipline in each parish, to present refractory offenders to the next monthly synod, and in the meantime to debar them from the Lord's table.

II. Monthly synods to be held of all the incumbents within certain districts corresponding to the rural deaneries; in these a suffragan or rural dean to preside; the majority to decide; and to be empowered to censure errors of doctrine appearing within their districts, with liberty of appeal to the diocesan synod.

III. Diocesan synods to be held once or twice in the year, consisting of all the suffragans in the diocese with a select number of the incumbents out of each rural deanery; the bishop or superintendent, "call him whether you will," to be moderator, and the majority to decide.

IV. The provincial synod to consist of all the bishops and suffragans, with representatives chosen by the clergy of each diocese within the province; the primate to be moderator. And both the primates and provincial synods to constitute a national council to meet every third year, "wherein all appeals from inferior synods might be received, all their acts examined, and all ecclesiastical constitutions which concern the state of the church of the whole nation, established."

to desire its total overthrow. The more influential part of its clergy, and the preponderating majority of the laity, were in favour of the parity and freedom of presbytery; though a considerable number as yet sought no more than the reformation of the existing establishment. The parliament was similarly divided in sentiment. Few of the members were, at this period, presbyterian in principle, and perhaps still fewer were decided episcopalians. The majority in both houses were Erastians, conceiving it to be the prerogative of the civil magistrate to model the government of the church as he pleased, without any reference to the authority of scripture. All parties, however, with the exception of the royalists, to whom the epithets malignants or cavaliers now began to be applied, were decidedly bent upon a thorough reformation of the government and discipline of the church.

In this state of public feeling the general attention of the nation was naturally directed to Scotland. Here they beheld an ecclesiastical establishment in full vigour, and free from those abuses which they lamented in their own; and here too, they were aware, existed a kindred spirit of opposition to the arbitrary power of Charles, whose encroachments on the rights both of their church and of their state, the Scots had so recently and successfully resisted.

Accordingly, in July, the parliament opened a correspondence with the General Assembly met at St. Andrews. They state, in their letter, the distractions into which the nation was plunged by "wicked counsels and practices of the malignant party;" they condemn "the avarice and ambition of the bishops;" they express their desires to avoid a civil war with the king, and to "return to a peaceable and parliamentary proceeding;" and trust that they will thereby be enabled to secure the honour of his majesty, the peace of the kingdom, and especially "the glory of God by the advancement of true religion, and such a reformation of the church as shall be most agreeable to God's word." To this communication the Assembly replied, by repeating their deliberate conviction, that there could be no reasonable hope of tranquillity to England, or to their own nation and church, nor yet a well-grounded peace between the two kingdoms; till the anti-christian system of prelacy be removed, and one form of ecclesiastical government established throughout the empire. They state that as prelacy, so far as it differs from presbytery, is almost universally acknowledged to be merely a human contrivance, it could therefore be the more easily abolished, "without wronging any man's conscience;" and they conclude by assuring the parliament that "what may be required of the kirk of Scotland for furthering the work of uniformity of government, or for agreeing upon a common confession of faith, catechism, and directory for worship, shall be most willingly performed" by them. Thus was commenced that correspondence between the two kingdoms, which afterwards led to the most memorable results. The Scots had as yet stood neuter between the king and the parliament; and had even been endeavouring, as mediators, to effect a reconciliation between them. When this was found to be impracticable, both parties sought to secure their co-operation; the king, on the ground of gratitude for his past favours to their church and nation, and the offer of additional privileges; the parliament, on the ground of their mutual safety, and the extension of their favourite system of ecclesiastical polity. The latter considerations prevailed, and the Scots, by espousing the cause of the parliament, rendered it ultimately triumphant.

The reply of the Assembly, so decided on the abolition of prelacy, and the conduct of the king in setting up his standard at Nottingham a few weeks after it was received, quickened the parliament in their proceedings respecting the church. Accordingly the commons on the first, and the lords on the ninth, of September, concurred in an answer to the Assembly's letter. In this declaration, they express their desires for unity of religion in all his majesty's dominions; they condemn the government of bishops as hostile to the liberties of the nation, and the occasion of many intolerable grievances;

"upon which accounts," they say, "and many others, we declare that this government, by archbishops, bishops, their chancellors and commissaries, deans and chapters, archdeacons and other ecclesiastical officers depending upon the hierarchy, is evil, and justly offensive and burdensome to the kingdom, a great impediment to reformation, and very prejudicial to the civil government, and that we are resolved the same shall be taken away." They conclude this celebrated paper by requesting the Scots, to join with them in petitioning the king to assent to their bill for an assembly of divines, that one confession of faith and directory of worship might be compiled for the three kingdoms.

Both houses were thus solemnly pledged to abolish prelacy and to call an assembly of divines, "as soon as may be." In the mean time, the progress of the war prevented them from taking any immediate step towards carrying these memorable resolutions into effect. When hostilities were suspended by the approach of winter, the parliament renewed their negotiations with Charles at Oxford, and submitted to him several propositions, as the foundation of a permanent peace. Among these, they required his confirmation of their "declaration for taking away of bishops, deans and chapters;" and his assent to their bill for convoking an assembly of divines. At the same time, to testify their determination to abide by their resolutions, a bill for "the utter abolishing and taking away" of prelacy, was introduced into the commons in December, and finally passed the lords on the twenty-sixth of January, 1643. The king's consent, however, could not be procured, either to this bill or the other propositions of the parliament. The negotiations at Oxford were consequently broken off; and both parties resumed hostilities in the spring with greater vigour than before. The alarming successes of Charles in the commencement of the campaign determined the parliament to make an immediate application for aid to the Scottish nation. To prepare the way for this application, it was evidently necessary to enter more vigorously on the work of ecclesiastical reform. In no other way could they satisfy their expected allies, that they were sincere in their desires for uniformity of doctrine and discipline between the two nations; and therefore, though reluctant to act without the king's concurrence, they at length, on the twelfth of June,[22] converted their bill for an assembly of divines into an ordinance, and summoned the persons therein mentioned, to meet at Westminster, to assist them in "settling such a government in the church as may be agreeable to God's holy word, and bring into nearer agreement with the church of Scotland, and other reformed churches abroad."

This celebrated assembly, though forbidden to meet by a proclamation from the king, commenced its sittings upon Saturday the first day of July. It consisted of ten lords and twenty commoners as lay-assessors, among whom, was Sir John Clotworthy of Antrim; and of one hundred and twenty divines, among whom, the only one connected with Ireland who attended, was Joshua Hoyle, D.D. for many years fellow and divinity professor in Trinity College, Dublin.[23] It possessed no ecclesiastical jurisdiction or authority. It was simply a council to advise and direct the parliament in such matters, as they might submit to its consideration; and its decisions were of no force, until confirmed by their ordinance.

Having set in motion this important engine for the reformation of the church, the next step taken by the parliament,

22 The dates of these various proceedings in the English parliament, on the subject of prelacy, are taken from the "Journals," as quoted by Godwin in his "History of the Commonwealth," vol. i. Many of these dates, as given by Neal and several other historians, are inaccurate.

23 Joshua Hoyle was elected Fellow of Trinity College, Dublin, in 1609. In 1623 he was appointed professor of divinity. He was a member of the Irish convocation in 1634. In 1648 he became master of University College, and King's professor of divinity, Oxford. Dub. Univ. Col. for 1833. Thomas Temple, D.D. another member of the Westminster assembly, had also been a fellow of Trinity College; but he had removed to England and settled at Battersea, near London, several years before. Brooke's Puritans, iii. 100.

who had no time to lose, was to despatch commissioners to Scotland, to the convention of estates and the General Assembly of the church, to obtain their assistance against the victorious arms of Charles. "The negotiation was not attended with much difficulty. With a commendable firmness and zeal, the Scots determined to support the English parliament, and to maintain the common cause by force of arms, undismayed by the perilous situation in which affairs in England then stood."(24) The English commissioners were anxious to promote merely a civil LEAGUE between the two kingdoms; but the Scots strenuously insisted on rendering it also a religious COVENANT. Both objects, however, were embraced, and both terms employed in the contemplated bond of union.

In preparing this bond, no difference of opinion appeared in the articles involving civil engagements between the two nations. The only point which gave rise to discussion, related to the model or plan by which the projected reformation in England was to be conducted. At length, the general, though by no means ambiguous declaration, that it should be conducted, "according to the word of God and the example of the best reformed churches," was unanimously adopted; both parties being content to leave the settlement of such modifications in the government and discipline of the church, as might be requisite in the peculiar circumstances of England, to the deliberations of the Westminster Assembly, to which commissioners from the church of Scotland were now added. The result of these negotiations, which were carried on in private between the English commissioners, and committees from the convention of estates, and the General Assembly, was—THE SOLEMN LEAGUE AND COVENANT.(25)

24 Godwin, i. 178.

25 The following is Baillie's account of the deliberations in Edinburgh on this interesting occasion:—"In our committees we had hard enough debates. The English were for a civil league, we for a religious covenant. When they were brought to us in this, and Mr. Henderson had given them a draught of a covenant, we were not like to agree on a frame; they were,

On the seventeenth of August, this memorable bond was introduced into the General Assembly,—"in the which, at the first reading, being well prefaced with Mr. Henderson's most grave oration, it was received with the greatest applause that ever I saw any thing, with so hearty affections expressed

more than we could assent to, for keeping of a door open in England to independency. Against this we were peremptor. At last some two or three in private accorded to that draught, which all our three committees, from our states, from our assembly, and the parliament of England, did unanimously assent to." Letters, i. 381. After the Restoration, and the death of Sir Henry Vane, a story was circulated by the royalist writers, that at these conferences, Vane, one of the English commissioners, outwitted the Scots by procuring the insertion of the qualifying phrase, "according to the word of God," by which it was left undetermined, as they alleged, whether presbytery or independency should be established in England. But, whatever may have been the duplicity of Vane, no such ambiguity, so far as I know, was ever attached by himself or his party to that stipulation; while, on the contrary, it was invariably pleaded as completely securing the establishment of the presbyterian polity in England, though certain modifications might be required to render the system, in its details, more suitable to the state of that kingdom. Burnet in his "Memoirs of the Dukes of Hamilton," published in 1677; and Clarendon in his "History of the Rebellion," written about 1670, but not published till 1703, are the only authorities for this piece of secret history, quoted by Neal, Laing, and a host of other anti-presbyterian writers; all of whom seem to take a delight in representing the leaders in the negotiations respecting the covenant, as meanly striving to over-reach each other.—I find an earlier authority than Burnet, for this anecdote respecting Vane, in a "Life of General Monk," published in 1671, by Thomas Gumble, D. D. another royalist writer; and as his version of the story is not generally known, I subjoin it for the information of the minute inquirer into these "Curiosities of History."—Speaking of the covenant, he says, "Sir Henry Vane would by all means have it called a league, as well as a covenant; and disputed it almost all night, and at last carried it. Another debate he held about church government, which was to be "according to the example of the best reformed churches:" he would have it "according to the word of God," only: but after a great contest they joined both, and the last had the precedence. One of his fellows afterwards expostulating his reason, that he should put them to so much trouble with such needless trifles, he told him, That he was mistaken and did not see far enough into that matter; for a league showed it was between two nations, and might be broken upon just reasons; but not a covenant. For the other, That church government in the tears of pity and joy, by very many grave, wise and old men."(26) In the afternoon of the same day it was adopted by the convention of estates, and the next morning transmitted to both houses of parliament in London. By them, it was referred to a special committee of their own members, and of the Westminster divines, "to the intent that some expressions might be farther explained, and that the kingdome of Ireland also might bee expressly taken into the same league and covenant." (27) These alterations having been accordingly made, it was finally approved by the commons, and Monday the twenty-fifth of September was appointed for the solemn swearing of it, by the members both of the parliament and the assembly.

Being convened in St. Margaret's church, Westminster, the Rev. Mr. White of Dorchester opened the meeting with prayer. The Rev. Philip Nye of Kimbolton, one of the commissioners who had been at Edinburgh, justified the covenant from Scripture, and displayed the advantage the church had received from such sacred confederacies. The Rev. Alexander Henderson of Edinburgh, who was attending the Westminster assembly, as one of the commissioners from

according to the word of God, by the difference of divines and expositors, would be long enough before it be determined, for the learnedest held it clearly for episcopacy; so that when all are agreed, we may take in the Scotch presbytery." Life of Monk, p. 23. For further remarks on this incident, see Brodie, iii. 456; and Cook's Hist. of Church of Scotland, iii. 63, 64.

26 Baillie, i. 381.

27 See a curious and valuable pamphlet, entitled, "The Covenant: with a narrative of the proceedings and solemn manner of taking it by the Honourable House of Commons and Reverent Assembly of Divines the 25th day of September at St. Margaret's in Westminster. Also two speeches delivered at the same time; the one by Mr. Philip Nye, the other by Mr. Alexander Henderson. Published by special order of the House." Lond. 1643. 4to. pp. 34. This was the first appearance of the Solemn League and Covenant in print. A copy of it is annexed to the ordinary editions of the Westminster Confession of Faith and Catechisms.

the Scottish church, spoke next, and declared, that the estates of Scotland had resolved to assist the parliament of England in carrying into effect the ends and designs of the covenant. Then Mr. Nye read it from the pulpit, article by article, each person standing uncovered, with his right hand lifted up bare to heaven, worshipping the great name of God, and swearing to the performance of it. Dr. Gouge concluded with prayer; after which the commons went up into the chancel, and subscribed their names in one roll of parchment, and the assembly in another, each of which contained a copy of the covenant.[28] On the fifteenth of October it was, with like solemnity, taken by the lords, after a sermon from Nehemiah x. 29, by Dr. Temple, formerly fellow of Trinity College, Dublin. It was subsequently ordered to be taken by all persons in England above the age of eighteen years, under pain of being punished as enemies to religion, and to the peace of the kingdom. With this view, copies were forwarded to every military commander in the service of parliament, that it might be taken by the soldiers; and to every minister, that he might tender it to his people and obtain their subscriptions.

A similar course was pursued in Scotland. The alterations made by the Westminster divines, were immediately submitted to the commissioners of the estates at Edinburgh, as well as to the standing committee of the church; both of whom,—" after a day's deliberation, did heartily approve the alterations as not materially differing from the form read in the assembly. So on Friday, [the thirteenth of October,] in the New church, after a pertinent sermon, by Mr. Robert Douglas, [one of the ministers of Edinburgh,] the commissioners of state at one table, the commissioners of the church at another, the commissioners from the parliament and assembly of England at a third, did solemnly swear and subscribe with great joy and many tears. Some eighteen of our

[28] Rushworth, v. 475.

Lords were present that day; and copies were despatched to the moderators of all our presbyteries, to cause read and expone the covenant the first Sunday after their receipt, and the Sunday following, to cause swear it by men and women, and all of understanding in every church of our land, and to be subscribed by the hand of all men who could write, and by the clerk of session, [in each congregation,] in name of those that could not write, with certification of the church censures, and confiscation of goods presently to be inflicted on all refusers."[29] The covenant, thus introduced, was everywhere received and subscribed, with the greatest enthusiasm and delight.

This seasonable measure tended most materially to ascertain and unite, the friends of true religion and liberty, throughout the whole empire. In those critical times, a bond of union, which might operate as a test of fidelity to the great cause in hand, was indispensably necessary. Such was THE COVENANT. It could be consistently, and, in point of fact, was actually, refused by none except by the violent partizans of Charles. It was no doubt pressed with great earnestness on all, and those who refused to subscribe it were viewed—and the result almost invariably proved the truth of the surmise—as hostile to the cause of truth and freedom. These persons were consequently discouraged, and, where the safety of the cause required it, were deprived of their places of trust, and laid under restraint. But in what other way could the Scots and the parliament, now united to restore and uphold constitutional monarchy and secure the liberties of both kingdoms, expect to attain success? Self-preservation demanded, when in a state of open warfare, that they should clearly ascertain both their friends and their adversaries, for the purpose of uniting the one, and repressing the other. And how could this end be attained, but by the enforcement of a test suited to the existing emergency? Had the covenant been

29 Baillie, i. 393.

simply a civil league, and merely the test of a political party, it would be much more favourably regarded by the present generation than it is. But, in accordance with the spirit of those times, it was both a civil and a religious bond,—an ecclesiastical as well as a political test; and it is in consequence of its bearing this two-fold character, that such diversities of opinion have existed with regard to its expediency then, and its authority now.

It must, however, be carefully remembered, that civil and religious concerns were so intimately connected, that it was impracticable, had it been desirable, to separate them in the public transactions of that period. The friends of constitutional freedom were the friends of scripture-truth, and reformation; and the abettors of despotism in the state, were either the bitter enemies of protestantism, or the bigoted adherents of prelacy in its most intolerant form. It was not *then*, as it is *now*, that men, of almost every creed and church constitute the same political party; or that men, united in the fellowship of the same church, are found to entertain opposite political sentiments. In the present state of society, a bond of a mixed character, like the covenant, would be palpably unsuitable and inefficient. The individuals who would now confederate to promote a civil, would be far from uniting to advance a religious reformation. But at the period under consideration, the covenant was a most judicious and suitable bond of confederacy; "for the matter of it, just and warrantable; for the ends, necessary and commendable; and for the time, seasonable." It was obnoxious only to the opponents of the civil and ecclesiastical reformation of the kingdom. Its objects were,—to secure the liberties of each kingdom, to preserve the privileges of both parliaments, and to maintain the constitutional authority of the sovereign;—to consolidate a firm concord among all parts of the empire on the basis of a federal alliance, and to secure the mutual defence of the subscribers without division or defection,—to preserve the reformed faith in Scotland, and to promote the further reformation of religion in England and Ireland,—and to bind each subscriber to study personal reformation, that "they, and their posterity after them, may live, as brethren, in faith and love, and the Lord may delight to dwell in the midst of them." The promulgation of the covenant, and the spirit which it excited and sustained, led to the most important results. A large army from Scotland soon after marched to the aid of the parliament, against the victorious arms of Charles, and immediately turned the scale in favour of their allies.

As the covenant included Ireland in its provisions, measures were promptly taken to transmit it to this kingdom.

On the fourth of November, the celebrated Owen O'Connolly, who had probably accompanied Sir John Clotworthy in his visit to England a few months before, was despatched by the parliament to the British and Scottish commanders in Ulster, to apprize them of the state of public affairs, and prepare them for entering into that engagement.[30] Such important changes had meanwhile taken place among the contending parties in Ireland, that the protestants of Ulster received the intelligence with heartfelt joy; and anxiously desired an opportunity of joining with their brethren in the sister kingdoms, in their SOLEMN LEAGUE AND COVENANT.

30 Carte, i. 486.

END OF VOLUME FIRST.

APPENDIX TO VOLUME FIRST,

CONSISTING OF

ORIGINAL PAPERS HITHERTO UNPUBLISHED.

See INTRODUCTION, page 32.

SINCE this part of the work was printed, I discovered among the manuscripts in the British Museum, the following account of the conference between Sir James Crofts and Dowdal, Roman catholic archbishop of Armagh, which took place at Mary's Abbey, Dublin, in June 1552, and which, so far as I know, has never been printed. It is a curious relic of the religious discussions of that age; and affords another illustration of the feeble and inefficient opposition made to popery in Ireland, compared with what it encountered in the sister kingdoms. How differently would Knox have handled the argument with the archbishop! See the discussion which that strenuous reformer maintained with a popish dignitary in Maybole, just ten years afterwards, on the same topic, the mass, in M'Crie's Knox, ii. 62–73.

[Donat. MSS. Mus. Brit. No. 4784, fol. 35–37.]

The discourse that passed at a meeting between Sir James Crofts, the lord deputy, and George Dowdall, archbishop of Armagh.

Sir James Croftes haveing intelligence that there were severall of the dissenting clergy with George Dowdall, who dissented themselves from the king's edict for the establishing of the liturgy of the church, to be read or sung in English, armed himself beforehand for to dispute with George Dowdall, and soe tooke with him Edward, [Staples] bishop of Meath, and Thomas, [Lancaster] bishop of Kildare, the day following. The meeting was in the great hall belonging to St. Mary's Abbey. A dispute hapned as Sir James foretould, which was occasioned upon a discourse concerning the masse as followeth:

G. Dowdall. My lord, why is your honor soe for my compliance with these clergymen, who are fallen from the mother church?

Sir J. Crofts. Because, reverend ffather, I would feign unite you and them, if possibly.

G. Dowdall. How can that be expected, when you have demolished the masse to bring in another service of England's makeing?

Sir J. Crofts. Most reverend ffather, I make noe doubt but here be those who will answer your grace, which behoofes them best to answer in this case, as it belongs to their ffunction.

E. Staples. My lord sayes well, as your grace was talkeing of the masse and of the antiquities of it.

G. Dowdall. Is it not auncienter than the liturgy now established without the consent of the mother church?

E. Staples. Noe, may it please your grace, for the service established by our gratious king Edward and his English clergy, is but the masse reformed and cleansed from idolatry.

G. Dowdall. Wee shall fly to hie, wee suppose, if wee continue in this strain. I could wish you would hearken unto reason, and so be united.

E. Staples. That is my prayers, reverend Sir, if you will come to it.

G. Dowdall. The way then to be in unitie, is not to alter the masse.

E. Staples. There is noe church upon the face of the whole earth, hath altered the masse more oftener then the church of Rome; which hath been the reason that causeth the rationaller sort of men to desire the liturgy to be established in a known tongue, that they may know what additions have been added, and what they pray for.

G. Dowdall. Was not the masse from the apostles' dayes; how can it be prooved that the church of Rome hath altered it?

E. Staples. It is easily proved by our records of England; for Cælestinus, bishop of Rome, (in the fourth centure after Christ,) gave the first Introit of the Masse, which the clergy was to use for preparation, even the psalm, Judica me Deus, &c. Rome not owneing the word masse untill then.

G. Dowdall. Yes, long before that tyme; for there was a masse called St. Ambrose his masse.

E. Staples. St. Ambrose was before Cælestinus, but the two prayers which the church of Rome hath foisted, and added unto St. Ambrose his workes, are not in his generall workes; which hath caused a wise and a learned man lately to write, that these two prayers were forged, and not to be really St. Ambrose's.

G. Dowdall. What writer dares write, or doth say soe?

E. Staples. Erasmus, a man who may well be compared to either of us, or the standers by; nay, my lord, noe disparagement if I say so to yourself, for he was a wise and a judicious man, otherwise I would not have been soe bould as to paralell your lordship with him.

Sir J. Crofts. As for Erasmus his parts, would I were such another; for his parts may paralell him companion for a prince.

G. Dowdall. Pray my lord, doe not hinder our discourse, for I have a question or two to aske Mr. Staples.

Sir J. Crofts. By all meanes, reverend ffather, proceed.

G. Dowdall. Is Erasmus his writeings more powerfull then the precepts of the mother church?

E. Staples. Not more then the holy catholique one, yet more then the church of Rome, as that church hath runn into severall errors since St. Ambrose his dayes.

G. Dowdall. How hath the church of Rome erred since St. Ambrose his dayes? Take heed lest you be not excommunicated.

E. Staples. I have excommunicated myself already from thence; therefore with Erasmus, I shall averr, that the prayers in St. Ambrose his masse, especially that to the blessed Virgin Mary, appears not to be in his auntient workes; for he had more of the truth and of God's spirit in him, then our latter bishops of Rome ever had, as to pray to the blessed Virgin, as if she had been a goddesse.

G. Dowdall. Was not she called 'blessed,' and did she not prophecie of herselfe, (when she was to beare our Saviour Christ Jesus,) that shee should be called by all men, 'Blessed.'

E. Staples. Yee, shee did soe; but others be called, Blessed, even by Christ himself. In his first sermon made by him in the mount, Blessed, saith he, bee the meeke, be the merciful, be the pure of heart; Blessed be those persecuted for righteoussnesse sake, and those that hunger and thirst after the same; and he blessed the low-minded sort, of which few or none of the bishops of Rome cann be sayd to be soe called since Constantine's reigne. Christ alsoe, to all those who shall partake of his heavenly kingdome, will likewise say unto them, 'Come yee blessed of my Father,' &c.

G. Dowdall. Why, pray, is it not probable that St. Ambrose desired the blessed virgin's mediation for him, as she is mother of Christ; are not children commanded by God's commandments to reverence and obey their parents; therefore as he is a man, why may not he be subject?

E. Staples. St. Ambrose knew better, that he ought to apply to Jesus the sole and onely Mediator between him and God; and that, as Christ is man, hee is the Mediator. If the blessed virgin, therefore, cann command her son in heaven to mediate, then St. Ambrose would have made her a goddesse or a coadjutor with God, who is of himself omnipotent. And lastly, if wee make her a mediator, as well as Christ, wee doe not onely suspect Christ's insufficiency, but mistrust God's ordinances, thinkeing ourselves not sure by his promises to us and our forefathers, that Christ should be our Mediator.

G. Dowdall. To the lord deputy. My lord, I signified to your honor, that all was in vaine when two parties should meett of a contrary opinion; and that your lordship's paynes therein would be lost, for which I am heartily sorry.

Sir J. Crofts. The sorrow is mine, that your grace cannot be convinced.

G. Dowdall. Did your lordship but know the oathes wee bishops doe take at our consecrations, signed under our handes, you would not blame my stedfastnesse. This oath, Mr. Staples, you took with others, before you were permitted to be consecrated. Consider hereon yourself, and blame not me for persisting as I doe.

E. Staples. My lord deputy, I am not ashamed to declare the oath, and to confesse my error in so sweareing thereunto: yett I hould it safer for my conscience to breake the same, then to observe the same. For when your lordship sees the copie thereof, and seriously considers, you will say it is hard for that clergyman (soe sweareing) to be a true subject to his king, if he observe the same: for that was the oath which our gratious king's royall ffather caused to be demolished, for to sett upp another, now called the oath of supremacy, to make the clergy the surer to his royall person, his heires and successors.

Then the lord deputy rose and tooke leave; soe likewise did the bishops of Meath and Killdare, who wayted on his lordship.

See Introduction, Page 33, and Note 66.

I could obtain only a very cursory glance at the letter of the lord chancellor Cusacke to the duke of Northumberland, preserved among the manuscripts in Trinity College, Dublin. I have since, however, had an opportunity of perusing it more leisurely, having met with a copy of it among the Harleian MSS. in that very valuable and accessible storehouse of historical records—the British Museum. I found the two passages quoted by Leland; and at the same time made the following transcript of the greater part of that portion of the letter which relates to Ulster. This very curious and important document cannot fail to be interesting to every reader, as it is both the earliest and amplest account of the state of Ulster, which has yet been published.

[Harl. MSS. Mus. Brit. No. 35, fol. 188 v. —194 v.]

The chauncellor of Ireland to the duke of Northumberland relating the state of Ireland. Anno 6, Edw. VI. May 8, 1552.

—— Next to Breany, [Cavan] is M'Mahon's country, called Oriell, wherein be three captaynes, the one in Dardarye, the other in Ferny, and M'Mahon in Leightie. These countryes [part of Monaghan and Armagh,] are lardge, fast and stronge; amonge whome there contynued intestine warre before tyme, wherby the most parte of the countrye was made waste, neverthelesse they be tall men of the number of lxxx horsemen, cc Kearne and vi^{xx} galloglas,* and all these for the most parte doe occupie husbandrye except the Kearne, and yett some of them doe occupie likewise: and nowe of late before Easter, by appoyntmente of my lorde deputye, I resorted to them to see their countryes ordered: and they all assemblinge before me, I caused them not onlye to finde, at their own chardges yearlie vi^{xx} galloglasses to serve the kinge, and to attende uppon an Englishe captayne of the Englishe pale, which hath the order of the countrye committed unto hym for the keepinge of the king's majestie's peace, the maintenance of the good and the punishmente of the evell. But alsoe I caused them to putt in their pledges to my handes, as well for the findeinge of the galloglas, as for the due performance of the orders which I tooke betwixt them; which thinge was done without force or rigor, and they as people most gladde to lyve in quyett, applyed to the same, which is great towardnes of obedience. Besides this, they have and yealde to all sesses to the souldiers of Moynehan [Monaghan] and in other places, beeves and carryadge, like as others in the English pale doe.

The next countrye betwene that and M'Gynnose's [Magenis's] countrye called Iveache, is O'Hanlon's countrye called Orres. The same O'Hanlon is an honest man, and he and his countrye lyeth readye to obaye all commandements.

The next to O'Hanlon, is M'Gynnose his countrye afforesaid,

* The *kerne* were the undisciplined foot soldiers of the native chieftains, usually armed with pikes and skeans. The *gallowglasses* were foot soldiers who wore armour, and carried swords and battle-axes.

wherin the Myorie, [Moira] Mr. Marshall fermer, is situated. The same M'Gynnose is a civell gentleman and useth as good order and fashion in his house, as any of his vocacion in Ireland; and doth the same Englishe like. His countrey is obedyent to all sesses and orders; the same Iveache hath bene parcell of the countie of Downe, and he beinge made sheriffe therof, hath exercysed his offyce there as well as any other sherriffe doth; soe as with them there lackes noe honest obedyence.

The next to that countrie is M'Cartan's countrye, a man of small power, wherein are noe horsemen, but Kearne; which countrye is full of bogges, woodes and moores, and beareth with the captayne of Lecaille.

The next to that countrye is the Duffreyn, wherof one John Whight [White] was landlorde, whoe was deceiptfully murthered by M'Ranills Boye his sonne, a Scott; and sithence that murther he keepeth possession of the saide landes; by meanes wherof, he is able nowe to disturbe the next adjoyneinge on every side, which shortlye by Godes grace shal be redressed. The same countrye is noe greate circuyte, but small, full of woodes, water and good lande, meet for English men to inhabitte.

The next countrye to the same eastwardes is Leicaille, where Mr. Brereton is farmer and captayne; which is a handsome playne and champion countrye of ten myles length, and fyve myles breadeth, without any woode groweinge therin. The sea doth ebbe and flowe rounde that countrye, soe as in full water noe man cann enter therin uppon drye lande, but in one waye which is lesse then two myles in length; and the same countrye for Englishe freehoulders, and good inhabitants is as civile as few places in the Englishe pale.

The next countrye to that, the water of Strangeforde, is Arde Savage his countrye, which hath bene meere Englyshe, both pleasaunte and fayer by the sea; of length about xii myles and iiii myles in breadeth, about which countrye the sea doth ebb and flowe; which countrye is now in effecte for the most parte voyde.

The next countrye to Arde Savage is Clanneboy, wherin is one Moriertaghe Cullenagh, one of the O'Neils, whoe hath the same as captayne of Clanneboy. But he is not able to maintayne the same. He hath viii tall gentlemen to his sonnes, and all they cannot make past xxiiii horsemen. There is another captayne in that countrye of Phelim Backagh his sonnes, tall men, which take parte with Hughe M'Neile Oge, till nowe of late certayne refused him, and went to Knockfergus.

The same Hughe M'Neile Oge, as your grace hath hearde, was prayed by Mr. Marshall, whoe hath made prayes uppon others of those confynes for the same, soe as he is noe looser, but raythen a gayner by his paynes. He sought to have his matter hearde before my lorde deputye and councell, wher-uppon a daye was prefixed for the same till Maye; and nowe lately I repayred to his countrye, to talke further with him, to tracte the tyme till grasse growe; for before then the countryes being so barren of victuall and horsemeate, noe good may be done to destroye him, whereby I perceyed that he was determined as he saythe to meete me, and conclude a further peace. Yett he hearinge of the arryval of certayne Scotts to the Glynnes refused to come to me, contrarye to his wryteinge and sendinge; and went to calle M'Connill, whoe landed with vi or vii^{xx} bowes, as was reported, and thought to bringe them with him to warre uppon his next neighboures; soe as there is noe greate likelye-hoode in him of any honest conformetye: and perceyveing the same in escheweinge his countrye, I appoynted, and planted in the countrye a bande of horsemen and footemen for defence therof against the Scotte yf they doe come; and upon the assemblinge of the councell which shal be within these iiii dayes, God willinge, suche good conclusions shal be taken for the defence of the kinge's majesties subjects in those quarters, and for the revenge uppon the rebells, as yf the Scotte did come, they shall rather repent their prosperitye by their cominge.

This countrye of Clanneboy is in woodes and bogges for the greatest parte wherin lyeth Knockfergus, and soe to the Glynnes, where the Scotte doe inhabitt. As much as this countrye as is neare the sea is a champion countrye, of xx myles in length, and not over iiii myles in breadeth or little more. The same Hughe hath two castles; one called Bealefarst [Belfast] an oulde castle standinge uppon a fourde that leadeth from Arde to Clanneboye, which being well repayred, being nowe broken, would be a good defence betwixt the woodes and Knockfergus.

The other called Castellrioughe [Castlereagh] is fower myles from Bealfarst, and standeth uppon the playne, in the middest of the woodes of the Dufferin; and beinge repayred with an honest companye of horsemen, woulde doe much good for the quyett and staye of the countrye there about; havinge besides a good bande of horsemen in Lecaille contynuallie to resorte and doe servyce abroade upon everye occasion; then such men of small power as Hughe is, must be content to be at commandement; for which purpose, there be devises a making which, by God's grace, with haste shall take effecte.

Next to the Glynnes where the Scotte resorte, M'Quoillynes [M'Quillan's] countrye is, adjoyneinge by the sea, and soe to the Banne; a countrye of woodes and most parte waste, by their owne warres and the exacions of the Scotte, and maye not make past xii horsemen. But they were wonte to make lxxx. When the Scotte doe come, the most parte of Clanneboy, M'Quoillynes and O'Cahan, must be at their comaundemente in findinge them in their countrye, and harde it is to staye the comeinge of them, for there be soe many landinge places betwene the highe lande of the Raithlandes and Knockfergus; and above, the Raithlandes [Rathlin island] standeth soe farr from defence, as it is verye harde to have men to lye there continuallie, beinge so farre from healpe.

The water of Banne cometh to Loghe Eaughnaie [Lough Neagh] which severeth Clanneboy and Tyroon and M'Quoillynes and O'Cahane's countrye.

O'Cahan's countrye [Derry] is uppon the other side of the Banne, and is for the most parte wast. His countrye joyneth by the sea and is not past xx myles in length, and most parte mountayne lande. They obeye the Baron of Dongannon, but what the Scotte take against their will.

The next countrye to that, on the other side of the Banne is Tyroon, where the Earle of Tyroon hath rule; the fayrest and goodliest countrye in Irelande, universallie, and many gentlemen of the O'Neills dwellinge therin. The same countrye is at least lx myles in length, and xxiiii myles in breadeth. In the middest of the countrye standeth Ardnaght, [Armagh] pleasantlye situated, and one of the fayerest and best churches in Ireland; and rounde aboute the same is the bishop's landes;

and thoroughe occasion of the Earl and Countesse his wyffe, they made all that goodlie countrye wast. For wheras the countrye for the most parte within this iii years was inhabited, it was within this xii moneth made wast, thoroughe his makeinge of prayes uppon his sonnes, and they uppon him, soe as there was noe redresse amongst them, but by robbinge of the poore, and takeing of their goodes; whereby the countrye was all waste. Wheruppon my lord deputye appoynted a bande of men, being Englishe souldiers, to lye in Ardnaghe; and left the Baron of Dongannon in commission with other to see for the defence of the countrye and quyett for the poore people, whereby the countrye was kept from such raven as before was used: and the Earle and Countesse brought to Dublyn, there to abyde untill the countrye were brought in better staye. And they perceyveinge the same, and that they could not retourn, they sent to the Irishe men next to the Englishe pale, and soe they did to other Irishemen, that they shoulde not truste to come unto my lorde deputye nor councell. This was reported by part of their owne secrett frindes.

By reason wherof O'Railye, O'Karrol, and divers other, which were wonte to come in withoute feare, refused to come unto us: Wheruppon I went to meete O'Railye to knowe his mynde what he meant. He declared he feared to be kepte under rest as the earle was. And then I toulde him the cause of his retayner was both for the wastinge and destroyenge of his countrye; and for that he said, he woulde never care for the amendinge of the same for his tyme, and yf there were but one ploughe goeinge in the countrye he woulde spende upon the same, with many other undecent wordes for a captayne of a countrye to saye. And O'Railye hearinge the same, saide, that he deserved to be kepte, and soe did he, yf he had done the like. Soe saide O'Karroll, and other of his countrye. And then Shane O'Neill, the earle's youngest soune came to Dongannon, and tooke with him of the earle's treasure viii[c]. lbs. in goulde and silver; besides plate and stuffe, and retayneth the same as yett; whereby it appeareth that he and she were content with the same. For it coulde not bee perceyved that they were greatlye offended for the same. Shane, being at peace till Maye, hearinge of the arryvall of the Scotte, did send to them to give them entertaynmente; and soe he sent to divers other Irishe men to joyne with him, and promysed to devyde his goodes with them, which they, for the most parte, refused to doe; but some did. And I hearinge the same, one Maye daye, went to him with suche a bande of horsemen and Kerne of my frindes, to the number of ccc. men, and did parlye with them, and did perceyve nothinge in him but pryde, stubbornes, and all bent to doe what he coulde to destroye the poore countrye. And departing from me, beinge within iiii. myles to Dongannon, he went and brent the earle's house; and then perceyveinge the fyer, I went after as fast as I coulde, and sent light horsemen before to save the house from breakinge: and uppon my comeinge to the towne, and findinge that a small thinge woulde make the house wardeable, what it wanted I caused to be made upp, and left the baron's of Dongannon's warde in the castle. And havinge espyed where parte of his cattle was, in the middest of his pastures, I tooke from him vii^c. kynes, besides garranes; and they sessed in the countrye cc. galloglas, and joyned all the gentlemen and souldiers of the countrye with the baron; wherewith all they were contented and pleased, and swore them all to the kinge's majestie: soe as I trust in God, Tyron was not soe like to doe well as within a shorte tyme I trust it shalbe: and doe trust, yf a good presedent were there, to see good orders established amongst them, and to putt them in due execution, noe doubte but the countrye woulde prosper.

Next to that countrye is O'Donnell's countrye, named Tyreconell; [Donegall,] a countrey both large, proffitable, and good, that a shipp under sayle maye come to fower of his howses. And bemeane of the warre which was betwene him and his father, the countrye was greatlye ympoverished and wasted, soe as he did banishe his father at last, and tooke the rule himselfe. And nowe the like warre was betwene him and the Callough O'Donnell, so as the warres did in effect waste the whole countrye. And I beinge sent thether to pacifie the same, did bringe them to Dublyn, where order was taken betwene them. But as yett they keepe the kinge's peace, and perfforme orders.

The next countrye to O'Donnell is Ferranaghe, [Fermanagh,] M'Guyer his countrye; a stronge countrye, and

M'Guyer, [Maguire,] that is nowe a younge handsome gentleman, and maye make cc. kerne, and xxiii horsemen. And he, the Calloughe O'Donnell, Tirraghe Lynnaghe O'Neyll, Henri M'Shane, and all the rest be joyned with the baron of Dongannon to serve the kinge's Majestie, and all these be younge men, and of most power in the North, soe as yf the earle and O'Donnell were at suche libertye as ever they were, without those they had noe power. And so by Gode's grace the thinge well followed, as I trust in God it shall, this summer will make a quyett Irelande.

Irishemen be soone brought nowe to obedyence, consideringe that they have no libertye to praye and spoyle, whereby they did maintayne their men, and without that they woulde have but fewe men. And the pollecye that was devysed for the sendinge of the earles of Desmond, Thomonde, Clanricarde, and Tyroon, and the baron of Upper Ossorie, O'Carroll, M'Guyres, and others into England, was a greate helpe of bringinge all those countryes to good order. For none of them that went to England committed harme uppon the kinge's majestie's subjects. The wynninge of the earle of Desmonde, was the wynninge of the rest in Monster with small chardges. The makeinge of O'Brian, earle, made all that countrye obedyent. The makeinge of M'William, earle of Clanricarde, made all his countryes dureinge this tyme quyett and obedient as it is nowe. The makinge of Fitzffadricke baron of Upper Osserye hath made his countrye obedient; and the havinge of their landes by Dublyn, is such a gag uppon them as they will not forfayte the same throughe willfulle follye. And the gentlenes my lorde deputye doth use amonge the people, with wisdome and indifference, doth profitt, and make suer the former civilletye. Soe as presidents in Mounster, Connaghe, and Ulster, by Gode's grace, will make all Irelande, beinge made shire lande, that the lawe may take the right course, and yll men throughe good perswacion brought to take their landes of the kinge's majestie to them and their heyres for ever after. And preachers appoynted amongst them to tell them their dutyes, towardes God and their kinge, that they maye knowe what they ought to doe. And as for preachinge, we have none, which is our lacke, without which the ignorante cann have noe knowledge, which were verye needfull to bee redressed.

No. I.

See Chapter II. page 119, Note 11.

The following is a summary of the names and residences of all the ministers settled in the dioceses of Armagh, Raphoe, Derry, Down and Connor, in the year 1622; hastily extracted, —and therefore, perhaps, not free from inaccuracies,—from the 'Ulster Visitation Book,' preserved among the manuscripts in Trinity College, Dublin. There is no report for the diocese of Dromore. As the old names of parishes are scarcely known beyond their own limits, I have subjoined the nearest principal town, or added such other marks as may enable the general reader to ascertain the locality in which each minister laboured; and, by this means, form an idea of the supplies of preaching distributed over the greater part of the province at that early period. I have also given, in a separate column, a few occasional extracts from the 'Observations' of the several bishops. These were Hampton of Armagh, Knox of Raphoe, Downham of Derry, and Echlin of Down and Connor.

[MSS. Trin. Coll. Dub. E. 3. 6.]

DIOCESE OF ARMAGH.

Parishes.	*Ministers.*	*Observations.*
Armagh.	Robert Maxwell, M.A.	Dean of Armagh. [See introduction, note 105, p. 58.]
	Lewis Ussher, M.A.	Archdeacon, [no parish stated.]
	John Symmons, M.A.	Precentor, [no parish stated.]
Tynan.	William Lord, B.A.	Resident and serveth the cure.
Derrinoose, between Tynan and Keady.	Oliver Gray, B.A.	Resident and serveth the cure.
Criggan, near Newtonhamilton.	Wm. Moore, M.A.	Curate and resident.
Lavileglish, or Loughgall.	William Nicholson, M.A.	Has a curate, a preacher, resident at Killnaman, a chapel of this church.
Kilcluney, near Markethill.	Henry Leslie.	Non-resident,—hath a sufficient curate.

Parishes.	*Ministers.*	*Observations.*
Clonfeckle, or Moy.	Thomas Grant.	Chancellor, resident, and serveth the cure.
Aghaloe, or Caledon.	Ibid.	Non-resident,—hath a curate, Robert Berry.
Dungannon.	John Mony, M. A.	Resident, and serveth the cure.
Donaghmore, or Castle-caulfield.	Ibid.	Non-resident, but hath a curate, Daniel Berkins.
Termonmaguirck, or Six-mile-cross.	Roger Blythe, M. A.	Non-resident, but goeth every third Sunday himself, and keepeth a curate, Daniel Kirk, brought up in the college, and readeth Irish and English.
Ballyclug, near Stewarts-town.	Thomas Bradley, B. A.	Also holds Artrea, adjoining Ballyclug.
Donaghendry, or Stewarts-town.	William Daniel.	
Clonoe and Arboe, between Stewartstown and Lough-Neagh.	Robert Maxwell, M. A.	Non-resident, but keeps a curate, Mr. Glass.
Ballinderry and Tamlaght, or Coagh.	Michael Berket.	
Desertlyn, or Moneymore	Thomas Hartford.	
Lissan, near Moneymore.	Ibid.	Serves every second day; Gregory Sturton readeth Irish.
Magherafelt.	Ezekias Smyth, M. A.	Also holds Kildress.
Desertcreight, between Cookstown and Dungannon.	William Swan, M. A.	Also holds Tullaniskin.
Derriloran, or Cookstown.	Wm. Darragh, M. A.	
Carenteel, or Aughnacloy.	Robert Sutton, M. A.	
Killeshill, between Ballygawley and Dungannon.	Robert Hamilton.	
Errigle-Kerogue, or Ballygawley.	Hugh Carter.	

The remaining parishes of this diocese lie in the province of Leinster, and therefore need not be given here.

DIOCESE OF RAPHOE.

Parishes.	*Ministers.*	*Observations.*
Raphoe.	Archibald Adair, M. A.	An eloquent scholar, and a good preacher of God's word, given to hospitality and good conversation. [Afterwards bishop of Killala, see chap. vii. p. 261. And of Waterford, p. 290.]
Leck, between Letterkenny and Raphoe.	James Scott, M. A.	Church decayed, but repairing.
Killygarvan, or Ramullan.	Alexander Dale, M. A.	Resides at Ramullan, consisting of 100 British indwellers.
Taughboyne, or St. Johnson.	Thomas Bruce, M. A.	Archdeacon, presented by the duke of Lennox. [See chap. v. p. 227.] The ancient church decayed, and the re-edifying thereof is staid by Sir John Stewart, knt., who obtained a warrant at the council-table to build a new church quickly at a town called St. Johnston, laying out L.100 toward the building of the same, and the rest to be at the parishioners' charges.
Stranorlar.	Robert Connell, M. A.	
Drombome, or Ballintrae, between Donegall and Ballyshannon.	John Knox, M. A.	
Inver, or Mount Charles.	Alexander Cunningham, M. A.	
Killomard, between Inver and Donegall.	William Hamilton, M. A.	Resident at Killibegs, but cure served by Andrew Murray.
Clondehorke, or Dunfanaghy.	John Aiken, M. A.	Understandeth the Irish language, and hath an Irish clerk. [See chap. vii. note 46. p. 330.]
Tullaghobiglie, near Dunfanaghy.	Ibid.	Has a converted priest, Owen O'Mulmock, who has L.10 per annum.

Parishes.	*Ministers.*	*Observations.*
Ray, or Manor-Cunningham.	William Paton, M. A.	Assisted in the cure by Thomas Fraizer, M. A. In the parish, is a bawne and house building by William Stewart, Esq. [ancestor of the present Londonderry family,] and the like is done by Sir John Cohoon of Lusse.
Athinish, now joined to Tully, near Ramelton.	Ibid.	Dischargeth the cure by himself, and by Brian O'Downey, a converted priest. [See chap. ii. note 9. p. 117.]
Conwall, or Letterkenny.	Dugald Campbell, M. A.	Understandeth the Irish language, and able to preach therein,—church to be removed to a market-town, called Letterkenny, where there is eighty families of British inhabitants.
Kilmacrenan.	John Hough, M. A.	Resident, and serveth the cure.
Meavagh, or Carrigart.	Ibid.	Cure discharged partly by himself, and partly by Tirlagh O'Kelly, a reading minister both in English and Irish.
Tullaghfernan, or Ramelton.	Wm. Connyngham, M. A.	Resident and serveth the cure. [See chap. ii. note 9. p. 117.]
Gartan, beside Kilmacrenan.	Ibid.	Assisted in this cure by a reading minister in English and Irish, Mr. John Ross.
Clondevadocke, or Fannet.	Robert Whyte, M. A.	Has L.10 per annum from the incumbent, Thomas Knox, B.D. who is non-resident; [probably the bishop's son and his successor in the bishoprick of the Isles in Scotland] he is assisted in the cure by Owen O'Downey, who readeth the common-prayer book in Irish, and is clerk of the said parish.
Aghanunshen, between Letterkenny and Ramelton.	Claud Knox, M. A.	Dischargeth the cure by himself and Brian O'Downey, a converted Irish priest: [probably the same who assisted Mr. Paton in the adjoining parish of Aughnish.]
Inniskeel, north of Killibegs.	Ibid.	Serveth the cure to all the Irish inhabitants by Owen Congall, a very good minister, reading in the English and Irish languages—the ancient church is in an island, but ought to be transported to Killdownie, where there is already a chapel of ease.

DIOCESE OF DERRY.

Parishes.	*Ministers.*	*Observations.*
Derry.	Henry Tutton, M. A.	Dean.
Moville.	Robert Kean, M. A.	Also dischargeth the cure of Coldaugh [Culdaff] as occasion is offered, there being one English family within the parish.
Clonca, or Malin.	Edward Boucker.	An honest man, but no licensed preacher; fit, notwithstanding, to catechise and to speak and read Irish, and sufficient for a parish wholly consisting of Irish—church fallen down and altogether decayed.
Clonmany, in Ennishowen.	John Sterne, M. A.	
Carndonagh in Ennishowen.	Patrick M'Tally.	An Irishman of mean gifts, having a little Latin and no English; but sufficient for a parish consisting wholly of Irish.
Disertegney, north of Buncrana.	Ibid.	Assisted by an Irish clerk, the whole parish consisting of Irish recusants.
Donagheady, between Derry and Strabane.	Robert Semple, M. A.	
Leckpatrick, and Camos, or Strabane.	Henry Noble, M. A.	The parish of Camos being small, and the town of Strabane built in the confines thereof, I united, in the former incumbent's time, these two parishes, and think them fit to be united; the rather because there is a fair church begun by the late earl of Abercorn, intended to serve these two contiguous parishes.
Clonroy, or Lifford.	Thomas Turpin.	The old church is ruined, but instead thereof, a fair new church is to be built in the town of Lifford, the foundation whereof is already laid by the executors of Sir Richard Hansard, Knt.
Donoughmore, or Castlefin.	Ibid.	Resides in the town of Lifford, but maintains a curate here.
Aghadocy.	Ibid.	Non-resident, but keeps here a curate, who is M. A.
Longfield, or Drumquin.	James Baxter, M. A.	Also holds Termonomungan, near Castle-derg.
Drumra, or Omagh.	Richard Walker, M. A.	

Parishes.	*Ministers.*	*Observations.*
Cappagh, near Omagh.	Gervais Walker, M.A.	Resides in a house given by Sir John Drummond, Knt.—holds also Badony or Gortin, consisting wholly of Irish recusants.
Drumachose, or Newtonlimavady.	Luke Astry, M.A.	The church is ruinated—the meeting of the parish is at a house in Newton, for which they pay a yearly rent of L.1, 6s. 8d.—he also holds Tamlaghfinlagan or Ballykelly, by dispensation.
Balteagh, between Newtonlimavady and Dungiven.	Arch. Brooke, M.A.	Also holds Bovevagh, beside Dungiven.
Banagher, near Dungiven.	Edward Harrison, B.D.	The church of this parish is at Dungiven—he also holds Comber by dispensation.
Tamlaghard, or Magilligan.	George Major, M.A.	
Aughanloo, near Newtonlimavady.	Ibid.	On the Haberdashers' property, where he has a curate.
Faughanvale and Glendermot, both near Derry.		Served by two curates, the one a preacher, the other a reader.
Dunbo, near Coleraine.	John Richardson, D.D.	Resident and serveth the cure—also holds Ardstraw or Newtonstewart. [Archdeacon of Derry, and afterwards bishop of Ardagh.]
Macosquin, between Coleraine and Newtonlimavady.	James Osborne, M.A.	Resident and serves.
Killowen, adjoining Coleraine.	Robert Baker.	Dwells within half a mile of the church—an ancient grave man, who hath preached heretofore, but now, by reason of his great age, sparely.
Errigal, or Garvagh.	Ibid.	Cure for the most part discharged by an Irish scholar, the whole parish almost consisting of Irish recusants.
Desertoghill, between Kilrea and Garvagh.	John Craigie.	An honest man, but no preacher nor graduate.

Parishes.	*Ministers.*	*Observations.*
Ballyscullin, near Castle-dawson.	Thomas Tonis.	A preacher, but no graduate—resident and serveth the cure himself.
Maghera.	Ibid.	Not resident—but repaireth hither every other Sunday—in his absence the clerk taketh upon him to serve the cure.
Tamlaght-O'Creilly, near Port-glenone.	Oliver Mather.	Preacher,—resides and serves.
Killelagh, near Maghera.	Ibid.	Not resident—but sometimes (as once in three weeks) he resorteth to the church, where no man cometh at him, the whole parish consisting of Irish recusants.
Kilrea.	Robert Hogg, M. A.	An ancient master of arts—is resident and serves the cure—the church repaired by the Mercers.
Desertmartin.	Ibid.	When the incumbent is absent, the cure is served by a curate.
Termoneeny, near Tober-more.	Wm. M'Teggart.	Late, by the Pope's grant, dean of Derry; but now being conformable to the reformed religion,
Kilcronaghan, or Tober-more.	Ibid.	was (by the appointment of the last lord deputy) preferred to this small parish, and that of Kilcronaghan.

DIOCESE OF DOWN AND CONNOR.

Bangor.	John Gibson, M. A.	Dean—resident and serveth the cure, and maintained by a stipend from Sir James Hamilton—church repaired. [See page 102, and note 36, ch. i.]
Downpatrick.	John Watson, M. A.	Curate to the incumbent, John Gibson, and resident—one church repaired, but not the cathedral.
Ballydrean, or Tullnakill, near Comber.	John Christian, M. A.	Archdeacon—serves the cure and resideth—church a ruin.
Kileleif, near Strangford.	John Curlet.	Curate to the incumbent, John Christian, and resident—church ruinous.
Drumbo, between Belfast and Lisburn.	Wm. Forbes, M. A.	Curate of this parish, and also of Drumbeg, beside Lisburn—church at Drumbeg repaired—the other ruinous.

Parishes.	*Ministers.*	*Observations.*
Philipstown, or Portafer-ry.	Malcome Hamilton, M. A.	Chancellor—church ruinous. [Made archbishop of Cashel in 1623, and continued to hold this parish in commendam. Ware's Bishops.]
Rathmullan, near Kil-lough.	John Mitchelhill, M. A.	Also supplies Ardquin, being maintained in the bishop's [Echlin] house—church ruinous.
St. Andrews, or Kirkcub-bin.	Arthur Moneypenny, M. A.	Prebend of St. Andrews—no church.
Killileagh.	John Boyle, M. A.	Resident—church ruinous. [See chap. v. p. 249.]
Talpeston, or Talbots-town. [*I have not been able to ascertain the locality of this parish.*]	George Porter, M. A.	Curate and resident—maintained by a stipend from Sir James Hamilton—the prebend of Talpeston is vacant, Pat. Hamilton being deprived by the lord primate for non-residence—church repaired.
Ballee, near Downpa-trick.	Richard Hackett, M. A.	Incumbent—resident and serveth the cure.
Donaghadee.	George Creighton, M. A.	Curate to the incumbent, Rd. Hackett—maintained by a stipend from Sir Hugh Montgomery—church repaired.
Kilmore, near Ballyna-hinch.	Patrick Savage.	Hath lately accepted this place; he is one of the college of Dublin, and now resident—the parishioners natives—the church ruined.
Glenavy.	John Wilkinson, M. A.	Also serveth the cures of Magheragell, and of Anagalldanagh, [Aghagallan ?] where he resides,—all the churches ruinous.
Ballinderry.	Thomas Peers, M A.	Serveth the cure—also those of Magheramisk and Derriaghy—all the churches ruinous.
Albavado, alias Belfast.	Robert Morley, M. A.	Incumbent—resident and serveth the cure—church built from the ground, and repaired.
Coole, or Carnmoney, between Belfast and Carrickfer-gus.	James Glendinning, M. A.	Incumbent—resident and serveth the cure—church a ruin. [See chap. i. p. 100.]

Parishes.	*Ministers.*	*Observations.*
Muckamore, between Antrim and Templepatrick.	Henry Lesley, M.A.	Serveth the cure of Emgall, part of Killead, at Muckamore, whither the people resort, not being able to maintain a curate—also serves the cures of six small adjoining parishes, including Crumlin and Killead—church a ruin.
Cregyvad and Holywood.	Robert Cunningham, M.A.	Resident at Holywood—serveth these cures and maintained by a stipend from Sir James Hamilton—church repaired in part.
Dundonald.	John Letham, M.A.	Resident—serveth the cure and maintained by a stipend from Sir James Hamilton—church ruined.
Newtonards.	Robert Montgomery. M.A.	Resident and serveth the cure—church repaired.
Comber.	James Fresall.	Resident and serveth the cure—church repaired in part.
Carrickfergus.	Robert Openshaw.	Resident and serveth the cure.
Templecorran, or Ballycarry; also called Broadisland.	Edward Brice, M.A.	Serveth the cures of Templecorran and Kilroot—church at Kilroot decayed—that at Ballycarry has the walls newly erected, but not roofed. [See chap. i. p. 98. And chap. iv. p. 201, note 17.]
Inver, or Larne.	Hugh Ross, M.A.	Serveth this cure, and that at Glynn, and is maintained by a stipend from Sir Moses Hill, [ancestor of the Downshire family.]—the churches both at Larne and the Glynn, repaired in part.
Rashee, near Ballyclare.	Donnell O'Murray.	Prebendary of Cairncastle—serveth the cure here—church decayed.
Kilbride and Donegore, between Antrim and Ballyclare.	John Sterling, M.A.	Resident, and serveth the cure—also serveth the cure at Ballynure—church decayed.
Ballymartin, or Templepatrick.	Christopher Tracy, M.A.	Resident and serveth the cure—church ruinous.
Antrim.	John Ridge, M.A.	Resident and serveth the cure—church and walls newly erected. [See chap. i. p. 100.]
Connor.	Henry Leslie.	Vicar here, but no curate—church decayed.
Drumaul, or Randals town.	Hugh M'Lerrenan.	Serveth the cure—also that of Dunean or Toome—both churches decayed.

Parishes.	*Ministers.*	*Observations.*
Aboghill.	Gavin Gray, M.A.	Resident and serveth the cure —church decayed.
Rasharkin.	Robert Dunbar, M. A.	Resident and serveth the cure—church decayed. Also serveth the cures of Finvoy and Ballymena.
Ballymoney.	William Todd.	Resident here and serveth the cure—church walls decayed and fallen to the ground.
Coleraine.	William Vincent, M.A.	Resident and serveth the cure —church standeth well slated and well repaired.
Milton, or Ballywillan.	Andrew Thompson, M.A.	Resident and serveth the cure —church decayed. Also serveth two other cures.
Derrykeichan, or Dervock.	William Wallace, M.A.	Resident and serveth the cure —also that of Dunluce—both churches ruinous.
Billey, or Bushmills.	Andrew Moneypenny.	Resident and serveth the cure —church walls stand with an old roof—also serveth the cure of Ardmoy—church unrepaired.
Ramoan, or Ballycastle.	Patrick Felles, M.A.	Resident and serveth the cure —also two other cures—churches decayed.
Layde or Cushendall.	Samuel Todd.	Resident and serveth the cure —church ruinous.
Teckmacrevan or Glenarm.	William Fenton, M.A.	Resident and serveth the cure —church decayed—also that of Cairncastle, [between Glenarm and Larne] where is no church, but the walls fallen down to the ground; there is a house builded in the churchyard at the charge of the parish, where they assemble together.

No. II.

See Chapter iv. page 194, note 15.

The following narrative of the public discussion at Belfast, between bishop Leslie and the presbyterian ministers, was circulated in manuscript, shortly after the meeting. The bishop impeached its accuracy, so far as he was concerned; and felt so annoyed by its getting abroad, that when he printed his sermon on the occasion, he appended to it a lengthened 'Answer' to the objections, urged at this Conference, against kneeling at the communion. See chap. iv. note 11. p. 188. How far the account which was circulated was deemed inaccurate, the bishop does not condescend to state. He contents himself with merely declaiming, in a very coarse and vulgar strain, against it, as "falsely traducing all his proceedings;" and apologizes for the "abject style" of his Answer by saying, "the very reading of that libell hath infected my pen with barbarisme." It is rather singular that an account of this 'Conference' was never before published. The Rev. Dr. Campbell of Armagh, the learned and eloquent vindicator of the presbyterians of Ireland, appears to have possessed a copy of it. See his "Examination of the bishop of Cloyne's Defence of his Principles," &c. Belfast, 1788. Note at p. 170. This was the only intimation I had of a copy being extant, until I discovered several in the Advocates' Library, Edinburgh, from a careful collation of which the following is printed.

[Wod. MSS. Bib. Jur. Edin. Rob. iii. 2. 2. No. 3.]

Collated with Rob. iii. 3. 1. No. 22, and Rob. iii. 3. 3. No. 8.

Conference between the bishop of Down, Mr. Robert Cunningham and other Scots ministers, August 11, 1636.

August 10, 1636. The bishop of Down taught on Matth. xviii. 17, in the afternoon; and after the calling of the names, the bishop called Mr. Brice, Mr. Ridge, Mr. Cunningham, Mr. Colwart, Mr. Hamilton, and declared, that whereas he had taken pains with them at the last visitation in private, and the report had gone, that the victory had passed on their side, therefore he would never any more talk with them in private. But if they on the country's charges, would travel to any university in Europe, he would travel on his own charges, and there would reason the points contraverted, and submit to their judgment. 'But if you,' says he, 'who are many, and I but alone, will reason before this assembly to-morrow by two o'clock, I hope they are judicious, and will consider of our reasoning;' to which last offer they did consent.

He also challenged Mr. Cunningham, that when he gave the communion at Holywood, he adjured the people never to take the communion kneeling; for which if he should prosecute, he said it would bring Mr. Cunningham to greater trouble than he would be able to bring him off again. But Mr. Cunningham declared upon his honesty, that he had not done so.

August 11, 1636. Being come to church, the bishop called Mr. Brice, Mr. Ridge, Mr. Cunningham, Mr. Hamilton, Mr. Colwart, to know if they would subscribe the first four canons, or if they were ready to lay open their objections, and he would answer in behalf of the church, to defend all that was commanded.

Ridge: Seeing he had done them that favour to offer them an hearing, they were ready to lay open their doubts; and that there might be no confusion, the company had entrusted to Mr. Hamilton to lay open their minds, to whom they prayed the bishop to give audience with patience.

The bishop says, It is well, Mr. Hamilton, what have you to say?

Mr. Hamilton answers, I bless the God of heaven who put in your mind and mouth, both in your sermon, and also in your public speech yesterday, to declare that it ought to be free, and it should be free to us modestly to propone our doubts against such things as are enjoined us to be subscribed, whereby I hope it shall be manifest that hitherto we have refrained to do as we are directed, not out of contention and stubbornness, but upon reasons prevailing with our judgments, which here I will unfold; providing (whereof we doubt not,) that this present liberty be not to our prejudice in time to come.

Bish. It shall not.

Ham. Further, lest we wander from the point, I desire and am content that we hold the rules of dispute and formal reasoning in objecting and answering.

Bish. I am content.

Ham. I conceive the case stands thus: If we can subscribe the first four canons, we are to enjoy our ministry, but if we do not subscribe them all, we are to be silenced.

Bish. So it is.

Ham. That which a man, in his own judgment, for sound reason disallows, he cannot subscribe unto; divers things contained within the compass of the first four canons, we disallow of in our judgments for sound reasons: ergo, &c.

Bish. Prove your minor.

Ham. My first argument is this: known corruptions in translation of the holy Scripture we disallow in judgment; but in some part of that, to wit, the book of common-prayer, which we are to subscribe, are divers known corrupt translations of the holy Scripture; therefore we justly disallow them.

Bish. First, you are not bound to a corrupt translation. Secondly, I deny that there is any material corruption in the translation of such Scriptures as are contained in the book of common-prayer.

Ham. I prove by subscription to the book of common-prayer, I am tied to the corrupt translation; for it is so in the third canon, 'that form of divine service, which is contained in the book of common-prayer, and no other shall be used.'

Bish. Well, it is so said in the third canon.

Ham. Now, I prove that there is some material corruption in the translation of the Scriptures that is contained in the book of common-prayer, thus: Where there is contradiction to true Scriptures, additions, detractions, altering of the same, and making nonsense of true Scriptures, there is corrupt translation; but so it is in the book of common-prayer: ergo, &c.

Bish. You draw to a dispute before this audience, which the people cannot understand, leading me to reason concerning the Hebrew language. But to save you a labour, I am content it bear your subscription, that whereas there are some corrupt translations in the book of common-prayer, it shall be free for you to read the best translation that ye can find in your church.

Ham. In so far we are satisfied, and accept of the offer.

Bish. You shall have it.

Ham. The second reason whereby I declare our just reasons in disallowing subscription, is this: Where apocrypha Scriptures containing untruths, are appointed to be read to God's people, we justly disallow; so it is in the book of common-prayer: ergo, &c.

Bish. Prove your minor.

Ham. Upon the fourth day of October, the twelfth chapter of Tobit is to be read, which in the ninth and fifteenth verses, contains errors

Bish. I never counted that book Tobit worthy the reading. Can ye say there are any further errors in the book of Apocrypha which is to be read?

Ham. Yea; upon the tenth day of October, the ninth chapter of Judith is to be read, which in the second, tenth, and fifteenth verses, contains errors. So also upon the seventh day of November, the twenty-fourth chapter of Ecclesiasticus is to be read, which in the fourth verse, contains an error.

Bish. Ye shall be free to read other Scriptures and to omit these, as it is usual with us on varieties of occasions to change one or both the readings, as at a visitation, at a burial, &c.

Ham. But our subscription is an obligation standing upon record for all ages to come. An hundred years hence, when our subscriptions shall be seen and compared with the thing subscribed unto, then these errors which we discover, may be laid on our shoulders, whereas your connivance, that we read it not, will be forgotten.

Bish. It shall be inserted in your subscriptions, that ye are free from all such chapters in the Apocrypha as contain untruths and errors.

Ham. My third argument against subscription is this: That which commands Apocrypha by name of holy Scriptures, and with this narration, that that which is read is most edifying, and may be less spared, whereas much canonical Scripture is spared; that, I say, is not to be subscribed unto; but such is the book of common prayer: ergo, &c.

Bish. When Apocrypha is called Scripture, it is taken in a large sense.

Ham. But by name of holy Scripture, is meant particularly canonical; yet mine exception is not only for that it is called Scripture, or holy Scripture, but farther, for that it is read and counted more edifying, and less fit to be spared than that which is not read, albeit much of it be canonical.

Bish. It shall be insert in your subscription that ye shall be free from reading all Apocrypha.

Ham. My fourth argument is, that form of divine service, (which and no other is to be used,) which excludes the reading of much canonical Scripture, is not to be subscribed unto; but the book of common-prayer is such a form which is to be used and no other, and directs such reading, when much canonical Scripture is left unread, and especially the book of Revelation which discovers antichrist, whom we might have better known, if the Revelation had been read five times every year, as other parts of the New Testament, since the Reformation: therefore the book of common-prayer is not to be subscribed unto.

Bish. When ye are directed to use no other form of divine service than that which is contained in the book of common-prayer, the meaning is, that ye are not to use any other form of liturgy.

Ham. We consent to use no other liturgy; but we say we cannot follow this direction, to forbear the two books of Chronicles, Solomon's Song and the Revelation.

Bish. The book doth not forbid you to read these Scriptures.

Ham. It commands not the reading of them, and the third canon, establishing the book, forbids any other form of serving, than is established in the book.

Bish. Though ye be not commanded to read these books, yet ye may preach upon them as much as ye will; and to speak truly, the book of Revelation is so hard, that not many people will understand it the better, though they hear it read.

Ham. Yet the Holy Ghost saith, Rev. i. 3. 'Blessed is he that readeth.'

Bish. With my blessing, both read it and preach upon it, all the days of your life. Are ye now satisfied?

Ham. My fifth argument is, that which avoucheth uncertainties for truths, and even in prayer to God, is not to be subscribed unto.

Bish. Prove your minor.

Ham. It says in the Collect, on Christmas day, 'O God, that gave thy Son this day to be born, &c.' Now, it is uncertain that Christ was born upon the twenty-fifth day of December; therefore it avoucheth uncertainties for certainty.

Bish. I confess it is uncertain when Christ was born, some avouching the twenty-fifth day of September, some the fifth day of December, some the twenty-fifth day of March, though it be most usually attributed to the twenty-fifth day of December; yet, when it is said, 'this day,' the meaning is, this representative day which the church hath set apart to remember Christ's birth.

Ham. It were better not to observe a day which hath been superstitiously doted upon for many ages, yea, regarded more than God's Sabbath, than to say expressly in our book, 'this day was Christ born.'

Bish. Ye are not to teach the church what is better to do than is appointed.

Ham. I press the apostle's words, Gal. iv. 10. 'ye observe days and months, times and years, I am afraid lest I have laboured amongst you in vain.'

Then spake one Mr. William Fitzgerald, a clergyman of wealth, not of his diocese, 'I beseech your lordship, ask Mr. Hamilton, how he expounds these words of the second psalm—'thou art my son, to-day I have begotten thee.'

Ham. If any man appoint the second psalm to be read only upon the twenty-fifth day of December and no other day, I would say that there is superstition to press that psalm at such a time, to countenance that uncertain day for a certain.

Ham. My sixth argument is, that which avoucheth impossibilities, is not to be subscribed unto: but so doth the book; ergo, &c.

Bish. Prove your minor.

Ham. It avoucheth that Christ was born seven days together, as appears by the preface appointed for Christmas holidays; and that the Holy Ghost descended seven days together, as appears by the Collect upon Whitsundays and two days following; and by a general rule in the book, that the Collect of every Sabbath shall be read the whole week thereafter. Therefore it avoucheth impossibilities; for it is impossible that Christ should be born seven days together, and the Holy Ghost descended only one day, to wit, the day of Pentecost. Acts ii. 1.

Bish. This last objection of yours clears the answer to the last, to wit, that the church means a day for representation, and not to tie the history to a certain day. And, in a word, 'this day,' signifies generally an indefinite time whereof the church is then remembering.

Ham. This exposition is unusual.

Bish. There are some other matters which ye keep off, that I expected you would insist upon.

Ham. I come even now unto it. I argue thus, that book that presses constitutions that are not able to abide the trial of the rules of God's word, is not to be subscribed unto; the book of common-prayer presses some constitutions that are not able to abide the trial of the rules of God's word; ergo, &c.

Bish. Prove your minor.

Ham. That which makes us, without a warrant, to serve our God as idolaters serve their gods, cannot abide the trial of the rule of God's word, to wit, Deut. xii. 4, 30, 31. The book of common-prayer presses some constitutions which make us without any warrant to serve our God, as idolaters serve their gods; ergo, &c.

Bish. Prove your minor.

Ham. That which presses a constitution to kneel before the elements at the Sacrament, or to kneel at the receiving of the Sacrament, makes us, without a warrant, to serve our God as idolaters serve their god: the book of common prayer makes us to kneel before the elements at the Sacrament, or at the receiving of the Sacrament; ergo, &c.

Bish. I deny your minor.

Ham. The papists kneel before the elements in serving their breaden God in the Sacrament; and we, kneeling before the elements, serve our God; therefore we serve our God as idolaters serve their god.

Bish. That cannot be a right syllogism.

Ham. To kneel before the elements in receiving of the Sacrament, is to worship our God unwarrantably, as popish idolaters worship their god: ergo, to press kneeling before the elements, is to cause us to worship our God, as idolaters worship their god unwarrantably.

Bish. I deny, though we kneel, that we worship God as the papists do, for they worship the bread as transubstantiated, and become God; we do not so.

Ham. Mark, I beseech you, I do not say we worship their

God, which we would do, if we imagined the transubstantiation of the bread; but I say, we worship our God, as they worship their god, which is contrary to Deut. xii. 4, 31, 'ye shall not do so to the Lord your God.'

Bish. I deny kneeling before the bread to be any worshipping, it is but accessory to worship;—no, it is no more worship than the kneeling before my bed to pray.

Ham. This is the difference; when one doth kneel before the bed, he doth it not in reverence to the bed, and he kneels before that wherewith idolatry hath never been committed. But when we kneel before the elements, we do it reverence of the mysteries, and before that wherewith idolatry hath been committed.

Bish. What is this to the purpose? Take away the abuse and keep the use.

Ham. In things ordained by God, it ought to be so; but not in things ordained by men, and abused to idolatry, against which I reason thus: That which provokes God to jealousy should be avoided; kneeling before the elements provokes God to jealousy; ergo, &c.

Bish. God is a Spirit, and discerns the thoughts of the heart, which if they be free from idolatry, he is not jealous of the outward behaviour.

Ham. Yet by this argument he is pleased to deter us from outward appearance of idolatry, as in the second command, from making and bowing down to images, and in 1 Cor. x. 22, from eating things sacrificed to idols by them who knew the lawfulness and not the expediency of it, as appears there, verse 23.

Bish. I will prove that the kneeling at the receiving of the Sacrament is not evil: We are commanded to kneel before the Lord our maker.

Ham. I hope the bread in the Sacrament is not the Lord our maker.

Bish. Well, Sir, ye take me too short, ye are too nimble with me. But this I say, I may kneel when, in a special manner, I appear before the Lord, as I do in receiving the Sacrament.

Ham. That is not always necessary, as in hearing of the word; but it is more specially to be avoided when there is an idolizable object before us, as the bread in the Sacrament. For these six hundred years past, it hath been committed idolatry with.

Bish. There is nothing in the world but is idolizable, if you term it so, the sun, moon, stars and things necessary, as well as bread in the Sacrament.

Ham. Therefore I argue thus, where an holy or necessary thing is, or hath been committed idolatry with, seeing the necessary holy thing cannot be removed, the appearance of idolatry with it, or worship towards it, ought to be removed and avoided.

Bish. I answer, it is not necessary that always the appearance of worship be removed, unless there be worship in effect. Now, in our kneeling, there is no worshipping.

Ham. I prove there is worshipping in kneeling. Where both soul and body worship, there is worshipping; but in kneeling, both soul and body do worship; ergo, in kneeling there is worshipping.

Bish. The worship which is altogether inward, is to be directed to God and not unto the elements; and for the outward gesture of the body, it is no worship at all.

Ham. By alleging that worship is directed to God and not to the elements, it would seem to turn aside the imputation of idolatry, but not of will-worshipping. For we may possibly worship God in an unwarrantable worship, which is called will-worship, Col. ii. 23, as well as false worship with an idol. But whereas you said, that the outward gesture is no worship, I prove it thus:—If God takes notice of an honest worshipper from a false worshipper, and an idolater in the outward behaviour, then there is worship in the outward behaviour. But God takes notice of an honest worshipper from an idolater, as in that passage, Rom. xi. 4, 'I have reserved to myself 7000 that have not bowed the knee to Baal;' therefore there is worship in the outward behaviour.

At this time the lord Claneboy, the lord Chichester, and the bishop of Derry, with captain Chichester and others, came into the church. And it is to be remembered that in all the words which were spoken by the bishop of Derry, the opponent, to wit, Mr. Hamilton, either answered not at all, as when the words were rather bitter than to the purpose: or if the bishop of Derry's words seemed to be to the purpose, and required an answer, then the opponent still directed his speech to the bishop of Down who was before him, and not to the bishop of Derry, who was behind his back.

Bish. For answer to your last argument, I say, however God take notice of a false worshipper, by bowing of the knee to Baal, yet that proves not that bowing of the knee is worship, but only a sign of worship; and the speech is a metonomy of the sign for the thing signified.

Ham. To prove that there is an outward worship, as well as an inward; and that, both in true and false worship, I reason thus:—All appearance of evil is to be avoided: In kneeling before the elements in the Sacrament, there is an appearance of evil, for even now ye called it a sign of worship; therefore kneeling is to be avoided.

Bish. But I deny your minor.

Ham. It is the appearance of will-worship and bread-worship; therefore it is the appearance of evil.

Bish. I deny that it is the appearance of any of them.

Ham. Where the body goes as far as it can go, if it were to commit bread-worship, there is the appearance of bread-worship: In kneeling before the elements, the body goes as far as it can go if it would commit bread-worship; ergo, &c.

Bishop of Derry. My lord of Down, in good faith I commend your charity, but not your wisdom, in suffering such a prattling Jack to talk so openly against the orders of the church. My lord, it is more that ye can justify yourself in to the state.

Bish. My lord, I was willing to give them open satisfaction to their doubts. But for answer to your last words, Mr. Hamilton, you speak of the appearance of evil; every man may allege appearance of evil in the best action of the world.

Ham. I distinguish the appearance of evil; the one is imaginary which lies only in the imagination of a man, and this I confess may be fantastical; the other is real, when the thing is as like evil as can be; and this last, the apostle, 1 Thess. v. 22, doth forbid. And of this sort, kneeling before the elements in the communion is. For, as I said, the outward behaviour is as like the idolatrous kneeling as can be, so that none can tell whether the man worship God or the bread. Yea, I suppose that a papist newly converted, and come to church not having his understanding cleared from his old error, must receive the Sacrament at the altar, as all are bound by the book to do, hath he not opportunity left him to commit idolatry, as he did before?

Bishop of Derry. Worship thou the devil, if thou wilt.

Bish. Though the kneeler, in receiving of the elements, be as far with his body as any idolater may be, yet this is not worshipping, seeing the intention of worshipping is not present.

Ham. Who can tell when the intention of worship is present, or will come or does come, to make a worship; seeing the heart quickly alters; and howsoever I say the intention be not present, yet it is an outward appearance of bread-worship or will-worship.

Bishop of Derry. It were more reason and more fit this fellow were whipped, than reasoned with.

Ham. I propose another argument against kneeling. Where kneeling before the elements is pressed, and idolatrous kneeling with the elements is not suppressed, that is a sin. But even now in this kingdom, kneeling is pressed, and idolatrous kneeling not suppressed; therefore to press kneeling in this kingdom before the elements, is a sin.

Bish. I deny your minor.

Ham. To tempt God is a sin: to press kneeling before the elements, and not to suppress idolatrous kneeling is a tempting of God; ergo, &c.

Bish. Prove it to be a tempting of God.

Ham. It is as much in effect as to say, kneel idolatrously and nothing shall be done to you; but, if ye kneel not at all, ye shall be sure to be troubled.

Bish. Frame an answer, and I shall answer it.

Ham. Where the commands of God are made of none effect by your tradition, God is tempted; when kneeling before the elements is pressed, and idolatrous kneeling not suppressed, the commandment of God is made of none effect by men's traditions; therefore therein God is tempted.

Bish. I deny your minor.

Ham. When the commandments of God are broken, and no punishment inflicted on the breakers of them, while men's traditions are urged; there the commandments of God are made of none effect by men's traditions. But when kneeling before the elements is pressed, and idolatrous kneeling not suppressed, God's commandments are broken, and no punishment inflicted upon the breakers of them, while men's traditions are urged: Ergo, when kneeling before the elements is pressed, and idolatrous kneeling not suppressed, the commandments of God are made of none effect by men's traditions.

Bish. Your major is so long, I cannot repeat it.

Bishop of Derry. That fellow talks clear nonsense.

Ham. If I talk clear non-sense, then did Christ talk nonsense: but that is absurd; ergo.

Bishop of Derry. There is sweet reasoning; because Christ did not talk nonsense, therefore he cannot talk nonsense.

Ham. I prove Christ speaking to the same sense and purpose as I do now, in the 15th chapter of Matthew. The Pharisees there questioning Christ's disciples for not washing before meat according to the tradition of the elders, our Saviour answered, 'why do ye make the commandments of God of none effect by men's traditions;' and he proves it, because the fifth commandment of honouring thy father and mother was broken, which they repressed not. One might wonder what affinity hath the not washing of hands with that commandment, 'honour thy father and thy mother,' &c. and how our Lord's answer could be to a good purpose. But seeing it is certain, that our good Lord spoke to the purpose, this lesson rises out of it, that where God's commandments are broken, and no punishment inflicted, therefore then men's traditions are preposterously urged in God's worship.

Bishop of Derry. Get him helebore to purge his brain from madness.

Bish. Mr. Hamilton, if it were in my power to suppress idolatry, then your reason would strike at me if I did not suppress it.

Ham. If it is not in your power to suppress it, yet it is in your power not to press kneeling; at the least, that scripture demands it of you.

Bish. I am commanded by the magistrate to execute his laws ecclesiastical, according to mine office; and so to take order with you, if ye practise not kneeling.

Ham. Therefore I do the more freely speak to you, who get access to his majesty, and are heard oftener before the estates of the kingdom than men of our mean estate, that you may plainly advertise his majesty and the estates, that it is not according to Christ's mind to press kneeling before the elements, when idolatrous kneeling is not suppressed.

Bish. But can you find in your heart to leave your calling, and to separate from the communion of the church, because that is not amended, which neither lieth in your power nor in mine to amend. For I confess, 'si res staret integra,' it would be another matter than now it stands.

Ham. The question is not, that if I should leave my calling, but if, when ye are to put me from my calling, I should give this testimony against the pressing of kneeling at this time, to the end, that your bearing it into your memory unto a more seasonable time, should plainly advertise his majesty and the estates thereof.

Bishop of Derry. I would you should know that the heaviness of our church and state hangeth not upon the atlas shoulders of such bullrushes as you are.

Ham. Every watchman is bound, according to his power, and as he hath opportunity, to advertise of any evil that he seeth arising in the church or commonwealth, as I do at this time.

Bishop of Derry. Let the fellow sit down, and let another that can reason, stand up and argue.

Ham. Where Christ's example, which would prevent all idolatry, is avoided, and that course is practised which hath been, now is, and hereafter may be, idolatry; that is unlawful. But in kneeling at the receiving of the communion, Christ's example is avoided, which would prevent all idolatry; and that course which was, is, and may be idolatry, is practised: Therefore it is unlawful.

Bish. I have many things to deny in your minor: 1st, That Christ's example is avoided. 2d, Albeit, I should grant that sitting were Christ's example, and were practised, (I deny,) that all idolatry would be prevented; for a man may commit idolatry as well sitting as kneeling. 3d, I deny that there can be idolatry in kneeling, if a man should teach his people the sound doctrine which we hold against transubstantiation.

Ham. First, I prove that Christ's example is avoided. Table-entertainment is avoided; but Christ's example allows table-entertainment: therefore Christ's example is avoided.

Bish. By table-entertainment you mean sitting, which I deny Christ to have used.

Ham. I mean indeed table-gesture, which it is clear Christ used.

Bish. Though I grant that Christ sat at the table at the time of the passover, yet he arose from supper, and did wash his disciples' feet, and you cannot prove that ever he sat, that night, down again.

Ham. Yea, I prove it out of John xiii. 12. 'And after he had washed his disciples' feet, he sat down again.'

Bish. It may be it was a long time after that Christ gave the supper. And say, that he had given it sitting, it does not bind us any more to give it sitting, than to give it any more after supper, and in an upper room.

Ham. That was occasional, because of the passover that was joined with it, and so for that time was necessitated. But the Lord might easily, within that chamber, have changed sitting into kneeling, if he so had thought it expedient, which he did not; and that, as I said, to prevent all idolatry which hath these six hundred years reigned in Christendom.

Bish. That is it which I denied in the second place, that sitting prevents idolatry. For a man may commit idolatry as well sitting as kneeling.

Ham. The heart of man may commit idolatry as well sitting as kneeling. But a man cannot commit bodily idolatry sitting, which he may do kneeling.

Bish. Bodily idolatry is a thing unheard of.

Ham. Is it unheard of that men exercise idolatry with their bodies, as in that passage which I named, of the seven thousand that had not bowed the knee to Baal? Yea, a magistrate or a minister can do no more, for his part, when he would suppress idolatry, but curb the outward expressions of it. He that would draw men to idolatry, can seek no further than to see the body acting the outward expressions of idolatry. For the heart, no man can know whether it be committing idolatry or not, but by the outward acts.

Bish. Where there is no intention of idolatry, there is no idolatry.

Ham. I deny that: For every one will deny intention of idolatry, and yet there are innumerable idolaters. The heart being deceitful above all things, it is dangerous to refer all things to the intention of the heart.

Bish. Where there is no idolatrous opinion of the elements, there is no idolatry; and you may easily teach your people, that they have no idolatrous opinion of the elements.

Ham. Though there is no idolatry in that case, yet there is danger in the outward appearance of idolatry which we should avoid. And as for my teaching of the people, I will rather teach them Christ's manner, and exhort them at the table as Christ did, than take up another manner and want such exhortations. Is it not better to close a pit wherein possibly people may fall, than leave it open, and set one beside it, to bid people go about it?*

Bishop of Derry. I beseech your lordship to cause one read this paper unto him. It is an exposition of the intention of

* Hamilton had probably taken this idea from Beza's correspondence with bishop Grindal. Beza, in a letter to the bishop, in the year 1565, had said, "If ye have rejected the doctrine of transubstantiation, and the practice of adoring the host, why do you symbolize with popery, and seem to hold both by kneeling at the sacrament?" Grindal replied, that though the sacrament was to be received kneeling, yet the rubric accompanied the service-book, and informed the people, that no adoration of the elements was intended. "O! I understand you," said Beza, "there was a certain great lord who repaired his house, and having finished it, left before his gate, a great stone, for which he had no occasion. This stone caused many people, in the dark, to stumble and fall. Complaint was made to his lordship, and many an humble petition was presented, praying for the removal of the stone; but he remained long obstinate. At length he condescended to order a lanthorn to be hung over it. My lord, said one, if you would be pleased to rid yourself of further solicitation, and to quiet all parties, order the stone and the candle to be both removed."—Robinson's Claude. ii. 77.

kneeling, made by the first reformers of our religion, who have shed their blood for it, whose minds we should more reverence than such novices as these are.

The paper was given to and fro to be read; but at last the bishop of Derry read it himself. The effect was this; that whereas they had retained kneeling in the act of receiving the communion, their purpose was not to justify the opinion of transubstantiation, for Christ's body was in the heavens and not on the earth. Neither to adore the elements, for that would be flat idolatry; but to keep their hearts in reverence to God in the midst of so holy an action. Which being read, the bishop of Derry said, what can be desired more plain than this?

Ham. As for the first reformers of religion, we profess they came as far as they could attain unto in so short a time. But to imagine that nothing can be needed of further reformation after their time, would be amiss. It is well known that Asa and Jehosaphat were good men; yet the Holy Ghost blames them for their *altars*, (this word was spoken with an emphasis of purpose to meet with the new-fangleness in eating on altars) and the high-places were not taken away. Now, we commend neither Asa nor Jehosaphat for leaving the high-places, nor condemn we their persons. So we allow the first reformers of religion to have done very much; but this we take notice of, that some things were left which was the appearance of, or might be the inducement to the very act of idolatry, to wit, the kneeling in the very act of receiving.

Bishop of Derry. There is no idolatry but in thy brain, I dare say.

Ham. As I said before, I say again; the body doth as much as it could do, if it would, commit idolatry; and therefore I propone this argument:—No human needless ceremonies which have been, at this time are, or hereafter may be, abused to idolatry, should be used in God's worship; kneeling in the act of receiving, is a needless human ceremony which hath been, now is by many, and hereafter may be, abused to idolatry; therefore, kneeling in the act of receiving should not be used.

Bish. I deny kneeling to be a useless human ceremony.

Ham. That which is devised by man, and that which well

enough may be wanted, is needless: but such is kneeling in the act of receiving the communion; therefore kneeling is needless and human.

Bish. That which the church hath ordained is not a needless human ceremony. Now, the church hath ordained kneeling in the act of receiving the communion.

Ham. That which the church hath ordained according to the rule of God's word, is not needless, I grant; but I deny that the church hath ordained kneeling according to the rule of God's word. I desire to know by what Scripture is such kneeling ordained.

Bishop of Derry. Give him Scripture for a peck of oats to his horse!

Bish. The church hath ordained kneeling according to that place of Scripture; 'Let all things be done decently and in order.'

Ham. As for these words, 'Let all things be done decently and in order,' the meaning must either be, let all things, ordained by God, be done decently; or otherwise, do what you will, and let it be done decently and in order. I deny kneeling at the communion to come under the first exposition, for it is not ordained by God; and that it should come under the second exposition, it hath but a weak ground.

Bish. The Sacrament is ordained by God, and kneeling is a decent receiving of it.

Ham. The Sacrament is ordained by God, and that Scripture will infer, Let the Sacrament be received decently and in order. But to receive the same Sacrament kneeling, is not ordained of God; and if it were ordained, the text would only infer, kneel decently and in order.

Bish. Whereas ye desire that the thing which is to be done decently and in order, be ordained of God, I hope ye will allow if it be either commanded in general rules or particular directions.

Ham. If kneeling in the act of receiving, can be proved to be ordained by God, either in general or particular directions, I shall allow of it.

Bish. But it is commanded in that general,—'Let all things be done decently and in order.'

Ham. That is the thing now questioned; and also that rule must abide the trial of other rules of God's word, such as, 'abstain from all appearance of evil;' which rule, if it be not fulfilled, that of decency and order cannot have place. And I have already declared, that kneeling is the pregnant appearance of both idolatry and will-worship, in so much, that if a man would seek to give appearance of these evils, his body can go no farther.

Bish. What think ye of the church of Poland, that approve of kneeling, standing and any other gesture, save sitting, and that because of some Arians that would maintain an equality with Christ; and this equality with Christ, your countryman Calderwood allows.

Ham. I do not think that he holds an equality with Christ; I know and profess, that in the Lord's Supper, our communion and fellowship with Christ is sealed; but an equality with Christ, no sound minded man will allow; and as for the church of Poland that decreed so, I know not how most of them are affected to the ubiquity of Christ's body. I take the most part of them to have been Lutherans, and therefore no wonder that they have established kneeling. But this I know, that the same church of Poland, in the same synod, have uttered their mind thus: 'Sed ob ritus externos, pios homines ferire, nec Domini voluntas, nec purioris ecclesiae mos est:'* And this he repeated the second time.

Bish. I prove that ye should or may kneel in the act of receiving, thus: where a man should or may pray, there he should or may kneel; that in receiving the Sacrament, we should or may pray; therefore, &c.

Ham. I distinguish your major; where a man may or should pray, as the principal and chief action taking up the whole man, he should or may kneel, I grant. But where a man should or may pray by an ejaculatory prayer, as a matter in the bye, but not in the main, that there he should or may kneel, I deny. For, in the receiving, it is not our main action to pray, but to meditate on the passion of Christ, and our prayers made for the

* It is neither the will of God, nor the practice of the church in her purer days, to punish godly men for their non-conformity to external rites.

time are only ejaculatory; and it is not fit then to kneel, there then being peril of will-worship, or idolatry, or the appearance thereof at the least, as often hath been said. But whatsoever may be done, I prove you may not press kneeling in receiving; thus:—That course which at any time forces me to break one of God's commandments, you cannot press me unto. The pressing of kneeling upon all in the act of receiving the Sacrament, forces some men at sometimes, to break some of God's commandments; therefore, &c.

Bish. Prove your minor.

Ham. Since men, if they must kneel in receiving of the Sacrament, must either break the command, 'Take, eat, do this in remembrance of me,' or otherwise eat doubting and damn themselves, contrary to Rom. xiv. 23.; therefore kneeling must break some one of God's commands.

Bish. He may blame himself for his doubting; and that is his misery, that whether he do it or not, he sins.

Ham. God allows that every man be fully persuaded in his own mind in what he does, Rom. xiv. 5, which privilege I crave to myself, and all others justly doubting of kneeling; as is allowed us in the whole fourteenth chapter to the Romans, throughout, and 1 Corinthians, the eighth chapter, throughout.

Bishop of Derry. If that hold, farewell all government.

Ham. Where the matter is civil and the loss civil, we submit unto it. But where the matter is God's service, and the peril damnation; we crave our privilege allowed us in the foresaid chapter, and thus reason:—That for which you cannot despise me in your judgment, you cannot execute some severe sentence upon me for it. But for nothing which you confess indifferent, such as kneeling, by your own confession, can you despise me in your judgment: therefore you cannot, for the omission of kneeling, censure me, which you are about to do.

Bish. When Paul wrote Romans xiv. chapter, there was no canon made for the church. But if constitutions had been then made, he had not so pleaded for the transgressors thereof, as ye do out of that place.

Ham. You say then that Romans xiv. chapter, hath no place after cannons be made, in that particular concerning which canons are made. But I say that all canons are liable to the examination of that xiv. chapter to the Romans, and we plead now our privileges from thence.

Bish. You cannot have privilege thereby, seeing canons are made.

Ham. Yet I am persuaded that these words, 'Let every man be fully persuaded in his own mind,' stands good to the world's end. And further, I argue thus;—That which Christ avoided in all the sacraments in the Old and New Testaments, that, we should avoid: But all adoration before the elements in all the sacraments of the Old and New Testaments, Christ did avoid: Therefore all adoration before the sacraments we should avoid.

Bishop of Derry. I will leave you my lord Down; and I will assure you, ye cannot answer it that you should have given them such liberty to-day.

Bish. I will attend your lordship. And then he said to the register, adjourn the court to two o'clock in the afternoon.

Bishop of Derry. Sentence them first.

Bish. I must do it and am sorry for it.

The court was adjourned to two o'clock in the afternoon; and from that time adjourned again, until the next day which was Friday.

No. III.

See Chap. viii. page 342, Note 4.

The following is the minute of the "Committee for Common Burdings,"—a kind of sub-committee appointed by the general "Committee of Estates" in Scotland,—authorizing the delivery of certain arms to Mr. Edmonstone of Broadisland, [see chap. i. pp. 98, 9.] and reciting the power of attorney given him for that purpose by lord Chichester, captain Arthur Chichester, his son, afterwards earl of Donegall, sir Arthur Tyringham, and captain Arthur Hill of Kilwarlin, near Hillsborough, the founder of the Downshire family.

[MSS. Records, Gen. Reg. House, Edin.]

Register of the Committee for Common Burdings; for 1641—1645. Fol. 18.19.

21*st Januar,* 1642.

Conforme to ane act of the seventh of this instant, ordaneing the number of armes yairin specifeit, to be deliverit to James Edmondstowne, in name of the Lord Chichester and some others in Ireland, upoun the securitie contained in the said act: The clerk producit this day the commissioun grantid to the said James Edmondstowne, to resave the saidis armes and to grant securitie for the same, togither with the act of secreit counsell of the dait, the sext of this instant, ordaneing the samyn armes to be delyverit, and the band subscryvit be the said James Edmonstowne for the pryce of the samyn armes, daitit the seventh of this instant. Quhilk commission, act of counsell, and band aforesaid, the commissioneris ordaines to be insert in the saidis buikis, to have the strenth of their decreit: Followis the tennor of the said commissioun:—

Know all men by these presentis, that in regaird of the present want of armes in the countie of Antrym, to arm men withall, quhairby we may be bettir enabled to contribute our best indevoires, to the suppressioun of the present rebellioun, and the furtherance of his majesties service, as it becometh all dewtiefull and loyall subjectis to doe; we, Edvard Viscount Chichester, of Carrickfergus, captane Arthur Chichester, eldest sone and air apparent of the said Edvard, sir Arthur Tyringhame, knight, one of his majesties most honorable privie counsell for the kingdome of Ireland, and Arthur Hill of Kilwarlen in the cowntie of Downe, Esquyre, have sent and imployed our trustie and weilbelovit friend, James Edmonstoune of Broadeyland in the countie of Antrym, Esquyre, to the citie of Edinburghe in the kingdome of Scotland, or to any other pairt of the said kingdome, to bargane and buy for our use these armes following, that is to say, ane thousand musketis with bandeliers, [cartridge-boxes] twa thousand swordis, fyve hundreth and fourtie pickis, fyve hundreth horsemens peicks with snaphances, [a kind of cavalry firelock] or for want of such, fyve hundreth carbynes, and thrie field peices of thrie or four pund bullet: And we doe also heirby constitute and appoynt the said James Edmonstoune, our trew and lawfull actornay for us and in our names, to signe, seal, deliver and perfyte any band or bandis, to any persone or persones quhatsoevir, quho shall give him and us credite for the saidis armes, for the trew payment of quhat sowme or sowmes of money, the saidis armes shall amount unto: And doe heirby also give the said James Edmonstoune, full power and authoritie to put our names to the saidis band or bandis, and affixe our seales to the same, and to doe all uther act and actis, thing or thingis, quhich shall be thought requisite by the lawis of yat kingdome, for the trew perfectioun of the said band or bandis; ratefieing, allowing and confirmeing all such act or actis, thing or thingis, which he, the said James, shall doe tuitcheing the premisses, as if we ourselwis wer personally present to doe and performe the same: In witnes quhairof, we have heirunto put our handis and seales, the sext day of December, in the sevinthtene yeir of the reigne of our soverane lord, Charles, by the grace of God, king of England, Scotland, France and Ireland, defender of the faith, anno Dom. 1641. Sic subscribitur, Edward Chichester, Arthur Chichester, A. Tyringham, Arthur Hill.

Signed, sealed and delyverit, in presence of Alexander Colwill, Johne Edmonstown, Johne Dalway, Richard Gressenor. Johne Rawlin, Not. Pub.

Then follows the act of privy council referred to, dated 6th January 1642; and the bond by James Edmonstone for the arms, amounting to L.13,702, 3s. 4d. Scots. In the minutes of committee, dated 26th January, there is another obligation by him for L.795, 17s. The amount of both these sums in British money is, L.1208, 3s. 4d.

END OF THE APPENDIX TO THE FIRST VOLUME.

Milton Keynes UK
Ingram Content Group UK Ltd.
UKHW042308181223
434467UK00008B/72

9 783752 533439